The
BOAT

Clara
Salaman

HEAD
ZEUS

First published in the UK in 2014 by Head of Zeus, Ltd.
This paperback edition first published in 2014 by Head of Zeus, Ltd

9 7 5 3 1 2 4 6 8

A catalogue record for this book is available from
the British Library.

Paperback ISBN 9781781855850
Ebook ISBN 9781781855836

Printed and bound by CPI Group (UK) Ltd, Croydon, CR0 4YY

Head of Zeus, Ltd
Clerkenwell House
45–47 Clerkenwell Green
London EC1R 0HT
WWW.HEADOFZEUS.COM

For Paul.
And for David Sanders RIP.

DROWNING

JOHNNY WENT ABOUT the business of suicide with a remarkable soundness of mind. When he was satisfied that the entire sea was his alone, land being so far away that even birds had been dropping and dying with exhaustion on the deck, he took his hand off the tiller and let the bows of the boat nose round into the wind. He stared out at the red-tipped waves, lit by a dawn that beckoned nothing good. The sails were thrashing about furiously above his head but he didn't hear them. After a long while he turned and looked up at the flapping canvas with eyes that had already died; they shone a dull green from his dark, sun-beaten face making him appear much older than his twenty-one years.

He stood up, rolled in the genoa, uncleated the mainsheet and stepped up on to the deck. He began heaving down the heavy mainsail, folding it back on itself, tying each sail-tie with methodical care, his body balancing easily on the rolling deck while the dark water beneath winked pinkly up at him. When the sail was neatly packed away for the last time he went back down into the cockpit and disappeared below deck.

The saloon was a mess: spilt food all over the floor, clothing that he only faintly recognized tossed here and there, cups and glasses, empty cartons and plastic wrappers, the detritus of various lives strewn across the boat. He wondered that he hadn't noticed the mess before. The dividing panel between the galley and the saloon had a big dent in the cheap wood, a scar he vaguely remembered. He went through the boat, picking up armfuls of rubbish and chucking it into black bin bags before stuffing the bags into the lockers underneath the saloon seats. He emptied the shelves and put the books and other assorted obsolete things into his old sleeping bag, which he bundled inside a cupboard.

The only thing of any beauty on board was the brass sextant. He picked it up and held it in his fingers; it was no more than a relic now, much like himself. He stepped out into the cockpit and stood at the stern facing the rising sun, which was hanging precariously above the sea, a bold pink globe carrying on regardless. He threw the sextant as far as he could out into the water, the red light bouncing off the brass as it spun through the air. He didn't watch its splash but turned and went back down to the saloon to get on with what had to be done.

When everything was cleared away, pots and pans in lockers, cushions stuffed into crevices, he caught sight of himself in the bathroom mirror and was surprised by what he saw: he was wearing a black suit and a dicky bow as if he'd stepped out of some fancy party. Both the jacket and the trousers hung loosely on his skinny frame but they seemed as good as any other clothes to die in. He kicked off his trainers and went through to the galley, breathing in deeply, looking out at the dawn light beyond the cockpit, his body as always in tune with the irregular movement of the boat; from the soles of his feet to the tips of his fingers, he was primed and balanced to the rhythm of the waves, the muscles in his core always that one beat ahead of nature's drum. Only his eyes were unmoving, focused somewhere beyond horizons.

His fingers moved first and reached for the galley drawer. He pulled it open and found the big kitchen knife. It had served many purposes and now had one more vital role to perform. But it needed to be sharp. He sat down on the galley step and spent a few careful minutes sharpening the blade, watching the sun dance about on the gleaming surface.

Then he paused before making his way through the saloon to the heads. He bent down on his knees beside the toilet and hung his head as if in prayer, despising the weakness of his own body – he was trembling all over. He took another deep breath, raised the knife and determinedly cut through both the outlet and the inlet pipes, watching as the water began to pour in. There was no going back now. Slowly he stood up, eyes fixed on the gushing pipes, the coldness of the seawater reaching his feet. It sloshed about the floor as the boat rolled in the waves. He watched, mesmerized, as it filled the cubicle floor, rising over his toes, immersing his feet and spilling over the base of the door frame and into the saloon. He turned, sloshing through it, and went back to his seat on the companionway steps, detached and yet fascinated as the water swept noisily from side to side, filling every cranny, darkening all in its path, seeping fast across the naff carpet, consuming everything in its way. It rose up the table legs and continued its journey in silence. He sat there quite transfixed, feeling the sun burn on the back of his neck, knowing that he would be next; he too would soon be swallowed up.

When the water rose to his knees, he stood up. Everything that was going to float was doing so. The toilet brush was bobbing about with the salt and pepper pots by the shelves; a small armband floated through from the forepeak cabin. He stared at the cartoon dolphins on the transparent plastic, watching as it bobbed jauntily across the chart table. He turned around and climbed the companionway steps and stood in the cockpit looking out into the empty sea: 360

degrees of nothing. He looked up into the pale morning blueness of the sky, aware of a throbbing in his body as the blood pumped around him noisily; it seemed ironic that right now he should be feeling more alive than he had done in a long time, as if life was giving him a little reminder out of pure spite. If he could have wept he might have wept then but his eyes were dry, all spent.

It didn't take long before the detritus spilt out into the cockpit and pretty quickly the weight of the water began to gently but firmly tug the stern downwards. Johnny stepped out on to the transom and smoothly slid his body into the water where the coldness took his breath away, biting at his skin. He should have been prepared for that. He kicked his legs and swam away from the boat. He didn't want to go like that, sucked down with her and her dirty cargo. He turned to watch her sink, feeling the weight of his clothes clinging to his body, dragging him down. On her stern he could see where he'd painted over her name: a futile gesture; as if he could ever have erased that curled looped lettering from existence: *Little Utopia*. Then suddenly the bows began to tip up into the air as the pull of the deep overwhelmed her, the top of the mast plummeting towards him, pointing accusingly as it fell. He trod water as she began to sink, dipping his head beneath the waves, the rush of the cold sea filling his ears and eyes. He blinked into the blue. There she hung half suspended, the wrong way round, belly up, leaning to the port side. He came up for air; they were almost graceful, her dying moments, her nose proudly sniffing at the sky, the last rise before the fall. Then she began to drop, quietly and smoothly slipping beneath the waves.

All that was left was a vortex of bubbles and a faint pulling at his legs. He snatched another breath and ducked his head beneath the waves to see her dropping fast, like a stone, pitching and rolling as she waltzed to her death. He watched until she was just a shadow and the blue became an inky black and he could see her no more. He lifted his head out of the water and gasped for air, staring at the surface where a foamy flatness had taken her place. Two large bubbles, final belches from the deep, burst into the air and then there was nothing – just him and the knowledge that his own absence would be next.

He could hear the sharp outtakes of his own breath as the waves lifted and dropped him like a piece of flotsam. He wondered then whether perhaps he should have weighted himself down, tied himself to the mast or strapped himself to a berth, but the very idea of being forever entwined with that boat made him glad he'd not thought that far ahead. He wouldn't last long, he was sure of that; he'd taken all the aspirin left in the medicine tin. He would drift off soon. He closed his eyes, laid his head back into the water and opened out his body to the sky.

He wasn't cold any more. His body felt unusually weightless. As he lay there he could feel the water becoming his ally; it carried and caressed him, was as soothing as a balm. He let himself move as one with the waves like a turtle floating on the surface, his spread-eagled limbs seemingly indistinguishable from the water itself, the same temperature, formless, merging together. The warmth of the sun was the same as the warmth of his own body; there was no divide between himself and his environment and he didn't remember ever feeling such extraordinary unity with his surroundings. Except with *her*, of course.

He must have drifted off for when he opened his eyes again the sun had slunk right down the sky and he'd forgotten that he was drowning in the Mediterranean Sea. He thought for a moment that he was lying on the sand dunes or in the back garden, a cool wind rousing him from his slumber. He gazed up through the canopy of blue, his mind seeking the blackness beyond. Thousands and thousands of feet above him he could see the faint white trail of an aeroplane. He thought of the people up there, all dry and safe, going about their businesses, opening sachets, adjusting headrests, shuffling newspapers, snoozing, heads full of meetings or mergers, leading their lives, being alive, unaware of the end of his small existence. Then the feathery trail melted too quickly into the blueness and an intense, unbearable loneliness took root in him.

He tried to keep hold of the good feelings, the unity, the lack of otherness he had felt a while ago, but the good feelings were all gone now, replaced with a hollow kind of dread. His body had lost its lightness; the weight of the suit was dragging him down. Even the elements had turned hostile: the waves were breaking over his face and the chill of the water had begun to sting his flesh and the shadows of clouds crossing the sun kept stealing his warmth. The sun itself was abandoning him; he watched it bounce about on the edge of the world like a great orange ball. He lifted his head and with each rise of the waves he checked the horizon: snatches of emptiness everywhere. There was nothing and nobody at all to die with. And it would be dark soon. A tiny flag of panic waved from somewhere in his gut; such smallness and insignificance could terrify a man who didn't want to die. He hadn't thought it would be like this; he had thought that drowning was meant to be swift. But he understood that the guilty do not deserve the luxury of an easy death. He should have tied himself to the mast and sunk to the bottom where he belonged.

He looked down at his hands shining greenly through the water. He was aware now of the roughness in his throat and the stinging of his lips. A pain jabbed across his middle; he needed to pee but felt incapable of doing so; his stomach was tight. At last he felt the warmth of his urine spread across his thighs and only when he had finished did it strike him how incredibly cold he had become. The sky in the east was already darkening and the wind was up, white horses dancing on the sea.

Then something else caught his eye. He thought he saw the pale hull of a cargo ship on the horizon, dipping and bobbing in and out of his sight. Instinctively he kicked his legs, his body betraying his mind. What did he care about rescue? There was no salvation for him. He stopped moving, laid his head back in the water and looked up at the sky. A wave broke over his face and he coughed and spluttered for air, downing a mouthful of sea water. He caught a flash of the ship again, this time realizing that they were on the same bearing. Only he'd got the scale of it wrong: it wasn't a ship at all. It was a fender – a white fender that he recognized. It must have come up from the deep, risen from the wreckage. He felt an affinity with it. There they were, two floating things in a watery wilderness.

He could barely move his limbs even if he'd wanted to, they'd become leaden and useless, waving like planks of wood as the coldness rattled in his bones. Panting and spitting water he watched as the fender bobbed towards him, only a matter of feet away now, taunting him with a brief respite from this struggle. He couldn't stop himself, he reached out and grabbed hold of it, hauling it in towards his body, resting his head against its scratched, solid surface, gasping for air, his eyes focusing in on all the scuffs and stains, wondering whether this was going to make dying easier or harder.

Something soft brushed against his legs and he looked down at the trailing fender rope. He pulled it up with his clumsy, frozen fingers. The rope was caught on a heavy piece of fabric. He brought it up to the surface. A small, cracked cry escaped from his throat and his heart thrashed about violently in his chest, briefly pumping life into the numbness. It was her prayer mat, all darkened and made heavy by the water, but most definitely it was her little prayer mat! A tiny piece of her had come back for him. She would have called it *a sign*.

His fingers, rigid as rods of steel, made heavy work of untangling the rope. His juddering teeth proved more capable and he bit his way down it, loosening the carpet inch by inch until eventually he worked it free, heaving it out of the water and on to the fender, passing the rope behind his body, his hands grabbing uselessly at each other. He tried jabbing the end of the rope through the eye at the top of the fender. By chance he succeeded and tightened off the slack, but it was dark by the time he'd tied the two half-hitches needed to keep him there and his body had begun to tremble uncontrollably.

1

THE BEGINNING

JOHNNY'S DAD HAD asked Rob and him to look out for the girls on the beach while he went to the chandler's in Padstow. They'd intended to do the brotherly thing, but Rob had ended up buying some dope off the lifeguard and they'd sat on the sand dunes getting stoned in the sunshine. They'd lost track of the girls hours ago. The last Johnny had seen of them, they were mucking about in the rock pools doing whatever it was that eleven-year-old girls did.

Johnny lay there sifting hot sand through his fingers, turning a perfect heart-shaped little piece of slate over in his hand, feeling the warm sun on his back, discussing the merits of trimarans versus catamarans with Rob, when his attention was caught by Sarah's little friend over Rob's right shoulder, up high in the sand dunes beyond. She was perched at the very top, back to the sea, poised, knees bent, arms stretched out in front of her. He wondered what she was doing. She looked like an animal about to pounce, her attention firmly fixed on the whispering grasses in front of her. Then, to his immense surprise – he was pretty wrecked – she threw herself backwards high up into the air, forming a perfectly piked backwards somersault, gracefully flying through the blue Cornish sky. She landed neatly on her feet at the bottom of the dune, facing the sea, before skipping forwards on to the harder wetter sand.

Johnny choked on the spliff. 'Rob! Did you see that?'

Rob gave a cursory glance over his shoulder. 'No,' he said. 'Watch Clemmie!'

So they both watched as she climbed back up the dune, scrabbling nimbly up the sand, like a sun-kissed nymph in her blue and white stripy swimming costume, Johnny noticing the tan lines on her perky little bum. She jumped sideways to avoid Sarah who was doing rather heavy forward rolls down the dune.

'Wait for it!' he said to Rob, leaning on one elbow, making himself comfortable, eyes on this new vision: her strong, brown limbs, her copper hair blowing about wildly in the salty breeze. How on earth could he not have noticed her before? Even the sunlight seemed to be lighting her differently today, as if she were something that had to be highlighted. Two minutes ago she hadn't even registered in his mind – of course he'd known her for years as his little sister's friend, and she'd been down to Cornwall a couple of times, but he'd never paid her any real attention. For the first time he was *seeing* her, as if he had borrowed some binoculars and there she was in sharp focus, Sarah's friend, a whole new species: a 'Clemency Bailey'. Once again, she took her position, frozen, poised, and then threw herself backwards fearlessly, arching and twisting against the sky but this time, open-bodied, slow and leisurely.

Rob sat up and wolf-whistled her. She turned around then and saw them watching her and she took a deep, flourishing, theatrical bow before scrabbling back up to the top again.

'She's going to be a right little heartbreaker,' Rob said, but Johnny could tell that his mind was back on trimarans, which suited him just fine; he preferred watching her over his shoulder, having her all to himself.

Then later that night everyone had gone for a walk along the surf because the moon was full – his mum was always coming up with hippie reasons for excursions – and on the way back to the cottage Clemmie had declared that she was going to go swimming and he had found himself deliberately dawdling, saying to no one in particular, 'I'd better keep an eye on her, there's a rip tide.' Even when she'd said she didn't need an eye on her, she was almost twelve, big enough to swim without eyes on her, still he'd sat down on the dry sand at the water's edge as the others wandered back.

'I'll have a smoke then,' he said and she'd shrugged her shoulders.

'It's a free country.'

And he'd been quite taken aback by the carefree way she had pulled her dress over her head and taken off her knickers without so much as a backwards glance at him. Then he'd watched her run into the sea, shrieking in the waves as they knocked her over, the moonlight shining on her naked body.

'Come in!' she yelled to him as he sat there on the sand and it had felt good to be invited into her watery world where all the fun was going on. She wasn't to know that Johnny never went *in* the cold British sea, only *on* it. Even when capsizing dinghy sailing, he prided himself on never getting wet; he'd neatly step on to the centreboard, straddling the hull and righting the boat, barely wetting a toe.

'Chicken Licken!' she shouted, diving under a wave, disappearing into the water, the starry night her backdrop.

'Come in, Johnny!' She was waving at him, slippery and shining. He felt for the first time as if he was in the wrong place, here, dry on the beach, when it looked so much better over there with her in the water.

'Help!' she cried, pretending to drown. 'Shark!' She went under and stuck her legs up in the air, walking on her hands.

Then, quite out of character, Johnny found himself ripping off his clothes and running in. 'Emergency services are here! Worry not!' he shouted, splashing into the icy water. 'Holy shit!' he yelled as the water hit his nuts. The thrill of the chill, the suck and the pull of the current made him whelp. Clemmie was swimming towards him, faking struggle, and he grabbed her hand and pulled her manfully into his arms, picking her up like a damsel in distress.

'I've got you. You're safe! Now where's that naughty shark?' he said, flexing a bicep.

She gave a throaty chuckle – he'd noticed that laugh of hers – and wrapped her legs around his waist and her arms around his neck. He could feel her nakedness against his stomach, the coolness of flesh on flesh. She turned her face to his. They were inches apart, locked together, not laughing any more but serious, intense, staring into each other's moon-shining eyes, and a strange sensation went through Johnny: a warm rush seemed to flood through his entire being as if a void he had never known existed was being filled up and it struck him that he had been waiting for this moment for all of his fourteen years; whatever it was, this was it! This was the essence of life! He wanted time to stop just for a moment until he had fully grasped it but already she was slipping out of his arms. She had let the water pull her away and was lying on her back looking up at the stars.

For she had felt it too; she lay there, floating, eyes to the heavens, surrendering herself to the waves, pleasantly startled by what had just occurred, this new sensation in her body, all slippery and buzzing. She felt alive. Something had shifted inside her, away from childish things. She let the waves wash over her and carry her back to the shore, suddenly aware of her own nakedness as she stood up and ran back through the surf to the dry sand.

A little while later they sat in silence watching the sea, wet, dripping and newly intimate. She was wearing his jumper; it hung gigantically around her small frame. She'd tucked her knees up to her chin inside it to keep herself warm, drops of seawater running down her cheek.

'Do you believe there are monsters out there?' she asked him, squinting out at the dark horizon.

'Yes,' he said. 'Why not?'

She liked that. She believed in monsters. She believed in everything.

'That red dot could be an eye,' she said, pointing far out to sea.

'Or a fishing boat.'

'Look! There's a green one!'

'Same boat. She's turning.'

'How do you know?'

'Red light's left side of the boat – port. Green's right – starboard. It's white now, that's the stern. She's heading out. West.'

'Where's it going?'

'Fishing.'

'I know that, Johnny. I meant if it carried on going straight, where would it end up?'

'America, I suppose. No, Canada even.'

'Wow.' She sucked the end of a piece of salty hair. 'Have you been to America?' she asked.

'No. Not yet. But I will one day. I'll sail there.' He liked it when she looked at him like that, shining her light at him; he didn't want her to look away.

'Really?'

'Yup. I'm going to build my own boat, mono-hull, ketch – wooden, of course. Teak decks, double-ended. She'll be the most beautiful boat on the ocean. And then I'm going to sail her single-handedly around the world.' He couldn't help showing off a bit. But it was true, that was exactly what he was going to do.

She was staring at him. Whatever it was that had shifted earlier on inside her, she could feel it starting again and it most definitely came from *him*. It was as if he knew her; it was as if they were connected. He was everything she wanted to be – chiefly, an adventurer. 'Johnny, can I come? Can I sail round the world with you?'

He laughed. 'Then it wouldn't be single-handed.'

'Who cares? We could do it double-handed.'

He smiled, getting out his tobacco. 'Well, perhaps we could.' He started rolling a cigarette.

'Roll us a ciggie!' she said, all excited now that they had some sort of arrangement. 'A nice big fat one like you were smoking on the dunes.'

'Do you smoke?' he asked, pleased that she'd been watching him.

'Not yet. Johnny? Why did you call a boat a "her"?'

He turned in towards her, away from the wind, to roll the cigarette. 'Because of the shape – all curves and elegance, like a woman.'

'Oh!' she said. 'Am I curved and elegant?'

'Well, you're only eleven.'

'Yes,' she said, annoyed with herself; eleven seemed a ridiculous age to be, neither one thing nor the other. 'And three-quarters.'

'I stand corrected.'

14

'I've got a boyfriend,' she said, as if that might make her a bit older.

'Yeh?'

'Yup. Roger Benson. We've touched tongues and everything.'

Johnny whistled. 'Go for it, Roger.'

He cupped his hands and struck the match, the red flame of the phosphorus briefly blinding him. He felt her watching him and he liked it. He inhaled and blew the smoke out into the air and then passed her the cigarette. Their fingers were clammy with dampness and the cigarette stuck so he held it to her mouth as she tentatively leant forwards. He could feel the softness of her lips against his fingertips.

She coughed. 'Yuck,' she said, spitting out a strand of tobacco.

'It's disgusting at first. You have to get used to it.'

'Do I? Oh, I will.' She was determined to get it right; her lips sought out the cigarette again. He fed her another drag. This time she breathed in without coughing but clearly not enjoying it.

'Good girl,' he said and she smiled proudly. He noticed for the first time how her two front teeth crossed a little and he thought that one day a boy might get obsessed with teeth like that.

'Johnny? Have you got a girlfriend?'

He leant back on his elbows and watched the fishing boat. 'Not exactly,' he said.

'What does that mean?'

'It means *not exactly*.'

She twisted around and lay on her front, looking at him. 'OK. I'll decide,' she said. 'Have you touched tongues?'

He looked her in the eye, straight-faced. 'Yes, we have.'

'Then yes, you've got a girlfriend,' she said, as if it were the most obvious thing in the world. She sat up again and went back to watching the fishing boat winking out in the Atlantic. Of course he had a girlfriend: looking like he did, smoking like he did, being an adventurer like he was.

'Are you going to marry her?' she asked.

Johnny laughed. 'No.'

'Why not?'

He took a long, slow drag of the cigarette. 'Because she's already married.'

She turned to him slowly, her jaw dropping, her eyes widening, her lungs filling. 'Wow! How old is she?'

'Thirty-five,' he said, watching the thrill dart about her lovely face.

'Oh my God!' she cried, delighted. 'She's an old woman, Johnny! You're only fourteen.'

A couple of months ago Johnny had been babysitting for a friend of his mum's when she'd come home unexpectedly early, smelling sweetly of red wine. She'd stopped him in the hall, slipped some cash into his breast pocket, told him he was the sexiest young man she'd ever come across and then, to his immense surprise, pressed her blue lips against his. One thing had led to another and she'd whisked away his virginity on a Superman blanket on the sofa, minutes before her husband came home. He'd been doing a fair amount of babysitting since then.

'Don't tell Sarah, Clemmie.'

'I won't,' she said, zipping her mouth and leaning back on her hands. She liked secrets. But she didn't quite know what to do with this one. She let it churn about her head for a bit but whichever way she looked at it, it kept making her feel peculiar.

The fishing vessel had turned south now, only its port light visible. They were sitting very close, watching it progress, the warm westerly wind blowing the hair off their faces.

'Johnny,' she said quietly, her dark eyes looking up at his. 'Will you marry me one day? When your girlfriend dies?'

He laughed.

'I'm serious,' she said.

His laughter ebbed away and he became serious too – she was exactly the kind of girl he would marry some day. 'OK,' he said.

'Promise?' she said.

He nodded.

'You have to give me something, so it's a real promise.' She seemed to know, even then, that time needed to be marked.

'I haven't got anything.'

Then he remembered. He put his hand in his pocket and brought out the little heart-shaped piece of slate he'd been smoothing on the beach.

'Jonathan Love, will you marry me?'

Johnny was standing in the hall by the kitchen where the phone was. She'd rung during supper and his dad, Rob and Sarah were all listening in case it was for them.

'It *is* Johnny, isn't it?' she said.

'Speaking.'

'It's Clem.' He must have paused. 'Clemency Bailey. Remember me?'

He certainly did.

'Clemmie,' she said. 'Only I'm Clem now.'

'Well, hello there!' he said. 'Of course I remember you.'

She sounded different to how he remembered: her voice was deeper. Then again she was probably just grown up. If he was seventeen now, she would have to be fifteen. Her family had moved out of Putney years ago but had recently returned and presumably she'd rung up to speak to his sister.

'Has your girlfriend died yet?' she asked.

He didn't know what she was referring to but he didn't fancy being overheard so he shut the hall door with his body, spinning the flex around his finger. It was pure chance that it was he who'd answered the phone rather than Rob or Sarah. He'd only just got back from crewing on a delivery to the Caribbean and was shortly off to take another boat over so he felt lucky to have caught her.

'What are you talking about? I haven't got a girlfriend,' he said.

'You said you'd marry me when your girlfriend died.'

'Did I?' He was smiling. 'What girlfriend was that then?'

'The married one.'

The affair with his mother's friend was long over. Her husband had found Johnny's sock under the bed with his name tape on it and had gone a bit mental.

'Well?' she asked.

'I am indeed available for marriage,' he replied. 'How about meeting up first though, just to go through dates and times?'

He met her in the Blue Anchor by the river in Hammersmith just as the sun was setting. The tide was high and the ducks were swimming in the trees. He'd come on his bike, a Triumph Tiger Cub he'd bought for a song in *Loot* which he was now doing up. Although he'd put brand-spanking-new spark plugs in, she'd stalled on the bridge and he'd had to push her to the pub, so he was a bit late.

He recognized Clemency Bailey straight away. She was sitting at a table outside, smoking a cigarette – like a pro, he noticed. She stood up when she saw him and waved. He was dazzled by her as he had hoped he might be. In some way she seemed responsible for, or at least a part of, the magnificent pink altostratus cloud display behind her. She was wearing jeans and a loose white top and he could see her cleavage, the soft roundness of her little tits, and he remembered with a pang how he had once held her naked body in the sea. Only she had been a child then. 'Hi,' she said.

He ran a hand through his helmet-flattened hair. 'Well hello, Clemency Bailey,' he said, putting his bike helmet down on the table. He leant forward and kissed her cheek. She smelt musky, like linseed oil, like freshly laid teak decking.

'Hello, Jonathan Love. You're looking well.'

So was she. She looked bloody amazing but he wasn't going to tell her that – you had to keep girls like her on their toes. 'I make an effort,' he said. He meant it sarcastically; his T-shirt was streaked with engine oil. But she wasn't looking at his T-shirt, she was staring him straight in the eye.

'I'm sorry to hear about your mum,' she said.

His mum had died the year before – from cancer. It had spread everywhere by the end. The only good thing about it was that no one had commented on him failing all his exams and dropping out. 'You saw my sister?'

She nodded.

He didn't want to talk about his mum. 'What are you drinking?' he asked.

'I'll have whatever you're having.'

She was underage of course, but so was he come to that – landlords never seemed to give a toss. He went in and got two Ram and Specials, brought them outside and sat down opposite her. She watched as he poured them both out and pushed one glass towards her. They chinked their drinks.

'So,' he said, looking into her lovely eyes. 'Down to business… will you be wearing white?'

Later, when a few drops of rain had turned into a torrent, they went inside and sat in the corner. There was a telly on at the bar with the sound down showing the cricket, the first Test match at Edgbaston and the West Indies were making mincemeat of England. Johnny hadn't met a girl who liked cricket before; he even felt faintly jealous when her attention truly switched from him to the telly. And he loved cricket. She told him how she preferred to listen to it on the radio, how she loved the commentary, how she could lie in bed for hours listening to the plummy tones of Henry Blofeld. While she spoke, Johnny's mind wandered; he pictured her lying in bed listening to the cricket, with him lying next to her caressing those little tits of hers, admiring that smooth, taut stomach, running his hands over her body.

He watched as she rummaged around in her bag. It seemed to contain a mammoth amount of crap. She started dredging through it, pulling various things out and placing them on the table: bangles and chewing gum, an assortment of pens and sketches she had made on random bits of paper. Eventually she found what she was looking for: her bulging wallet. She took it out and began going through it with the same thoroughness. It was hard to believe that one person could carry around so much junk – he'd come out with a tenner and a spanner.

'That's him,' she said with some awe, producing a rather tatty-looking photograph. Johnny looked at it: a tall man in stupid glasses wearing a big foppish bow tie standing underneath a palm tree in the Caribbean somewhere holding a bat. *To Clemency* was scrawled across the bottom of the photo. *Battings of love, Henry Blofeld*. Johnny, who wouldn't have minded being the recipient of such wonder, thought he looked like a bit of a git.

'In my opinion,' Clem said, eyes back on the screen where Botham had just hit a six, 'Botham has single-handedly saved England from total embarrassment.'

Johnny got up, smiling at her, tapping his pockets. He wanted to put a song on the jukebox. 'I like your strong opinions,' he said.

She was slightly taken aback, not quite sure whether he was criticizing her or not. 'Well, they're always open to change,' she said, her voice lilting optimistically. It was true, she did have strong opinions but usually she was just trying them out, seeing how they sounded, so much so that sometimes she wondered whether she really had any opinions of her own at all. She certainly hadn't intended to make him laugh. She watched as he wandered across the room with a smile on his face. He leant against the jukebox flicking through his choices and he looked so handsome and so familiar to her. She remembered how kind he had always been to her as a child, how mortified she had been when he'd found her in the middle of the night in the bathroom in Putney. She'd wet the bed and was trying to dry the sheet with bits of loo paper; he'd put the sheet in the laundry basket and given her a towel and told her to put it on the wet bit and just go back to sleep. She used to go home from the Loves' house aching to have a brother of her own. But now she was glad that he wasn't her brother.

He put on a song, something she didn't know, and came back over to the table, sitting slightly closer to her than he had been before. She liked the way he knew the words and was singing along as he drank his beer. She liked the sound of his voice. She liked the way he looked at her, with those eyes which were as green as dirty bathwater. In fact she liked everything about him. She thought that whatever happened, this song would always remind her of him.

Later, Johnny got up and ordered a couple more Ram and Specials from the bar, tapping his foot along to Aztec Camera. She'd put 'Oblivious' on four times in a row – he wished he'd never started it. As he turned back to the table with the drinks he caught her slipping her thumb out of her mouth and was momentarily embarrassed for her. He'd forgotten that she sucked her thumb. He remembered her down in Cornwall sucking away, the way her other hand lazily fondled herself as she did so.

It was irrelevant anyway; he was already hooked by then. He returned to the table, placing the bottle and the glass in front of her and picked up the photograph that was still lying there amongst the beer rings. 'I sailed there last year,' he said casually, dropping the photo back down. *Beat that, Blofeld.*

'Where?' she asked, her attention all his now, her eyes shining that wonder on to him.

'The West Indies. Barbados.'

'No! On your own?'

'There were two of us. Me and the skipper.'

Her eyes widened as she took this in. She stared at him; he was actually living his dreams. Nobody *did* what they said they were going to do when they were fourteen. He had sailed across the Atlantic. He was the real thing. He was everything and more than she had hoped he would be.

'Weren't you scared?' she asked.

He laughed. 'Of course not.'

'I would have been. What was it like? Travelling all that way, arriving by sea? Was it incredible? Is it paradise?'

Johnny took a sip of his beer, almost thrown by her intensity, Blofeld blown right out of the water now.

'Well… it was something else!' he said. It really had been. Seeing Barbados appearing on the horizon after weeks of being becalmed in the Atlantic had felt like a miracle. He'd gone a little bit mad, but he wasn't going to tell her that.

The crossing had taken six weeks; they'd barely had any wind, and the isolation had really got to him. He'd become convinced, for one reason or another – a nuclear explosion perhaps or a collision with a comet – that life on planet Earth had ceased to exist. He had become so embroiled in his own apocalyptic fantasy he was quite sure that the boat he was on was the last vessel left on the planet and for the first time in his life it hit him with acute clarity, now that they were all dead, how much he loved his friends and family. Clem wouldn't know it, but even she had come into his thoughts then, as an example of all the opportunities missed, how life had to be grabbed by the balls. He'd smelt the land before he saw it. It had never occurred to him that land would have such a strong smell: rich, lush and earthy. Planet Earth smells of earth. He'd come out on deck as they approached the island and when he saw the greenness of the mountains and the turquoise waters of the shores he'd searched frantically for evidence of human life. Then when he found it through his binoculars, the boats and the bars, a little plane in the sky, he had felt an exquisite happiness and love for the human race. Barbados had indeed seemed like paradise – not for the reasons she might have thought, but for the fact that the human race was still going.

'It *is* paradise,' he said to her. 'I'm going there again in a couple of months' time.'

A little wind was knocked out of her sails. It didn't make any sense, she knew that; she had gone for years without seeing him at all, yet suddenly the imminent prospect of his absence filled her with bleakness. 'Can I come with you?' she asked but he laughed and she felt foolish. She'd got carried away; she'd have to watch herself, she was always leaping ahead. He was an adventurer and adventurers went on adventures. She would just have to do her adventuring on her own. She would be as brave as he.

'Maybe we can meet up. I'm going travelling too,' she said, pouring her Ram into her Special from a height, watching the top turn into a creamy froth. 'I've got to see the world, Johnny. I don't want to be stuck here for the rest of my life with my mum.'

He'd been watching her carefully and had a strong desire to lean forward, turn her face to his and to kiss those lips. For the first time it occurred to him that he might actually rather be doing something other than sailing.

'I tell you what, Clem. Sod the delivery. Let's go travelling together,' he said and he thought that he might do or say anything at all just to see that look in her eye. 'After the wedding, of course.'

She laughed, not quite sure which bits were the joking bits. But it didn't matter. Sitting here with him making make-believe or real-believe plans made her happiness so acute it almost hurt.

'Where do you want to go?' he asked her, clinking her glass, his fingers brushing against hers, his eyes soaking her up.

'Let's go east,' she said.

Everything about her turned him on: how comfortably she wore her own skin, the way her top lip rested on her bottom one, the naughty glint in her eye when she looked at him, the way she wore her clothes, the woody smell of her. It was visceral. When Botham hit another six and she gripped his thigh and let her hand rest on his leg for a moment, he thought she might notice his stonking great hard-on. He'd had it for hours.

When it was dark and they were middlingly pissed, he said he'd take her home on the Tiger Cub – assuming he could get it started. They walked around the corner to where the bike was. She seemed impressed with his handiwork, or pretended she was. He gave her his leather jacket and his helmet and did up the strap for her, his fingers touching her cheek. He wanted to kiss her then but she was too excited about getting on the bike and he knew he'd have to wait – he should have done it in the pub. He climbed on the bike and told her to get on behind him and hold on tightly, which she did. The Tiger started first go, the faithful beast.

She hadn't been on a bike before. She kept leaning the wrong way, which he didn't like. She was clinging on to him for dear life, which he liked a lot, and she was screaming in his ear, which he also liked. It felt so good to be the wielder of thrills.

Unfortunately, as they sped down Rocks Lane heading for Putney, he noticed a police car too late, right after he'd over-taken it. He turned left as soon as he could and ignored the blue flashing light in his mirror but when the car pulled up alongside he was forced to acknowledge it. The copper in the passenger seat was making that slow dabbing gesture policemen like to do. Johnny waved, signalled – or would have if he'd put the bulbs in – and pulled over by the church where the homos do it in the woods.

'Don't worry, Clem,' he said, keeping the engine running; he didn't like to turn it off in case it never started again. Clem didn't look that worried. In fact she looked rather excited.

'Here,' she said brightly, rummaging around in her enor-mous bag. She'd never been in trouble with the police before but she wasn't at all bothered. There was something invin-cible about Johnny. With him she felt safe, he was brave and fearless – he'd sailed across the ocean. 'Have a pear drop so they can't smell the booze.'

He took one. He hadn't had a pear drop for years, that sweet–sour taste of childhood.

They watched the police car stop and the doors open. Two of them got out. One was on a walkie-talkie and the other, a tall bloke with a swanky gait, was putting on his helmet. As he approached, the shorter one started giving the bike a once over.

'Turn the engine off!' he said to Johnny.

Johnny pretended he couldn't hear him.

The tall one joined in, 'Turn the engine off!'

'If I turn it off, it might not start up again,' Johnny said loudly.

The short arse took it upon himself to turn it off. Then he stepped back from the bike and began prowling around the front of it. 'Well! Well! Well! What have we here?'

He actually said 'Well, well, well,' as if he'd learnt it in pig school. 'No brake lights? No indicators? No helmet?'

No insurance. No MOT and no licence either, but that could wait.

'No rear numberplate?' chimed in the tall one. Johnny didn't know why they were asking all these things as questions, but didn't feel obliged to answer.

'Can I see your licence, sir?'

'It's not on me,' he said, to which the short-arse made a grand show of getting out his notepad.

'Name?' he said.

Johnny wasn't an idiot. He wasn't going to give his name – that was for sure. He looked about him for inspiration.

'Hood,' he said. The policeman started writing it down. 'Robin Hood.'

He felt Clem give him a little pinch on his waist, but she didn't say anything. The policeman's upper lip curled as he looked up suddenly from his pad. But Johnny could see that he'd already written HOO…

'Don't you waste my time, you little jerk.'

'Honest,' Johnny said. 'That's my name. Robin Hood.'

The policemen looked at each other. 'Are you fucking deaf?' That was the tall one.

'That's my name, sir,' Johnny said, all meek and humble.

'Well, you can come down the station and write it out for us then.'

'OK,' he said, weighty with emotion now. 'Look, I can't help it if my parents were jokers. I've had to take grief all my life and I swear I'm going to change it soon as I get the chance but what can I do? Robin Hood is my name. I'll get my birth certificate if you want.'

Johnny could see a little chink; the short-arse was wondering if he was full of shit after all.

'Do I look like I was born yesterday?' the short-arse said, but he was definitely wondering.

Johnny shrugged, depressed by his life's burden. 'It's the truth.'

The copper glared at Johnny and then turned to his mate. Eventually he wrote it down in his little pad before turning his attention to Clem. 'And you, love?' he asked. 'What's your name?'

She leant forward, peering at his jottings. 'Marion,' she said clearly. 'Maid Marion.'

2

THE HONEYMOON

IT WAS QUITE chilly now that the sun was sinking down behind the mountains. It was the end of March and the evenings were cool. Johnny was on the upper deck looking back across the fishing boats out to sea to where they had just come from: Turkey. The land was no longer visible; it had merged with the royal blue of the horizon. He stepped up on to the wooden guard rail for a higher angle but there was still no sign – visibility had been poor all day. He looked back along the *Old Rangoon* and marvelled at her ugliness. She was a hundred feet of quite spectacular bad taste, a millionaire's plaything, a floating tower block of unseaworthiness, a flash pile of plastic made for sipping cocktails in some poncey harbour. He had never imagined himself aboard such a monstrous vessel. But then again, there were lots of things he had never seriously imagined – like being married to Clemency Bailey, for one, and having the world unfurl before them.

He got down from the guard rail and rolled himself a cigarette. Down on the pontoon some young Greek boys were standing about transfixed by the *Old Rangoon*'s British skipper, Charlie, who was busy folding out a portable bicycle beside them with the curt efficiency of a man accustomed to being stared at. The bike was comically small and Charlie was unusually tall and as he clicked things into place undoing various bolts and locks he seemed to be giving the impression that he was about to start some kind of circus act. A small but keen audience was gathering, watching expectantly for the juggling or sword-swallowing to commence atop his strange little bicycle. Instead, with an unnecessary scissor- jump manoeuvre, Charlie mounted the bike, nodded a cursory farewell to his fans and peddled off with out-turned knees towards Kos customs house. The boys looked up at Johnny questioningly as if he were somehow responsible for Charlie and his lack of derring-do. Johnny shrugged his shoulders and lit his fag.

Johnny himself had only met Charlie six hours earlier when scouting for work along the quayside in Bodrum harbour. He'd come across him standing on the stern deck of the *Old Rangoon* involved in a discussion with the fat man from the marina who they often used to see parading about in his shiny uniform being important. The fat man had been posing offi- ciously at the back of a large lorry with a GB plate parked not ten feet from the stern of the motor yacht, examining the lorry's contents from the rear sliding door. He was too huge to actually get up into the truck but was managing to exert his authority just by leaning against the back frame and mumbling into his crackling walkie-talkie from the pavement.

Johnny, observing the proceedings, had wandered round to the back of the truck himself to have a look inside. As far as he could tell some wealthy bastard was moving house: it was piled high with grand pieces of furniture and huge Harrods boxes.

A spotty Turkish youth stood between the Uniform and Charlie, attempting to translate. Johnny stood behind them eavesdropping, sensing an opportunity. He had a gift for being noticed, for appearing at the perfect moment, and right now, at this juncture in their travels, they badly needed some work. He and Clem were totally skint – work had dried up in the boatyard and they were living in a tent behind Attila's restaurant with the equivalent of three pounds left to live on. That meant two days before they'd have to start nicking food again.

There was a military precision about Charlie, accentuated by his habit of clicking his heels together as a means of punctuating his speech. Both his accent and his beard were tightly clipped. He was quite clearly used to being obeyed and made no attempt whatsoever to speak slowly to the Turks.

'We leave the truck here at customs as agreed, and the proprietor, as I have already explained, will be here tomorrow morning at zero eight hundred hours. The proprietor will remove the truck from your premises. Understand?'

The spotty youth's version of these instructions sounded considerably shorter. The Uniform grunted, shook his head and waved his hands and the youth looked gloomily back at Charlie. 'No truck,' he said.

'My boss has already paid you to take it,' Charlie insisted, clicking the heels for emphasis.

The translator translated but the Uniform shook his head again and lit up yet another cigarette. 'OK,' Charlie persisted. '*We* unload the belongings from the truck and leave them with you to be collected at the aforementioned hour.' Neither the translator nor the Uniform was impressed by this idea either.

'Take it to Kos!' the Uniform said, turning away with a nonchalant scratch of his balls.

'Need any help?' Johnny said, stepping forward. 'We're looking for work.' He nodded in Clem's direction; she was crouched down on the quayside repacking their maroon bag that his dad had made them out of the sail of a Cornish Crabber. She was a hoarder, she collected everything – sweet wrappers, matchboxes, any old tosh – and now had it all laid out on the quay like she was holding a jumble sale. Charlie rubbed his beard, his attention still on the receding oval figure of the Uniform. 'Bloody idiot,' he said. 'Thinks I'm made of money…'

It seemed a fair enough assumption; Charlie certainly had the reek of money about him. He had that casual yet pressed cleanness that the rich favour: his dark neat jeans were rolled up just so, his ironed shirt was whiter than white and his deck shoes were gleamingly unscuffed.

'Is she *not* your boat then?' Johnny asked, looking down the *Old Rangoon*, wondering whether it was worth hanging around or not.

Charlie eyed Johnny suspiciously. 'For God's sake, man, do I look like a mighty great shipping magnate? Would I be taking this sort of codswallop if I were at the top of the food chain?'

Not once in his entire life had Johnny ever heard anyone use the word *codswallop*.

'Oh no, I can assure you,' Charlie continued. 'I'm just the monkey who sails the boat.'

Johnny strolled round to the back of the truck. 'Who does all this belong to then?' he asked, nodding at the truck.

'My boss is responsible for this truck.' He directed everything he said not at Johnny but at the Uniform, who was further along the harbour side squeezing himself into his tiny black booth and peering out of the minute window hole, giving the peculiar impression that he was wearing a burqua.

'What's he doing, your boss, moving house?' Johnny asked.

'Not him – his very important friend.' He raised his voice for this last bit so that the Uniform might hear. 'An *exceptionally powerful man*, I'll have you know.'

'If he's so powerful why didn't he get his own truck?'

'Good question!' Charlie said, spinning round. Johnny had at last got his full attention. His beady eyes inspected Johnny's scruffy appearance. 'How do you think the rich get richer, young man? They don't ever spend their own money, that's how. He heard that we were going down to Fethiye and asked if he could put "one or two things" on board our truck, which was coming out from the UK with a few pots of paint in it. One or two things, I beseech you!'

Charlie laughed at the audacity of it and Johnny tried to look suitably outraged.

'My boss is livid. Livid!' The thought of his boss's fury clearly quite excited him. 'I've never seen him like this. There's going to be trouble. He told me to dump the stuff here at customs but that walrus over there in a box…'

Charlie folded his arms and looked over at the Uniform Then an idea struck him. He turned his attention back to Johnny. 'Can you work hard?'

'Yes,'

'How do I know that?'

'Well, you can ask anyone at the Gündüz yard. We've been working there for the last four weeks, twelve hours a day.'

'And the girl?' he said, looking over at Clem, who was now ambling towards them. 'Is she strong? She looks a bit puny.'

'No, my wife is small but she's strong.'

'Your wife?' He laughed. 'You look like you're not long out of short trousers yourself. Do you have passports?'

'Of course.'

'How long have you been in the country?'

'A month or so. We're meant to be travelling through. Heading for Iran, Iraq, maybe make it to Pakistan, India.

'All right, all right, I don't want your bloody life story. You're hired. I'll pay you ten pounds each for the day. Unload the truck. Put it all on this deck. We're going to Kos.'

So with a couple of Charlie's Turkish crew Johnny and Clem had spent the next three back-breaking hours unloading the contents of the truck on to the stern deck and the three of them had motored across to Kos in the monstrous floating hotel that was the *Old Rangoon*.

Johnny flicked his cigarette into the oily water of the marina and wondered what Clem was up to. The Greek boys had ambled further down the quay and were fiddling about with their fishing rods. He looked down on to the deck beneath brimming with the curious unwanted cargo: piles of boxes filling all available space, a white Steinway piano backed against the marble statue, a giant oak table standing on its side with a chandelier hanging from one leg, a four-poster bed carefully taken apart, the entire contents of some Turkish millionaire's garish home wedged on to the back of the boat.

His back ached. He stretched and yawned. With any luck they should get it all unloaded and be back in Bodrum before midnight in time for a swifty with Aussie Dave with twenty quid in their pockets. He took a deep breath of the fresh evening air and thanked his lucky stars; then he turned around and set off to look for Clem – she had to be somewhere on this vast vessel of vulgarity. He opened the sliding glass panel beside the controls and slipped inside, finding himself in a corridor along the starboard side of the boat. He hadn't been on the upper level yet.

'Clem?' he called. Hung along the walls was a stream of photographs, in enlarged pixels, featuring a heavily made-up, bleached-blonde middle-aged woman striking various jaunty poses. She was not a woman who benefited from either enlargement or jaunty poses. He stopped at the last photograph where she had been joined by her family. No wonder Charlie obeyed Mr Shipping Magnate's every command: he had the face of a boxer and the eyes of a killer. He was twice the size of his wife – which was saying something – and his banana-sized fingers, dripping in gold, looked as if they might very easily squeeze the life out of living things. In front of the happy couple were three fat-faced, metal-braced girls who would one day clearly have an issue with hair removal.

'Clemmie?' Johnny called again. She was probably snooping around like him. He opened a door to his left and the décor hit him right between the eyes. He found himself in some kind of safari theme park. A zebra skin complete with head gaped up at him from the floor; a leopard-skin throw had been tossed with careless precision over a leather sofa stretching across the beam of the boat. To his side a galloping wooden giraffe chased by skinny wooden men with spears was glued to the floor and above the fake log fire hung a large oil painting of a herd of elephants traversing the African plains.

He found her in a room marked 'Emperor Suite'. He opened the door and would have whistled had whistling not been bad luck on a boat – his lips made the movement without the sound. The cabin was enormous, acres of fluffy white carpet leading to an emperor-sized bed covered in an army of red satin pillows. Clem was lying spread-eagled on the satin covers. The only reminder that they were actually on a boat and not in a hotel room was the swaying view of the harbour through the porthole above the bed.

He walked across the room, leaping to her side, landing face down on the pillows

'Oh! Yes!' he sighed, his voice muffled. 'A proper bed!' It had been a long time since they'd slept on a bed. The grass underneath their sleeping bags in the tent had long since been squashed flat and the sweltering canvas had lost its cosy romance a while ago.

Johnny kicked off his trainers and rolled on to his back. For a minute or two it seemed as if they both might fall asleep there and then, but he could never resist her for long. He ran his hand along the curve of her hip and up her arm, the hairs bleached bright white by the sun, her skin a honey tan that he was convinced no other human being possessed.

'One of the boxes...' she said, lifting her legs up into the air and pulling off her jeans and her knickers in one swift movement, '... had a dress in it with a price tag on for three thousand dollars. How can someone spend three thousand dollars on a dress?'

Johnny helped her with her shirt, gently brushing his lips against the softness of her nipples. 'Think of what we could get with that money,' he said. 'We'd get our boat... the gorgeous, double-ended, teak-decked, sixty-foot ketch. We'd cross the Pacific, go wherever we fancied... whenever we fancied...'

She looked down at him and smiled. Sometimes her heart ached with all the love she bore him; she'd had no idea that it was possible to love another person this much. Sometimes their love felt so infinite, so boundless, she felt like an astronaut floating in it. She gently kissed the top of his head and ran a hand through his hair, which was standing up in tufts from all the salt water.

'I'd catch fish for you,' he said, pulling himself up and kissing her lips. 'I'd dive for you. I'd get pearls or sponges...'

She was used to being adored by him; it was just the way things were. Life before they got together now seemed vague and unimportant. Ever since that night they'd spent kissing in the police cell in Barnes after Johnny got arrested, they had been inseparable. To her mother's dismay she'd moved in to his squat in Roehampton on her sixteenth birthday. Her mother had never approved of Johnny; she thought he was a waster, that he'd never get a proper job and earn a decent living, which meant that she was missing the point entirely:

those were the precise reasons why Clem loved him. Her mother had never understood her; ever since Clem could remember she had looked at her with a kind of bewildered disappointment in her eyes. And though it made Clem feel treacherous to admit it – because after all, her mother had been the only constant in her life – she was frequently embarrassed by her: her lack of imagination, her conventionality. Sometimes, especially when they were all together at the Loves and her mother would make some banal comment about the weather or the tea, she actually felt ashamed of her. However, since travelling, she had noticed a change in her own heart; with the distance, the irritation had been replaced with a fondness, from a thousand miles away she could actually appreciate her mother. She promised herself that she would try and behave differently towards her whenever she got home again. The truth was that Johnny's family had become her family; she adored them and they had embraced her in the same way they embraced life. When they stayed in Putney, Johnny's dad would come into their bedroom in the morning bearing tea and reciting sonnets, pulling open the curtains with an ode or two. '*Shall I compare thee to a summer's day*,' he'd say to the summer's day. He employed them at his building company and if they weren't earning money doing that they were usually to be found in bed in the tower block in Roehampton. They'd heaved a huge mattress right up to the window so that they could look out over Richmond Park. They didn't have sex *all* of the time; sometimes they just lay there for hours on end staring into each other's eyes as only lovers or loonies can do, in sheer amazement, always reeling from the miracle that two parts of the same thing had united and become one. Clem pulled away from Johnny's lips. 'Isn't Mr Magnate's friend going to be furious? When he finds out that all his stuff has been dumped at Kos when he thought it was going to Fethiye?'

'Not our problem, Clem,' Johnny said, rather wishing that just occasionally she would concentrate on one thing at a time. He breathed in her lovely teak-decking smell and pretty soon they found themselves making love on the millionaire's slippery red satin sheets.

They didn't hear him come in. Clem saw him first; she sat up very slowly, not bothering to cover herself up and she tapped Johnny on the shoulder. He turned around to see Charlie Potts holding the door wide open staring at them.

'Oh, there you are,' Charlie said, seemingly not noticing that they were mid-coitus, showing no signs of embarrassment or backing out. 'If you're going to do that sort of thing I would rather you didn't do it in here. There's a room on the lower deck available for breeding purposes.'

Johnny ran a hand through his hair. They certainly weren't breeding – she was on the Pill.

'Anyway, there's no time for any of that...' Charlie said with a brisk click of his heels, walking right into the room and over to the bed and handing Johnny a sheet of blue paper. 'It's a telegram from the boss,' he said, keeping his eyes exaggeratedly averted from Clem's bare breasts. Johnny held the telegram in his hands and Clem leant in close to read it: 'SINK ALL POSSESSIONS STOP IN INTERNATIONAL WATERS STOP'.

Both Clem and Johnny laughed and looked up at Charlie but his expression was deadpan. 'He's not serious?' Johnny asked, wiping the sweat from his glistening forehead.

'My boss is not known for his jocularity.' This fact could be backed up by one glance at his photograph.

'Won't they take it here?' Clem asked.

'Have you seen customs? It's the size of a sentry box.'

'He wants you to chuck all those things overboard? The piano? The furniture? The gold mirror?' Johnny asked. 'Into the sea?'

'Affirmative. We'll do it tonight and then we'll go on to Fethiye. I'll pay you an extra fifty plus your fare home. Does that sound satisfactory?'

'But if he knows we're going to Fethiye he'll be there waiting, won't he?' Johnny said despite himself; he didn't want to talk himself out of the money.

'Be that as it may. If there's nothing on board, there's nothing on board.'

Johnny and Clem looked at each other. It was a no-brainer. 'All right,' Johnny said, looking up at Charlie. 'Let's do it.'

Charlie nodded curtly. 'And now I would suggest you either bring your extra-curricular activities to a halt or finish it off quickly and get yourselves ready for some hard work.' With that he double-clicked his heels, turned around and walked out of the room.

The *Old Rangoon* pulled out of Kos marina, the sky behind a streaky pink. Clem couldn't resist a little tinkle on the ivories. She sat down at the Steinway and commenced a rather complicated Beethoven sonata, aware that Charlie was watching her. She could play the first twenty bars or so of quite a few impressive tunes rather well and then would feign distraction or indifference and the playing would conveniently dwindle out just as she got to the tricky bit. It gave the illusion of brilliance that she liked. Johnny was on to her even if no one else was.

Charlie stood on the upper deck He was keeping an eye out for boats, bending over into the microphone every so often to impart some instruction to his young crew on the stern deck.

His voice came out clearly and efficiently through a speaker beside Johnny, who stood there bare chested and sweating, surrounded by lumpen duvet bags loaded with goods, still not quite believing that they would shortly be throwing nigh on a million quid's worth of belongings into the sea. He kept half expecting a boat to pull up with a message from the boss saying that he wasn't serious, that it had all been a joke. One crate in particular was causing Johnny concern. It contained a brand new ship's compass and satellite-navigation system, worth a small fortune. He'd pointed it out to Charlie who'd said, 'Marvellous. That'll sink a treat.' And when Johnny had persisted, Charlie had looked calmly at him and said, '*All* possessions, Jonathan. You read the telegram. The police will be in Fethiye waiting for us. I assure you that Turkish police are not much fun. Have you seen the film *Midnight Express*?'

As the sun set leaving dark purple scratch marks across the blue, they sorted everything out by weight. Gold was good but marble was better. Silver was OK. And wood was useless. They filled a fridge freezer with crockery and cutlery, they attached the ship's compass and a garden statue to the mahogany table, they rammed the brand-new outboard motor into a wardrobe, tying it down with various garments including the three thousand-dollar dress which turned out to be made of a useful stretchy fabric. They worked quickly and efficiently for hours, filling Harrods duvet covers with all the leftover junk-like jewellery, vases and perfume bottles. They worked until their limbs ached and their hands had callouses and now they were just awaiting Charlie's word to begin dumping it overboard.

It was pitch dark by the time his crisp, curt voice came out of the speaker to their side, two small electric bulbs shining on to the deck. 'Radar's off. Engine's off. Navigation lights off. No other vessels about. Action stations!'

A blast of sinister choral music burst from the speakers and they both looked up at him with surprise. 'Verdi's Requiem,' he said over the speaker and gestured in the dim light for them to get a move on. The boat was swaying to and fro on the water. Johnny unclipped the wire at the stern between the two wooden guard-rail posts and went back for the first weighted sack. It contained the boat engine and most of the jewellery and the heavy gold mirror – there was no way it would float. They heaved the sack along the deck holding two corners each, dragging it to the edge of the stern.

'OK, Clem,' he said and slowly they heaved the sack up and began to swing it between them, higher and higher, rising with the crescendo of the music. 'One… two… three…!'

They let go and watched as it flew clunkingly through the air, a disfigured swollen white shape, landing inelegantly in the water. They both darted forward to the edge and leant over the guard rail watching the white mass float for a moment before the sea slowly consumed it, sucking it down into the darkness, gobbling up a good twenty grand in one salty mouthful.

They stared at each other, appalled and elated at the surreal situation they were in.

'And again!' she said. 'Let's do it again!'

So they continued with the next sack, this time weighted with a large marble lamp and all the silver candelabras. They lifted, swung, counted and threw. They rushed to the edge to watch it sink. What with the Verdi playing at top volume and the wind blowing and the boat rolling in the choppy water in the moonlight and the sheer insanity of what they were doing, their strength knew no bounds. One, two, three and over the sacks went; over went the four poster, the wardrobe and chest of drawers, the moose's head sticking out of the duvet, his glassy eye catching the light from the bulb as he floated for a moment before sinking. Ultimately everything was just *stuff* – priceless junk headed for the murky depths of the Mediterranean. They worked until the stars had followed their course halfway across the sky, Verdi had long since ceased and the yellow fingernail moon had clawed its way up the sky

They left the piano until last, the largest object deserving top billing. Charlie himself came down to help with the Steinway. Clem ran her fingers along the keys, the notes jammed and jarring. The three of them wheeled it to the back of the deck, got behind it and pushed it as fast as they could forward. It tipped over the edge of the deck, landing gently with a strangely melodious chord, floating for a while before taking a lopsided dive into the deep.

For a moment the three of them stood there on the empty deck, quite still, staring out into the sea. Everything had gone without a trace as if it had never existed. Not a single piece of bubble wrap left as evidence of what they had done.

'Mission accomplished,' Charlie said. 'Now get some rest, chaps. I'll wake you when we get there.' And he climbed the steps up to the wheelhouse two at a time and disappeared.

They lay on their bunk in a small berth near the stern in the crew's quarters, nose to nose, eyes locked, reeling as if drunk on what they had just done, on the glimpse they'd had into this beautiful upside-down world, on the sweet taste of release. They were so physically tired they could barely move. 'Charlie says if they ask us, which they won't, we tell the police nothing. We act completely innocent. We never unloaded any truck. OK, Clem?'

'OK,' she said with a yawn. Her whole body ached.

Johnny gently stroked her hair back behind her ears until she fell asleep. It wasn't long before he closed his eyes and they both slept a deep and dreamless sleep.

The strange thing was that the police weren't waiting for them in Fethiye. The *Old Rangoon* arrived just after dawn and customs came on board in their fluorescent jackets and their big moustaches, smoking their filterless cigarettes and flashing their torches. They mooched about a bit, asked no questions, got Charlie to sign a few papers and then left.

The trouble didn't start until they got back to Bodrum.

It was late by the time the dolmush pulled in at the bus station. Stars were scrawled across the sky like spilt paint and a wind was blowing wildly from the sea, swirling bits of litter into the air and ballooning the men's long shirts as they rushed to the mosques, called to prayer from the tower. The floury waft of baking bread mixed with the pungent sweetness of flowers whipped past their noses as they stepped off the bus. The town no longer felt alien to them; their arrival seven weeks earlier on the little fishing boat from Naxos felt like a lifetime ago – the yellow lights of the harbour winking out at them through the darkness from miles out long before the small white buildings and the castle became visible, the call from the mosques luring them in. Only later did it strike them that they were actually out of Europe, on a different continent, in a Muslim country. Apart from the man in the kebab shop in Hammersmith and the old bloke in the tower block who wouldn't use the lift, neither of them had ever knowingly even met a Turk before. But now, getting off the dolmush, Bodrum felt like home.

They had decided that with a little money in their pockets for once they would treat themselves and stay in Genghis's guest house for a few nights before finding more work in the boatyard; they'd save a few bob, pack up the tent and start heading east in the next few weeks.

Johnny flung the big red bag over his shoulder and stepped off the bus; it was half the weight it normally was as the majority of Clem's stuff was still in the tent. It contained only their sleeping bags, some of her junk and a change of clothes. If it was down to him they would always travel like this.

Clem was in high spirits after her little purchase in the dolmush. Somewhere during the first hour on the bus the driver had stopped at the side of the road to pick up a pile of carpets. Johnny had watched through the window as the pile stood up and climbed on to the dolmush all of its own accord. It came up the steps and made its way down the aisle of the bus to the back where they sat. His heart sank; as tourists they were like beacons to salesmen. The bus had been pretty much empty, save for two old women and a pervy old bloke a few seats further down. The pile of carpets stopped and sat down right next to Johnny in the back row. He caught a glimpse of a weathered old hand and a dark creased eye somewhere in amongst the fabric. *Here we go.*

'Eenglish?' a voice came from within as the vehicle lurched forwards along the bumpy road, the undercarriage clanking loudly. Johnny pretended not to hear him.

'American?' the voice said. The carpets were rubbing against Johnny's arm; they smelt musty but not unpleasant. Johnny shook his head without looking up from his book.

'English,' Clem confirmed across Johnny's lap, her hand reaching out to touch the fabric of a blue and red carpet halfway down the pile. Johnny looked at her aghast. He knew, just as the carpet man did, that he had a taker. The blinking eye went berserk and the weathered hand tugged at the carpet.

'Beautiful, hand-made, one hundred per cent natural dye… prayer mat…' he said, the words tumbling out.

'No lira,' she said to him.

'God hears your prayers on this carpet… magic carpet… Sterling?' he said, the eye glinting excitedly at the mention of money. 'Sterling good,' he said. 'For you special price… only four hundred pounds this carpet, very special.'

Clem laughed and shook her head. 'Four hundred pounds? You're joking!'

'Three hundred ninety… come quickly.' The hand flapped beckoningly at them as if it wouldn't be offering this crazily good price for long. But time was the one thing they did have. He sat next to them for six hours and he didn't stop selling for one single second. They ignored him, politely at first and then plain rudely: they talked between themselves and then later Johnny rolled up bits of tissue and stuffed them into his ears and dozed off for a while, only to discover when he awoke that the man was still gabbling figures at his side.

Then somewhere into the fifth hour of the journey, after a puncture and a scrap down at the front between the two old women, Johnny began to tune in to what the man was saying. His voice was quiet, his tone deflated now, his eye rolling exhaustedly, but his stamina and the price he was now offering were quite remarkable.

'Did you say *four* pounds?' Johnny turned slowly and stared at the carpets. The eye appeared through the pile, refocusing, blinking itself out of a trance-like state.

'Four pound sterling, yes please,' he said wearily.

'It's a deal.'

Clem was thrilled. She had spent the rest of the trip folding and unfolding the prayer mat. It wasn't big, maybe three feet by two feet, but she had no doubt that the carpet seller was right: it was a magic carpet. Its prayers would be answered. She could feel its power. Its past and future history lay in her hands. One day she would show it to her grandchildren and tell them how she and Johnny had bought it on a bus for four quid.

Back in Bodrum she carried it rolled up tightly under her arm as they made their way through the square. She was looking forward to showing it to Genghis. He was a man who knew a thing or two about everything and would surely be impressed with her bargain.

They wandered through the throng and down to the front where the trees were all painted white from the waist down as if wearing petticoats to protect their modesty. They shook their leaves loudly as the wind swept through them. Someone had hung some lights in a tree and they bounced about in the breeze. Groups of men hung around on the street corners doing nothing in particular as the older ones sipped tea and played Okey. As usual they stopped talking and turned their heads as Johnny and Clem passed by. Just beyond the jazz café an old man with an enormous nicotine-stained grey moustache yelled something at them, waving his hand.

'What's his problem?' Clem said. Johnny took her hand and walked a little faster. He hated the way the men here looked at her. Sometimes they even reached out and touched her – her crotch or her breasts, with him right by her side. He walked a little faster. Little dots of rain began to darken the pavement. They made their way down along the harbour where the dim lamplights dotted along the front of the quay shone double on the water's speckled surface. Deserted boats tied to the heavy iron loops bounced up and down in the waves and others anchored further out in the darkness could be seen bobbing about, their rigging tinkling loudly in the wind. A yellow moon flashed sporadically through the clouds silhouetting the castle over on the far side as the sounds from the bars and restaurants filtered across the water.

The rain was falling a little harder now and they jogged the last bit to Genghis's *pansiyon*. Up near the marina they could see some activity going on: various police cars and uniforms were wandering around in the darkness flashing their torches along the boats. Johnny knocked on Genghis's door but there was no response. He knocked again a little louder. A shuttered window on the first floor opened and Genghis stuck his head out. He said something in Turkish which they didn't understand before glancing nervously up and down the street. He shut the window quickly and they heard him running down the stairs. The door opened.

'Come quickly,' he said, pulling them in, shutting the door behind them fast. He leant against it as if keeping someone out.

'What is it?' Johnny asked. He'd not seen Genghis looking in such a state; he was usually a man with an easy smile on his lips.

'You must leave, Johnny,' he whispered. 'You must leave Bodrum immediately.'

'What? Why?'

'I don't know what has happened... but they are everywhere looking for you.' Genghis looked truly terrified, his mouth twitched and his eyes kept darting to the door.

'Who? Who is looking?' Johnny said, worried now by the state of him; the wonder and thrill of last night's events suddenly dimming into something sinister.

'This morning they go to your tent, they pull it down, they take your things. They go to Attila restaurant, they pull up a table, he say nothing...'

'Who, Genghis? Who does this? The police?'

'Maybe. I don't know. I don't think so... Bad men. They go to boatyard, they take Australia man...'

Johnny's heart dropped. 'They took Aussie Dave?'

The Australian was not a man to get on the wrong side of. They had spent weeks working for him. He'd built his own boat out of ferro-cement specifically for smuggling purposes. He smuggled guns, carpets and God knew what. He would personally be after them if these other people didn't get them first.

'He's in the hospital. They smash his boat up.'

'Oh my God,' Clem cried, the colour draining from her face.

'They were here this morning asking me questions about a truck from the UK. They know you were in Kos. They go to Kos. They come back. They go to Marmaris. They come back. They wait. You must leave before they find you. Go, I say. Go!'

'But it was nothing to do with us, Genghis...' Johnny said.

'Don't tell me anything. I must know nothing,' he said, holding up his hands, a look of pure fear in his eyes. 'You have made enemy. Just have to leave!'

'What do we do?' Clem turned to Johnny expectantly. Johnny heaved the bag back over his shoulder. What indeed? They stood out a mile. There were barely any foreigners in Bodrum – tourist season was still a long way off.

'They're coming back,' Genghis said. 'I thought you were them. You're not safe here. You must leave. Come out of the back.'

He led them through the *pansiyon*, his slippered feet scuffling quickly across the mottled tiled floor. Johnny grabbed Clem's hand; he could feel her trembling, or it might have been him, his heart was punching at his ribs, his head spinning. 'Let's just get the hell out of here, see what's left in the tent and maybe if someone at the marina can give us a lift.'

'No tent,' Genghis said, opening the back door quietly. 'No boatyard. No marina. Just leave. You don't understand... this is not your country. This is very different. You don't want police. Try fishermen. You have money?' He was rifling in his pockets now.

'Yes, we're fine, Genghis.'

'Not marina, OK? They wait for you.' His round happy face was so serious and his kindness so touching that Johnny leant forward and hugged him.

'Thank you, Genghis,' he said.

'Turkish people good people. I'm sorry.'

Then he opened the door a little wider, checking first that the way was clear. They dashed out of the *pansiyon* into the rain, glad of its cover, and climbed over the little wall at the back and crossed the road to get out of the light from the street lamp. They set off up the lane at the back of the *pansiyon* before realizing it passed the field where their tent was and, sure enough, a car was parked near by, blocking the lane. They turned slowly and as they rounded the corner they started to leg it back down the hill, stopping at the harbour road.

'Maybe we should just explain ourselves to the police,' Clem whispered, panting, the prayer mat clutched tightly underneath her arm. 'It was nothing to do with us. We're not to blame.'

'No,' he said. *Never trust policemen.* His mind was racing. The rain had started to pour hard. He watched it fall in slants in the light from the street lamp. Up at the marina he could see a car turning round, headlights flashing across the water.

'Someone's coming,' Clem whispered, looking behind them back up the lane where heels clicked in the darkness. Johnny was eyeing the road, his head trying to play catch-up, not quite believing or understanding what was going on. Down the road, the men from the tea houses had all gone inside, out of the rain, all except the man with the moustache who stood under an umbrella on the next corner looking around. Johnny squeezed Clem's hand and dragged her forward, running across the road into a small area of scrub between the quay and the front. They ducked down into the bushes. He had to think; he had to come up with something. Above the noise of the rain, he thought he heard the crackle of a walkie-talkie or a radio. The fat man from customs had a hand in all this, he was sure of that.

'We need to get to the road,' he said.

'Not down there, not past that guy,' Clem whispered.

'No, let's get to the other side of the harbour.'

They scuttled out of the bushes and ran across the quay, jumping down on to the shingle beach where the fishing boats had been pulled out of the water. They pressed themselves up against the wall, catching their breath.

'Are you scared, Johnny?' Clem said, still clutching the carpet, her soaked hair flattened against her cheeks by the rain.

'Shitting it,' he said.

She rather wished he hadn't said that. She felt the last of her own bravery ebb away. He mustn't say things like that. He mustn't be scared – as long as he wasn't scared they would always be all right, nothing could ever harm them. She could feel the panic welling up. He took her hand and they ran along the shingle beach in the darkness, their footsteps lost in the pounding rain. When the shingle ran out they climbed back up on to the quay, Johnny keeping the bag on his shoulder, hiding their faces. They walked quickly along the water's edge in the semi-darkness, ducking in and out of the line of moored gulets, all empty and locked up, past the fishing boats and the abandoned wrecks. Clem's hand was small and slippery in his. They needed to get past all the boats and up to the road.

They passed the café with the yellow awning; laughter and noise spilt out through the rain. As they rounded the quay two men holding torches appeared from directly ahead where the road they needed joined the harbourside, which made the dash for the road unviable. One of the men shouted something to the other and Johnny and Clem backed into the darkness on to the stern of a gulet, Johnny swearing under his breath.

'Johnny,' Clem said in a small voice, her body twisting round. 'There are four men behind us...' He turned quickly and, sure enough, behind them in the darkness, maybe fifty yards away, four men were walking towards them.

'Get in the boat,' he said and they clambered aboard over the cleats and ropes, shuffling forwards in the rain, creeping over the transom into the cockpit. He thought perhaps they could nick one of these boats. But it was no good, they had to get past the marina, they'd never be able to slip away.

'We just need to get over there,' he said peering over the stern, nodding towards the lane where the men were still lurking. 'Unless we go the other way...' He looked over towards the castle and the rocks beneath it.

They waited in the cockpit, keeping their heads down, until the men behind them had caught up and split off into two groups, one of which stood under the yellow canopy of the restaurant and the other turned back towards the marina. Instead of using the quayside, they quietly clambered over the boats, beam to beam, Johnny with the bag across his shoulders now like a backpack, Clem still clutching her carpet, climbing from one boat to the next in the darkness.

There was a shout from behind and a flash of torches across the rigging and decks of the boats further behind them. Their only option now was to leg it quickly towards the rocks beneath the castle where the huge man-made, wave-breaking boulders piled up against each other.

They were both nimble on their feet and they ran as fast as they could through the driving rain. Behind them they could hear the cry of voices as torchlight flashed across the water but neither of them turned until they got to the rocks. Breathless, soaked and terrified they began to scrabble across the boulders on all fours, slipping in their panic. Clem cried out with pain; she'd gashed her face. Johnny grabbed her wrist and pulled her along, gripping her so tightly that her fingers throbbed and her arm socket ached. Not until they got to the promontory did they stop and pause and look behind them through the downpour. They'd lost the men with their torches; two of them were on the boats going the wrong way and the others had disappeared along the road.

'Jesus Christ.' Clem was choking, the tears running down her face. 'What do they want from us?' She was shaking uncontrollably. Johnny watched the men scrabbling across the boats. Some of them were running back towards the marina. He leant back against the rock.

'What are they going to do to us?' she cried.

'I don't know,' he said, his eyes frantically searching the harbour. How the hell was he meant to know everything? He pulled her in out of the flashing torchlight and they huddled against the rock as far out of the rain as was possible until the cries and footsteps ceased. They sat there for a long while, both of them shocked and frightened, their breathing rapid, their hearts pumping furiously. They sat there until there was quiet, until the only sound was that of water: the sea crashing against the boulders; the rain lashing the rocks. And he wondered what the hell they were going to do.

Clem pulled away from him, tucking herself into a ball, her forehead resting on her knees, motionless. Somewhere in the distance a rumble of thunder rolled across the sky. She lifted her head and looked out across the sea. There was nowhere to go to. There was nothing to say.

When she did speak, her voice was flat. The panic had been replaced by an eerie calm.

'Why do we always end up in scrapes, Johnny?'

'We don't *always*,' he said.

'We do.'

He couldn't really deny it. They were always in scrapes. In France they'd worked for an awful man who'd conned them out of their money, in Italy they'd been mugged not once but twice and they'd ended up on a very strange hitch-hike through Yugoslavia with a man who kept changing his clothes for no apparent reason. Even their wedding had been a disaster, topped off with him forgetting to take any money to the fancy hotel in Padstow so they'd had to do a runner out of the window down the drainpipe.

'It's just what happens when you go travelling,' he said, but inside he was wondering how other people managed to avoid scrapes – Rob and his girlfriend only ever came back from their travels with suntans and tales of dreams fulfilled.

She didn't say anything, just carried on staring out at the horizon. She closed her eyes and rested her head on her knees again and started imagining. She could do this easily; she could almost transport herself out of any situation. She could imagine somewhere else so vividly that sometimes it seemed as real as the real thing. She let the rain lead her. She took the sound and turned it into Cornish rain. Only now it was lashing down against the windows of the cottage behind the curtains and she was all warm inside beside the fire, sitting in the faded armchair watching a film on the crappy black and white TV. Johnny was sitting at her feet, leaning on the chair, and his dad was lying on the sofa in his shorts, his hands behind his head, his wild white hair standing up. Every now and then the picture on the telly would go fuzzy and Johnny or his dad would have to get up and fiddle about with the coat hanger that was sticking out of the back.

'I'm sorry, Clem,' Johnny said.

The rain was seeping down the back of her shirt; she could feel it running down her back into her pants. 'It's all right,' she said wearily, turning her face towards him, eyes still shut.

He knew what she was doing. But it did them no good thinking like that. Even up shit creek with no paddles you could always use your hands or get out and push. He stood up and looked about him, out to sea, reaching into his pocket to check that he still had their tobacco. He dried his fingers on his shirt and rolled himself a cigarette under his jumper and lit up, keeping the flame covered by his hand. They'd wait here for an hour or two and then make their way back to the road; it would be fine. She'd see. They'd get up the hill and hitch a lift and by tomorrow evening they'd be laughing about all this. When he turned back to offer Clem a drag, he found her kneeling on the carpet, her palms pressed together, her lips mumbling.

'What are you doing, Clem?'

'I'm praying on my prayer mat. That's what it's for.'

'Only if you're a Muslim.'

'God's not bothered what religion you are.'

He flicked the soggy cigarette into the water. He knew she believed in angels and ghosts and her own private god, who thought church was a waste of time yet enjoyed getting the odd request, but he'd never seen her praying before, not on bended knee. He felt he'd really let her down then. She shouldn't need to turn elsewhere for comfort. He hated the idea of her depending on someone other than him.

God, if you're listening to her, get us out of this.

They both heard the music at the same time. It seemed to ooze through the pouring rain, the gentle strumming of a guitar accompanied by a pure, almost angelic female voice. It was coming from somewhere very near, from the rocks just around the corner, out of sight, as if a mermaid were sitting there, singing to them, luring them in. Quite stunned, they stared at each other, neither one of them moving a muscle, the clear voice briefly transporting them from out of their miseries. She sang of a bad moon rising. She made earthquakes and lightning, hurricanes and overflowing rivers sound like the most wonderful things in the world.

The mermaid was singing to *them*, voicing their worries. Slowly Johnny raised his chin up to the heavens and closed his eyes, feeling the rainwater washing his face, the music seeping into him.

Completely enchanted, they both moved slowly, as if any sudden action might disturb the singer. Johnny bent down and gently picked up the sail bag and Clem carefully folded up the prayer mat, tucking it under her arm, and then she took Johnny's hand, both of them following the voice, their ears finely tuned, lightly tripping from rock to rock now that there was a new hope, now that their hearts had been lifted.

A small, barely populated bay crept into view. The strange thing was that they had never come across it before; it seemed to have popped out of the nothingness entirely for their benefit. The bay beyond this one held the boatyard which they had travelled to every day. But this bay was invisible from the road.

A smattering of small boats littered the water and through the darkness a few white houses stood out along the shore.

There was only one light on in the entire bay, a warm yellow glow shining from a small boat moored by a short jetty not fifty yards away, bobbing about in the choppy water. The boat was stern to with the cabin doors ajar, light spilling out on to the cockpit dancing a zigzag across the choppy water to their feet, illuminating the slicing rain between them.

It was from this boat that the mermaid sang, her voice pouring out like rays of sunshine, touching them with its warmth.

Her voice had been joined by another. The second was the voice of a child and together they sang in perfect harmony about that bad moon on the rise.

Now that Johnny and Clem could see properly with the light of the boat to guide them the rocks seemed less slippery despite the relentless rain; their feet found it quite easy to grip. It poured harder and the thunder rumbled closer. They heaved themselves up from the rocks on to the pier and walked twenty paces or so to the beginning of the little wooden jetty, the voices fading a little now that the boat was beam to. Johnny adjusted the sail bag on his shoulder and took Clem's hand. They stepped on to the jetty, their sodden shoes making no noise as they slowly moved down the planks towards the boat, stopping right at the stern. Written on the transom in curled looped lettering was the name *Little Utopia*.

That was exactly how it seemed to them: a heavenly place full of warmth and light and music.

3

THE *LITTLE UTOPIA*

THE *LITTLE UTOPIA* was a small boat, not much more than thirty feet in length. The wooden sliding hatch was pulled across to stop the rain coming in but the cockpit doors were slightly open, for the rain was pouring from the other side, the starboard bow. Above Johnny's head, hanging from the backstay, was a Union Jack transom flag flapping wildly in the wind. They stood there motionless, hand in hand, soaked to the bone yet oblivious to the weather, quite transfixed by the light and sounds from within. The angel's voice had brought them here. The song was coming to an end and despite the wet and the cold neither of them wanted it to stop, for the mermaid to become human. Right now just the promise of safety was enough.

When the strumming of the guitar ceased and the rain took over the night again, Johnny cleared his throat. 'Hello?' he called out above the cacophony of the elements. A bolt of lightning flashed above them.

A moment later the hatch was pulled back and a man stuck his head out. He was a big, fine-looking man, dark and unshaven, almost bearlike. He shielded his eyes with both hands from the light within to see them better.

'Hello?' he replied, stepping out into the cockpit. His

T-shirt was dry and pale and the rain darkened it almost immediately in 45-degree stripes across his chest.

They watched him take them in, his expression changing from caution to concern. Johnny realized how desperate they must look. He turned to Clem and in the light from the saloon he saw how her chin was cut and the blood had run down on to her shirt, a mess of red smeared across her chest. She'd lost a shoe and her hands, feet and ankles were covered in grazes. Underneath the wetness and the blood she looked barely more than fifteen years old. He knew that he himself didn't look much older.

'Jesus. Are you all right?' the bear man asked but neither of them could think of anything to say. It seemed quite evident that they were not all right. The man glanced down the quay towards the shore as if there might be more of them. Johnny too looked around him but the bay was deserted, the other boats all empty. Another growl of thunder rumbled across the sky above them.

'Please,' the bear man said, gesturing. 'Come in out of the rain!' He offered his hand and Johnny passed him the soaked sail bag and turned to Clem. She was unable to move, her limbs locked frozen.

'It's all right, love,' the man said to her, helping her carefully on to the boat, taking her hand in one of his giant paws and her carpet in the other. 'You're safe here.'

She looked up at him and suddenly the kindness of a stranger proved too much and the tears spilt freely from her eyes.

'Come on now,' he said gently, opening the cockpit door with his foot, putting the soaking sail bag over his shoulder. 'Get yourselves inside and let's get you warm.'

Johnny led the way down the companionway steps and stood there dripping water on to the floor of their dry warm boat. A woman, presumably the mermaid, was sitting on the port side of the saloon, a guitar on her lap. Next to her was a young child, not more than four or five years old. She was the spit of her mother but with her father's dark colouring. Neither of them said anything; their identical unblinking eyes stared at the strangers from underneath their identical skew-whiff fringes. The child's gaze swung solemnly from Johnny to Clem and down at their bleeding, torn legs.

'Why's that lady crying?' she asked her mother.

'OK. Bed now, Smudge,' the woman said, standing up, taking the child's hand. The girl wriggled free and scurried away from the strange new arrivals into the forepeak, her big, dark eyes peering from behind the door as she slowly closed it.

'Annie, get the first aid,' the bear man said to his wife, his voice low and soft. Then he turned to Johnny.

'Do you speak English?' he said.

Johnny nodded. 'We are English,' Johnny said.

'Were you attacked?'

Johnny shook his head. The man nodded and began to wash his hands in the galley sink. 'You better get your wet stuff off.' He leant into the berth beside the chart table and pulled out a bundle of towels before approaching Clem and raising her chin with one of his giant fingers. He stooped down to examine her cut.

'That's nasty,' he said, his mop of dark, curly hair falling over his eyes.

She nodded. 'I fell on the rocks,' she said as he dabbed at her chin with the towel, his eyes flicking up to hers but flicking away again when no explanation was forthcoming. It was hard to know where to begin, so instead she stared at him for she was quite stunned by the course of events. A part of her was still standing outside in the pouring rain, wretched, not knowing where to go.

'There is a road, you know,' the bear man said with a wink. She was studying his face; he was old, in his late thirties, his eyes were very dark, his skin was weathered and his jaw unshaven, but it was his smell that struck her most. He smelt of something familiar: her father. He used the same soap that her dad used to use. She shut her eyes and let him tend to her.

Johnny peeled off his clothes. His drenched jeans and shirt sat in a pile on the floor. He was standing there in the galley stark naked, rubbing himself dry with a towel when the woman and the little girl came back into the saloon. 'Oh, sorry,' he said, covering himself up.

'Nothing we haven't seen before,' the woman said with a smile as she put the medicine box down on the table. There was something quite striking about her when she smiled; her face seemed to transform. The little girl placed a pile of clothes beside the box and the woman said, 'You can find something in that lot.'

'Thank you,' Johnny said to the little girl, who hid behind her mother's legs, those unblinking eyes never leaving his as he started to go through the clothes.

'Back to bed, Smudge,' the bear man said and the girl just stood there staring.

'Do what Daddy says,' the woman said, rubbing the girl's dark hair. She scurried off and the woman opened up her medicine box, inside of which appeared to be every remedy known to mankind. The bear man rifled through it and began applying one thing after another to Clem's grazes.

'You all right, love?' he said to her in his soft, low voice. She opened her eyes and nodded, watching as he turned back to the tin, his large but delicate hands putting a lid back on a tube. She noticed then that the tips of two of his fingers on his right hand were missing.

'Well, that should do it,' he said, dabbing at her and giving her a smile, revealing even white teeth. 'You'd better get your wet stuff off!'

Johnny was already in some dry clothes, a pair of enormous shorts with a belt tied in a knot and a huge sweat shirt belonging to the bear man. Clem did exactly as she was told and peeled off her soaking trousers, staring at her own gashed legs as if they belonged to someone else. Thin brown sea urchin spines stuck out of her ankles and feet. Slowly she undid the buttons of her shirt, took it off and handed it to the woman, who picked up all of the wet clothes and took them though to the wet locker. Clem stood there naked but for her knickers, which left nothing to the imagination, gazing at her blood-stained body. Johnny covered her in a towel and began to carefully rub her dry.

'We can get those out,' the woman said, looking down at Clem's feet, pulling out a pair of tweezers from the box. 'Put this on!'

She handed her a large T-shirt dress and helped her into it, wrapping a cardigan around her shoulders. Clem sat down at the table with Johnny at her side, watching in silence as these strangers quietly passed each other scissors and plasters and various implements and set to work on her feet and ankles.

Johnny's body began to prickle as the warmth seeped through his skin. He leant back against the saloon seat and listened to the rain beating down against the coachroof above them and he actually thanked Clem's god and her prayer mat for delivering them to these people. He watched them working away. The woman had a frown of concentration set on her brow, her top lip biting the underneath one. She was probably the same age as his mother had been when she died. Her eyes were a pale blue and sloped downwards at the edges, giving her face a peculiar sadness. She looked up and caught him staring and smiled. Once again he was quite taken aback at how quickly the sadness seemed to dissipate, how she looked like an entirely different person when she smiled.

'All right?' she said to Clem, wiping her tweezers and putting them back in the medicine box. 'That's the worst of them out.'

'Thank you,' Clem said. She was warm now and mended. She felt blessed. Her prayer mat had worked. These people had saved them. She reached out and took Johnny's hand in her own and kissed his fingers one by one, both of them watching as the man took out some tumbler glasses from a cupboard in the galley above the hob. He wiped them on a tea towel slowly and thoroughly in his great big hands, put them on the table then leant over the woman, his huge tipless fingers resting on her shoulder. He grabbed a large bottle of raki from the shelf behind them, slid open the coolbox and pulled out a bottle of water.

It was exactly what they needed. They watched him pour out the raki into the glasses and add the water so that the cloudiness swirled around the glasses like smoke in the air, releasing that sweet aniseed perfume.

'Get this down you!' he said, taking a seat next to his wife, pushing the glasses across the table towards them. They picked them up, raised them and knocked back the raki. Johnny felt it burn down the sides of his throat, a shaft of flame soaring down into his gut, into his centre. The bear man topped him up immediately.

'Thank you,' Johnny said, sucking in a quick breath to cool his palate. 'We owe you an explanation.'

The bear man looked up at him, his dark brown eyes twinkling. 'You don't owe us anything,' he said, reaching behind him on to the shelf for his cigarettes. It was a soft packet and he tapped it hard at the bottom and caught the cigarette in his lips. He tilted his head to the side and lit the cigarette quickly, smiling, chucking down the lighter on the table, watching it slide across the wood towards Johnny.

'Are you hungry?' he asked. Not waiting for a reply he stood up with bended knee, as did his wife, and from the seat beneath them pulled out a large bag of crisps and tore it open in his giant hands. He laid it open on the table, gesturing for them to tuck in while he himself picked up the guitar at his side. It seemed to Johnny that the man was in perpetual motion, his fingers now strumming chords in an easy, relaxed way, as if the tune would eventually and organically materialize of its own accord.

Johnny and Clem were ravenous. They devoured the crisps while the man and his wife went about their business as if having bleeding, needy strangers turn up in their company was an everyday experience. He played his guitar while she sewed a button on to a garment on her lap. Johnny paused in his eating when the woman began to sing again, at once mesmerized by that voice. He put his hand on Clem's thigh and she smiled. *See!* his eyes said. *We always get out of our scrapes.* He really believed it. He would never ever let her down. She smiled, happy now that she was warm and safe. She knocked her glass against his and made herself comfortable, tucking her feet up under her knees to listen to the bear man strumming and the woman singing and the waves bashing against the hull and the rain pounding the decks.

'We thought you were a mermaid,' Clem said when the woman stopped her singing.

She looked up from her sewing, laughter transforming her features.

'Or an angel. When we heard you from the rocks,' Clem said, 'you sounded like an angel.'

'Did I?'

'I thought you *were* an angel.'

'I assure you, I'm not,' the woman said, her face losing its lightness. A frown creased her brow as her attention returned to her needle and thread.

'But you do have the voice of an angel,' the bear man said, looking at his wife as he strummed.

'Yes, but I'm not one, am I?' she replied, her pale sloping eyes holding his gaze. She picked up her glass and knocked back the rest of her raki.

'We're Frank and Annie, by the way,' the bear man said.

'Johnny and Clem,' Johnny said, saluting him with his glass.

A roar of thunder cracked so loudly over their heads all four of them jumped.

'Christ Almighty!' the man said as the lightning flashed on and off like faulty wiring. He got up and moved to the companionway, pushing open the cockpit door. Johnny thought he noticed a slight limp as Frank climbed the steps. He was wearing long, baggy shorts and his legs were strong, covered in a fuzz of dark hair; a long scar ran down the inside of his calf. He leant out into the cockpit and looked up towards the mast.

Johnny turned around to look out of the Perspex window behind him. Fork lightning jabbed at the hillsides, lighting up the bay. There were other boats bobbing about, mainly fishing boats, getting pounded by the weather. But none of them were occupied; there wasn't a soul out – there was nobody looking for them, he felt certain of that.

'Quite a storm,' the bear man said, closing the doors behind him and sitting back down at the table, picking up the guitar again as his wife continued with her sewing. They were quite comfortable without conversation and that felt like a relief. Johnny could enjoy the wonders of the raki in peace; he loved the way it clouded his mind with its pleasant aniseed fog. He looked about him then, taking in every aspect of the boat. He was always puzzled by charter boats, their tubby ugliness, their lack of elegance, their uniformity. They were practical and buoyant, floating blobs of functionality. All the interior woodwork looked as if it were made of 2-mm ply.

'Are you holidaying?' Johnny asked the man.

'Holidaying?' he said, pausing mid-strum. 'No, no. We live on her. The *Little Utopia* is our home.'

'Oh,' Johnny said, quickly rearranging his features into an impressed expression. He swigged back another mouthful of the firewater, feeling it ease over any faux pas. The man strummed again and began to sing in his low, soothing voice, seemingly making up the tune as he went along.

'Clem,' Annie said as if hearing the name for the first time. 'What's that short for?'

'Clemency,' she said. 'But no one calls me that.'

'Like Smudge. Her real name's Imogen. But we don't call her that either.'

'Where are you from?' the bear man asked them.

'London. Putney,' Johnny replied.

'We're from the other side. Kentish Town,' he said.

'How long have you been living on the boat?'

Frank rested the guitar on his lap, his forearm lying on the curve. Johnny was thinking how smooth and clean the bear man's hands were for someone who lived on a boat; his own were gnarled and ingrained with grubbiness no matter how hard he cleaned them and this guy had almost twenty years on him. Then Johnny too noticed the missing fingertips on his right hand.

'Six years…?' the man said, looking at his wife.

She nodded.

'We've been coast-hopping all that time,' he said. 'Started off in France and here we are.'

That sounded like heaven to Johnny – though on a classic boat, of course. Not a pile of plastic like this.

'We never spend more than a week in one place, if we can help it,' the man said. 'You were lucky to catch us tonight; we would have moved on if it wasn't for the weather.'

'Where are you heading?' Johnny asked.

'We're travelling round the great Turkish bay and then onwards. At least that's the plan.'

Johnny and Clem caught eyes briefly, both of them hearing the same thing: a lift out of here. Johnny pulled out his tobacco and took the packet of Rizlas from the pouch. The papers were soaked and came out in a long white stream. The bear man pushed his soft cigarette packet Johnny's way.

'Have one of these,' he said. 'I imagine you'll need somewhere to kip tonight… This turns into a double.' He nodded at the berth he and Annie were sitting on.

'What about your daughter?' Johnny asked.

'She's fine. She likes to sleep in with us.'

'Thank you,' Johnny said. 'Thank you so much.' He tapped out one of Frank's smokes. He felt Clem poke his leg with her finger. 'Sorry to be cheeky,' he said. 'But is there any chance you could drop us off at the next place down? The next village or the next town?'

'We've got money,' Clem added.

The bear man and his wife looked at each other. 'Sure,' he said. 'I don't see why not.'

'Oh, thank you!' Clem cried. 'Thank you so much! I could kiss you!' she said and the bear man and his wife laughed.

'Feel free!' he said, raising an eyebrow, giving a flash of his neat white teeth and raising his charged glass.

It didn't take much to get Clem drunk. Johnny watched her blow kisses to their hosts across the table. The raki had made her cheeks flush and her dark eyes shine. She looked truly lovely. And the bear man too saw her loveliness. Johnny watched it happen. Frank was leaning forward to pick up his lighter when her beauty struck. He was momentarily thrown; his smile froze before slipping slowly from his lips. Occasionally, when Johnny witnessed how her beauty could disarm people, he thought of it as a sort of weapon. Frank looked as if Clem had just pulled a gun on him – there was the briefest flash of pure helplessness in his eyes.

'You two look like kids, if you don't mind me saying,' Frank said, looking away, back to the safety of his guitar.

'Well, we're not. We're married,' Clem said proudly, draining her glass, oblivious to her effect on people. 'I'm nearly eighteen.'

'I noticed the ring,' Frank said. She looked down at the tiny sapphire on a sliver of gold on her finger. Johnny had won a game of poker and they'd bought it for thirty-six quid in Kensington market before they left.

'We're on our honeymoon actually,' she said, suddenly remembering that herself, a wavelet of melancholy passing through her as she recalled the night's events. She took Johnny's hand, which was no longer damp but warm and flushed like hers. She ran her fingers over his, smoothing his skin, pressing away the bad things. 'We're travelling east – going to try and keep on going. It might be the longest honeymoon ever,' she said.

'Before you go home and settle down?' Frank asked.

'Oh no, we're never settling down.' She laughed, fiddling with one of the plasters on her ankle.

'Don't you want children?'

'Of course we do. I've got all their names ready. We'll have loads of children.'

'Not loads,' Johnny said, flicking his ash into the butt-piled ashtray. He wanted to wait to have kids, wanted to buy a boat for them to live on first – a proper boat that needed a bit of work: a sleek wooden ketch or a big Dutch barge, not a bucket like this. Boats like this should be banned. Any boat designed by a potato brain should not be allowed to set sail.

He looked up. He was as drunk as a skunk and not quite sure what he was saying out loud and what he was keeping to himself.

'Soon,' Clem said, taking the cigarette out of Johnny's fingers and stealing a drag. 'We're going to have babies soon.'

'In about ten years,' Johnny said. The man and his wife laughed although he'd not meant it as a joke. Frank offered Clem one of his cigarettes. She took one and leant forward with that extra concentration that drunkenness requires and he lit it for her.

'Do you want boys or girls?' Frank asked her.

'Both.'

'Girls are good,' he said. It was hard to judge the sobriety of a stranger but Johnny reckoned the bear man was pretty sloshed too. They all were. Raki should carry a health warning. 'Are *you* going to have more children?' Clem asked, turning to the woman. But she didn't answer. A shadow crossed her large, pale eyes and the rain rattling on the coachroof rattled that little bit louder.

Behind Clem a beautiful brass sextant was resting on the chart table. Johnny reached for it. 'Nice sextant,' he said, changing the subject. 'Where did you get it?' Johnny's dad collected sextants; he'd like this one.

'It was on the boat when we bought her. I don't think it works.'

Johnny felt its heavy weight in his hands and peered through the glass. He saw no reason why it shouldn't. 'Where did you buy the boat?'

'France,' he said.

'Was your daughter born there?' Clem asked Annie.

'No. Here,' Annie said.

'In Turkey?'

'No. Here on this boat.' She laughed. 'Right where Johnny's sitting actually.'

Johnny instinctively flinched and they all laughed; he'd been inadvertently funny again. He didn't mind them ganging up on him, was quite happy to play the joker. He was rather enjoying making this woman laugh, seeing the light switch on in her face.

'It's all right, I washed the covers,' she said, gently tapping herself out a cigarette, one eyebrow raised. 'Frank delivered Smudge himself,' she said looking proudly up at her husband.

'Are you a doctor then?' Clem asked.

'No,' Frank said, strumming the guitar again as he spoke, his head cocked a little as if the chord he was searching for was just out of reach somewhere. 'But I've watched enough of them do their stuff,' he said and it sounded almost like lyrics to the tune he was playing.

She waited for him to illuminate them further but he was

lost in his music now. She thought he might be an artist of some sort; he had those abandoned kind of good looks, like a film director, perhaps, or a set designer. They listened for a while and knocked back more raki. Frank stopped playing; he laid the guitar flat on his knee, picked up his cigarettes, shook the packet in his big hands and tapped one out, catching it in his mouth again. He was properly flash.

'I like how you do that,' Clem said and Johnny knew she'd be practising it for hours, choking and gagging on fags until she got it right. She leant over and lit it for Frank.

'What do you do about school?' she asked. 'Does Smudge go to school?'

'Bollocks to school,' Frank replied, taking a deep, hot drag, sucking the life out of the cigarette. 'Over-rated.'

Johnny liked that. That had always been his thinking too.

'We teach her ourselves,' Frank said, emptying the dregs of the bottle into their glasses. 'She can get by in three languages. She can pretty much read, add up, knows about history. What can school teach her that I can't?'

'Are you all right?' Annie was looking at Clem who was trying to open the hatch.

'I'm just a bit hot,' she said, feeling a little worse for wear now.

'You're drunk,' Johnny said cheerfully.

'Yes,' she said. 'Oh, Johnny, I'm very drunk and very hot.' She sat down again and he took off her cardigan for her.

'You do look a bit flushed,' Annie said, leaning across the table and tenderly pressing her silver-ringed hand against Clem's forehead, her pale blue eyes blinking with concern. It was an intimate, feminine gesture and through the foggy drunkenness that had rapidly taken hold in him, Johnny found that it had cut him to the quick.

'You feel OK,' the woman said to Clem, sitting back down next to her husband. 'It's probably the raki. Have a little lie down.'

Clem took her advice instantaneously and lay down right where she was, resting her head on Johnny's lap. She sighed heavily and curled on to her side, putting her thumb in her mouth, her other hand fiddling with the slate heart around her neck. He knew she'd be asleep within a minute or two; she had an uncanny ability to fall asleep the moment she chose to. He positioned the cardigan around her legs and ran his fingers through her hair, letting the ringlets spring back into shape like the suspension springs on his dad's old Norton.

'My mum used to do that,' Johnny said, looking up at Annie. 'My mum used to do exactly that when I was a kid.'

'Exactly what?'

'The hand thing.' He copied the way she had put her hand on Clem's forehead.

'Did she?' Annie said smiling at him. 'I guess it's just something mums do.'

'Maybe.' He hadn't thought of his mother for a long time. The drunkenness had made him nostalgic. 'I used to have a radiator by my bed and sometimes in the mornings if I didn't fancy going to school I'd press my head against it and kick the sheets about and moan a bit and Mum would do that; she'd lean down and feel my head with her hand just like you did and she'd look all concerned and say, "Yes, you are hot, Johnny, I'll ring school." And hey presto! I'd get to lie in bed all day masturbating to my heart's content.'

Annie and Frank both laughed. He was quite the joker today. 'There we go,' Frank said. 'That's exactly why I don't want boys.'

Annie turned to a pile of laundry at her side and picked

up a little dress and began pressing it down on her lap, smoothing it with her palm, ironing it flat. Frank leant forwards against the table, one giant paw gently wiping the surface as if he'd spotted some crumbs. Then he looked up at Johnny, his smile gone now. 'So you lost your mother, did you, Johnny?' he said. And Johnny, quite taken aback, could only stare back, confused. He didn't remember saying anything about her dying. But then again he wasn't quite sure what he was saying at all.

'Don't worry, Johnny,' Annie said, pausing in her ironing, looking up at him with those wide, sad eyes, seeing his confusion. 'Frank can see things other people can't see.' She looked at her husband with a strange mixture of pride and defeat. 'He sees everything.'

'Yes,' Johnny said, looking into Frank's dark eyes. 'My mother died.'

'You were what, mid-teens?' he said and Johnny must have nodded. Frank's voice was so gentle it was as if he was inside Johnny's head, swirling around with the raki, drowning in the stuff. He felt as if he was melting from the inside out; he'd tell this man absolutely anything if he asked.

'Hard for you,' Frank said quietly. 'Boys need their mothers.'

Johnny nodded again. He remembered her touch more than he remembered the details of her face: that cool, loving hand against his forehead, the coldness of her rings, the hardness of her nails. They were always painted a shiny pale pink. He was overwhelmed by the clarity with which he could remember those hands.

Annie stopped her folding and moved her fingers cautiously across the table and rested them on Johnny's. He couldn't help himself, he was too drunk to care; he lifted her hand and pressed her palm to his forehead, all self-consciousness gone.

He smiled and shut his eyes. He felt so overwhelmed by every-thing now – the evening, their escape from those men, this haven they had found, the kindness of these people, taking them in, tending their wounds, the raki, the music, being here so far away, his love for Clem and his dead mother – that his eyes began to sting and the table swirled about the cabin in a watery flurry and he thought that he must be crying.

'It's all right, Johnny,' Frank said softly. 'You've had a bad night. You found yourself in a tight spot. But you're safe now.'

Then Johnny felt Frank's great hand smoothing his hair gently, femininely. No man had ever touched him like that before. 'It's OK,' Frank said in that low, soothing voice of his and Johnny laid his head back against the shelf and closed his eyes, feeling the weight of Frank's hand on his head, Annie's hand on his wrist and Clem's head on his lap; he was surrounded by touch. He listened to the rain on the deck, which was softer now, like drumming fingertips beating out a complicated rhythm. He thought that he must be very drunk indeed. He felt Frank take his hand off his head, heard him pick up the guitar again and start playing some chords. Both of them were humming now, softly, a very long way away, and Johnny let their voices dance through his head and he thought what a strange and wonderful time he was having. He felt as if somebody had taken the plug out of him and he was pouring out. How good it was, this sweet release.

When he opened his eyes they were both smiling at him. He smiled back and Annie returned to her pile of laundry, ironing with her palm.

'This will be me and Clem one day,' Johnny said. 'This life – living on a boat with a kid.'

Frank rested one elbow on the table and grinned at Johnny. 'Good lad. It's the only way.'

'Is it?' Johnny sat up straight, all his melancholy gone as quickly as it had arrived. 'Tell me!'

The bear man's dark eyes twinkled at him and he sighed heavily. 'Well,' he said mysteriously, as if he were about to reveal a secret. 'We're on a boat, aren't we? We're under the rule of no land. We live how we want to live. We're free of all those ridiculous values that society places on us, rules that other people live their lives by: how to behave, how to conform, how to treat each other, how to bring up our children. Nobody should tell us how to live, what children should or shouldn't be learning, how they should or shouldn't think. Here on the *Little Utopia* we think for ourselves. No rules, no fetters, no chains, no labels. You know what this is, Johnny?' he said, slamming his glass down, the raki spilling on to the table. He was drunk all right. 'It's the fucking Golden Age.'

Johnny slammed his own glass down too. He didn't know what the fucking Golden Age was but it sounded fucking fantastic. He was grinning now; he'd not met a man like Frank before in his life. Everyone else seemed to have compromised somewhere along the line. Not this man: he was living on his own terms. Johnny swore to himself that he would be like him, never settling for less. He'd never live a half-arsed life in a half-arsed relationship with a half-arsed job like so many people. Even his dad had compromised. Frank was brave. Johnny would be brave.

Frank tapped out another fag and caught it in his lips – how cool was that – and lit it in that snatched, hurried way and then passed it to Johnny. He then tapped out another for himself. No man had ever done that to him before.

'I'm with you,' Johnny said, a major slurring of the tongue going on now. 'What the hell happens to most people as they get older?' he cried, feeling pretty heated now, pretty let down by the rest of the world. 'Why do they just opt out?'

'Fear,' Frank said. 'People live in fear. Not us, my friend! Not us on the *Little Utopia*!" And he tipped his raki glass against Johnny's.

'To the *Little Utopia*!' Johnny cried, with one too many t's. Annie knocked her glass against his and Johnny noticed then how pissed she was; her eyes were as skew-whiff as her fringe and her pile of laundry looked like the leaning tower of Pisa.

'To international waters!' Johnny added, suddenly thinking of the moose's head staring into the darkness from out of a chest of drawers somewhere in the deep, the white keys of the Steinway piano tinkled by no one and the satnav pointing the way to nowhere, all down there in the dark, at the bottom of the deep blue sea sea sea. Could that really have only been twenty-four hours ago?

'Under the rule of no land!' Frank cried, standing up to chink Johnny's glass and in so doing catching a glimpse of Clem sound asleep now on Johnny's lap, flat on her back, her chest rising and falling under his hand, her thumb hanging loosely from her lips as Johnny's fingers twirled the little slate heart hanging around her neck.

'Look at her!' Frank gasped, amazed, wobbly on his feet. 'She's sucking her thumb!' Johnny nodded and Frank laughed and fell back down into his seat heavily, a seriousness taking hold of his rather fine features.

'I like you two,' he said. 'You have something rare and precious.'

'Too bloody right we do,' Johnny said. He was unattractively drunk now. But it didn't matter. Nothing mattered. This was a new kind of freedom.

Frank slowly blew out a jet of smoke and put his cigarette

down. 'Yes,' he said, staring hard at Johnny, pinning him with his dark, intense eyes. 'I like you two very much.'

Then he snatched up his guitar again and strummed loudly and sang with abandon the same old song about that bad moon that the mermaid had been singing – he sang of nasty weather, of an eye for an eye, of getting things together, of being prepared to die and Johnny cocked his head to listen.

Not until then did the lyrics strike Johnny as strange.

At night, the house in Putney had creaked and breathed in a different way to its daytime life. Johnny lay in bed and listened to the rain lashing against the rattling windows and the asthmatic groaning of the boiler in the cupboard. But it wasn't the storm that had woken him up. He kicked off the covers and got out of bed. His room was next door to the bathroom and he could hear someone retching through the wall. He opened his bedroom door and quietly leant against the bathroom door. He pushed it open.

His mother was on the floor on her knees, head in the toilet bowl, being quite violently sick.

'Hey, Mum!' he said and knelt down beside her. He put his hand on her back and felt her heave. He pulled back her hair from her face and held it back while he waited for her to finish.

She sat back and wiped her mouth, exhausted and pale. 'I must have eaten something...'

Johnny leant over and flushed the toilet and then filled the red plastic toothbrush holder with some water and gave it to her. She rinsed out her mouth and spat into the toilet bowl. He helped her up and she sat on the edge of the bath. He ran the flannel under the tap and gave it to her. She wiped her mouth and hands.

'Sorry I woke you, love,' she said.

'You're shivering,' he said and went into his bedroom and got his dressing gown. It was way too small for him, he'd had it since he was twelve, but it almost fitted her.

'Go back to bed,' she said.

'I'm not tired.'

She was still perched on the edge of the bath. She looked him in the eye, a smile on her pale lips. 'My lovely boy,' she said quietly.

'Are you going to chuck again?'

'I bloody hope not. It's exhausting,' she said and rubbed her face. Outside the rain was hitting the window in loud gusts and they both looked towards the frosted glass.

'Fancy watching the storm downstairs?' she asked.

A while later they were settled into the low armchairs, angled towards each other, under the glass refectory at the back of the house in the animal room. They were silhouetted against the darkness, snug and warm, listening to the howling wind, watching the rain fall in sheets against the glass. His mum had a blanket wrapped around her and was leaning back looking up through the ceiling at the torrent of water as the guinea pigs and gerbils roamed freely at their feet. The room smelt of sawdust.

'I'm glad none of you are out sailing in this.' The wind howled louder as if responding to her. 'When's Rob off?'

'October.'

'You've got to take your dad sailing, Jonts. He misses it. He needs a change of scene.'

She leant forwards and picked up one of the guinea pigs but it scuttled off her lap and landed with a scratch on the tiles. Johnny spied his dad's rolling tobacco that was sitting amongst bits of motorbike on the shelf in front of him. He picked it up.

'Why did Dad sell *The Gull?*' he asked, rolling himself a cigarette with already-experienced fingers. 'I loved that boat.'

'I'm surprised you can remember it – you were very little.' She smiled; the memory of the boat was clearly a good one. She ran her hand through her hair and sighed. 'It got too difficult with all you kids. Sarah was on the way. You and Rob kept chucking things overboard like it was going out of fashion. I'd had enough....'

'Nothing to do with Uncle Tim then?'

She stopped looking up at the glass roof and turned to her son. 'Maybe.'

They sat in the rain-lashing silence. 'What a way to go,' Johnny said eventually. 'On a night like this.'

'They say drowning's not so bad, you know.'

'And how the hell would they know that?' he said and the wind rattled the glass. 'Pass the matches, Mum.'

'Jonathan, you're fifteen,' she scolded half-heartedly, bending forward and chucking him the matches.

'Does he talk about it, with you?'

'About Tim? No,' she said and crossed her legs in the chair, smoothing the blanket with her hands. 'But still waters run deep.'

'What do you mean?'

'Every now and then he wakes me up in the night, shouting out for Tim in a voice I don't recognise.'

Johnny stared at her. He didn't want to know this; his dad was a man who never showed any fear. In fact he was a man who allayed other people's fears. Patrick Love could be guaranteed to find a solution for any problem.

Johnny struck a match into the darkness and lit his ciggie. 'What was Tim like?' he asked.

'They were like you two, your dad and his brother,' she said fondly. 'They were great friends, really good brothers. They were fanatical climbers; they'd climb anything. One night they climbed right to the top of Albert Bridge. Have a look when you're next there – Tim's tie is still up there. And they got all the way back that night to his flat in Fulham without once touching the pavement.'

'Impressive.'

'That's what I thought.' They laughed together, they had the same laughs.

'Tim was rather like Rob, you know,' she said.

'Obsessed with sex?'

She laughed again. 'He *was* actually, now you come to mention it. He always had a different girlfriend. Let's just say he wasn't fussy.'

There was a flurry of activity at their feet, claws scratching on the tiles as a pair of guinea pigs scuttled across the room and skidded into a corner. A flash of lightning lit up the sky and they both counted for the thunder, both imagining being out there, drowning in a storm like this. The thunder rumbled in the distance.

When she spoke, her voice was low and quiet. 'I just hope it was quick. I hope he died quickly.'

Johnny sucked on his cigarette. 'I don't know… he probably died of hypothermia.'

'Do you think?'

'And I don't think it's quick. It's meant to be a bit surreal, you start seeing things that aren't there.'

'Or maybe they are there, Johnny,' she said. 'Maybe they're there to comfort us.'

'You're such an old hippie.'

She smiled and the wind howled. It seemed to have woken

up the gerbils now; one of them was going berserk on its wheel. He watched it spinning round like a lunatic in the shadows.

'Unless he panicked – they say that panic is what kills you,' his mother said. And then almost to herself, 'God, I hope I meet death without a panic.'

Johnny watched her. He wanted to ask her what was going on, what she wasn't telling him. He sucked on his cigarette, held the smoke inside himself before blowing it out slowly into the room.

'I've heard you be sick before, Mum,' he said quietly but her expression didn't change, she was still looking upwards. He waited for her to say something and the seconds began to feel rather long.

'Mum?'

'I've got a sensitive stomach.'

'And your back? Why does your back keep hurting?'

'It's nothing, Jonts. Arthritis.'

'You've got arthritis? You're only thirty-seven.'

'Well, I'm having tests. Arthritis is most likely.'

She reached out her hand for the cigarette and Johnny passed it to her, watching her elegant fingers take it and bring it to her lips. He hadn't seen her smoke for a long time. He watched the end of it burn like a fierce little sun in the darkness as she inhaled.

'And this weather doesn't help,' she said.

He didn't understand what she meant about the weather but he said nothing.

'Well if it is arthritis, I'll wheel you around, don't worry. I'll strap you to the trapeze and use you as ballast on the Fireball.'

She gave him a big smile and then she leant over and squeezed his hand. 'Don't mention it to the others, eh, Jonts?'

Afterwards, he was always to wonder whether he should

have mentioned it to the others, whether it would have made any difference.

Johnny awoke to the sound of the engine running. Without moving, through the port window he could see grey sky. He turned his head and felt the thud of a hangover follow a moment behind. Clem was at his side fast asleep still wearing the dress she had been in the night before. He didn't remember going to bed at all but they appeared to be lying lengthways where the saloon table had been last night, an unzipped sleeping bag thrown across them. Then he remembered. They were safe. They were getting a lift out of here. He watched Clem sleeping for a moment, and then reached out a hand and undid the button at the top of her dress to see her tits better. He ran his fingers over her soft brown nipple and slowly up her throat and gently stroked her lips. She opened her eyes sleepily and smiled, nuzzling in closer to him and shutting her eyes again. Then she opened them suddenly.

'We're moving!' she said.

He nodded. 'See, Clem. We do get out of scrapes.'

She smiled at him until another thought struck her. 'What day is it?' she whispered.

It was Friday. 'Is it Friday?' she said, looking worried.

'I'm not sure.'

'It is,' she said. 'It's Friday.'

'Clem,' Johnny said, putting his arm around her. 'Don't be ridiculous.'

She sighed and turned on to her back. He could feel her thinking, lying there looking up through the hatch at the white blotting-paper sky. They had had to change many plans over the years in order not to leave on Fridays. Then, as if Frank knew this and was mocking her, from out in the cockpit he started a shrill operatic whistling. Clem turned her head and glared hard at Johnny, her eyes widening. He smiled at her.

'It's not funny,' she whispered. He shouldn't be laughing. He of all people should understand the importance of superstition. His own uncle had drowned in a storm off the Cornish coast. He'd tripped on deck whilst putting a reef in and fallen overboard in the dead of night and Johnny's dad had tacked up and down for two whole days looking for him, calling out until he had no voice left. The body hadn't washed up for another week. It turned out that not only had they left port on a Friday but they'd also just painted the hull green – another glaring mistake. Clem liked sailing because the superstitions were already there and she didn't need to make them up. She'd made up lots of rules for other things, for most things in fact. If she was in a car, she had to hold her breath between lamp-posts; if she was on her bike, she had to wiggle the front wheel at post boxes or red buses. There were special ways for making sandwiches, running baths, drawing curtains, getting dressed. Before she met Johnny it had never occurred to her she was unusual, she reckoned everyone had their own particular ways of doing things. Johnny always put his socks on in a certain way that took for ever and he always brushed his teeth for five minutes. She never mocked *him*.

'Clem, we're just getting the hell out of here. We'll get off at the next village, take a bus east. That's all. We're not going on a *trip*.'

She stared at him for a moment and then she kissed him. She loved his straightforward thinking. Left to her own devices she got carried away in the detail. She pushed her body in closer to his and kissed him again. He put his hand up her dress to find her hotness.

'Tick tock, tick tock…'

They both lifted their heads in unison from the pillow. There was someone else in the saloon. Sitting on the end of the bed was the little girl from last night; Johnny couldn't remember her name. She was wearing a red velvet buccaneer jacket with grubby, frilly white cuffs. But apart from that she was stark naked, her dark hair sticking up wildly from her head, a cuddly toy hanging from her hand.

'Hello,' Johnny said. 'There's a pirate on the bed.'

'I'm not a pirate, I'm Captain Hook.'

He didn't correct her. 'Where's your hook?' Clem asked.

'I dropped it in the sea when I was hunting.'

'What were you hunting?' Johnny asked her.

'Sea monsters,' she said as if everybody knew that.

'Of course! Have you caught any?'

'I can see your bosom,' she said. The dress had slipped off Clem's shoulder. She pulled it up.

'And I can see yours,' Clem replied.

'But I'm a man,' the little girl replied, frowning. 'Men's bosoms don't work.'

'And who's this?' Clem asked, looking at the mauled and chewed monkey thing she was holding in her arms.

'Gilla,' she said. 'He's a grilla. Sea monsters don't like grillas.'

'I used to have a little monkey like Gilla,' Clem said, looking at its lopsided face, remembering how passionately she had once loved her own toy.

'It's my birthday soon,' the little girl said.

'Is it?' Johnny asked. 'How old will you be?'

'Five and a half. My real name's Imogen. Imogen means "It's not my fault" in Irishness.'

'Smudge?' The bear man's voice boomed down from the cockpit. 'I said not to disturb them. Let them sleep! I want you up here.'

Through the hatch Johnny caught a flash of Frank. He must have been doing it on purpose – he was wearing a green shirt. Johnny couldn't even remember why green was unlucky; something to do with sailors missing home and homesick sailors making for an unhappy ship. Clem would know.

Smudge jumped off the bed and scrabbled up the companionway steps like a little feral beast dragging her Gilla. This boat was evidently her playground; she was as nimble as a weasel as she scuttled into the cockpit. Johnny got up on his knees and peered out of the saloon windows. On their port side they were passing the outskirts of Bodrum: the castle in the distance behind them, white houses dotted along the bay. On the starboard bow about a hundred yards away was a small speedboat. There were a couple of men on board looking at the *Little Utopia* through binoculars. Johnny ducked.

Frank appeared in the companionway leaning on the hatch, eyes on the horizon ahead. 'Yeah, you might want to wait down there,' he said to Johnny. 'That boat's been hanging round for a while. You didn't bring any drugs on board, did you?'

'No,' Johnny said.

'Wave at them, Smudge! There's a good girl.'

Clem came up beside Johnny. 'They're not still looking for us, are they?' she said.

'I doubt it. Still want to hang around till Saturday?' he asked her, his eyes watching the speedboat. There weren't any other boats about apart from the odd fishing boat heading out from the harbour behind them. The tourists were only just discovering Turkey – no doubt one day Bodrum would have its own airport.

'Get yourselves some coffee, it's on the hob,' Frank said, standing there in the cockpit, displaying the full extent of his greenness. He was wearing khaki shorts.

'We'll be getting off in a few hours,' Johnny said, turning to Clem. He got off the bed and made some coffee and Clem packed away their bed and turned it back into the kitchen table. They sat down and waited until eventually Frank stuck his head down.

'Coast is clear,' he said. Johnny came out on deck and looked around him, taking in the grey sky and the lack of wind. The coast was quite literally clear: there was nothing there at all. It was utterly deserted as far as the eye could see: a barren mountainous scrubland punctuated by the occasional shack. They were barely a mile out off the shore, motoring at a steady four knots, dragging a tender behind them, a little wooden rowing boat that had seen better days.

It was hard to believe there had been a storm raging last night; save for the swell in the water and the crisp cleanness of the air there was no evidence of it; there wasn't a breath of wind now and the low cloud was beginning to melt away leaving a thin, watery blue in its place, the sun nothing more than a dull white ball shining hazily on to the slate grey sea. There were no other sailing boats, no other boats at all.

In the unforgiving daylight, both Frank and Annie looked older than they had last night – he might even be forty. Unlike Johnny, Frank seemed unhampered by a hangover. He had a fag on and looked like he hadn't bothered with bed at all. Annie on the other hand did look hampered; she was in the corner with her knees up drinking coffee, her eyes shielded by large sunglasses, trying to ignore Captain Hook who was climbing over her shoulders. 'Stop it, Smudge!' she said wearily, gently wrestling her daughter off her.

'I don't think anyone's going to find you now,' Frank said.

'No. But where the hell's the next village?' Johnny looked out into the nothingness.

'Have a look at the charts,' Frank said.

Clem joined them up on the deck, clutching her cup of coffee. 'Morning!' she said over-cheerily. Johnny could tell she was trying hard not to be bothered about the greenness of things and the whistling and the leaving port on a Friday. She sat down slowly on the starboard side of the cockpit, looking out at the barren surroundings.

'Johnny's good luck on board a boat,' she said apropos of apparently nothing.

'Is he?' Frank asked, turning towards her.

'He was born lucky.'

'Ah, well then…' Frank said, bending over, putting his hand on the lever adjusting the throttle slightly.

'He was born in the caul. He came out in the sack. It was completely unbroken. His dad said he looked like he was covered in clingfilm.'

'That's good luck, is it?' Frank asked, tipping his ash over the side.

'Kept me fresh,' Johnny said, stepping down the companionway steps to have a look at the chart laid out on the chart table.

'It means that he's never going to die from drowning,' she said.

Johnny spread the chart out on the table. It was unbelievably rudimentary, not a lot more helpful than a postcard. Villages were not marked, but now, looking out at that barren scenery, he was beginning to wonder whether there were any. The bigger towns, the ones that would have bus stations and possibly train stations were on the next bay, Datça and Marmaris, and he thought he remembered Frank saying last night that they 'coast-hopped'. They would surely pass a village – they could get out, find a road and hitch a lift. It wouldn't be a problem.

'No. It's true,' Clem was saying as Johnny stepped back out into the cockpit. 'In the olden days sailors would go to a lot of trouble to get someone like Johnny on board. It meant that as long as he was on the boat, it was never going to sink.'

'Am I in a coal?' Smudge looked up at her mother from her lap.

'*Caul*. No, darling.'

'You believe in luck, do you, Clem?' Frank asked her, an amused expression on his face.

'Don't you?'

'No. How's it looking, Johnny?'

'Well, villages aren't really marked but there's bound to be something along here soon, we'll just get off and hitch.'

'Eventually we'll hit Datca, won't we?' Frank said.

'We'll be off before that, thanks, Frank.'

'But some things just *are* lucky,' Clem was saying to Annie. 'And some things aren't. Everyone knows that.' But no one backed her up. 'You don't believe in luck at all?' she asked Frank, unable to fathom the idea; even Johnny never whistled on boats.

'I don't believe in anything that aims to inspire fear in people. Good luck and bad luck, they're just a means of control. They create fear. Religion does it. Governments do it. It's just another form of manipulation by the authorities.'

Clem stared at him, wondering whether he was serious.

Johnny had forgotten quite how much he had liked this man last night and suddenly remembered how off his trolley he'd been – he had a vague embarrassing recollection of weeping. 'Sorry about last night,' he said to them, rolling himself the first fag of the day. 'I think the raki got me.'

'Never apologize for the way you are, Johnny,' Frank said,

flicking his cigarette overboard and looking Johnny right in the eye. 'That's bullshit.'

'So you think that we make our own luck then, Frank?' Clem asked, still working things out, her eyes focused far out to sea.

'Indeed I do,' he said, turning to her. 'Cause and effect.' And with that he started to whistle again.

They chugged along all morning enjoying the peace and solitude, watching the blueness of the sky take hold. As the sun began to shine Annie helped Clem hang up the contents of their sail bag along the guard rail with washing pegs, their entire wardrobe hanging out for inspection. There was very little of it: a couple of shirts, a couple of pairs of trousers, two jumpers, the prayer mat and their sleeping bags drying in the weak morning sunshine. Smudge was tagging along copying them and when they'd finished they took cups of tea to the bows and spread out towels and Johnny could see Clem chatting away earnestly with Captain Hook while he and Frank sat in the cockpit smoking cigarettes and drinking milkless tea, eyes scanning the coast for signs of life. The further they got from habitation the more Johnny began to get that strange yet familiar feeling of isolation, of slipping over the edge of the world.

From the saloon Cat Stevens sang about first cuts and bad luck on the car cassette-radio that was rigged up to two speakers.

'So you've done a bit of sailing, have you, Johnny?' Frank said.

'Mainly dinghy… but I've done a couple of crossings.'

'Crossing what?' Frank asked, looking up from his tea-stirring.

'The Atlantic.'

Frank paused, spoon and eyebrows raised, nodding his head, impressed.

Johnny rolled himself a cigarette and Frank chucked him the lighter and they sat in silence for a while looking at the women, the sea and the scenery, sipping their drinks. Johnny was never happier than on a boat. Something changed inside him when he was on the water. It felt fundamental, as if there were shifts going on at a cellular level. He had always felt far more comfortable on the sea than on land, ever since his dad had taught him how to sail the Mini-Sail down in Cornwall when he must have been about Smudge's age.

Johnny sighed, put his feet up on the cockpit seat and stretched out, thinking that life was good, that this was the best way to travel by far; they'd get off at the next place, hitch a ride and go wherever the driver was going as long as it wasn't back to Bodrum. He scanned the water for evidence of wind, itching for Frank to get the sails up. It would be a shame to be on a sailing boat and not get a bit of sailing in.

The sun was shining brightly now; it had swallowed up all the haze. Johnny was watching the little girl pouring way too much suntan lotion on to Clem's back, getting the white liquid all over her yellow bikini straps. Her mother was clearing up the mess, scooping handfuls off Clem's back and rubbing it into her own body. It always intrigued Johnny to see how free and easy women were with each other's bodies; the three of them were like grooming primates.

He sipped at his tea watching Clem shift around, lying down on her tummy. Annie began to smooth the extra lotion into Clem's thighs and up the steep rise of the start of her buttocks and he could feel himself getting hard. He looked away briefly but when he looked back, Annie had put down the bottle and to his great surprise, pulled her T-shirt clean off over her head and was sitting there bare-breasted looking out to sea, rubbing the remaining lotion into her chest. The tea hovered at Johnny's lips. It was unignorable: she had unexpectedly glorious tits.

He stared for a little too long and then turned away just so that it didn't look as if he was staring and he put all his energy into being fascinated by several large birds flying fast by the boat, almost skimming the surface of the slate-grey waves in their search for fish, swooping and lurching inches above the water.

'Wonderful, aren't they?' Frank said, putting the cup to his lips. 'Boobies.'

Johnny turned sharply and looked at Frank. 'The birds, I mean,' Frank said, looking back at Annie. 'They're called boobies!' Then he threw back his head and roared with laughter; they both did. Frank laughed so much he had tears running down his cheeks.

'They're pretty wonderful too,' Johnny said, because they really were but then he wondered whether he'd gone too far. However Frank was laughing so much that Annie and Clem were looking round at them wondering what the joke was.

All afternoon they motored on with barely any wind at all. They passed no signs of civilization and Johnny went down below deck to examine the chart again. There was a small town, possibly a village, at the innermost point of this small bay but it appeared to be quite a way inland so that was no good. He went back out with the binoculars and scanned the hillsides: miles and miles of nothing, barren scrub dotted with the occasional goatherd or shack. He watched skinny black beasts ambling up and down the hills. He swung the binoculars back round and took a surreptitious look at Annie's tits again. He refocused and moved the binoculars down her body. She was powerfully built, strong and fit. She had her legs up and he zoomed in on a series of small white scars along the inside of her thigh. He lowered the binoculars, turned around and leant back against the coachroof and found himself drifting in and out of sleep, dozing in the warm sunshine, his mind ablaze with breasts and legs.

Later in the afternoon Frank asked him to take the helm while he took Smudge down for her afternoon nap. Johnny and Clem played cards with Annie by the tiller. She taught them how to play Five Hundred, an incredibly complicated game, like Bridge but even more confusing, where the two of diamonds was the big bad trump. It involved partners, bidding and dummies. He noticed the scars again as she dealt the cards; they were all over both thighs, fine white lines like little caterpillars crawling up towards her crotch.

The breeze did come in the late afternoon but Frank preferred for them to find a bay and hunker down for the evening. Johnny would have much preferred to have got the sails up now that the wind had arrived, he loved night sailing, but it wasn't his boat and another night on board sounded just fine to him. The further away they got from Bodrum the better. They were bound to come across somewhere tomorrow. Even if they found a house with a car they could pay for a ride; they still had all Charlie's money.

So the *Little Utopia* chugged in closer to the coast and nosed about for a suitable harbour as the sun slunk down the sky. It didn't take long to find one. They motored in, the vast mountainous scrub sheltering them from the wind. Johnny and Clem stood at the bows checking the depth of the water with Captain Hook pointing out fish. The bottom was rocky with sandy patches and when Johnny dropped the anchor it caught quickly and the boat swung round, nose to the breeze.

When Frank at last turned the engine off the sudden peace was blissful. Johnny forgot how much he hated engines;

people had managed for hundreds of years without them and somehow they had now become indispensable. A couple of years ago, Rob, Clem and he had delivered a boat from Gibraltar to Falmouth without an engine in it at all. It was such a rare event that they used to get rounds of applause as they sailed into harbours.

For a while the four of them stood about the boat, silenced by the silence, just staring out at this stunning piece of nature they had found themselves in, listening to the breeze rippling on the water, the waves lapping against the boat, the occasional cry from a bird of prey on the sloping golden mountains. They were in the middle of a beautiful piece of nowhere, the sinking sun on their backs, their shadows long and lean reaching over the water, up the rocks to the foothills.

There was a general clearing up of the cockpit and the deck and Captain Hook had a tantrum at the removal of her grubby pirate jacket and the attempt to put other warmer clothes on her naked goose-bumping body. Johnny managed to distract her with the very important job of looking out for the 'green flash', the mythical moment when the sun disappeared below the horizon and a green light shot up into the sky. He told her how he had spent his whole life looking out for it but had never seen it because his eyes weren't clever enough. Smudge had stopped crying then and climbed on to his lap and stared at the sun with wide eyes, trying hard not to blink while Annie had put some warm clothes on underneath the Captain Hook jacket, brushing a hand through Johnny's hair in thanks.

The sky became streaked with pinks and purples that spread out like long, tapering fingers over their heads towards the east where the first stars were already out. Frank and Clem, bearing thick jumpers and tumblers full of red wine, joined them in the cockpit and the five of them sat and waited for the green flash as the red ball sank down the sky. Captain Hook was the only lucky one – she saw it several times, she said, when the others must have been blinking. She described it in some detail, how the colours of the rainbow flashed as well, how very clever her eyes must be. But for the rest of them the sun kissed the horizon and slid out of view without a hullabaloo.

As the stars prickled the sky and the moon got into its swing, they ate pasta on plates on their laps. Annie put Captain Hook to bed; she fought it briefly, they could hear a tired protestation from the forecabin but shortly Annie joined them again with fresh supplies of wine. Clem made room for her, getting up to join Johnny on the other side of the cockpit, lifting his feet and placing them on her lap, her knuckles gently massaging the balls of his feet. Frank was sitting next to Clem at the stern, his legs hanging over the tiller, his eyes looking up at the heavens, his finger following the trajectory of the orbit of the stars in the galaxy. It was impossible not to talk about the tiny scale of their little lives on Earth. If Betelgeuse, visible over there, was the size of an orange, he said, planet Earth was smaller than a pinprick. Clem was leaning in close to see exactly which star he was pointing at. She was wearing Johnny's polo neck and her hair was caught down the back of it, with just a few coils springing out around her face, and Johnny was thinking how much he'd like to have sex with her right now. He even thought of getting up and taking her hand and saying, *Excuse me, guys, I'm going to go and have sex with my wife, won't be long.* He was pretty sure no one would mind. He drank from his glass and saluted Annie who was topping up her own glass in that quiet way she had. Their silences were comfortable; they sipped at the warming red wine listening to the waves lapping at the boat.

'This has been the most unexpected and wonderful day,' Clem said to no one in particular.

'The best kind of wonderful day,' Frank said to her, his eyes still on the sky.

She sighed heavily, pleasurably, and hung her head back, looking out at all the millions of stars above them. 'I suppose one day mankind will discover all the mysteries of the universe,' she said, her fingers pressing into the arch of Johnny's foot. 'Even work out what black holes are.'

Frank made a quiet sound of agreement, 'Hmmm,' as did Johnny, but his was to do with the massage.

'When we *do* know all the answers, that'll probably be it – the end of the world,' she said.

'I bet you we already know the mysteries of the universe,' Frank said in his low soothing voice. 'They'll be staring us in the face.'

She repeated his sound of agreement: 'Hmmm.'

'I think that's the divine joke,' Frank said. 'That we actually know all the answers already.'

'Maybe,' she said, not convinced, pausing in her massage, as if it were too much to listen and rub at the same time. Johnny wriggled his toes a little to remind her. 'Or we once knew them and then we forgot them.'

'Yes,' Frank said, turning his head to get a better look at her. 'Exactly! Perhaps our whole purpose here is to rediscover them.'

'Or maybe we don't have a purpose,' Johnny added and heard Annie chuckle.

'Oh, Johnny,' Clem said, pressing her knuckle hard into the sole of his foot. 'Don't be ridiculous, of course we do. Otherwise what's the point?'

'Ah, we agree on something, Clem.' Frank flashed his straight white teeth in a smile.

'What do you think the point is, Frank?' she asked. 'You said "divine joke" a moment ago. So you do believe in God?'

Frank was looking up at the sky as he spoke, picking each word as carefully as if choosing a particular chocolate from a superior selection. There was something about the way he spoke that made you have to listen, not to miss a thing. Frank would have been a great teacher. If schools had had teachers like him, Johnny might have paid a bit more attention.

'I don't believe life is pointless,' he said slowly. 'I don't believe in God as such but I do believe in a universal force, that there is an order to the chaos.' He was looking at Clem but including them all. 'And I most definitely have faith that one day human civilization will return to a second Golden Age.'

Clem picked up his cigarette packet. With the slightest tilt of her head, Johnny saw her asking whether she could take one of the cigarettes. Frank must have signalled yes but it was too dark for Johnny to see, because she took one out of the packet and Frank twisted his body round and lit it for her. He looked surprisingly old in its red flame; his brow fell in creases over his eyes and Johnny wondered whether Clem had noticed that.

'What *is* the Golden Age?' Johnny asked him.

'Ahh!' Frank said, as if recalling a fond memory. He swung his legs off the tiller and pushed himself upright. He picked at the cuff of his holey old jumper. 'According to many ancient texts it was a period in history where we human beings lived in accordance with the Natural Laws.'

Clem was listening attentively, inhaling her cigarette. She had become an elegant smoker over the years, like a twenties' film star.

'A time when bliss and harmony reigned supreme – man in utter harmony with nature,' he continued.

'What's a Natural Law?' she asked.

'A Natural Law is a law set by nature but whose ramifications exist in everything.'

'I don't understand. Like what?' she said.

'Well, probably the most obvious one…' Frank replied slowly in his low, gentle voice; Johnny had to strain a little to hear, he didn't want to miss a single word, '…is that we are all part of the same thing. We, us, planet Earth, the universe, are all made up of the same chemical elements. There is the same potential in you as there is in a star being born trillions of miles away up there.'

Johnny began rolling a cigarette, slowly as he always did, nice and thin, the tobacco evenly distributed along the paper, tearing himself a little cardboard from the Rizla packet for the perfect roach. What Frank was saying was perfectly obvious really, that there were a finite number of elements from which the universe and everything in it was made, but it was the *way* he said things that made them sound original and fresh. Johnny felt glad that they had this extra night on board; he wanted to hear more. He also rather wanted Clem to start massaging his feet again but she appeared to have forgotten about them; her attention was now entirely on Frank.

'Think of an acorn!' he was saying, leaning forward, looking at them now. 'In that tiny little seed is the capacity to become the mighty oak tree. Surely life is just the realization of our potential, the unmanifest becoming manifest.'

Both Clem and Johnny were quite still. He had entranced them. He was looking into their eyes, his own lit up by some internal fire. 'Or think of it like this: deep inside each of one of us is a mine full of precious stones. All the riches of the Earth are available to us. Perhaps our duty as human beings is to excavate those mines, bring those diamonds out into the light. It might be perfectly possible to live in a state of sparkling bliss all of the time if we so chose.'

'How do you get down there?' Clem asked him, her voice breathy with wonder.

'Simple. You tap into your potential.'

'And how do I do that?' she asked, suddenly tiring of the weight of Johnny's feet altogether, pushing them away and tucking her knees under her chin. Frank sighed a sigh full of unknowable longings and shifted his body slightly towards her.

'You have to follow all of the other Natural Laws and it will happen automatically. The first thing to understand is that you are in control of your life. You are not a victim. The world is what you want it to be. I always tell Annie that. Don't I, love?'

He wasn't expecting an answer; he didn't even look at her. Johnny did. She was knocking back the wine as though she'd heard it all before. There was an attractive feistiness behind that sorrowful façade that he was warming to. But Johnny hadn't heard it all before and he wanted to hear more. In all his life he had never heard anyone talking in this way.

'You have to start taking responsibility for yourself and by that I mean for all your responses to life and to do that you have to break down your own defences.'

'I can't control my responses to things, I just respond,' Clem said.

Frank laughed and sat back. 'You're absolutely wrong. Of course you can.'

'I can't.'

'Just try *witnessing* the choices you make as you make them.'

'What do you mean?'

He sat still, leaning forward again, his legs apart, his finger-tips and the two stumps tapping together as he thought. Then he looked at her, straight in the eye – they were close. 'I mean this quite sincerely, Clem,' he said and then paused. Both Clem and Johnny leant forward a little more. 'You are one of the most beautiful women I have ever come across,' he said, not taking his eyes off hers.

There was a hiatus, a tiny moment when Time's pendulum hovered. Johnny noticed the way Clem tried to hide her delight; the corners of her mouth tightened a little and she looked away from Frank, her eyelashes fluttering. She tossed Johnny a careless glance as if she were embarrassed. If there had been daylight he would have seen her blush. And Johnny himself felt a wave of something new and bitter wash through him.

'OK,' Frank said, pulling out his packet of cigarettes. He tapped one out and caught it in his lips and lit it in that snatched, hurried but easy way. 'You chose to be flattered,' he said as if it had been nothing but an experiment, the compliment false. He lit the cigarette, leant back and blew out a steady stream of smoke. 'It was a choice you made. You could have chosen to be insulted by that remark.' He turned to Johnny. 'And, Johnny, you too, your ego might well feel dented by another man calling your wife beautiful.' He paused. 'But it is *still* a choice.'

Johnny didn't want Frank to think that he was like other weaker men whose egos were easily bruised. He wanted to be better than other men. Clem *was* beautiful, that was a fact, and Johnny *wanted* other men to think her beautiful: he revelled in it. He chose to forget about that wave of bitterness and the moment he made the decision he could feel it subside. He chose *not* to be offended. It felt good. He felt in control. He suddenly understood what Annie had meant when she said that Frank could *see things*. He looked over at Annie; she was slumped, her hair fallen over her eyes.

'I shall choose to take it as a compliment to my astonishingly good taste,' Johnny said, lighting his roll-up. Frank smiled at him and nodded approvingly, which made Johnny feel even better, as if he'd most definitely passed some kind of test.

'OK, I get it, Frank,' Clem said, putting on a voice that Johnny hadn't heard before, like a student trying to impress the teacher, all combative and feisty. 'I'm not flattered. So someone thinks I'm beautiful. So what?'

'That too is a choice, Clem.' Frank was still speaking slowly and carefully as if he only had a limited supply of words, as if the chocolate box was almost empty. 'But you'll find that there is always the *right* choice to make in any given situation.'

'How do you know what the right choice is?' she asked.

'The right choice is the one that makes you and everyone around you happy,' he said, his dark eyes glinting at them, first Clem and then Johnny. 'You know it in your gut. Start trusting your gut: it always knows the answer.'

No one had ever told Johnny to trust his gut before – his Dad always told him to use his initiative, which was firmly based in his head. He had no doubt that what Frank was saying was right.

'The pair of you, if you start doing this, I swear you'll be amazed at the outcome. The usual barriers that enclose you will drop like clothes from the body.'

'Talking of which,' Annie said. Johnny had thought she was asleep but she pulled herself abruptly to an upright position. 'Frank says we shouldn't be wearing clothes at all. They were all naked in the Golden Age.'

'You're drunk, love,' Frank said to her, not unkindly.

'Sorry,' she said, hanging her head again, looking down at her feet. He leant over and took one of her hands in his, looking up at Johnny.

'Annie's had a difficult life,' he said tenderly. 'Haven't you, my love?'

She looked up with her pale, sad eyes but said nothing.

'Is that true what you said?' Clem asked quietly after a pause when it was clear Annie was not going to enlighten them any further. 'Was everyone naked in the Golden Age?'

'Yes, it's true,' he said, letting go of his wife's hand. 'Wearing clothes is just another form of division. Clothes are yet more defences, more barriers between us and the world. Only in nakedness can we be truly open, can we begin to let go of our psychological inhibitions. Only naked can we truly reveal ourselves.'

'Wouldn't everyone just be having sex all the time if we were naked?' Johnny said, both appalled and excited by the idea of a general abandoning of clothes. He flicked his cigarette overboard and watched it fly like a burning comet into the sea.

'Initially perhaps they would, but I don't think it would last,' Clem said. 'Not if that was all you ever knew.'

'I agree,' Frank said.

'Maybe you're right,' Johnny said. 'We'd get pretty blasé. We'd have stripteases in reverse – the big finale in a woolly jumper.' Only Annie laughed at his joke.

'Are you naturists? Do you normally go around naked?' Clem asked them.

'Alone on this boat, if it's warm enough, we're always naked, aren't we, Annie?'

Annie nodded. The image of her breasts swung back into

Johnny's head; he flashed a look at them as he knocked back the last of his wine. He glanced over at Clem, who was fiddling with a coil of her hair, looking at Frank, smoking, thoughtful. He liked the general idea of nudity and revelation but knew in reality he wouldn't fancy sharing Clem's nakedness with other people. Her body was his alone.

Annie stumbled into a standing position and ruffled his hair. 'Don't look so worried,' she said to him. 'Bed… if Smudge isn't hogging it!'

Not long after Frank followed her down and Johnny and Clem retired to their quarters all of two and a half feet's worth of toilet away from Annie and Frank. Johnny spent a little while brushing his teeth in the cockpit, glad for a moment alone; there was something niggling him that he couldn't quite put his finger on. He looked up at the moon. It was almost full, just a wedge off the right-hand side; it lit a jagged path across the water linking them in white light. The stars were out in their billions and he felt the smallness and insignificance that he momentarily sought. 'Drop it,' he said to himself, 'just drop it.' He spat out the toothpaste into the water and returned to the saloon.

When he came back in, Clem had made up the bed. She was zipping together their two sleeping bags and had pulled to the dividing door. Johnny took off his clothes and climbed in, making himself as comfortable as he could. But he found that he couldn't just 'drop it', *it* lingered. He didn't feel like waiting for Clem as he normally did, pulling back the cover to let her in and then covering her up, warming her in his arms. He didn't want to turn away either, that would have been too much of a statement, so he lay there still on his back while she took out her earrings and did all that night stuff that seemed to take women so much longer than men. He put his hands behind his head but he was longer than the berth so he had to tuck his knees up.

She turned the light off before going out to brush her teeth and he was glad of that, he didn't particularly want to be visible. He thought of feigning sleep but she would know something was up; he never went to sleep before her. Instead he lay there listening to the gentle lapping of the waves against the boat, the thoughts tossing about his head, the bright moonshine flashing across the saloon as the boat rose and fell in the water. Next door he could hear Frank's rumbling voice come to a halt.

Clem on the other hand had a wonder and new lightness in her heart. She stood in the cockpit looking up at the moon. She stayed up there for a while; she wasn't remotely tired. Quite the reverse, she felt exhilarated. Somewhere inside her, near her core, she could feel a fluttering, like wings taking flight, as if something contained was being set free. She stared up at the billions and zillions of stars and understood for the first time her connection with them, with the whole universe. There was no *otherness*; separation was an illusion. She knew with a certainty that she was just a part of all this, the same elements that formed her made up everything. She felt capable of absolutely anything. She took a deep breath of the clear night air, of the stardust, and hoped that she would remember this feeling. She needed to share it with Johnny or write it down. She came hurrying back down from the cockpit and began getting undressed in the saloon, unable to think of quite the right words to describe her feelings; besides, he was lying on his back looking away from her. She climbed into bed but he didn't turn around so she snuggled in close, tucking his arm around her. But still he didn't respond.

'What's the matter, Robin Hood?' she whispered.

'Nothing.' He was meant to say, *Nothing, Maid Marion*, but he couldn't. He felt distant from her. He couldn't feign warmth. What he really wanted was for her to apologize for something she wouldn't understand that she had done. He was as immobile as was possible; it was all he could think of to do until he worked out what was going on inside his mind.

'Something's wrong,' she said, leaning up on her elbow, worried.

Johnny kept quiet until he heard her sigh and lie back down. Then he turned his head away from her a little and tried not to make a sound, tried to be invisible. But it was no good. 'Do you fancy Frank?' he whispered, as casually as a whisper of such a nature could be whispered.

There was a brief pause and then he heard the swish as she turned her head sharply to face him. 'What are you talking about?' And he felt small and stupid. 'Are you jealous?' She sounded surprised, even a little bit pleased, she had never known him jealous before.

'I'm not jealous,' he said. 'Why would I be jealous?' Then he gave a little laugh at the outrageousness of the idea. 'You just seemed really flirty, that's all.'

'Flirty?'

'Yeah,' he said, his tone implying that everyone had noticed her embarrassing behaviour.

'I wasn't flirty.' He was spoiling everything. All that wonder and magic she had felt not a moment ago on deck was now gone. Slowly she turned around, away from him.

He hadn't wanted it to go like this. It was his fault. He wished he didn't love her so utterly; he felt like a great gaping sore she could chuck salt on. He sighed heavily hoping she could read all his complicated and conflicting thoughts with that one exhalation. Jealousy was an ugly, repulsive thing that should lurk in the shadows. He turned his face away and felt her move round to face him: a kindness he didn't deserve.

'I'm sorry, Clem,' he said and she forgave him immediately and moved down a little and rested her head against his chest. After a while she began to lightly run her fingers through the hairs on his chest. He shut his eyes and tried to lose himself in her touch. She lifted her head and put her hand on his face, turning him towards her, and she kissed the hollow beneath his cheekbone where her lips fitted; then she kissed his lips, which he resisted for a second or two, just to punish her a bit before giving in. Then she began to kiss him with an urgency to let him know that she was his. She knew just what he needed; she was going to make love to him.

'Hang on,' she said, pulling away, and he watched as she got up, her lovely body silver in the moonshine. She rummaged around amongst all her bits and bobs that lived in the zip pockets of the sail bag and pulled out a cassette and held it up to him. It was her Otis tape.

She knelt on the seat as she worked out how to operate the tape machine on the shelf opposite, her bottom cheeks looking as ripe and edible as a peach. Already his desire began to outweigh the jealousy. He doubled up the cushion beneath his head to appreciate her: the contours of her body, the smoothness of her back, the white tan line around her buttocks like living marble, swaying slightly in the flashes of moonlight. Then Otis began, 'These Arms of Mine'. She was so obsessed with this song she had recorded it on a loop and it played for forty-five minutes. She turned the volume up as far as she dared, aware of the others sleeping, and slowly she began to sway her shoulders in time with his haunting voice.

She gave Johnny a little throwaway glance over her shoulder – a sit-back-and-enjoy-me smile. As she leant back her head, the coils of her hair falling down her back, she looked unearthly to him, like God's very own blueprint for beauty. Then she began to move with the music, her body responding to every mournful Otis pang. This dance was purely for him, to tell him that she was all his, and as he made himself comfortable to enjoy her; he felt her love go through him like a tonic, the antidote to that bile. He could feel the remnants of his jealousy being washed away by his lust. He was gagging for her. He loved her more than he had ever loved her, as much as any lover had ever loved.

Sometimes he found sex almost too intense. He felt as if he might burst when he was inside of her, as she sat straddled across his lap; surely no human being could survive such extremes. It didn't seem possible to love another person this entirely without shattering into a million pieces.

'Slowly, Clem,' he said, gripping those peachy cheeks, feeling her teeth on his shoulder, her gasps in his ear, and he could bear the pleasure no longer.

That was then when he saw the glint of an eye in the little gap between the panels of the dividing door. The moonshine swung across it. Johnny drew in a breath sharply and his body froze but the eye disappeared in a flash before he could be *absolutely* certain.

4

CLOSE TO THE WIND

THE SKY WAS overcast on the second morning, just like the first, and there was a faint breeze in the air. They breakfasted in the cockpit; the setting was so solitary and tranquil it was hard to believe that they would ever come across civilization again. The only sounds were the gentle lapping of the water against the hull and the constant chirruping of the crickets over on the hills. They were probably about fifty yards off the rocky shore. Everyone was so at ease with each other that Johnny had begun to wonder whether he had imagined someone watching them making love the previous night. It seemed quite absurd now in the clear light of morning.

Annie was peering through the binoculars, scouring the little bay slowly as if she were looking for something in particular. Clem was sitting on her prayer mat and had a fishing line thrown over the bows of the boat and Frank was teaching her how to fish. He and Smudge had risen early and rowed ashore to find insects for bait and returned with a cupful of dead flies and bugs.

Johnny and Smudge were sitting on the coachroof playing games. She was still wearing her Captain Hook jacket and nothing else. Johnny was distracted, keen to get the sails up, and kept looking over at the horizon to see if any more wind was coming their way; what wind there was blew in from the west and, having had another look at the useless chart, Johnny rather wanted to get going as he was now beginning to think that there was a possibility that they might not find a town for a good few days. Frank, however, was much more interested in fishing than sailing; he didn't seem remotely bothered about the direction of the wind, or finding a village, he was quite content to motor from bay to bay exploring the coast, fishing and pootling around on the shore. His only agenda seemed to be whatever was going on in the moment; their plans were vague and sprawling – to reach southern Turkey before the summer.

Johnny was inventing a game with Smudge: Olympics, or Limpets as she called it. Gilla the grilla was exceptionally agile, an all-round competitor, and had reached the finals of every single sport and was now warming up for the diving finals. He hovered on the boom wearing Smudge's goggles and the dolphin armbands and was preparing nervously for the big one: the triple twist backwards half-loop. Johnny had attached string to his arms and Gilla was in the process of a lengthy warm-up, bending and stretching to calm his nerves. Smudge thought Johnny's commentary hilarious. She screamed with terror every time Gilla mustered up the nerve and tiptoed forwards along the boom and then she screamed with delight when the fear got the better of him and he'd have to pull out quaking and trembling as the paramedics saw to him. But this time he boldly flew into the air, leaping from the boom, twisting and turning into the sea. Smudge cheered and rushed to the guard rail and hauled him out, a little soggier and heavier.

'And he's got a perfect ten from all the judges!' Johnny cried in his best commentator voice, pulling the string in. 'Yes,

siree, Gilla the Grilla has taken the gold for Great Britain!'
Smudge and he clapped and cheered before she leapt up and
scurried below deck to get something.

'You've got a little admirer there,' Frank said, coming
along the deck and bending down to rummage in the bucket
for bait. 'I think she's got her first crush.'

Then Smudge reappeared in the companionway, holding
out a gold coin of some sort attached to a ribbon, a great grin
on her face. 'Look! Gilla's gold medal,' she said proudly.

'What's this?' Johnny asked her, taking it from her hand.

'Daddy's medal,' she said, hauling herself back up on to the
coachroof. 'But it can be a Limpet medal too.'

Johnny looked over at Frank, who was bending the fish
hook into shape in his enormous fingers. 'Frank's medal?'
Johnny repeated, looking down at its golden face, the profile
of some King and Queen, four pale blue enamelled leaves
coming off from the centre. There was writing inscribed
around the edge; he turned it around in his hand to read it:
For God and the Empire.

'What is it?' Johnny asked Frank. 'An OBE?'

'Something like that,' he said, concentrating hard on
attaching a centipede to his hook.

'The Queen gived it to him,' Smudge said.

'*Gave* it, Smudge,' Frank said, biting the hook carefully
between his teeth. '*Gave* it.'

'The Queen *gave* it,' she said. 'Come on, Johnny. Let's do
the prizes.'

'Wow! What for?' Johnny said, turning it over in his hand.
'What did you do?'

'Nothing much. Just my job,' Frank said disinterestedly,
piercing the flesh of the centipede with a pop.

'What was your job?'

'A boring one,' Smudge said, pulling at Johnny's arm. 'Come on, Johnny!'

Frank winked at his daughter. 'The Met,' he said, gently tugging at the centipede's curled body. 'I worked for the Met.'

Johnny stared at him, his mouth a perfect circle of surprise. 'You're a copper?'

'*Was. Was* a copper. I got early retirement after a nasty incident with a ten-ton truck on the M4.'

'Are you joking?'

'No joke,' he said, the centipede swinging in the air in a ball of death. Johnny searched Frank's face for clues – a smile perhaps. But Frank was poker-faced.

'I thought you were against the establishment and everything they stand for?'

'And from what better place to challenge the order of things...' He carefully flicked a bit of centipede gunk into the water with his toe and then turned to smile at Johnny. '... but from the inside?'

Johnny rubbed the back of his neck, staring down at the medal. 'What did you get this for?'

'Let's just say I was good at getting people to open up.' He wandered down the deck towards Clem. 'It's not a big deal, Johnny. The establishment's approbation... it doesn't mean anything.'

'Then why did you accept it?' Johnny called out after him.

Frank laughed as he flicked the line over the bows. 'It would have been churlish not to,' he said.

'Why aren't they biting?' Johnny heard Clem ask as she leant over the boat looking down into the shallows beneath. She sounded different and he knew that she was all wide-eyed and freshly impressed by him; he could hear it in her voice.

'Patience, Clem. All good things come to those who wait,' Frank said, putting a finger to his lips.

Clem seemed to have forgotten all about green shirts and bad luck, quite happy to spend her time aboard the boat. Johnny knew he was being childish; they were having a wonderful, unexpected couple of days – even if they were doomed to have coppers in their lives.

'There are berries over there!'

Johnny turned to the stern. He'd forgotten about Annie. She had put down her binoculars and was pointing up into the hills. 'We could have some apple and blueberry pie for lunch.' She smiled at him and then raised her voice at the others, 'After the fish course, of course.'

'Don't hold your breath...' Clem said out of the corner of her mouth as Frank cast the second line out into the water, chucking a handful of sweetcorn overboard, leaning back as he settled in for a wait.

By the time they had tidied things up and found Smudge's other shoe and bags to put the berries in and a clean bottle to carry some water and watched Clem let several fish slip away, it was late morning before Annie, Smudge and Johnny climbed down into the little tender. It was an old boat and had a few bodged leaks along its faded white wooden planks; various corks from wine bottles had been shoved into holes. The bottom was wet but not uncomfortably so.

Johnny let his hand trail in the cool water as Annie rowed them ashore, the grey sky clearing now, evaporating into a weak, watery blue, changing the colour of the water before their eyes. There were plenty of fish down there; he turned and looked back at the boat. The *Little Utopia* didn't look so tubby from this low angle: she looked almost sweet. Frank was showing Clem how to cast a line; he was behind her, his arms around her, and it looked as if they were in some kind of embrace, their bodies locked together, and Johnny felt that same wash of bitterness pass through him. He looked at Annie; she was oblivious. He thought about what Frank had said, about choices, and he turned his back to the boat and made a better choice. Annie was watching him.

'That wasn't an OBE,' she said. 'It was a CBE. One up.' It was a fact not a brag.

'Blimey.'

'*Row, row, row your boat, gently down the stream,*' Smudge started to sing. Johnny listened to her sweet voice. She was leaning over the water, her face inches away, looking down into the depths. He knew what she was doing; she spent quite a lot of her time looking for monsters. '*Merrily, merrily, merrily, merrily, life is but a dream,*' she sang, her clear voice tripping across the water and bouncing off the rocks.

'He never gives up on anything,' Annie said, her voice as flat as the water. 'You ought to be aware of that.' Johnny had no idea what she was talking about but he had no trouble believing her; everything about Frank was different from other people. He watched Annie row. She was tall and strong and it took no time to reach the rocks. She pulled in on a scrap of chunky sand. Johnny and she jumped out and heaved the boat with Smudge still inside up on to the crunching shore. He felt slightly reckless away from the *Little Utopia*, here on dry land, just the three of them, some space between them and the boat. He chucked the rope round a rock, wondering whether he still remembered how to tie a one-handed bowline. Yep. He did.

'Flash bastard,' Annie said, getting the bags out of the tender, leaning over, flashing a look up at him. He could see her cleavage beneath her chequered shirt as she did so.

He pretended to strut a little. 'You've either got it or you haven't, babe,' he said, making her laugh, making her face light up again.

'Where did you see the berries?' he asked, looking up into the scrubby landscape. It was warmer on the land; he could feel the difference in temperature immediately, a wave of heat seemed to be slipping down the hillside and hitting them front on. It was going to be a warm day.

'Up here,' Annie said, taking Smudge's hand and setting off up the hill. Johnny followed behind Captain Hook, who was as quick and nimble as her mother, her red costume shining in the light, Gilla dangling at her side, one paw dragging through the prickly scrub. The earth was a pale orange and surprisingly lush – the storm must have soaked everything. Hundreds of tiny flowers seemed to be unfurling around them and small birds darted in and out of the bushes. A lizard scampered across their path and Smudge spent some time trying unsuccessfully to catch it.

As they trudged up the hillside, the sun came out properly, the haze disappeared and the sky became a rich blue. They stopped halfway up to have a drink of water and looked down at the boat and the small figures of Clem and Frank at the bows, one so much smaller she looked like a different species altogether. They were sitting separately now, either side of the bows, and Johnny felt better about that.

'Daddy!' Smudge shouted down, waving at the boat, but neither he nor Clem looked up. They were playing music down there; a faint beat echoed across the water but he couldn't tell what song it was: the stern was facing away from them. The water around the boat was a turquoise blue, so clear and crisp that from up here he could see the anchor line and the pile of rocks it had caught on.

'See!' Johnny said, turning to Smudge at his side, crouching down to her level. 'No monsters today.'

'They hide in the daytime,' she said all matter of fact. She turned her face up to his. 'Have you ever seen a monster, Johnny?'

He looked down at the water. 'No, *I* haven't. But I once sailed with a man who'd definitely seen a monster. He was out in the Pacific, thousands of miles away from land. He told me that he was on watch one dark and moonless night and out of the water, right in front of the boat, two big luminous green eyes rose up, either side of the bow. Then the eyes went higher and higher as the monster came out of the water. Up, up, as high as the mast.'

Her eyes were getting bigger and bigger as she listened, her lips parted. 'What did it do?'

'Nothing. It just stared at him and slowly went back down.'

'Did he catch it?'

'No.'

'I would have caught it in my net,' she said, putting her little hand in Johnny's and hanging on a bit tighter than before.

Annie was absolutely right: there was an abundance of berries up here, hundreds of them wherever he looked. He bent down and started to pick them off the spiky little bushes and soon his bag began to fill up. For a while Smudge stayed at his side and helped although the majority of her berries never made it to the bag, just the occasional squashed handful she peeled off her palm.

'Save some of them for lunch, Smudge,' Johnny said.

'I'm not eating them,' she said, looking up at him, her mouth and chin smeared with black juice.

He ruffled her already ruffled hair. As soon as she was full up she got bored of berry-picking and wandered off a little;

she squatted down to play in the earth and began humming a little song to herself. Annie was further along, higher up, picking fast and furiously in the sunshine.

Small blue butterflies swooped around him, some landing on his shirt mistaking him for a flower. He watched a couple of lizards darting about his feet and a large spider scurrying away from them. The place was teeming with life. Soon his bag bulged heavily with bilberries; he had the knack now and could get eight or nine in one picking. He liked the feeling of being self-sufficient, getting produce from the land and the sea; this was a good way to live. He could see himself and Clem doing this one day on their own boat, their double-ended, teak-decked wooden ketch. He wiped the sheen off his forehead and looked round for Annie. She was higher up the hill busy picking.

'Johnny,' whispered a small voice over in the bushes.

'What?' He made his way over to Smudge, who was crouched down in the scrub, her Captain Hook jacket caught on various brambles; it stood out like a tent revealing her naked bottom underneath. She was cradling something in her hands. 'What have you got there?' he said.

She opened her palms and inside was the tiniest, most perfect miniature tortoise. At first he thought it was a toy but then it lifted its little head up at him. He knelt down beside her. It must have only just come out of its egg, and it was exquisite. 'Captain Hook!' he whispered. 'You've found treasure!' He ran his finger along its soft shell. 'Where did you find that?'

'Over there. There's lots of them,' she said, pleased at her own cleverness.

'Show me!' he said. She leapt up and jerked her jacket off the brambles, making an additional hole or two, and she skipped off. He followed in her quick little footsteps as she jumped through the bushes, stopping to scratch the occasional itch.

'Here!' she said, stopping suddenly. Sure enough, there at her feet a large mother tortoise was ambling through the scrub with five little babies following her, struggling to catch up, taking ten steps to her every one. Johnny silently crouched down to observe them. Smudge came up to him, put her arm around his neck and balanced herself against him, still holding one of the babies in her hand, the other ruffling his hair in much the same way he had ruffled hers. She smelt of bilberries and soap. He watched as she squatted down and tried to ram a bilberry into the baby tortoise's mouth, mumbling words of encouragement to it. She was such a little thing herself with her turned-up nose covered in freckles, her baby soft skin, the bilberry-stained lips, her big, dark eyes so wide and clear.

Annie was much further up the hill, her back to them, picking away. Down on the water he could see Frank and Clem in the same places still fishing.

'I don't think she wants it,' Smudge said, looking up at Johnny. 'Do tortoises drink milk?'

'No,' Johnny said. 'They're reptiles.'

'Orangina?' she asked.

'No.'

'Does it bounce?'

'No.'

'It looks bouncy.'

'Well, it doesn't bounce.'

'This one is my pet.'

'You'd better keep it with its mummy,' Johnny said.

'No,' she said as if that was a very bad idea. 'She's mine. I've given her a name.'

'Oh, what's she called?'

'She's called "Granny".'

'Granny?'

'Yes.'

'That's nice,' Johnny said stroking one of the other little tortoises. He sat down on the earth. 'Do you have a granny, Smudge?'

She shook her head. Then she nodded, scrunching her nose up as she thought about it. 'Well, I do have one. I heard her on the telephone. She doesn't like us.'

'I'm sure she does.'

'No, she doesn't. She called my mummy a *stupid bitch* and said my daddy should be *locked up and they should throw away the key.*' She shouted out the last bit in a slight Irish accent and then bent down to shove another bilberry into the mother tortoise's mouth.

'There's a good tortoise,' she whispered into her cupped palm. 'We'll have a nice bath and a cup of tea.'

Johnny looked up. Annie was waving at them, holding up the bottle of water. He beckoned her to come over. 'What about cousins?' Johnny asked Smudge but she shook her head. 'No other family?'

She shrugged her shoulders. 'I want a big brother but my mummy doesn't want another baby but my daddy does.' She looked up at him, squinting into the sun. 'I know how you get babies. Four million sperms have a race – you can't see them coz they're teeny weeny weeny – but they're all trying to get to the egg that the lady's hatching in her winkle.'

'I see,' said Johnny, pretending to be suddenly fascinated with what the tortoises were up to and shortly Annie came over and joined them, her bag full of berries. She'd tied her hair back into a ponytail and her skin was glowing with perspiration. Her face lit up when she saw the tortoises.

'Oh, look!' she said, crouching down to examine them.

'I found them,' Smudge said proudly.

'Aren't they sweet? Oh, Smudge, clever you!'

'This one's my pet.' She opened her hand and showed her mother the tiny tortoise on her palm.

'No, love, you can't keep it. It belongs with its mummy.'

'No, it doesn't.'

'Well, you can look after it for a while,' she said.

'It can be my birthday present,' she said as if this was the obvious solution.

Annie kissed her forehead. 'Drink this!' she said, holding up the water to Smudge's lips. Smudge drank a little and then dribbled some out into her palm for Granny, who dipped her head obligingly.

They watched the tortoises for a bit longer and then Annie and Johnny moved over into the shade of a large olive tree, sitting down and leaning against its trunk, shoulder to shoulder, the crickets pausing their cacophony. Annie offered him the water. 'After you,' he said and watched her drinking thirstily. She passed it over again and he drank.

The view was beautiful. Only the tip of the *Little Utopia*'s mast was visible from here; it swung from side to side over the top of the rocks like the pendulum of a metronome. The water in the bay was a patchwork of turquoise and green and further out where it turned into a darker blue Johnny spied a boat with its sails up, a white triangle slipping along the curve of the Earth; there was a good breeze out there and he yearned to be in it. He shut his eyes and listened to the crickets, which had started up their racket again, comfortable with their presence now. In the distance he could hear Smudge's tuneful little voice singing her made-up hums to the tortoises. He drank more water, one eye on the dozens of blue butterflies fluttering by. He wiped the sweat from his brow, his elbow brushing Annie's arm.

'When's Smudge's birthday?' he asked her.

She'd been dozing and opened her eyes. 'In a couple of days.'

'She said she was going to be five and a half.' Annie smiled and shut her eyes again. He watched the smile drop slowly from her face, like melting wax, as the sadness took hold. Life had disappointed her somewhere along the line and he wondered *how* life could disappoint, whether it happened suddenly or insidiously. She opened her eyes and he quickly looked away.

'You must think I'm a rotten mother, Johnny,' she said. 'A sad old drunk.'

'No, of course I don't,' he said, sitting up a little. 'Besides, I don't know you.'

'No, that's right,' she said quietly, putting her hand over his, patting it gently. 'You don't know me.'

She took the bottle out of his hand, unscrewed the lid and took a swig. He looked over in the direction of where Smudge was playing. He couldn't see her from here but he could still hear her humming.

'He saved me, you know,' Annie said. She'd been looking far out to where the sea met the sky but she turned her eyes to his. 'I will always put him first, you know. Always. Whatever else Frank's done, he saved me.'

She'd lost Johnny now; he ran his hand through his hair. 'Saved you from what?'

She smiled at him and shook her head as if she'd been foolish to expect him to understand. 'From myself,' she said, looking back at the pendulum mast. Johnny was the one who felt foolish for not realizing what she'd meant.

'Well, he seems like an amazing man, your husband.'

She dragged her eyes from the mast back to Johnny's. 'Yes, he is.' She had that same flat tone to her voice and they sat there saying nothing for a while.

'I could never leave him, you know. Never.'

'No,' Johnny said, confused. 'Why would you want to?'

She made a sound like a little laugh but it got stuck in her throat somewhere. 'I'm a bad person, Johnny.'

He had the feeling that she was going to cry and he had no idea what to do about it. 'Of course you're not.'

She looked away, out at the bay again, and so did he. He wanted to help her, to cheer her up, to stop this melancholy that he couldn't fathom. He pulled out his tobacco and rolled a cigarette, lit it and passed it over to her.

'Thanks,' she said, touched by the gesture. He could feel her watching him as he rolled himself a cigarette and it made him slightly self-conscious. When he looked up to light his own cigarette she was still watching him. This time he didn't look away.

'I've seen the way you look at my breasts, Johnny,' she said, exhaling the smoke, moving nothing but her lips, blowing cool air on to his skin. He paused, flicked his lighter off and took a drag. He wasn't sure if she was mocking him or not. He felt short of air, his breathing was high and quick and he thought that if he spoke his voice might come out cracked.

'You can touch them, if you like.' She said the words so quietly he thought about pretending that he hadn't heard. But they both knew that he had. She started to undo the buttons of her shirt, slowly and steadily, keeping her eyes on his, and he sat there not sure where to look or what to do, so he did nothing; she was smiling slightly as if she found him amusing. When she had finished undoing all the buttons she opened wide the shirt and, because it would have been humanly impossible not to, Johnny looked down at her breasts and felt his heart quicken. She had the sort of tits that a man might risk everything for. When he looked up again at those pale eyes of hers, he saw something new in them: a boldness, a determination. Frank was right. *Only naked can we truly reveal ourselves.* 'Touch them, Johnny,' she said.

He must have signalled something because she reached out and took his bilberry-stained palm and pressed it to her breast. It felt warm and slightly moist and unbelievably full in his hand. His fingers moved across her skin and he gently pinched her nipple between his thumb and forefinger and she tilted back her head and gave a little sigh. He hadn't seemed to consciously make any choices at all and yet his mouth was wet and his cock had gone as hard as rock.

'Mama!' Smudge's voice came from further up the hill and he pulled his hand away quickly. 'Mama?' she cried. 'By mistake accidentally I think I've broken Granny...'

Johnny leapt to his feet, knocking over the water bottle and righting it as Annie calmly and methodically did up her buttons, keeping her eyes on him and a teasing smile on her lips.

Clem had caught two fat fish which were, as far as she could tell, pretending to be dead in the bucket behind her. Frank had caught five. They were motionless but if she prodded them they flapped about a bit then went back to playing dead. She was sitting at the bows ready to catch her third, holding her line expectantly, looking out at the beautiful, glistening sea, humming along to 'Space Oddity' as Frank came along the deck with a couple of cups of coffee. He'd taken his shirt off and was surprisingly fit and tanned, an imposing figure. He bent down and put one of the cups on her prayer mat and then sat down at the starboard bow next to her and picked up his rod, his back to her. She looked away. She hadn't seen him topless before and it felt oddly intimate.

She looked out at the sea and listened to Mr Bowie. Poor old Major Tom floating in his tin can. She thought of her dad, how he used to sing this song, how he used to strut about being Bowie or Jagger to make her laugh.

'They still together, your mum and dad?' Frank asked. It was uncanny how he did that – knowing what she was thinking about.

'God no, they divorced years ago.' She could hear the nonchalance in her own voice. She had perfected that over the years.

'Siblings?' he asked.

'Two half-brothers.' She used the same careless tone but it didn't trip off the tongue quite so easily, it had the ring of risk in it. It was being on the boat, it was the *Little Utopia;* she'd noticed how unbidden memories kept rising to the surface. There was something about the absence of distraction and the empty horizons that allowed dark, sunken things to pop up into the light like bubbles from the deep.

They sat in silence. She watched a bird swoop by, searching for fish. Frank shifted at her side, reaching for a cigarette, and she couldn't help but notice a large scar running down his back, glossy and smooth in the sunshine. His right shoulder blade had deep, rippled indentations down the bone as if some of it had been cut out. She found the disfigurement strangely beautiful, a stamp of his uniqueness. She wanted to reach out and touch it.

'It's not pretty, is it?' he said without turning around, feeling her eyes upon him. She looked away, embarrassed.

'Still, I'm lucky to be alive,' he said. He stretched out his legs and she caught sight of the scar on his calf. 'I spent six months at the Hotel NHS.'

She wasn't very good at telling when he was joking – she spent a few moments wondering why he'd stay in a hotel before she understood. 'Six months? How terrible,' she said.

'Not so bad in the end,' he said, picking up his coffee and taking a sip. 'I got around to reading all the books I'd been meaning to read for years.'

She swatted away a fly that was buzzing about in the heat and looked down at her line. She'd only recently started reading. As a child she had always been a doer, not a reader. 'Books like what?'

'Oh – the classics: Ovid, Hermes, Ficino. The philosophers.'

She hadn't heard of any of them but hoped her face didn't give this away. She wished she knew a little bit more about everything; it was beginning to dawn on her how badly educated she was. 'Did you study philosophy, Frank?'

'Not officially.'

'I want to study philosophy,' she said on a whim. 'I'd like to do some reading. I don't feel I've read very much in my life.'

He reeled in his line a little and shifted his position. 'What do you want to know about?'

'I want to…' *I want to be like you, know all the things that you know.* 'I suppose I want to start looking for the truth about things.'

'Ahhhh! The truth!' He turned and smiled at her and it was hard to tell whether he was mocking her. 'You're on a quest for knowledge.'

'Yes,' she said cautiously. But he didn't say anything else. 'Where do you think I should begin?'

'If you're looking for answers, I suppose the first thing is to start asking the right questions.'

Her mind went blank. She couldn't think of any questions at all.

'I don't mean now, Clem.' He smiled, looking at her so fondly that she didn't mind him laughing at her.

'Johnny and I are going to work our way to India. I thought maybe I'd go to a few ashrams.' He didn't proffer an opinion. 'Maybe find a guru,' she added, not exactly sure of what a guru really did, but Rob had met one and had raved about him.

'You don't need a guru, Clem. You're the one that has to answer your own questions. That's the beauty.' He winked at her and they fished for a while, which meant that they did nothing at all.

'Have you heard of Krishnamurti?' he asked her.

She pretended that she vaguely had and took a guess. 'Should I read him?'

He rested his arm on the guard rail. 'He was a fabulous man, a truly original thinker.' He was smiling at the mention of this Krishnamurti and she wondered whether Frank knew him, whether they were friends, what sort of things they got up to, whether they fished together, what kind of discussions they had.

'Wherever he went people wanted to know more, always asking him questions, until he had developed this immense following. Then one day, in front of three thousand hard-core disciples, he declared the whole thing finished. Told them all to piss off and get a life.' Frank seemed to find this incredibly funny. He was chuckling. 'People were weeping and wailing... it was like the end of the world. What were they going to do? Who were they going to follow?'

'Were you there?'

He turned round to look at her and laughed a little louder. 'I might be old, Clem, but this was in the nineteen twenties.'

She laughed too.

'But I've read the speech he gave. It's a beautiful speech; you should read that. I've got it somewhere.'

'I will,' she said. 'What did he say?' The fly that had been buzzing around her was now buzzing around him, dancing on his skin, and she felt a pang of envy for its boldness. He brushed it firmly aside.

'He told them that *Truth* was a pathless land, that they couldn't get to it via any religion or sect. He said that truth was limitless and unconditional, it couldn't be contained or organized and the moment that it *was*, it became crystallized and deadened. He told them that belief was an *individual* matter and if they followed someone else, they would cease to follow the *Truth*.'

She stared down into the water, empathizing with those weeping and wailing followers. How on earth were you meant to find your own truth?

'Do you think Jesus must be turning in his grave at the mass following that he's inadvertently created?' she said, hoping Frank might be rather impressed with her. Frank turned to her and smiled. 'Spinning like a top, Clem.'

They sat in a happy silence. David Bowie was still trying to get in touch with ground control and though she didn't want to have her dad in her head – he didn't deserve to be there – she found he kept popping up.

Frank tapped himself out a cigarette, caught it, lit it and passed it to her. 'It's hard to be true to yourself. Sometimes you have to go against the great majority.'

She rested her chin against the guard rail and caught the gash where she had cut herself. She sat back on her wrists, listening to Frank, wondering what majority *he* had gone against.

'Governments and religion need to control us. Believe me, I know,' he said in his easy, rolling voice. 'So we live by their rules.' He lit his own cigarette and turned to her, blowing the smoke up in the air above the bows. 'But whose benefit do you think those rules are really for?'

'For us all, I presume,' she said, striking out, trying to go against his majority.

'Maybe,' he said, leaning back on his hands but she could tell he didn't think so. 'Why is it illegal to kill a man who burgles your house and rapes your wife but perfectly legal to kill a total stranger in a war over oil that's nothing to do with you?'

She hoped he wasn't expecting an answer; she'd run out of strong opinions.

'You see, society needs us to think in a certain way for it to function, for it to use us. It needs to tell us who to point the finger at, who are the "victims" and who are the "perpetrators".' He was looking her directly in the eyes and she felt that he could see right through her. 'You have to set your own compass, Clem. Never forget that.'

His eyes were so dark and intense that for a moment she didn't notice that something was tugging at her line.

Clemmie was sitting in the front of the blue Cortina. She had never been on a trip with her dad, not just the two of them. Normally the three of them went on trips together so her mum would have been in the front and Clemmie would be sitting in the back holding her breath between the lamp-posts, listening to her mother talking and laughing. Sometimes she would lean forward to hear what she was saying after a particularly laughy laugh but she never got the joke and went back to her breathing tasks. They could make her feel a bit left out, her mum and dad, the way they laughed and talked all the time, not really including her in their conversations. If she tried to join in, pushing herself into the middle, taking both their hands, her mother would end up brushing her hair or wiping her mouth with a spitty handkerchief or tugging at her skirt or pulling her thumb out of her mouth. But today, this time, it was just her and her dad and he didn't care about those kinds of things. He cared about getting to the bar before closing time, not missing the match, England winning the cricket – sensible things.

The road was narrow with high hedges; she could only see through the windscreen kneeling and she had to keep her hands on the dashboard because her dad kept stopping to look at the map. He'd been to the hotel before but he liked to try different routes and time himself. The sun was shining straight into their faces so they both had the visors down and she kept glimpsing her own face looking down at her. Her mother had brushed her hair so that the top was flat and now she was worried that she looked like Violet Elizabeth Bott from *Just William*. She tried to pat down the curls.

'You look very pretty,' her dad said with a wink and that made her feel better. Apart from her hair, she had to agree with him. She had dressed with great care. She was wearing her corduroy turquoise smock dress with her favourite red tights underneath and so far no spills on either. However, her toes, tucked underneath her bottom, felt a bit squashed because she was growing out of her best shoes: her brown, size eleven, lace-up Start-rites. The ones that made the exciting clickety-click noise on the pavement and turned her feet attractively inwards like Sarah's. Pigeon toes were all the rage at school.

Her dad was singing along to the radio. '*My sweet Lord…*'

He was wearing his shiny blue suit with a wide-collared pale green shirt and the sun kept glinting off his gold neck-lace. His chin was covered in stubble. She didn't like him all prickly; he'd said he hadn't had time to shave and she wondered how long shaving took. He had his Starsky sunglasses on and was swaying with the music, dancing as he drove, making her laugh.

He was copying the singer exactly, pleadingly, desperately, making fun of him but serious all at the same time. He pretended to pass her a microphone and she joined in on the *Alleluia* bits.

'OK, are you ready?' he said after a while and she beamed at him. This was the best bit, the bit where her mother would say, 'Really, Jim, I'm not sure this is a good idea,' and he'd ignore her. They'd been doing it since she was tiny. Clemmie knew her cue. She clambered across the gear stick on to his lap and carefully took hold of the steering wheel. He let go, his hands raised in the air. 'She's all yours. Left a bit! Good girl, Clembo. Straighten up! Corner coming up...' He changed down a gear and she bumped up and down on his knee, peering over the wheel as she turned to the right. 'Round the corner, there you go! Give a hoot!' She was driving the Cortina, his pride and joy, for a good ten minutes or so all by herself except for the feet bit.

The sun had dropped low in the sky by the time they pulled up outside the hotel. Clemmie had fallen asleep and was momentarily confused to find herself at the seaside. They parked at the back of the tall, dark building and walked round to the grand entrance, carrying their bags. She stepped carefully in her Start-rites through the splatterings of white seagull poo on the steps up to the swirling glass door.

There was an old man in a uniform who seemed to know her father. 'Hello, Jim,' he said. 'And who's the beautiful young lady?' For a moment she wondered whom he was talking about and then when her father said, 'This is my daughter,

Harry. The most fabulous, cleverest, gymnastic young lady in the northern hemisphere,' her chest swelled with pride and she had to keep swallowing in case she looked like a smarty-pants – and *no one likes a smarty pants*, her mother was always reminding her of that. She couldn't help the smile so she turned it up to the old man in the uniform. She had never felt so grown up in her life and suspected it might have something to do with her red tights and the clickety-click noise.

The old man tried to take her spotty case off her but she held on tightly and he kind of dragged her through the lobby to the desk. Up above them in a high domed ceiling hung a giant chandelier and over on the left was a large lounge with three ladies sitting in a row at the bar, drinking from triangular glasses, all of them in fur coats though it wasn't even cold. Her father said hello to them as they checked in at the desk – he always said hello to everyone – and she liked the way the ladies all looked at her as though she was the luckiest girl in the world, which she probably was.

The bedroom had two enormous double beds in it on to which her dad flung the cases. He unpacked his own while she bounced on the bed near the window. Then he opened her suitcase and they both noticed that she'd forgotten to pack any clothes. She'd insisted on doing her own packing. She'd remembered the main things: her roller-skates and her Whimsy set and some boxes for collecting things but no nightie or toothbrush or clothes. She could see that he was annoyed with her but was trying not to be.

Her dad went through to the bathroom to have a shave while she carried on bouncing. He'd taken his shirt off. He was quite fussy about his clothes; he'd folded it up and hung it over the loo seat. He had a white foam beard like Father Christmas and was talking out of one side of his face.

'Where first? What do you fancy? A walk on the beach?'

'Ice cream,' she said, attempting a somersault.

'Good shout. Ice cream on the beach.'

'Yippee!' She tried again, succeeding this time. 'Can I have two?'

'As many as you want.'

'Six?'

'You can have all the ice cream you desire, Clemency Bailey.' Spin, spin, spin she went.

They walked along the shingle eating ice creams as the waves lapped the shore. He didn't tell her off when she mistimed a wave and got her Start-rites soaked. He said it didn't matter – he could dry them with the hair dryer when they got back. They started collecting special pebbles and the ones she didn't want in her box they threw back into the sea. It was much quieter without her mother. There wasn't all the talking and the laughing, just more wetness and ice creams and staring at the sea. Her mother wouldn't have gone in for any of that.

Clemmie was working her way through a Raspberry Mivvi, still chewing the bubblegum from the Screwball when she looked up at her father. He was looking up at the sky, frowning, a faraway look in his eye, his mouth like an upside-down smiley face. It made her feel all mistaken; she had presumed that they were having the best day of their lives but now she realized that it was only her. She could tell that he'd rather be somewhere else, with someone else, with her mother. She hated her mum then, for being such fun, for being so laughy, for having the love of Jim Bailey, for taking away some of the attention that rightfully belonged to her. She tried to think of something interesting to say.

'Did you know that sneezes come out of your nose at three hundred miles per hour?'

'No,' he said, his eyes off the horizon now; he was looking down at her. 'I didn't.'

'Yes, it's true. Sarah's brother Johnny told me that.'

'Did he now?'

'Yes. Sarah's brothers have magic bums – they can set off jets of fire.'

'They sound charming,' he said, taking out his cigar tin. She knew he'd give her the box when he'd finished them and she wondered how many he had left.

'Yes. I wish I had a big brother. They've got a shed in the back garden that smells of cigarettes. It's got a pool table and a dartboard in it. Johnny got *one hundred and eighty*.' She said *one hundred and eighty* in the same voice that Rob and Sarah had used, all sing-songy and hilarious. She remembered feeling a little left out then, when they'd all done that. They had proper family jokes that she wasn't party to. 'Daddy, can we get a pool table and a dartboard? Johnny said you can get them at Barkers.'

He was looking at her askance. 'I think someone might have a little crush on this Johnny…' He was nudging her arm, teasing her.

'No, I don't,' she said, not liking it. That wasn't what she had meant at all. He was spoiling things. Johnny was just a nice brother. That was all. She wished she hadn't said anything. She wished she hadn't tried to cheer him up.

They were walking along the front now, past the dark, tall houses covered in seagull poo. 'Hey, look!' he said. The lights of a funfair were in the distance twinkling temptingly against the sweep of sunset mauve behind. Clemmie forgot about his jibes immediately. She grabbed his hand and tried to pull him along, her damp feet beginning to warm up, the excitement rising in her chest as the wafts of toffee apple and candyfloss filtered through the air, with the snatches of music, the faint siren-like screams, beckoning them in.

Then there they were: the big wheel, the swing boat, the coconut shy, the bumper cars, the kids, the huge men with tattoos, the litter, the toffee apples – all the fun of the fair. A fat woman in high boots and mountains of hair eyed her father as they passed her stall, a small booth with painted-on curtains and 'Fortune Teller' written in fancy lettering on the top. She spoke without removing the cigarette from her lips, like a film star. 'Hey, handsome, wanna get your fortune told?' She sounded like a man. Clemmie squeezed her dad's hand to stop him walking on by. 'Oh please, Daddy!' she begged. 'I want my fortune.' She liked fortunes and things: she'd once had a red plastic fish on her hand that curled into a ball, which meant that she was *passionate*. So they followed the woman into her little hut and squeezed around a small table. A little brown dog raised its head from a basket underneath and blinked sleepily up at her but growled when she bent to touch it. The fat woman wanted money first and wasn't really bothered that the ash from her cigarette was falling all over her lacy tablecloth. Then she put on some reading glasses, which didn't seem very gypsyish, and asked for Clemmie's hand, breathing all over her, smelling just like the vicar at Christmas when he'd been drinking Christ's blood. Obediently Clemmie unfurled her palm and the woman twisted it this way and that, screwing up her eyes, which might well have been because the smoke was getting everywhere – she'd not taken the fag out of her mouth once. 'Yes indeed,' she said in her man-voice. 'I see a young and handsome prince… many children…' Clemmie stared at her, brimming with belief.

Her dad laughed. 'Steady on,' he said. 'She's only eight.'

The woman gave him a rather short look from over her spectacles. 'Tomorrow is Friday the thirteenth,' she said, opening her bloodshot eyes wide at Clemmie. 'Beware Friday the thirteenth!' She waved her hands in a mysterious circle, then stood up and sighed as if her prophecies had exhausted her.

'Is that it?' her father asked rudely.

They wandered around the fair and stood about watching and waiting as happy, loud people hopped on and off things with purpose. They stood on the edge of the Bumper Car ride watching the cars slow to a halt. Clemmie clutched her dad's hand as he pulled her through a mob of people rushing across the smooth plasticky floor and sat her down in a red one. Then off they went swerving and bumping, shouting and twirling. She leant back to watch the pokey thing making sparks along the ceiling.

'Where next? Where next?' she cried as he lifted her out of the car. He was as happy as she was now. He'd forgotten all about her mother. They played a shooting game and he won her a monkey toy. They wandered through the noisy throng with her new best toy. There was so much to see. The bright bulbs and multicoloured lights flashing on and off made the night sky behind shine a bold royal blue. She looked down at her Start-rites clicking amongst the litter and the spilt popcorn, shuffling along with a hundred other feet. Hers were chilly again, but she didn't complain. They stopped by the Waltzer and watched mesmerized as people in giant tea-cups and saucers flew across the floor, towards and away, in and out, spinning this way and that, missing each other by a hair's breadth, faster and faster in a whirl of ecstasy.

'This one! This one!' Clemmie cried, looking up at her dad.

'Are you sure?'

'Yes. This one!'

'It might make you a bit sick after three ice creams.'

'No it won't. It really won't. Please, Daddy.'

So they waited for the cups and saucers to stop and for the wobbly-legged people to get off. Then, still clutching her father's hand tightly, she climbed into the blue one that looked like the china at her nanna's house. Her dad stuffed Monkey into his pocket and they waited as the other cups began to fill up, the fair man hopping casually from saucer to saucer, holding out his tattooed hand for the money before slamming down the metal bars. 'Hold on tightly,' said a voice on a loudspeaker before some music blared out and then very slowly the tea-cups began to move. Whoosh. Whoosh. They swung out, nearly crashing into a couple of boys in the next cup. She screamed with joy, looking up at her father. *See, I told you it would be fun!*

Then slowly it began to speed up and Clemmie slid across to the edge and rather wished she wasn't wearing her slippery red tights. But it was still fun, everyone thought so, everyone was screaming. Her father was smiling, the wind making his curly hair stand up on end. He had his arm around her and she slid back into him as the tea-cup whooshed unpredictably about the floor.

Faster and faster they went: strangers' faces looming up and bearing away from her; her knuckles white as she gripped the bar. And still it got faster. Rather too fast now. Her feet couldn't reach the saucer. Her father had to remove his arm and hold on with two hands and she could no longer look round at him, she was doing all she could just to hold on. The tights and her lack of weight meant that she was sliding about all over the place.

Then suddenly it wasn't fun at all any more. She couldn't stop the slipping. She tried to ground her feet but she was too small and now she'd slipped forward she couldn't get back. She could feel herself sliding beneath the bar.

'Make it stop!' she cried. 'Make it stop, Daddy!' But he couldn't hear her. She was going to slide right out, she knew it. 'Make it stop!' She was screaming. The fear consuming her now, she was rigid with terror; she felt sick with it, she was going to die – she was going to go flying out and get squashed beneath the machinery, split into two pieces.

Still faster it went and as it hurled into a new direction Clemmie felt herself go, there was nothing she could do about it and, still clinging on, she slipped right underneath the bar, her body straight as an arrow flying through the air. But she didn't let go. She was looking up at the roof of the red tent and holding on for dear life, her legs flying about, her brown Start-rite shoes banging hard against things. She could hear her father swearing and shouting. She felt him grab her arm and pull her in but the force of the change of direction twisted her round; she was half in half out. He couldn't pull her in.

'Stop the fucking machine!' He was screaming. She had never heard him say that word before and she was glad that at last he understood why she had been screaming. She wasn't just being a scaredy-cat. He was holding on with one hand and holding her in the other. She lifted her head and she could see his face, the panic in his eyes.

'I've got you. Clemmie! I've got you! I won't let you go,' he yelled. 'I won't ever let you go.'

And she had really believed him.

5

IN THE WAKE OF THINGS

JOHNNY COULD HEAR Frank's low, soft voice from the tender; it rumbled across the water as he rowed. He wished he'd not left the boat, not gone berry-picking and certainly not felt Annie's breast up there on the hillside. He was returning to the boat carrying a new cargo of guilt. Only a couple of hours ago he had been convinced that it was Clem who would betray him and now the tables were turned: he had beaten her to it. His stomach was knotted in a confusion of lust and loathing. He hated himself for being at the mercy of his cock. It was definitely time to get off the boat, to find the nearest village, to leave them; he must make sure of that. The truth was that he didn't trust himself around Annie.

There she was right in front of him now as he rowed them back to the *Little Utopia*; she was letting her toes drag in the water, eyes closed, tipping her face up towards the sunlight, her elbows underneath her arched back and those tits of hers jutting tantalizingly forward, a lazy smile on her lips. She seemed unconcerned by what had happened up there, was acting as if everything was perfectly normal, paying Johnny the same attention as before, no more no less. It was as if no line had been crossed.

'Hey, Smudge,' he said, diverting his own attention. 'How's Granny doing?'

She was behind him at the bows, whispering sweet noth-ings into Granny's unlocatable ears having dropped her on a rock during a bouncing experiment.

'One of her legs is a bit dangly,' she said. Now that Granny's life expectancy in the wild had been seriously curtailed, Smudge had been allowed to bring her back to the *Little Utopia* as a pet.

Johnny rowed, watching the oars passing through the clear green water. He could hear Clem laughing and the splashy flick of a fishing line hitting the surface. He rested the oars in their rowlocks for a moment to listen to the quietness and looked up at the coastline to his left, miles and miles of unin-habited scrub, and it made him feel intensely claustrophobic. He looked back at Annie; she was watching him now and he quickly looked away. He must get Clem off the boat; they must leave, get back to their lives, back to the two of them. He glanced up along the coast to the north, land they had already passed, inlet after inlet of nothingness. There was no choice about it: they had to stay a little longer. There was absolutely nowhere to get off and go to.

'Hey, guys! We've got lunch!' Frank said, standing up, bare-chested, as they approached. He was holding up the bucket. Johnny couldn't meet his eye, so he settled on his chest, which was much less hairy than he'd have supposed. Johnny passed up the bilberries and the new crew member, then helped Smudge on board and got himself up over the guard rail, all without looking at Frank's face.

'Hey, Johnny,' Frank whispered, grabbing his arm in his hand, holding him behind as the others went below deck with their wares. Johnny had to turn around and face him then. Frank's eyes were mischievous, quizzical. *He sees everything*. 'You look like you need cheering up. After we've eaten, you want to get the sails up? Show me what you're made of?' he said.

Johnny nodded. That was exactly what he wanted to do; Frank did indeed see things. 'Absolutely,' he said.

Annie gutted the fish and Frank cooked them while Johnny patched up Granny's leg. He made her a splint out of an old lolly stick while Smudge and Clem built her a new home out of a cereal box, Smudge decorating the walls with felt-tip drawings of more able tortoises skipping about merrily in the scrub. They put Granny in the box with her lollipop leg. She seemed unimpressed; she stared at the murals, nonplussed by the unexpected turn her life had taken.

Johnny slid himself under Clem at the saloon table and put his arms around her. He squeezed her small body against his and buried his face in her hair. He whispered in her ear that he wanted to row her ashore and find a nice private stretch of shade. Smudge, sitting on the other side of the table, thought that sounded like an excellent idea, they could look for more tortoises – not quite what he had in mind. Instead the three of them chopped apples and made a crumble and Johnny didn't think about Annie's breasts at all until she came down to help them and he could see them jiggling underneath that shirt as she peeled the apples.

It wouldn't be long now; they might even find a village this afternoon.

After lunch was cleared and washed up, to Johnny's relief, they left the bay. He pulled up the anchor and Frank motored them out of the harbour. They chugged along the coast for a bit with Johnny waiting for the nod to get the sails up. He sat waiting, leaning against the mast, Clem at his side, the warm breeze on his face, turning every now and then to see if Frank was ready. He couldn't just put the sails up without Frank's permission; it would be like helping yourself to a drink in someone else's house. He wondered out loud what he was waiting for.

'He doesn't do anything without a reason,' Clem said, sucking loudly on a pear drop; she'd bought a stash of them in the UK and rationed herself to one a day so that they'd last her up to three months. 'Have you noticed that?' she said.

'I have,' Johnny said, his hand absentmindedly stroking her leg. They both looked over at Frank at the helm, his dark hair waving wildly in the wind, a cigarette dangling from his lips. There was something of Gregory Peck about him today.

'He saved us, didn't he?' she said. Johnny turned to look at her; she'd used exactly the same words that Annie had. 'The other night…'

'I suppose he did,' Johnny said, taking her hand. 'I think we should get off at the next village though, not wait for the town.' He looked out at the puffy white cumulus clouds bouncing along the horizon. 'Otherwise we might be stuck for a week.'

Clem turned sharply round to look him in the eye. 'What? Aren't you enjoying it?'

'I am… I am,' he said, backtracking, trying to sound reasonable. 'I don't want to outstay our welcome, that's all.'

'But we haven't. Frank says we can stay as long as we like.' Then she paused, screwing up her face in the sunlight, struck by a new idea. 'Why? Did Annie say something? What happened on the hillside?'

'Nothing,' he said, too quickly, a clenching in his gut. He squeezed her hand. 'Nothing happened.'

'Well, what's the rush then?' She looked over at the shore and he noticed that the ends of her lashes had been bleached by the sun. His eyes followed her gaze. *Nothing.* The bows of the boat were going up and down in the waves, ploughing through the water. An arrhythmic lull seemed to take hold of them both.

'I'm not ready to leave,' she said, smoothing his fingers. 'It doesn't feel like the right time. Let's wait until we get to a town.'

He felt both relieved and anxious to hear her say that. If the Annie thing hadn't happened he would be with her one hundred per cent. There was something different about these people, something alluring and attractive. The attraction wasn't a physical thing – well, it was, but it was much more profound than that. He didn't understand *what* it was quite yet. He could only think of it as though he had been swimming on the surface for a long time and someone had just introduced him to the snorkel and mask.

'OK,' he said, feeling that at least he'd tried. 'Well, let's play it by ear.'

'Don't get too comfortable!' Frank yelled from the cockpit. 'She's all yours!'

Johnny leapt to his feet and started undoing the sail-ties. 'Aye, aye,' he cried. 'Head to wind, Frank!' he called but Frank couldn't hear above the engine. 'Clem, turn her round, can you?'

Clem jumped down into the companionway and Frank turned off the engine and disappeared below deck, letting Clem take the helm. She nosed the boat round into the wind and Johnny grabbed the halyard and started to hoist the mainsail. The halyard jammed and Johnny jerked it free, heaving harder, balancing his weight, one foot against the mast. The sail was stiff and clean and flapped about wildly as it went up. The wind had shifted a little; they'd have to beat into it.

Johnny cleated the halyard off, pulled in the mainsheet and unfurled the genoa. Annie and Smudge sat huddled together on the port side watching his every move as he went to and fro along the deck checking the sails, looking up and leaning out, shouting instructions to Clem. Frank stood in the companionway in his fisherman's jumper, a big grin on his face as he watched Johnny get the boat going to its maximum capacity.

Johnny took the tiller and bore away into a close haul. The boat heeled over. Both Annie and Smudge let out identical little cries, their hands gripping the sides as if they thought the boat about to capsize.

The *Little Utopia* moved nicely. Johnny was pleasantly surprised. 'She's quite nippy for a fat bird,' he said, looking over at Frank, letting out the mainsheet just an inch or so.

They headed further out into the open water and Johnny felt his doubts and worries get swept away with the wind. This was all he needed; this was what he had been waiting for: the thrill of a little bit of speed. Speed fuelled by wind power alone. It wasn't just Johnny feeling the adrenalin; he looked at the others and could see that they were all feeling the rush. It was impossible not to. Clem came and sat by his side, slipping her hand into the back of his shorts, kissing the dip beneath his cheekbone where her lips fitted and for a while it felt good, but then he became aware of Annie sitting there on his other side with her breasts. He had to stop it. He tried to think about how old she was but that didn't work, it made him remember babysitting for the neighbours. He tried to think of her making love with Frank, but that didn't work either, that only intrigued him. He turned to Clem and kissed her lips in a perfunctory way, handed her the tiller and got up to adjust the genny. Only a couple of days maximum, he thought, looking over towards the land.

It was much windier out at sea without the shelter of the mountains. The bows of the boat thumped smack down into the water, the spray hitting everyone in the face. Smudge squealed each time it happened, licking the salt from her lips, grinning at Johnny. She was a brave, wild little thing. Thump, thump, thump went the bows.

'Oh my God!' Annie cried, anxiously looking up at Johnny, holding Smudge close. He squinted up at the main. He should probably put a reef in.

'Frank!' he cried. 'Do you want to put a reef in?'

Frank, still standing on the companionway steps looking out to sea, turned back to Johnny and then looked up at the sails. 'Up to you,' he said.

'Put one in!' Johnny said but Frank didn't move.

'Put a reef in, Frank!' Johnny repeated, thinking he hadn't heard. Frank looked up again at the sail and then back at Johnny.

'What's a reef?' he asked.

Johnny laughed. *What's a reef?*

'No, I'm serious,' Frank said, shrugging his shoulders. 'What the hell's a reef?'

Johnny looked over at Annie, who stared blankly back at him.

'You know what a reef is,' Johnny said, laughing, not knowing quite what was going on. 'You have sailed this boat before?' he asked, handing the tiller to Clem again.

Frank shook his head. 'No,' he said. 'I've never sailed any boat before.'

Johnny laughed again but he was confused, thought that perhaps this was some sort of test Frank was setting. He put the reef in himself. Then he came back down into the cockpit and changed tack, heading back towards the shore, and it began to dawn on him that this wasn't a test: the reason why the sails looked brand new was because they *were* brand new. Frank wasn't joking. When he'd said that they'd been sailing round the Med for the last six years, he meant *motoring* around the Med. He didn't know how to sail. Johnny stared at Frank in amazement. Why the hell would a man who didn't know how to sail take his family to live on a sailing boat? He had to be crazy, and the sheer insanity of it was kind of impressive.

'Why buy a sailing boat, Frank? Why not a motor boat?' he asked a little later on, when they were alone in the cockpit sipping at beers. Frank tapped himself out a fag, caught it in his lips and lit it, sheltering the flame from the wind. He sat back, spreading his huge frame out wide, a mischievous smile on his lips.

'Perhaps, like you, Johnny,' he said, 'I had to leave in a bit of a hurry.'

Johnny was intrigued. He waited for more information but Frank was unforthcoming and Johnny didn't want to ask, didn't want to pry, it would display a lack of something manly and he still wanted to impress Frank, for Frank to think he was different from other men, worthy of his friendship and respect. So instead he sat back himself and looked out at the horizon.

'I'll tell you one thing, Johnny,' Frank said, rewarding him for his patience. 'I did nothing that I'm ashamed of.'

Johnny looked away, up at the canvas. The wind had dropped a little and he adjusted the main and unfurled a little more of the genny and they drank their beers in silence. Below deck he could see Clem and Annie chatting in the galley. 'Have you never done *anything* that you're ashamed of?' Johnny asked him. Those generic kinds of questions were acceptable, he knew that.

Johnny watched as the wind blew the ash off the end of his cigarette. 'I take full responsibility for all of my actions,' Frank said and Johnny wished that he could say the same. 'We get what's coming to us, Johnny. We can't escape karma. That's why it's very important to witness the choices as we make them. Create good karma for yourself.'

A bit late now, Johnny thought.

'Stay until we get to Datca at least,' Frank said, as if they had been discussing his plans. He put his arm lazily around Johnny's shoulder. 'There's sod all along this coast.'

It was true. So the decision was made; it was easy. They would stay.

The sun crossed the sky and later on, far out on the horizon, another boat sailed by, but apart from that the sea was theirs. Johnny spent the rest of the afternoon busying himself – making small adjustments to the sail trim, rolling the genny out, rolling it in, putting a reef in, taking it out, tacking, gybing, whatever the fluky wind wanted him to do. Frank had liked that: there was no choice but to respond to the now, to each breath of wind as it came or went, no time to dwell on the past. Johnny had started showing him how to read the sails, how to rely on his senses and it had felt good that he was giving Frank something in return for all that Frank was giving them.

Annie and Smudge disappeared for a siesta and shortly Frank joined them. Clem remained at the bows sketching away in her black book while Johnny sailed the boat. He watched her up there, the methodical way in which she worked, and he wondered what on earth she was sketching because there was nothing to see but sea. He thought about how they would be doing this some time, sailing their boat, going wherever they fancied, seeing the world on their terms.

He'd stopped scanning the shore for villages now – what was the point? He had completely overreacted this morning; it was nothing, it was insignificant, it had clearly meant nothing to Annie and it actually meant nothing to him. He could wait another couple of days for the town; there was no point in getting stuck in some village. Now that he'd made that decision to stay, to relax, he knew it was the right one, he could feel it in his gut, just as Frank had said. He was so focused on the sails and the horizon and the sea that he didn't notice the feeling sidling back in, of the real world slipping away, their world being on this thirty-foot boat with a population of five where the rules seemed to keep taking him by surprise.

Annie was the first to come up, yawning, crease marks of sheet on her cheek. She was wearing one of Frank's shirts and not much else and Johnny pretended not to notice but was intensely aware that, with Clem dozing at the bows, it was just the two of them in the cockpit. She passed him a cup of tea and it was she who didn't meet his eye; she seemed distracted, unhappy, and he thought that perhaps she too was feeling bad about what had happened. She went back down below and he watched her pottering around the galley. She put on some music, Aretha Franklin, and began cooking something, reading a recipe. The wind had dropped and Johnny started fiddling around with the sextant. He'd cleaned up the mirrors and the lens and was lining up the horizon with the sun when Annie came back out holding a bag of potatoes. She undid the bucket hanging from the back and swung it neatly full of seawater, checking out the horizon as she did so. She emptied the potatoes into the bucket and began to peel them.

'This is the furthest from land we've ever been,' she said, looking over at the distant shore.

Johnny stopped squinting through the lens and looked at her as she peeled. 'Seriously?' he asked. She nodded, her pale eyes looking up at him; the first moment of intimacy since he'd touched her on the hillside. She shot a furtive glance down below deck and Johnny thought she was going to refer to it. He returned to the safety of the sextant lens.

'He can't even swim!' she said. There was something mocking, unkind in her tone.

Johnny put down the sextant and sat down. 'He can't swim and he can't sail?' he asked. It felt naughty talking about him. 'Are you masochists? Why the hell didn't you buy a house instead of a boat?'

She looked down at her hands and vigorously swiped at the potato. 'No one can find you on a boat, can they?' she said. Then she flashed another look down below, wiped her face with her sleeve and got up, as if she'd said too much.

Shortly Frank appeared from the forepeak in his shorts and Johnny watched as he pottered about the saloon, his large, tanned frame, the row of dents on his back, the broken shoulder blade. Clem said he'd been hit by a truck. It looked like he'd been run over by a tractor.

Much later, when the pleasant analgesic of alcohol had helped change the atmosphere to something more united, after they'd moored in yet another deserted bay and eaten their supper, after the sky had gone pink and the Earth had turned its back on the sun, after the girls had read bedtime stories to Smudge and were playing hippie music and dancing in the galley, and Frank and Johnny were drinking a bottle of red in the cockpit, the night sky put on the most spectacular display for them. Something big was happening up there: the sky was full of shooting stars wherever you looked. It had been going on for hours.

Frank was lying along the stern seat, his legs dangling over the tiller, his eyes watching the sky as he quizzed Johnny about his sailing experiences. Johnny was telling him about the one and only time he'd been in a full-on storm, where the wind was blowing a steady sixty gusting up to eighty in the Bay of Biscay. He and Rob had got caught in the force ten in a thirty-two-foot wooden yawl. The sea had been white; dense streaks of foam zigzagging across it. They'd dropped all the sails, harnessed themselves on and hoped for the best. He remembered clearly being down at the bottom of a freakishly huge wave and looking up to where it was breaking and all he could see was a tiny handkerchief-sized patch of sky, the rest was a living mountain of water about to come crashing down on them.

'Jesus,' Frank said, turning his whole body round to Johnny. 'And what was going through your mind?'

'I was just hoping the boat could take it.'

'Ah! But then you were born in the caul, let's not forget,' Frank said, swirling the wine around in his glass. Johnny laughed.

'Did you feel fear?' Frank asked and Johnny was pleased to see how impressed Frank was with him. He glowed a little, despite himself.

'Fear, excitement… It's much the same thing, isn't it?' Johnny said. He wasn't trying to sound flash, it really was true: the only thing he truly remembered feeling at the bottom of the wave was pure exhilaration.

Frank laughed. 'I like the cut of your jib, Johnny.' He sat up and tapped out a fag and leant back, one leg up on the seat, blowing the smoke up into the sky, tapping his foot in time to the music, eyes set on Johnny, looking at him in that intimate, almost sexual manner. It made Johnny uncomfortable in a not entirely unpleasant way. A dark and peculiar thought struck him: if he were a woman, Frank would be exactly the sort of man he could imagine falling in love with.

Frank was staring at him. 'I think I've been waiting a long time for you, Johnny. I think our paths were meant to cross.'

Johnny felt himself flush. He had never sought anybody's approval like this before. He tried not to be flattered, he tried to be cool but as he sipped his wine and looked up at the sky above, somewhere inside he was shining.

'I don't believe in coincidences,' Frank said, looking at him oddly as if he were seeing him for the first time. 'It's just opportunity and preparedness coming together.'

This was all new to Johnny, the whole idea that things happened for a reason. His mother used to talk like that and he had always liked it but since she had died he had become totally rational. You live, you die, and that's that. He sucked on his cigarette and listened to the comforting crackle of the burning tobacco.

'You like a bit of danger, don't you, Johnny?'

Johnny wasn't sure what he meant. He leant back a little, resting his head against the coachroof, and thought about the question. High up above a meteor shot through the Earth's atmosphere. 'I think I do,' he said.

Frank's voice was quiet. 'Did that feel dangerous today?'

'No, that was barely a five.' He blew out his smoke, slowly, and watched it disappear into the night.

'No, not the sailing,' Frank said, his voice still low. 'Up on the hillside… touching my wife.'

Johnny froze. He turned to Frank in the darkness, the music from down below blaring inanely, aware of the sudden thumping rhythm of his heartbeat, the tightness that seemed to have taken hold in his chest.

'Was it exciting?' Frank whispered.

Johnny sat up and leant forward. 'She told you?' He was whispering too.

'She tells me everything, Johnny.'

Johnny could only stare. He swallowed, trying to release the tightness around his neck. He glanced down below deck. Annie and Clem had stopped dancing around in the galley and were crouched over some book. Johnny shuffled forward along the seat. 'I'm so sorry, Frank. I'm so sorry. I don't know what happened... I don't know what I thought I was doing...'

'Hey,' Frank said, moving in a little closer. He placed his big hand on Johnny's shoulder. 'Relax. I don't mind. It doesn't matter.' He waved it away as if it was of no importance at all.

It doesn't matter. He felt Frank's huge fingers kneading his shoulder, relaxing him, absolving him. It didn't make sense.

'It's the "danger" that interests me,' Frank said, sitting back, sucking on his cigarette. 'Besides, Annie can do as she pleases. I don't believe in repressing people. We mustn't censor ourselves. We must be what we are.'

Johnny stared at him, confused. 'Really?' he said.

'Denial is against all my principles,' he said, serious yet with a glint in his eye.

'You're something else, Frank.'

Frank offered him a cigarette, which he took, his hand shaking a little.

'We have to be free to be ourselves, Johnny. This is life. There's no point otherwise!'

'You won't say anything to Clem?' Johnny asked, looking up at him, leaning in as Frank lit his cigarette for him, his face lighting up in the flame, dark and rugged.

'Not if you don't want me to.'

'Will Annie tell Clem?'

'What are you so afraid of?' Frank asked, letting the flame go out, his features retreating into the darkness. 'I thought fear and excitement were the same thing?' he said, smiling, ruffling Johnny's head as if he were a schoolboy.

Then he was still for a moment before leaning forward again. 'Fear has no place in love, Johnny.' Johnny stared at him, wanting to understand. Sometimes Frank made him feel as if he'd been looking at the world upside down for his entire life. 'You must see that! ' He tapped the side of Johnny's head slowly with his big knuckles. 'You need to start changing the way you're thinking.'

Johnny wanted to change; he wanted to see the world the way Frank saw it; he wanted to look out of the same window that Frank was looking out of.

'Fear is just the unknown, Johnny. That's all.'

Johnny nodded; he thought he understood that.

'Do you want to know how to get rid of the fear?' Frank whispered, smiling now.

'Tell me.'

'You embrace the uncertainty.'

Johnny didn't get it; he watched as Frank crossed one leg over the other and rubbed his chin thoughtfully. 'Why are you so scared about Clem finding out?' He wasn't expecting an answer. He carried on, his voice low, aware of the girls down below. 'You're worried about what? Some bullshit you've made up, like hurting her, upsetting her. So you lie, or you don't tell the truth. You protect her. Is that right?'

Johnny nodded.

'Well, that's fine, Johnny, but sooner or later, you're going to understand that the only life worth living is a *free* life. That's a life without lies, half-truths, censorship and misunderstandings. You touched Annie because you wanted to. There's nothing wrong with that.'

'Isn't there?' Johnny asked, because he was pretty sure that there was.

'No.'

'But it would hurt Clem if she knew.'

'Yes,' Frank said, his eyes shining. 'Because at the moment the pair of you are living in the prison of your past conditioning. You're still living with old thought processes, old values. There's no evolution in that, only stagnation and decay. You need to evolve, Johnny.' He made evolving sound like the most wonderful thing in the world. 'Real love has no limits,' he said. 'No boundaries.'

Johnny stared into Frank's eyes. He could feel something new fizzing away inside of him now, a glimpse of what life could be like, an absolution of any darker desires; he could sense all the potential that was lying in wait. He wanted to *evolve*. That had to be the point of it all – if there was a point – which he was now pretty sure that there was. As a species, evolution had to be our primary purpose.

'I tell you,' Frank said, flashing his white even teeth at Johnny. 'As soon as you accept uncertainty with an open heart, as soon as you step into the unknown, life is bloody magical. It's a blast, not some of the time, but *all* of the time.'

Annie stuck her head out into the companionway, holding out two tumblers. 'Hey, you two. Pour us some!' She'd washed her hair and looked clean and shining. Frank took the cork out of the bottle and poured the red wine into the glasses. 'Get yourselves out here,' he said. 'There are shooting stars all over the place. All our wishes can come true!'

'Smudge asleep?' Johnny asked, noticing that he could look Annie in the eye again now.

'Eventually,' she said. 'I'll have to move Granny. She's sleeping on the pillow.' She looked up at the sky for a moment and squeezed shut her eyes to make a wish. 'Fresh eggs for Thursday please,' she said, opening them again. 'We were just looking up cake recipes for the birthday girl.'

Annie turned back round into the saloon. 'Turn the lights off, Clem. Pass the guitar!'

Clem and Annie came out into the dark of the cockpit and sat down together opposite Johnny; the starlight and their cigarettes the only light. Annie began to play along with Fleetwood Mac, only it sounded entirely different when she sang it. Clem lay back, next to her, her body close to Frank's, her feet on Annie's lap and the four of them listened as Annie sang about the songbird while the meteors hurled themselves through the Earth's atmosphere and Johnny felt extraordinarily lucky to be alive. *This, here, now is magic.* He got it then, the power of uncertainty, true freedom, and it felt just like love to him. He was drunk, but that was irrelevant.

Annie's voice took them somewhere else as it always did and they followed it willingly; they went wherever she took them and she kept on singing and the stars kept on shooting. Eventually Johnny reached for the bottle and poured the dregs into Frank's glass. He was drunker than he thought and the empty bottle slipped from his fingers. Annie went to catch it with her legs but knocked it into a spin in the centre of the cockpit floor. It whirled around in a blur of darkness.

'Oh, yes!' Annie said, leaning forward, her fingers ceasing their strumming, resting her chin on the guitar. 'Spin the bottle...' She looked round at them all, one eyebrow raised. 'Who do I get to kiss?'

They laughed at first, but then gradually, one by one, they leant forward to watch it spin, all of them wondering, all of them quiet now. It seemed to take forever to slow down, for its bottle shape to re-emerge from the blur. Johnny was thinking about kissing her now, how he had wanted to up on the hillside, how he had wanted to press his face into those breasts. But this time, he didn't feel bad about it; he just let himself be free, he stopped the judgements, he wasn't going to think like that any more. The bottle began to slow down, slower and slower; round and round it spun, taking all his hopes around with it. *Step into the unknown.* The bottle stopped indisputably at Clem.

Clem leant back. 'Oh,' she said, surprised. 'It's me.'

She glanced across at Johnny; he could see the expectation in her eye: she wanted him to tell her what to do. He smiled and shrugged his shoulders, giving his consent, but Annie had already put her finger on Clem's chin and turned her face to her own. She leant forwards and kissed her tenderly on the lips. He could see that Clem was surprised; she had never been kissed by a woman. But he noticed that she didn't pull away so, after a moment or two, Annie kissed her again, so gently at first that Johnny could almost feel the softness of their lips. They began to kiss properly then, a real, deep, passionate embrace and he became so stiff he would have to undo his jeans if this carried on. He saw Frank lean back against the stern and spread his arms across the transom but it was too dark to read his expression.

'Your turn!' Annie whispered as she pulled away. Clem was a little breathless, her lips parted and moist. She was turned on, just as Johnny was, just as they all were. She briefly caught his eye and then bent down and flicked the bottle into a spin. They all watched it turning, the dark whir on the cockpit sole. It bounced off the side of the cockpit seat and came to a fast halt pointing towards the bucket tied to the stern. The only person sitting at the stern was Frank. Johnny could see her profile in silhouette: her mouth was open, her tongue on her lips and he knew that there was a light in her eye.

'Don't worry, Clem,' Frank said gently, his words low and soothing in the darkness. 'You don't have to play these games.'

She stared at him, motionless.

'No, go on,' Johnny heard himself say. 'Kiss him, Clem…'

And he watched as his wife stood up and bent down to kiss Frank; he heard the wet soft noises of them kissing, saw how his gentle giant hands held her head with such tenderness, the way those hands moved slowly down her back and how she pressed her body into his, giving herself to him.

6

SICKNESS AT SEA

THERE WAS BARELY any wind and the sails were flopping about. It had been like this for forty-eight hours. Every now and then a warm gust from the west would take the boat up the backside and she would pick up a little speed, enough for Johnny to think about putting the spinnaker up, but just as he decided that he would, the wind would drop and he'd stuff it back down through the hatch. They were moving slowly, about two knots; everything felt lazy, hazy and still. Occasionally an insect buzzed by or a bird swooped languidly past but everything had been stifled into quietness by the heat and lack of wind. Frank had said he wanted to save the last of the diesel for motoring in and out of bays.

Clem was lying on her prayer mat on the deck, feeling the warm sunshine on her skin, her feet resting on the boom, ostensibly to stop it gybing but more for her own comfort, her toes and hips moving almost imperceptibly to the Stevie Wonder drifting up through the open saloon hatch. She was thinking about what had happened two nights ago, her head still awash with moments and sensations, her body still buzzing, her face still tender from the scratches of Frank's beard. She had never kissed a man with a beard before – at first it had felt odd and cave-mannish after the extreme softness of Annie's face and lips. Then again, she had never kissed a woman before. She had never been with anyone apart from Johnny. She wasn't even sure that she found Frank physically attractive – he was so much older and bigger, a man not a boy. He definitely wasn't attractive in the same way that Johnny was. Yet there was some other connection that had turned her on, had made the sexual act seem something other than physical. She was aroused again, just thinking about it.

Johnny was watching Clem, his thoughts the only turbulence in the omnipresent stillness of their surroundings. His head ached. She was naked save for the heart necklace, thumb in mouth, right hand lazily seeking out the hot spots across her body. Her hands were like two little birds, the left nesting as the right flew off purposefully to find succour and bring it back. Usually, when clothed, she concentrated on her facial supply of hot spots, the bone beneath her eyebrow, her temple, the dip in her upper lip, the secret cave under her jaw bone, but lying there stark naked she evidently felt quite free to explore the warm softness of her breast or her hip or her armpit. This was only ever done when they were in bed. Alone. But for the last couple of days, she had clearly felt free to do it out in the daylight in front of anyone who was watching. Johnny didn't like it. He felt that she was being deliberately provocative, stroking herself here there and everywhere. She was doing it to titillate *him*. But the thing *was*, the fact that she hadn't seemed to have noticed was that Frank wasn't even watching her. He was sitting over by the genny engrossed in some history book. She was making herself look ridiculous.

His head was full of crap. He needed some wind to clear it all out.

'Hey, Smudge, need a hand?' he asked, envying the simplicity of her child world. She was standing on the galley step heaving various things over the lip and out into the companionway: a bowl full of water, various lotions and potions and towels and flannels and then Gilla, whom she'd strapped into her bikini – an ironic sight, since most of the humans weren't bothering with clothes. Then last but not least she brought out Granny who was sporting a colourful ribbon tied around her middle. She was wearing Frank's CBE as a belt.

Smudge plonked Granny down on the towel, which she promptly used as a toilet. Then Smudge herself climbed over in her Captain Hook coat which was looking even grubbier than normal. 'Naughty Granny doing a poo,' Smudge said, turning over poor Granny, exposing her pale underbelly to the world. She undid the ribbon and dabbed cotton wool in the water and started cleaning Granny up as if she were a baby.

Granny waved her legs in the air hopelessly, her little neck straining round, her wrinkled, old-man eyes blinking at up at Johnny.

'Now, Granny,' Smudge said bossily, turning her back over and dangling her over the bowl full of water. 'You can stop all this. I've had quite enough of your antiques. It's bathtime whether you like it or not.' She did a pretty good impression of Annie; she certainly had an ear on her.

Granny wasn't so keen. Smudge might have been a little more sympathetic to Granny's plight when she herself kicked up a notable stink at bathtime.

She picked Granny up and put her down in the water and poured some shampoo into her hand.

'Not shampoo, Smudge,' Johnny said, taking the bottle out of her hand. 'Granny's not got any hair. Just let her have a little dip... Smudge?' he said, bending down. Granny's feet had caught his eye, they had messy dabs of red paint on her claws. 'What have you done to her?'

'Oh. She wanted to play Beauty Salons,' Smudge said, shaking her head as if she herself had attempted to persuade Granny otherwise.

He sat back at the tiller, glancing over at Frank who was still engrossed in his book, sitting on a towel near the bows. Annie was sleeping down in the saloon, curled up on the seat, a sheet over her. There was always at least one of them asleep at any given time. Clem was still sunbathing. She'd stopped stroking herself now and was turned away from him. He was still reeling from what had happened, how quickly everything seemed to have changed and yet no one was referring to the fact that they had all fucked each other. *Only naked can we truly reveal ourselves.* Frank was right about that; they had reached a new level, the four of them. There was not a lot to hide now; the barriers had been removed. Nothing could be more intimate than watching another person orgasm. He was surprised by how quickly nudity had been normalized, how unselfconscious the others were, whereas he himself had categorized things: he was fine with it when they were sunbathing or washing or having sex, doing things where nakedness was an obvious choice, but he needed people to be wearing clothes when they were eating or having discussions or cooking. Yes, he liked boundaries; he liked a public and a private persona.

He couldn't work out quite how he felt about it all now. He'd been all right at first, even the day after, but today everything was odd. He couldn't help feeling as if he'd been robbed, or that he'd been careless, that he'd mislaid something precious. When they were lying about the boat like this, all in their own little worlds, it was hard to believe that it had actually happened, that he had willingly taken part and openheartedly given his wife to another man. Not that she had put up any resistance; he had watched as Frank had laid her down on the cockpit seat under the stars, his mouth pressed to hers; how she'd pulled up her skirt and pulled down her knickers and opened her legs as if she'd been waiting for him, dying for him, gagging for him. Johnny had felt proud of her, how beautiful she looked and how keen she was; he'd wanted Frank to be impressed by her; he'd wanted her to please him and for Frank to feel the gift of Clem from him, Johnny. *I give you my wife.* Then of course, it meant that Johnny could have Annie; his guilt was erased. She had got down on her knees and undone his jeans and taken him in her mouth and all the while Johnny had kept his eyes on Frank and Clem getting it on, watching as Frank had slipped his fingers down between her legs into her wetness. How he kept saying over and over, 'You little thing, you little gorgeous thing,' as he fucked her with his hand. How she had arched her back and moaned at his touch, or was it his words? But the thing *was*, the thing she hadn't seen, the thing that made her look foolish lying there touching herself in the sunshine, lying on her bloody prayer mat, was that while Frank was fucking her it was Johnny he was locking eyes with. When they were inside each other's wives, when Frank was coming, as he shuddered and juddered, at that point of pure abandonment when a man looks helpless and pathetic, it was Johnny Frank had been staring at. And Johnny, who was shortly to climax himself, had been half appalled and half aroused by it.

'Have you got me a birthday present?' Smudge said. She had wrapped a resigned Granny in a towel and was applying talcum powder liberally – no tortoise in the history of tortoises had ever been so pampered.

He had momentarily forgotten that her birthday was coming up. 'Maybe we do, maybe we don't,' he said, making his eyebrows dance up and down with suspense. 'You'll just have to wait and see!'

'Oh I can't,' she said, grinning her baby-toothed grin, crawling across the cockpit sole to him and climbing on to his lap. He ruffled her tangled mess of hair.

'Only one more sleep and you're five years old! Just think! Such a big girl!'

'Yes,' she said, a tremble of excitement running through her. 'Daddy says that five is the most important age in the world.' She swung her legs against his and turned round to look at him with a frown. 'What can big girls of five do that little girls can't?'

'Well, big girls can… swim, can't they?' he said. He didn't really have any idea about five-year-old girls.

'Yes they can,' she said, eyes wide with possibility. 'Will I be able to swim tomorrow?'

'Well, maybe not tomorrow but soon.'

'What else can big girls do?

'Um… big girls can read and write.'

Her eyes widened in wonderment at all the amazing opportunities that age was going to bring her. 'When I was a little girl of four I couldn't really write properly, could I?' she said as if it were already a distant memory, curling a lock of matted dark hair maturely round her ear. 'I just did really good scribbling…'

He laughed and looked up at Frank, who was watching them with a smile on his face. Johnny waved.

'If you wanted I could have my present early? Now, even?' she asked hopefully.

The day before, they had actually passed a bay that was occupied. It had two houses in it. Johnny had peered through the binoculars to examine it carefully. There was no vehicle that he could see but the houses were inhabited; there was washing hanging up on the line. They'd rowed ashore and a little old woman had come out from the far house to meet them. She welcomed them inside her extremely humble abode.

There was one stone room with a fireplace in the middle and a stone sink. There was no running water but there was a stream running down from the mountain that divided the two houses. The woman lived a completely isolated life; there was nothing in the whole premises to hint that Christ had come or gone. At the sight of a few lira she had gabbled away through rotten wonky teeth and taken them through the stone room to the back garden where an old, skinny donkey blinked dolefully at them from underneath the shade of a tree. She'd got down on her hands and knees and scrambled into a chicken coop, reversing out with a scrawny-looking chicken in one hand and an egg in the other. She'd handed over the flapping bird and laughed at their blank expressions, gabbled some more, taken it back and cheerily snapped its neck in two. When she'd spied Johnny rolling a cigarette, she'd helped herself to his tobacco and rolled herself a cigarette the size of a small baguette with her nimble chicken-killing fingers. On the beach where they'd left the tender, Johnny had found a piece of driftwood and Clem had collected a load of shells which some creature had thoughtfully drilled holes into and in the evening, as Smudge had slept, she had threaded the shells together into a necklace on a piece of fishing line and Johnny had sharpened the wood into a spear for killing monsters. So now Smudge not only had a necklace and a spear but it looked like they'd have chicken and a cake for her birthday as well.

Johnny looked up from Smudge, out on to the glassy water. 'Gybing!' he said. Smudge jumped off him and picked up Granny. Frank shifted as the genny flapped across him and Clem stirred, took her feet off the boom and sat up hugging her knees to her chest, ducking her head as the boom swung over and the *Little Utopia* dozily shifted through the non-existent wind. Clem got up from her prayer mat and wrapped a sarong around her naked body. Slowly, Johnny noticed, deliberately; she wanted Frank to be watching her.

'Bloody wind, where are you?' Johnny muttered under his breath, his headache banging at his temples.

'Bloody wind,' Smudge repeated, tucking Granny underneath one arm and Gilla under the other, standing up, looking out to sea, trying to pull the same frustrated expression that Johnny was pulling. Then she spotted her father and tottered down the deck to join him. He put down his book and lifted her into his arms, squeezing her tightly, blowing a raspberry on to her belly. 'And who is going to be five years old?' he cried in a booming, scary voice.

Clem stepped down into the companionway and put on her shades. Her hair was now so curly and bleached and her skin so dark, she looked quite different to the Clem he remembered in England; he felt slightly nostalgic for the other one, the one he knew really well, who was his and his alone. She slid down the side of the seat on to the cockpit sole out of the sun and smiled at him. It didn't feel like a real smile to him, it felt like a testing-the-water smile, a gauging-his-mood smile. They had been in some unspoken struggle ever since it had happened. She yawned.

'You shouldn't be tired, all you do is sleep,' he said. Everything he said to her seemed to have an edge to it today.

'Didn't know I was being monitored so closely.'

'Oh? I thought you did,' he said. 'I thought that was why you were lying around naked touching yourself.'

She paused. She turned her face up to his, taking her sunglasses off to see him better.

'He wasn't even watching you,' Johnny said, adjusting the tiller slightly. He wasn't proud of himself. He wasn't quite sure what he was even jealous of any more; he was just trying to pick a fight. She sat back up on the cockpit seat and glared at him. She'd never looked at him that way before. That was a look he'd seen her give her father.

'Why don't you just ask what you really want to?' she said. 'Why don't you ask me whether I prefer having sex with him or you?'

They had never spoken like this to one another – but then again, these were exceptional circumstances. Johnny reached over and picked up Frank's packet of fags, which was lying on the seat. He lit himself a cigarette, his fingers trembling just a little, hating her but hating himself more.

'Well? Did you?' he said as flippantly as he could.

She paused and took a cigarette of her own. 'It was different,' she said.

Wrong answer. He looked up to check whether the sail was luffing or if the wind had dropped or if the sky had fallen in or anything just as long as he didn't have to look at her. *He wasn't even looking at you; he was looking at me.* This was awful, ugly, being at war with her.

She sighed and turned her back to him, tucking her knees up to her chin. He couldn't see her face but he saw her wipe her eyes roughly as if they were betraying her. 'You started it…' she said.

He had made her cry. He wanted to reach out and touch her but he couldn't do it.

'You started it, Johnny. You did it too. And now you're acting like I'm the one that's done something wrong.'

It was true. He tried to tell her he was sorry with his eyes.

'Let's get off this bloody boat,' she said and he leant forward and wiped away a tear from her cheek with his thumb. He had meant to do it tenderly but it didn't come out that way. He didn't seem able to reach his tenderness any more. *Yes, they must get off the boat.*

'We need wind,' he said quietly. 'We're really low on diesel.'

By the afternoon the wind had completely died and the water had become flat and glassy for miles around. They were prisoners of the open sea. The sails flopped about and the boom banged. The boat barely moved and his head still ached. There were dolphins everywhere, a stream of them leaping and diving across the expanse of sea – the lucky things needing no wind. A pod of mushroom-coloured whales with bulbous noses passed by not more than a hundred yards away. Frank had looked them up in a book and Johnny had wondered out loud why everybody wanted to know the names of every-thing, couldn't it be enough just to see things, did we have to attach labels to everything? Frank had been watching him carefully since then, as if he were worried about him.

Annie was in the cockpit. Her back was slightly sunburnt so she had put her clothes back on, a flowery sundress that Johnny hadn't seen before. She was plucking the chicken; her dextrous and able hands firm and strong as she ripped out the feathers and flicked them overboard, leaving a trail behind the boat, piles of them getting caught on the bows of the tender, a soft, gingery moustache sitting on its wooden lip. Smudge was seated with Clem at the bows; they were singing together some repetitive nursery rhyme as they painted their toenails to match Granny's, the waft of acrylic hovering on the boat, being blown nowhere.

Frank was clattering about in the galley making coffee. He passed Johnny and Annie up a cup and then joined them in the cockpit with the guitar. He looked out over the glassy sea and began to strum it lazily as the boat drifted nowhere, the sound tripping far across the water and he wondered whether anyone on earth could hear them. Johnny squinted at the

162

horizon. It was a bitch of a day. They were becalmed; they could be stuck here for ever.

'I don't think you *should* leave us, Johnny,' Frank said, once again reading his mind.

'It would be an impossibility under present circumstances,' Johnny said, eyes as ever scanning the water for signs of wind.

'You and she will be fine,' Frank said quietly, glancing down the boat at Clem. 'You can't force solutions on problems, Johnny. Solutions emerge by themselves.'

Johnny picked up his tobacco, glancing at Frank as he did so, glad of the conversation. Annie ripped off another handful of feathers and chucked them overboard. Johnny watched them floating on the water, balancing on the surface, drifting with the boat.

'You two, you're at the beginning of your journey,' Frank said. 'And there's always pain with birth.' He tapped out one of his cigarettes, catching it in his mouth.

'Not that you'd know,' Annie said, rolling her eyes.

'Don't be annoyed with her,' Frank continued, ignoring Annie's remark, lighting his cigarette. 'Or us,' he said.

Johnny looked up at him. He didn't want Frank to stop talking.

'When you're feeling frustrated or upset by a situation or a person, Johnny, you've got to try and remember that it's *not* the person or the situation you're upset by, it's *your feelings* about them.'

He leant forward and lit Johnny's cigarette. Johnny sat back and inhaled deeply. 'Maybe sometimes it *is* someone else's fault, Frank,' he said.

'Yes, but they're still *your* feelings. They're not someone else's. You are responsible for your reactions, Johnny. And responsibility means not blaming anyone or anything for your situation.' He smiled again, his eyes full of kindness and understanding. 'Not even yourself.'

Frank had a way of calming him; his words worked as balm on Johnny's splintering thoughts. He only felt troubled when he felt out of control, that things were happening *to* him. He looked back at the scattered feathers in the glassy water; they lay in a straight line as far as the eye could see. The *Little Utopia* was moving. She had left a feathery wake. Time was slipping by just fast enough for the naked eye to miss it.

He shut his eyes and took a deep breath and when he looked inside himself, he found that his jealousy had lost its sting and he wondered why he had felt so fearful. After all, what *was* his big fear? That Clem might stop loving him? That she might love Frank? She would always love him. Wasn't that what his father had said after his mother died: *you can't lose the love*. So what if she loved Frank too? Johnny himself loved Frank. Everything was going to pass anyhow. One day they'd be looking back at all this. It was as transient as the blue cigarette smoke hovering over their heads.

Frank was strumming on the guitar again, playing something new, something familiar. A Beatles' song his mother used to play on the big old record player.

Johnny leant back and listened, his eyes as always scanning the water for wind. How did Frank manage to see through situations, to the core of things and find what was real in there, the seed of truth behind the bullshit? His mind worked like a sieve, straining out the waste. Annie was right; he did see everything. He wondered what Frank had been like when he had been his age. He would have liked to know him then.

Frank was watching him as he strummed. Then he stopped suddenly. 'Hey, Smudge?' he called down to the bows of the boat. Both Smudge and Clem looked up. There was something similar about them, not just their hair and nails, but their expressions. They could have been sisters: what with Clem being so small, the age gap seemed less.

'Why don't you give us a show?' her father said. Johnny knew that Frank was trying to cheer him up. He smiled. Smudge's face had lit up.

'Yes! Yes!' she cried, leaping up and down. She ran down the decks and into the cockpit, leaning over her father whispering something in his ear. He whispered back.

'Yes! Oh yes!' she cried. 'I have to get ready! I have to put my costume on!' With that she scampered down into the galley, shutting the cockpit doors behind her.

Frank reached across and rested his hand on Johnny's thigh. 'Stay with us,' he said quietly. 'You want to go east? Let's go east. Let's go through the Suez Canal, head for the Indian Ocean.'

When Frank said things like that Johnny couldn't imagine ever leaving them. It would be insane to turn down such an offer. Yet he would; they had to move on. He and Clem both knew that; they had agreed that. But the pull to stay was great; Johnny felt that he was halfway through some kind of metamorphosis, that if he left now, his transformation would be incomplete. He could see it clearly – his old life, lived in a happy kind of ignorance, and the new one, where wonder after wonder seemed to unfold before him. It was all a question of risk, stepping into that uncertainty.

'Sometimes you have to take risks to get the real rewards,' Frank said, those dark eyes looking right into him and reading him like a chart, the tip of his cigarette crackling fiercely as he sucked the life out of it. Annie was watching him from her husband's side, willing him to stay; he could see it in her face. Frank was almost whispering. 'When you start making the right decisions moment to moment, everything falls into place with absolutely no effort at all, Johnny. Don't force those solutions. This moment, the one you are experiencing right now, is exactly as it should be. It is the result of all your other choices.'

Johnny looked up at the sky and felt the moment, the one right now, and it felt fine. He smiled and watched as Annie tossed the plucked chicken into the bucket of seawater and began to wash it down. Johnny stared at the corpse, white and puny underneath all those feathers, like an old man's scrotum.

Then the cockpit doors opened slightly as Smudge pushed her nose and mouth around them. 'Ladies and gentlemen, take your seats!' she yelled. Then the doors were firmly shut again and Clem came down from the bows, put her book aside and sat down next to Johnny. He took her hand and she let him. They were all right. They were going to be fine. That night had just been a shock for both of them.

The cockpit doors flung open and Smudge was posing on the companionway steps dressed in some pink frilly knickers of Annie's and a matching bra stuffed with several pairs of socks and a pair of way too big wedged shoes. She looked extremely funny, especially because her expression was so focused, so intent. Johnny tried hard not to laugh.

Then Frank began to strum his guitar and it only got funnier. Smudge wasn't remotely distracted by their muted giggling; she began to wiggle her hips with the music, her face deadpan, one eyebrow raised. She had struck a pose and was going to keep it. Her arms held wide the cockpit doors, her knees were bent forward as she wiggled, her bottom sticking out, her sock-cleavage thrust forward, her head tilted back, her lips forming a kiss.

'*I wanna be loved by you...*' she sang in a breathy, sultry, perfectly mimicked voice. She was doing a Marilyn Monroe impression and she was doing it uncannily well. It was quite

166

the most extraordinary thing that either Johnny or Clem had ever seen: the sophistication, the perfect pitch, the sizzling expression. Smudge was mesmeric. Clem covered her mouth to contain herself, to plug the laughter.

Smudge must have seen the film because she struck the poses and sang the words with an incredible and almost disturbing accuracy. She was pointing her finger at Johnny and bouncing up and down when a pair of socks rolled out of her cleavage. But being the pro that she evidently was, she seamlessly bent down to pick them up again and stuffed them back inside and just carried on singing in that sweet child voice, hoiking up the giant knickers. Johnny wiped the tears of laughter from his eyes, trying desperately to keep a straight face, which he failed to do when during the instrumental she turned a little circle clunking in the heels before striking the finale attitude, hands on hips, lips pursed. They clapped and cheered and Smudge kicked off the shoes, looking quite thrilled by how well she had gone down. 'I'll do another!' she said and scurried back down into the galley.

'I think that'll do!' Frank called down after her.

'Oh my Lord,' Clem said, still laughing. 'She's going to be little performer. She's incredible!'

Frank, a big grin on his face, turned to the pair of them then and laid down his guitar. 'So are you two going to stay with us a little longer or what?'

Johnny and Clem looked at each other, the laughter dissipating. 'We'll see,' Johnny said. After all, decisions meant nothing right now floating in a motionless boat without a breath of wind.

Much later and in renewed spirits, Johnny turned the engine on and the *Little Utopia* spluttered into yet another deserted bay for the night. They'd barely travelled ten miles all day but Johnny had spotted vague wisps of cloud on the horizon and was sure there was wind on its way; wind that would carry them forwards. The hills were gradually getting higher; great mountains surrounded them on three sides and birds of prey swooped down the slopes looking for rabbit or rodent or whatever it was that they ate. The sun set and they drank wine in the cockpit and listened to the eerie howls of the wolves in the hills from the safety of their floating home.

By the early hours of the morning, the four of them were seated around the kitchen table, happily drunk but playing a game of Five Hundred in a concentrated silence. They'd been playing for hours, knocking back the wine. Five Hundred was a difficult game but Johnny and Clem had got the hang of it now. Clem had been dealt the mother of all trumps, the two of diamonds, three hands in a row and both she and Johnny were proving to be excellent players, giving Frank and Annie a run for their money. There was something refreshingly straightforward about cards that Johnny loved: there were clear rules, no room for negotiation, you won or you lost. He had always liked numbers, the precision of mathematics. He was partnered with Annie while Clem and Frank were together. Three of them were fiercely competitive; only Annie's modus operandi was all about trying not to mess things up for her partner. Johnny noticed that for some reason she had dressed up, she had a clean white shirt on, no bra, mascara on her eyes and some shiny stuff on her lips, as if she was going for a night on the town, which was certainly out of the question – God knew where the nearest town was.

Frank and Clem had won the last two hands and Frank was now dealing a new hand. Clem was busy sucking her thumb as the cards landed in front of her, her right hand determinedly stroking a hot spot just behind her earlobe as if her life depended on it, and yet her focus was entirely on the hand being dealt. Johnny poured the last of the bottle into their glasses.

'You look about Smudge's age when you do that,' Frank said to her. 'What are you doing with that other hand?' he asked. Johnny was wrong, he *had* been watching after all.

'Hot spots,' she said, reluctantly taking her thumb out to speak. Johnny thought he'd been unfair earlier. She hadn't been doing anything deliberately; her thumb was her comfort, it aided her concentration. Alcohol made him a much kinder gentler person: he must never forget that. He loved her fiercely then, in that moment. Everything was going to be just fine, moment to moment.

'Hot spots?' Annie asked.

'The parts of your body that are burning with heat,' Clem said.

'What parts?' Annie asked. She was being flirtatious; they all knew it. Clem locked eyes with Johnny and he smiled at her, genuinely. She slowly took out her thumb and placed her fingertips on Annie's temple.

'See? Your temple is warm. It's always warm, by the way. That's why it's a hotspot.'

'What a sensualist you are,' Frank said to her, dealing the cards slowly and deliberately. Johnny knew what was coming now. He could feel the electricity in the air. There was something alarming about it and yet intoxicating, irresistible. His body felt it first: a tingling in his groin. His brain had to play catch up. Moment to moment.

'I like it,' Annie said, placing her fingertips on Clem's temple. She always seemed to be the instigator and before Johnny knew it, there was only one thing on his mind. Clem surprised him; she was so able, so confident. She could turn it on so easily. He watched her and Annie touching each other's faces, softly, tenderly, with their fingertips. Frank had put down his cards and leant back, one arm on the couch behind Johnny, who, for want of something to do, pretended to study his cards; he wanted to delay the sexual game a little, to eke it out and prolong the excitement. He raised his glass to his lips and drank slowly, snatching a look at the girls.

'The best one...' Clem said, meeting his eye, making sure he was up for it. '... is this,' she said. He watched her undo the top two buttons of Annie's shirt and slip her hand on to the far side of Annie's breast, almost under her armpit. He was hard now.

He felt Frank's hand behind him, down the back of the cushion; he could feel his fingers brush against the base of his back and was unsure whether it was deliberate or not. He preferred not to know. His eyes were fixed on Annie's breast where Clem's fingers were, his breathing getting high and shallow; he didn't want Frank to remove his hand. Glancing down he could see that Frank was hard too. He could feel the sex in the air. He looked down at his cards open in his hand. Shit, what a time to get the two of diamonds.

'You have to shut your eyes,' Clem said to Annie.

'Oh, yes. I can feel it,' Annie said. Johnny could actually see her tits now, through the open shirt. 'Let me feel yours,' Annie said, taking the reins from Clem, leading the dance, opening her eyes, not waiting for a response, undoing the buttons of Clem's shirt. Clem looked over at Johnny again as Annie slid her hand inside and then shuffled back slightly and bent down to take Clem's brown nipple in her mouth, sucking at it gently. Johnny laid his cards flat on the table, abandoning all thoughts of the two of diamonds. He watched them sucking at each other and wanted to undo his flies and get out his cock without moving away from the touch of Frank's hand.

Johnny jumped when he heard the cry. It was brief but

high-pitched coming from the forepeak. He'd completely forgotten about Smudge, the fact that they had a child asleep next door. The cry killed the atmosphere immediately. He felt his prick softening. How could he have forgotten she was there? He sat upright, brushing himself down, glad he hadn't undone his flies. But no one else seemed to have heard her, not even Frank, who was closest to the door. Then Smudge cried out again, louder this time, and Clem heard; she pulled herself away from Annie and started quickly doing up her shirt.

'Frank! Smudge is awake,' Johnny said, nudging him on the leg and looking over at Annie, who was making no attempt to do up her shirt. Her breasts were out, her eyes on her husband. Frank cocked his head listening out for Smudge and slowly he withdrew his arm from behind Johnny and pulled himself upright. Johnny knew then that his hand had been there deliberately.

But nobody went to Smudge. Frank sighed, pulled the cork out of a new bottle and refilled their glasses. He turned to look at Johnny and said, 'Just as we were getting started.'

'Lucky we heard her,' Johnny replied, reaching for his tobacco. 'There might have been some explaining to do.'

'You don't need to worry about Smudge,' Frank said, his face losing its flush as he rolled the soft packet of cigarettes backwards and forwards in his hand. 'She's used to all this,' he said, his other hand waving across the table to including the cards, the booze, the sex, everything.

'What, just debauchery in general?' Johnny said as he sat back against the cushions, wondering whether they would be playing cards again but not wanting to appear too keen because then everybody would know that he had the two of diamonds. Smudge cried out again, a sleepy, dreamy moan as if she was going back to sleep now. Still nobody went to her.

Frank caught a cigarette in his lips. He chucked down the lighter and it slid silently across the table. 'It's a small boat,' he said scrutinizing Johnny's face.

'Yup,' Johnny said. 'Not a lot of privacy for nooky-making.'

'That's right,' he said, taking a tip-glowing suck. 'Besides, she doesn't like to be left out of all the fun.' He tapped his non-existent ash into the ashtray, smiling as he did so. 'Who does?'

Frank blew the smoke out from the corner of his mouth in a steady stream and Johnny watched it slip out through the hatch above their heads. Both Annie and Clem picked up their cards. Then slowly Frank raised his hand and put his arm around Johnny, resting his hand on the back of his neck, cupping him gently, those warm, tipless fingers against his skin, their faces close. Frank's pupils were indistinguishable from his iris, like two black holes.

'Fate brought you to me, Johnny. Like attracts like. This is no coincidence that you should come to us now, right at this moment in time.'

An uncomfortable silence filled the saloon. Johnny swallowed. His throat was dry and rough. 'What moment in time?' he asked.

Behind Frank, the forecabin door creaked open and they all turned to look. A very sleepy Smudge stood there naked beneath her Captain Hook coat, rubbing her eyes, her skew-whiff fringe standing upright, Gilla dangling from her arm. Frank let go of Johnny's neck and slowly leant forwards and picked up his daughter and sat her on his lap. She leant against her father, mumbling sleepily. Johnny stared at them, watching the caress of those tipless fingers against her skin. Not a moment before he had wanted that touch on his own flesh.

Something wasn't right. He felt a chill enter the saloon. It slipped beneath his skin and stole across his flesh making all the hairs on his body stand on end.

He looked across at Clem. She was sorting out her hand of cards, oblivious to anything else. He looked over at Annie and she was looking right back at him, her eyes flicking from Frank's hands to Johnny's face. She knew what he was thinking; he swore he saw a kind of thrill in her eye. He wanted to say something but his tongue lay heavy in his mouth while the rest of his body began to take on a weightlessness – he had the strange sensation that he was floating above the table, out of the saloon, that he was leaving, going somewhere else, the connections inside him closing down like lights going out in a building, leaving him fumbling around in the darkness. An unprecedented claustrophobia had taken hold of him; the sides of the boat were caving in on him. He felt nauseous, as if he was falling downwards from a great height. He had to get out of here. He stumbled to his feet, knocking the abandoned cards off the table, watching as the two of diamonds floated down to the floor. He turned, mumbling something about 'air' and made his way up the steps out into the pitch blackness of the night. He shut the companionway doors behind him and snatched lungfuls of the cold night. He looked out but saw nothing: 360 degrees of darkness. They were in the middle of absolutely nowhere.

He staggered blindly out of the cockpit and down the deck to the bows, hanging on to the forestay, still reeling, feeling as if he had just had the shit kicked out of him. He blinked, his eyes trying to adjust to the darkness. They were moored about two hundred yards out in the heart of a small bay surrounded on three sides by mountains. He could just make out strips of starlight over the water on the horizon and he wanted more than anything to be over there, off this boat. He sat down, back to the mast, hanging his head in his hands, trying to sort his head out as the air spun about him. Frank was a good man, an exceptional man, a man full of worthy longings, a man whose spirit soared higher than other men's, whose mind dug deeper, a man who saw through things, a truth-seeker, a philosopher, a lover of mankind; he was blessed, he had touched Johnny in a way no other human being ever had; he had opened him up and turned him on to the world, taught him to look at it, to accept instead of struggle. Johnny's gratitude had known no bounds; he would have done anything for him – he *had* done anything: he had given him his most beloved gift – Clemency Bailey. Johnny thought of him like a father, like a teacher, had even wanted him like a lover. But now the only impresion he had in his head was of Frank's fingers kneading Smudge's thigh. *My daddy should be locked up and they should throw away the key.*

He pressed the back of his head hard against the mast until his neck hurt, needing to feel some physical pain, needing to press the thoughts out of his mind; he clenched his fists into his middle, feeling a sickness sitting in his stomach like a stone.

He heard the companionway doors opening and turned to see Clem looking around for him, cupping her eyes, trying to block out the light from inside. *They* were spoilt; everything was tarnished; their love, she and he, it had all been tainted by him. She walked slowly down the deck towards him, pulling her cardigan tight around her body.

'I couldn't see you. You OK, Hoody?' she said, crouching down at his side, her hand on his thigh. He couldn't say anything; he didn't know what to say, how to express himself.

'I thought you wanted to...' she said, getting it all wrong. 'I thought it was all right.'

'We have to get off the boat,' he said, wiping his mouth.

'We will, as soon as we find somewhere.'

'I really need us to get off the boat,' he said and she heard

174

his desperation. He wanted to get in the dinghy and row right now. He didn't care where. He'd rather stumble around on the land than be here.

'I know,' she said. But she didn't. She didn't know anything. She was ignorant and innocent and he wanted her to stay that way. There she was with her hand on his thigh, touching, together, but he felt miles away from her. He had to try and close the gap, to explain himself, but words fell short.

'I think something's going on' he whispered. She turned her head and looked him the eye.

She was, shaking her head, wanting to understand. 'What do you mean?'

What *did* he mean? He could feel her eyes burning into him, waiting for him to explain himself. He had to calm down. He looked up at the stars softly twinkling over there on the edge of the world and he wiped his mouth carefully. He'd try a different tack. 'What did you think of Smudge's dance today?' he asked.

She looked at him, puzzled by the change of subject. 'What do you mean, *what did I think of it?*'

'What did you think?'

'It was funny.'

'Yes. That's what I thought,' he said, looking back out into the darkness. 'But I don't think we should have been laughing.'

'Why not?'

He turned to her. 'I don't trust Frank.'

She stared at him for a moment and then she blew out her disdain in a sigh. 'Oh, for God's sake, Johnny. I'm getting so sick of this.'

'There's something about him, Clem… I don't want you alone with him.'

'What!' she said, turning on him, annoyed. 'Why are you doing this? Why are you so jealous? It's just so boring.'

It was horrible to see her look at him that way; there was no love there at all. She wrapped the cardigan tight around herself again. 'I thought you were bigger than that,' she said and he heard the disappointment in her voice. 'I didn't think you'd be so... so...' She couldn't find the right word, but whatever word she looking for had a bad taste, he could see that. '... small-minded.'

She got up without even looking at him, shooing him away with her hands and he watched her go back down the deck. *Small-minded*. He really hoped that she was right, that the only problem was his small-mindedness. He peered through the saloon hatch and caught glimpses of Annie and Frank moving about inside, putting away the table, Clem joining them, picking up the fallen cards, and carrying on just the same as they always had. He stayed up there, watching the sky for hours, waiting and thinking, listening to the wolves over on the mountains howling into the darkness. He kept his eyes on the horizon waiting for their only salvation: wind. He listened to the waves. Every now and then an impotent anger churned about inside him, rose up and then subsided in a fog of confusion. At one stage he saw the port lights of a boat crossing the horizon and he wondered who was in it, what they were doing, what they were thinking. He envied them their everyday worries. The night seemed eternal, as if the sun was refusing to shine on the *Little Utopia*. But at some hour the wolves stopped their howling and the fingers of dawn crept slowly across the sky giving colour to the world, to the deserted, scrubby, mountainous backdrop behind, yet he could see no beauty in it. But with the light it seemed that all the demons of the night scurried away back into the darkness and he wondered whether the sea madness had started to get to him.

7

HAPPY BIRTHDAY

JOHNNY HAD NOT thought he would sleep but evidently he had. Someone had put a sleeping bag over him, a tender gesture he appreciated, whoever it was. He had a moment's calm before the shameful thoughts slunk into his mind, like sewage into the open sea. The certainties of last night had lost their edge, were now just fuzzy, indistinguishable shapes. In the glaring light of day they seemed absurd. He sat up and looked over the flat, windless water at the white-gold morning sun, pulling the bag around his shoulders.

All he and Clem had to do was get off the boat and everything would be fine. They would come across a village or a town, maybe even today, and there they could say farewell and disembark. That sense of urgent panic, of need for escape that he had felt last night, had abated. It seemed ridiculous now to think of himself rowing the dinghy out into the darkness, stumbling about in the wilderness. He was going stir crazy. Clem was right. This jealousy was new and he didn't like it. He had never felt inadequate before. He closed his eyes and felt the warmth of the sun caress his eyelids.

This was the first morning he could remember not waking up with Clem in his arms and he missed her. He felt alone. The hatch door beside him fell open with a bang. Smudge stuck her head up through it and was smiling from ear to ear. She was wearing her Captain Hook coat but was also wearing a paper crown on her head. 'It's my birthday!'

'Hey!' he said, pretending that he hadn't totally forgotten.

'Don't wake him!' Frank's voice called from inside the forecabin.

'It's all right,' Johnny called back. 'I'm awake!'

Nothing had changed. Everything was the same. Johnny and his jealousy just needed to get off the boat now; that was all. When he looked at Smudge's radiant smiling face he saw an untroubled soul. He wanted to hug her, to apologise. 'Happy birthday!' he said and she climbed out of the hatch and jumped at him, knocking him backwards, her wild black hair sharp against the blueness of the sky behind, her eyes as dark and impenetrable as her father's.

'Coffee, Johnny?' Frank yelled through the hatch.

'Please.'

'Mummy said I wasn't allowed to ask for my present.' She paused, staring at him hard, pinning his arms down. 'So I'm not.'

'You might have to ask Clem about that...' He would apologize to Clem.

'Why are you sleeping up here?' Smudge asked him, turning herself around, wriggling into a comfortable position, using his knees as arm rests.

He ran a hand through his hair. 'I'm looking out for wind,' he said as cheerfully as he could because there wasn't any at all, the sea was like a mirror. She looked out for wind as well and then after a while she turned round again.

'Shall we talk about *five*?' she said.

'Yes please,' he said. 'Tell me all about five.' He wondered whether Clem was up. He wanted to see her, to make amends, for things to go back to how they had been.

'Well, there's one and four. Then there's two and three. Then there's five and zero…' She went through it again in her head. He watched her soft, little, chubby fingers as she counted off the possibilities, the frown of concentration on her brow. She was adorable. He would miss her when they left.

'That's all I can think of,' she said.

'And six minus one,' he said.

'Oh yes, and seven minus two.'

'And two and a half add two and a half.'

Her eyes lit up. 'Who would have thought five was such a busy number? How old are you?' she asked, twisting her neck, looking up to his face.

'I'm twenty-one,' he said.

'How many fives is that?'

'Four and one left over.'

'I'm five,' she said as if that were an answer in itself. He nodded and kissed the top of her head and was glad she couldn't see his eyes and the ugliness that lay behind them.

'Coffee's up!' Frank was standing in the companionway, placing mugs on the coachroof, a cigarette dangling from his lips, his dark, curly mop of hair standing on end, the sweet, bitter aroma of the coffee filling the air.

'Today is going to be the best day ever. We're going to play musical statues,' Smudge said, pulling Johnny up and along the deck. 'We're going to have a picnic on the beach and Mummy's going to make me a cake.' She was grinning from ear to ear. 'We're going to eat roasting chicken and play hide and seek.'

Clem was in the cockpit. She had Smudge's presents in her hand. She had put the necklace into one of her collecting boxes and wrapped towels around the monster-killing stick. She looked up at him cautiously, gauging his mood. Johnny bent down and kissed her and she smiled and touched his hand. He was forgiven.

'This is from me,' she said, handing over the box to Smudge. 'And this one is from Johnny.'

Smudge was so excited she was bouncing with suspense, her little body rigid, her hands clutched to her chest. Johnny couldn't remember ever feeling such excitement over birthdays; his own family had never really gone in for them.

Annie came up from the galley while Clem was tying the necklace around Smudge's neck and Johnny noticed that she didn't meet his eye when he greeted her. She was smiling, carrying more presents, but when he spoke she didn't look at him and busied herself going up and down the steps. Even when Smudge opened her monster-killing stick, Annie admired it, said all the right things, but didn't once actually acknowledge him.

It carried on that way. When they played musical statues to some shitty Abba song, Annie didn't once look at him. No one else would have noticed; it was an accomplished ignoring. Briefly, as they hovered in frozen dance inches away from one another he caught her eye but she had looked away at once. She kept herself busy in the kitchen – taking the chicken out of the coolbox, wrapping potatoes in tinfoil, pouring out ingredients for her cake. It was subtle and it was working; he felt told off and troubled. He kept looking out at the horizon for signs of wind. But there was no chance of that today as he watched the bags full of food and crockery being passed out into the cockpit. Frank was in the tender loading the bags neatly. There was no going back: they were going to have a party on the beach.

Annie asked for Frank to come back for her in twenty minutes as she hadn't finished the cake and there wouldn't be room for everyone in the tender anyway. Frank sat down in the boat, balancing out the weight of the bags. He put the oars in the rowlocks and for a moment Johnny thought he was going to row off and how easy it might be to pull up the anchor and start the engine and maroon him on this deserted piece of shore with a tender full of food.

'Johnny, you row us,' Frank said. 'Pass me the birthday girl, please.' He stood up and held out one arm to take her.

Johnny lifted Smudge up. She had Granny in one hand, the spear in the other and a lollipop in her mouth; he passed her over the side of the *Little Utopia*, to Frank. Johnny found himself being particularly jovial as if to make up for the grimness of his thoughts.

So with the tender very low in the water, its holes bunged up with old corks from red wine bottles, Johnny got in and rowed the four of them ashore while Annie remained on board to make the cake. Frank was pointing things out to Smudge, explaining how the birds hunted their prey, how the shapes on the water's surface gave away where the fish underneath were, what the rock formations told us, his musings on primitive life forms and Johnny thought how lucky Smudge was being brought up like this, in this alternative childhood. He looked over at Clem and she smiled at him and he felt renewed, full of new hope for them. He wanted her all to himself. They really had to leave the boat now. It had been long enough.He looked over to the south, at the huge, majestic mountains shrouded by the deep blue sky, their reflections dancing on the glassy surface of the water, disturbed only by the ripples from the oars. It was like they were stuck inside a snow globe – a sunny globule of undisturbed time.

He rowed to the shore and they got out of the tender and pulled it up on to the sand. He took Smudge's hand and the pair of them and Granny went off looking for driftwood while Frank and Clem started building the fire.

"Shall I go and get Annie?' Johnny said after he'd dumped a pile of sticks and logs on the sand.

'Sure,' Frank said. 'Thanks.'

Johnny pushed the little dinghy back into the water, climbed in and began to row back to the *Little Utopia*. He looked up at the windless sky, the only breeze coming from his own movements through the water. Why did he still feel so trapped? He thought of the *Old Rangoon* and throwing all those things into the sea – how free and unhampered he had felt then. He yearned for such escapism again. He let his mind ride with fantasies: he and Clem could go for a row in the tender and just not come back to the boat, take their chances on land. Or they could row back to the old woman's cottage, although there wouldn't be much point in that: there was nothing there, no transport, no village, just the donkey. He should take another browse through the crappy old chart and try to find out exactly where they were. But he was only daydreaming, he knew that. He looked back at the mountains, at Frank and Clem making the fire, at Smudge in the shallows – they'd arrive somewhere soon enough. He would just have to be patient.

Clem sat on the sand watching Frank attaching the scrawny chicken corpse to the spit he'd made, his dextrous fingers manipulating the pale flesh as he dug the stick deep inside its body. Smudge was splashing about in the shallows with her fishing net and her monster-killing stick, naked save for her Captain Hook jacket. Clem looked away over at Johnny rowing the dinghy back to the *Little Utopia*. He had that frown etched on to his brow. She watched him pulling back the oars, drifting further and further away from her. She could feel the void however much they pretended it wasn't there. She was glad he had slept up on the deck last night, glad that he hadn't come down wanting sex with her. This was new, this distancing of herself. She was changing; she could feel it. Up until now she had always thought of Johnny as invincible; she was the flawed one and he was perfect. But it wasn't so. She could see the chinks in his armour and, though she knew it was shallow, it made him less attractive to her. She found his jealousy quite repellent; it magnified his immaturity. How silly she had once been to wish for it, to feel as if it were proof of love, when all it did was make him seem weak and less of a man. He should be learning from Frank, not jealous of him – Frank would never stoop to such neediness. Her father had once said that about her mother. *She's so needy.* She hadn't understood it at the time; she'd thought he was being callous and cruel, justifying leaving them. She had already learnt to dislike him by then; her mother had taught her that, with her drip-feeding of resentments. But her mother *was* needy, it was true, needy and preoccupied by the little things. She remembered her mother's outrage on discovering that Liz was eight years older than her and had *varicose veins* and *no style.* As if it was all about looks. But she was beginning to understand that attraction was a much more complicated thing.

'Penny for your thoughts?' Frank said. She took her eyes off the horizon and glanced at him, at his broad dented shoulder, his huge gentle hands picking out the dud matches from the box, putting them neatly on the stack of wood beneath the spit. She watched as he pulled out a live match and struck it firmly against the side of the box. The sunlight was so bright, the wind so absent, the flame so upright, it was almost invisible. He bent down and lit the rolled-up newspaper at the bottom of the pile. He blew out the match and flicked it on the pile, then sat back to watch the fire burn.

'I was thinking about my dad,' she said. Even she sounded surprised. Prior to this trip she rarely thought of him, let alone talked about him, not even with Johnny. He was not a feature in her life any more.

'You're not close, are you?'

'God, no. I've hardly seen him in years.'

Frank looked up at her. 'That's a shame.'

She shrugged. 'Not really.' But it was. She knew it was. She didn't like to think about all the *shames* that had stacked up over the years.

'For him, I mean.'

She smiled. She couldn't help herself; she needed that support. She watched the way he prodded the fire gently, the way the sticks caught light and spat hot sparks on to his skin, how he didn't flinch, how he just flicked them off at his own leisure. 'No, really,' he said, turning his head to make sure he had her attention. 'It's a pity that he doesn't know the wonderful young woman that you've become.'

'I don't know about that,' she said, embarrassed but loving it.

'Well, I do,' he said. 'You're intelligent, curious, open-minded, kind, positive, loving, good-natured. All the things a father could hope for. Oh, and you're not bad-looking either.'

His words made her dizzy; she wanted them written down so she could remember them for ever, so she could take them out and look at them whenever she chose. She could show them to him, Jim, her father. Proof.

She sieved the sand through her fingers and examined the grains, the broken colourful shells, crushed over millennia, but she soon found herself looking back up at the horizon where all the unremembered things seemed to lurk. 'When I was Smudge's age I thought he was the most amazing person in the world,' she said, laughing and then not.

'Disillusionment with one's parents is utterly normal.'

'I can't imagine Smudge ever being disillusioned with you.'

He looked over at his daughter, who was standing, poised, stock-still in the shallows with her spear raised, looking like a savage. 'She will be. I must accept that.'

'They let me think everything was fine. People should shout and argue before they split up. It's only fair.'

He was leaning back with his ankles crossed. 'Maybe everything *had* been fine,' he said.

This thought had never occurred to her. The memory of those first eight years had always been tainted by his betrayal; his final action had negated all the previous little happinesses. Even now, whenever she or her mother recalled things from those days their sentences always seemed to trail out into an emptiness.

'Sometimes people have to leave the people they love,' he said. 'It's just the way it is. You can't change what happened, Clem, whatever he did or didn't do. But you can change how you feel about it. You really can.' He was smiling at her. 'It's his loss. He'll know that. You should pity him – in the true sense of the word, you should have *compassion* for him.'

She felt as if she was going to cry. It was as if she was being given permission to love her father, a feeling she had not indulged for years. Everyone around her seemed to despise Jim; how nice it felt to allow the love back in. It took her by surprise, this tightening of her throat, this sudden stinging in her eyes. She was glad that Frank looked away, sensing her fragility. Briefly he reached out his hand to brush her knee. Then he got up to tidy up the camp and he busied himself with the Thermos, pouring the coffee into cups. It wasn't a bad feeling, the tearfulness; it was quite a relief. Besides, it passed as quickly as it came.

She looked over at the dinghy. Johnny was rowing Annie back now, only they seemed to have stopped; the oars were high in the air. She wished Johnny could be himself again. She liked sitting here with Frank. She liked everything just how it was. He passed her a coffee and sat back down next to her, both of them watching the others.

'Are things all right with Johnny?' he asked.

There was no point in lying. She didn't think she could ever lie to him. 'He's jealous of you.'

He paused for a moment, the coffee cup at his lips. Then he put it down and rearranged some of the sticks before taking his cigarettes out of his pocket. He tapped one out and turned to her, his expression thoughtful, puzzled. 'Why should he be jealous of me?'

She held his gaze for just a second and then she had to look back at the fire in case her eyes gave something away. She pulled her knees up to her chin and watched the flames as they whipped about noisily in the newly charged atmosphere. 'I suppose he thinks I might have feelings for you,' she said and although her eyes were now firmly fixed on the fire, her heart felt as if it were dangerously suspended, hanging in the air, exposed and raw, ready to be scorched just like the chicken over the flame.

'Well, he shouldn't be jealous of me. He's the one that's going to have your babies.'

She hugged her knees a little tighter and both the fire and her heart crackled loudly. Frank lit his cigarette and then he smiled at her in that calm, private way he had.

'It's nothing to be ashamed of, Clem – having feelings for

me,' he said in his rumbling, effortless voice. 'That's a beautiful thing.'

Then he stood up and went off to get more wood.

'Annie?' Johnny called as he approached the *Little Utopia* in the shabby old rowing boat. He rested one oar in its rowlock and balanced the other inside the tender, one hand reaching out to grab the toe rail of the bigger boat. 'You ready?'

She came out with a pan in her hand and passed it underneath the guard rail. He glanced at her briefly, not expecting eye contact now, and took the cake from her hands. She looked dishevelled. She reeked of alcohol, that sweet, sickly smell of whisky. He hadn't even known that they had whisky on board. He put the cake down on the floor between two bungs. It looked more like a paste than a cake, but then she'd had to make do without an oven. She'd stuck five candles in and dusted it with icing. She stepped over the guard rail and climbed down into the tender with another bag over her shoulder and sat down opposite him. She picked up the cake and held it in her lap as he pushed them away from the *Little Utopia* with one oar. They drifted out into the water.

For a while they couldn't see the others on the shore as they rounded the bigger boat. He was watching her, waiting for her to acknowledge him, but her eyes were downcast. She looked old and tired; even the holes in her ears where her hooped earrings hung were dashes rather than dots. Life had taken its toll. He wondered what he had ever seen in her: she had big dark freckles on her hands like an old person, her dress was covered in chocolate, her hair was all matted, she had downward lines around her mouth and broken dark veins on her thighs; she was drinking whisky in the morning, for God's sake.

They were still floating around the bigger boat, the oars out of the water, resting in their rowlocks, dripping on to the faintly rippled surface. She was staring at the cake and when she at last did meet his eye, hers were weighty with misery.

'I told you I was a bad person...' she whispered.

He stared at her, his hands tightening around the wood as he placed the oars flat beneath the water.

'Now you *know*,' she said, taking urgent little glances shorewards where the others were still obscured by the hull of the *Little Utopia*.

'Now I know what?' he said, clearing his throat.

'I saw you. You *know*...'

He stared at her, the oars hovering above the water.

'You want me to spell it out?' she said, her voice weak and shaky. His mouth went dry. He watched as several fat tears spilt from her eyes on to the dusted whiteness of the cake.

'Spell what out?'

It was her silence that spoke to him, slowly shining its light into his darkest places. He felt sick.

'Please don't hate me,' she whispered. He watched as she rummaged about in her bag and brought out a small bottle of Johnnie Walker. She unscrewed the top and drank thirstily.

'Say something!' she said.

But he couldn't.

'Johnny, say something!'

He shook his head. 'I don't know what you're talking about.'

'I used to be just like you,' she whispered as if they might be able to hear her from the beach. 'I was just like you. I thought it was awful when he first suggested it...'

'Shut the fuck up!' he said with a fierceness that stopped her.

She nodded eagerly, as if she liked his ferocity, as if she wanted more, for him to shout abuse at her, to punish her. 'But he taught me how to see things differently…'

'What the fuck are you talking about?' He was trying to shut her up; he didn't want to know any of this. He would rather be anywhere else in the world right now than here, listening to her. He dipped the oars in the water and took a long, deep stroke, as if he could get away from her. '

'We never hurt her. We would never ever hurt her!'

'For God's sake shut up!'

'She likes it. She enjoys making love.'

And then quite suddenly he stopped rowing and leant over the boat and vomited into the water, the oars dropping with a crash against the sides as he heaved into the blue. He drooled and spat and wiped his mouth then turned to her. Her eyes were as blue and piercing as the sky behind. He shook his head with horror.

'You're not fit to be a mother. You're not fit,' he said, his voice breaking with a kind of sob. 'You don't fucking deserve her.'

'No,' she said and she hung her head.

Johnny gripped the sides of the boat, his eyes scanning the horizon looking for a way out of this nightmare, but there was nothing but glassy stillness everywhere. 'Why, Annie? Why?'

'When I saw your face it took me back. I remembered,' Annie whispered, looking up at him from underneath her skew-whiff fringe, her face contorted into a pathetic plea. 'Will you save her, Johnny? Will you take her with you?'

He stared at her with disbelief. 'Are you serious?' he said. He turned away, cupping his hands in the water, washing his mouth out, splashing water on to his face. 'No, Annie. This is not my problem. Clem and I are getting out of here.'

Annie nodded then opened the bottle again and took another mouthful; then she scrabbled around in her bag for her cigarettes; a tangle of addictions. She struck the lighter a few times in a panic before it worked. She inhaled deeply, like a junkie.

Johnny wiped his face on his shirt and looked towards the shore. The others had slipped into view again, the dash of red of Captain's Hook's coat, the turquoise of Clem's shirt, Frank's larger, darker frame.

'Just leave him!' he said, because he wanted to help her. But he couldn't.

She let out a sort of laugh. 'Oh, Johnny,' she said as if he had no idea at all. 'You think he'd let me leave him? Let me take his daughter?' She sounded hollow and empty, all scooped out. She rested her head on her knees, facing out to sea, letting her hand trail in the water, lost in some unlovely reverie.

When she spoke it was as if he wasn't even there. She seemed calm and remote. 'I met him in a pub in Islington. He came in with six others, all in plain clothes, shouting and knocking things over, looking for someone. They were on a raid. Everyone was running about getting out of there but I just stood there and I stared at this man. It was as if I already knew him. And he stopped what he was doing and he looked right at me and I thought to myself, *You're the man I've been waiting for.*' She laughed and turned her face to Johnny. She had transformed like she always did when she laughed and he saw her then as a young woman in that pub in Islington.

'I can't leave him, Johnny. He is my destiny. I could never leave Francis Goodman. I love him.'

'Despite what he does? What he makes you do?'

But she wasn't listening. 'He wasn't just any old copper. He was brilliant. And he chose *me*, Johnny. Francis Goodman chose me. He could get confessions out of anyone, anyone at all. They put him on all the big, famous cases. All the IRA hard nuts, he'd have them crying like babies, crapping themselves in their cells.' She sat up and inhaled deeply, just like Frank, sucking the life out of the cigarette. 'They used to call him the Samaritan – because he killed you with kindness.'

She paused, those heavy, sad eyes back to looking inwards now. She tipped her ash into the water and Johnny watched it float downwards like a column collapsing in a quake. She drank more whisky and then offered him the bottle. He took it, resting the oars in the rowlocks, watching them rise up like wings high into the sky. He rubbed his forehead with the fleshy part of his palms, massaging his own head, trying to iron everything out. He looked over at Frank on the beach. He'd lit a fire; the smoke was going straight upwards, hovering above their heads, being blown nowhere for there was no wind. Over in the dead calm by the rocks, a fish jumped.

'There was a ring of them, you see,' she said, her words lingering in the air like the smoke. 'At the Met. They were all the same. Photographing themselves, making films with children, watching each other, one-upping each other. But they were careless. Someone found out, someone with a score to settle. Two of them were killed outright by these vigilantes, thrown from the tops of buildings. But Frank, the ringleader, they saved. They kept him for three days in a room. They used electric probes; they cut him up; they stuck things into him; they beat him with lead pipes, smashed in his skull, his back, his legs. They left him for dead.'

Johnny couldn't row any more; the strength had seeped out of him. He knew then that the sickness sitting inside him would not ever leave. It was too heavy to pass through. He looked over at the shore where Smudge was up to her waist in the water, spear poised above her head. He could see Frank moving, wandering around on the shore, bending to pick up wood. The limp that wasn't so obvious on a boat where there was nowhere to move was now quite evident. He was crooked to the core. He wished those men had finished him off.

'I was pregnant with Smudge at the time. I kept praying for a boy, I knew what his preferences were...'

Something about what she was saying didn't make sense. He tried to work things out in his head. Clem had told him that Frank was in hospital for six months. If she was pregnant then, how could she have given birth on the *Little Utopia* six months later? It didn't add up. 'How could you do it, Annie? How could you stay with a man like that?'

'Someone like you would never understand. You with your easy confidence. I bet life just rolls out for you. My life was nothing when I met him, I was nothing. I had more trust in him than I did in myself. He gave me everything. He taught me to believe in myself, Johnny. He taught me how to think. He showed me how to love, how to express my love. You have to understand I'm nothing at all without that man. Just nothing.'

She started to cry then. Those big fat tears fell down her cheeks. He was going to deny it, say it wasn't so, but he wasn't so sure. He thought of Clem. He was nothing at all without her. You couldn't wander around for the rest of your life being just a remnant of a person. 'What did the Met do?' he asked. 'Turn a blind eye, get you out of the country and give him a nice pension?'

She shrugged and looked up at the sky, her head hanging backwards. He could see the pale creases on her neck where the sun hadn't reached. Her voice was small and faraway. 'I *know* it's wrong, Johnny, what we do. I *know* I am a shameful, worthless human being. But he's different. He's proud of what he is. He's always been that way; which makes me so much worse than him.'

Despite the terrible things that she had done, he felt pity for her then. He wanted to reach out and touch her, to try and give her some comfort. But he didn't.

All he had to do was get through the next twenty-four hours and tomorrow they could get away from all this.

'Annie,' he said and slowly she lifted her eyes to meet his. 'I don't want Clem to know any of this. Do you understand? I don't want this… sick stuff… anywhere near her.'

Annie nodded and took a drag of her cigarette, blowing the smoke out in a weak, steady stream towards her bare feet. She looked as if she understood. As if she knew that Clemmie's innate sense of goodness and trust in the world must not be sullied by them.

'I don't want you *ever* to touch her again,' he said. 'Do you get it?'

She nodded again and when she looked up he saw the fear back in her eyes. 'But don't you see what he's doing, Johnny?' she said and Johnny felt the dread rise up in him. 'He's preparing you. He wants to share Smudge with you.'

He stared at her. Then his focus slipped behind her, to the flat, glassy water, almost indistinguishable from the cloudless sky. He looked over at Clem by the fire, at the upright smoke. There was not a breath of wind anywhere, from the curve on the edge of the world to the heights of the deserted, barren mountains. He wanted to lose himself in the stillness.

He picked up the oars and rowed the last twenty yards in silence. They both got out of the dinghy, Annie juggling the cake and the bag while Johnny pulled the tender up on to the beach. Annie went to join Frank and Clem on the blanket. They were drinking coffee from the Thermos and reading their books. Johnny walked towards them slowly; he had no appetite. He was watching Frank, pinning the new information he had about him on to the man he didn't know at all. He felt as if he were locked outside of himself, as if he were observing himself from somewhere else while his husk of a body went through the motions, made pleasantries, sat down on the blanket, carefully placing himself between Frank and Clem; he stretched his legs out, took the coffee that Clem passed him, smiled at her, admired the fire and the spit and swallowed the tasteless hot liquid. He did not behave at all how he might have imagined he would; there was no anger, no rage, no fighting because he felt derelict inside. He heard himself laugh a little when Frank made a joke; he could feel an idiotic grin stuck on his face. When he needed to remind himself that he wasn't a shell, that he was flesh and blood, he got up and went down to the water's edge and put his feet into the coolness. He wondered fleetingly what time of year it was, he'd temporarily forgotten; the air was warm but the sea was cold. It was still March, or was it April, he had no idea any more. He wondered how long they'd been on the boat – it seemed like a long time. He felt like a different person altogether from the old Johnny. The water felt good, bracing against his skin. He wanted to be swallowed up by it. He found himself going in, up to his knees, his groin, his waist, his chest, and he kept on going. Clem would be amazed if she was watching – which had begun to seem unlikely; she hadn't been watching him very much that day. He walked until he was out of his depth and then he dropped down under, at last finding some refuge beneath the surface, immersed in the coldness. He kicked his legs and let his body float up, head down. He opened his eyes and blinked into the green at the rocks beneath and once again he thought of all those things they'd chucked into the sea lying peacefully at the bottom somewhere never to be found and the thought of such undiscovered stillness gave him comfort. It was good to see the world from another perspective, to block out their voices, their existence. He rolled over, breathed out and looked up into the sky where, high above, a flock of tiny birds flew by, black against the blue, free to go wherever they chose.

His solitude did not last. He could hear cries and hollers – Smudge had spotted the opportunity for some fun and was swimming her way towards him. He shook the water from his hair, his ears. 'Johnneeee,' she cried. 'Wait for meeeee!'

She looked so small and vulnerable, splashing her messy jumping doggy paddle his way. He swam towards her and held out his arms for her. She was way out of her depth, so trusting, so reliant on the goodness of others, so easy to betray. He could see Frank watching them from the shore and wondered whether this was all part of some perverted plan, whether this was what lay ahead for her, to be passed from hands to hands. Of course Johnny could save Smudge if he really wanted to: get Clem and Annie in the dinghy, leave Frank under some pretence, get in the boat and abandon him. But Smudge was not his problem. She was Annie's. His priority was Clem.

Smudge clambered into his arms laughing, slippery, wriggly and naked. He wondered why someone this happy needed saving at all. 'I found a monster, Johnny!' she said.

So did I.

'Did you kill it with your spear?' he asked.

'No. I let it go.' Her eyelashes had matted together like a doll's eyes; she looked so perfect and fragile. 'Be the monster, Johnny. Be it!'

He dived under the water, staying still for a moment before grabbing her and lifting her high into the air, throwing her up with a monster growl. She screamed with a delighted terror. He could do this. He could pretend for just one day.

Johnny lay on his towel on the other side of Clem, who was reading her book – something Frank had given her by Krishna someone. The emptiness had subsided now; he was beginning to inhabit himself again. He rolled himself a smoke and watched Smudge lying dreamily in the shallows of the water, humming to herself. He was looking at Frank from the corner of his eye – he was turning the chicken on the spit – those tipless fingers, those dents on his back constant reminders of his crimes. Annie, trying hard to hide her drunkenness, was overdoing the sobriety. She had sat herself down inelegantly on the rug and was pouring coffee into cups, like a sloshed Mary Poppins, singing snatches of lift-music. She passed Frank more coffee. She was trying to please him. It was pathetic to witness. Christ, they *had* to get out of here.

His gaze returned to the horizon, to escape. There were faint wisps of cloud smeared along the edge. Smudge came running up out of the water and jumped on to her father, pressing her wet body up against his back. For different reasons both Frank and Johnny flinched. Frank put one hand behind his back instinctively to support her. 'Yuck! You're cold and wet!' he cried. 'Get off!' Johnny looked away.

'Is that the chicken that made the egg for my cake?' Smudge asked, sliding down the side of him, looking at the chicken upside down.

'Yes,' he said.

'The chicken that the old lady killed?'

'That's right.'

'The chicken in the bucket?'

'The very one.'

'But I want it alive again.'

'Well, it's too late. It's dead now and we're going to eat it in about an hour,' he said.

She slid right off him and on to the ground and turned on to her tummy in the sand, chin in her hands as she looked at the roasting chicken. 'So we just took everything away from it, its baby eggs and its feathers, we breaked its neck and we drowned it, and then we're going to eat it?' she asked, matter-of-factly, wanting to get the sequence of events straight in her head. There was no judgement in her tone: her father had taught her that all right.

'It's a nasty old world,' Johnny said, flicking the wet sand off his legs. He couldn't help himself; the water had unfrozen him.

Annie looked round at him, nervously. Clem yawned and stretched and put her book down. 'I think I fancy a swim,' she said and he watched her getting up, her lovely, strong golden body. He didn't want her to take her clothes off for Frank's dirty eyes to feast on her. But he could only blame himself for he had handed her to Frank on a plate. Now he suspected that whole escapade had been deliberate, that seduction of him by Annie on the hillside: it had been intended to feed his guilt so that he would want to make amends. He'd been taken for ride after ride. He'd been a total fool.

'Coming, Smudge?' Clem said, holding out her hand. 'Shall we jump off the rocks?'

Johnny watched the pair of them skip down the beach. Clem was doing cartwheels in a perfect straight line and Smudge was trying to copy her, both of them carefree and oblivious. He wanted it to stay that way. He noticed that Annie was uncomfortable now that it was just the three of them; he could see her hands trembling, but that might well have been the alcohol.

'You seem pretty detached today, Johnny,' Frank said after a silence, leaning back, his posture the exact echo of Johnny's, their ankles crossed, eyes out at sea. Detachment seemed a pretty straightforward choice right now, the best way to cope while partaking in this ugly little charade. He said nothing.

'Not that it's a bad way to be,' Frank added. 'Quite the opposite. Without it we're prisoners of helplessness and hopelessness, victims of mundane needs—'

'Will you just shut up for once, Frank,' Johnny said and it sounded so good to his own ears. He wasn't angry; it was just that he could no longer pretend. He was tired of all the bullshit. Frank turned around, taken by surprise, and Johnny shifted forward, picking at an old bite on his shin. He felt freed by Clem's absence. He didn't have to play this game any more.

'You can stop it all now,' Johnny said, turning to him, looking him right in the eye. 'I *know*.'

'You know *what*?' Frank asked, defenceless, intrigued.

'I know what you are,' Johnny said, lighting up a cigarette, his hand trembling a little, one eye on where the girls were. He saw Annie reach out for the black bag with the bottle in it.

'And what am I?' Frank asked. There was a faint smile on his lips.

Johnny blew the smoke out slowly. 'I don't care what you do. I don't care how you justify it, because I know you will. But I want nothing to do with it. Nothing.'

Frank took a breath as if he was going to say something but thought better of it. He took his focus out to the sea and uncrossed then recrossed his legs.

'By the way, you keep your filthy hands off my wife,' Johnny added. 'That's all over now.'

Frank held his hands up in a mock-hostage way. 'Whatever you say, Johnny.' Then he leant back against his palms, nodding to himself, working things out. Annie was cowering. She had the bag clutched in her lap; her hand had snuck inside.

'Annie, darling,' Frank said, not unkindly. Annie cowered further, hiding behind her hair and Johnny saw the immensity of her fear, just a flash of it as she glanced at her husband. 'What have you been saying to Johnny?'

'Nothing,' she said. Too quickly.

'Don't blame her,' Johnny said.

'Nothing at all, love?' Frank said, ignoring Johnny.

'The truth,' Annie whispered. Johnny saw her summon all her bravery. 'He knows the truth,' she whispered in a mouse-like voice.

'Oh, Annie,' Frank said, hanging his head and rubbing his eyebrows with a sigh as if this was all a great joke. 'What has she been telling you?' The way he looked up at Johnny was so resigned, so amused, as though this had all happened many times before, that temporarily Johnny was confused. 'What? That I was some kind of super interrogator? That I was the leader of some high-powered paedophile ring?'

Johnny took a drag of his fag. He could see Clem and Smudge holding hands jumping into the water from the rocks. 'That's right, Mr Samaritan.'

There was the briefest pause. 'Mr Samaritan?' He laughed. 'I haven't heard that one before. That's what they called me, yes? Was it the IRA?' He turned to Annie. 'Not the Foreign Legion, love? Not the SAS? Not SO19? There are so many versions, I forget where we are.'

'Please don't,' she whispered, unscrewing the lid of the whisky.

'I should have seen this coming,' he said to Johnny. 'I apologize. She does this every now and then. I should have noticed. It's all part of her... condition,' he said, waving his hand as if Johnny knew what he was talking about.

'Darling,' he said gently, turning to his wife. 'You should have told me. Have you stopped taking the yellow pills?'

She nodded. She was staring at Frank, her eyes full of some fresh torment. 'Please don't,' she whispered and they glared at each other, locked in some ancient battle. 'You mustn't, Frank.'

'I have to tell him, Annie,' he said gently and he turned his back on his wreck of a wife. She drank from the bottle.

'Did she tell you about herself, Johnny? No? How she's spent more of her life inside institutions than outside of them? How she's been sectioned more times than you could possibly imagine? How we had to leave in a hurry before they locked her up again? How living on this boat is the only way we can stay together? Do you know how many labels she's been given in her life? Psychotic, delusional, schizophrenic, pathological liar, criminally insane, a mythomaniac... the list goes on.' He spoke the words as carelessly as if they were ingredients for a recipe.

Annie started to sob. 'Is this true, Annie?' Johnny asked, utterly bewildered by the pair of them. She threw him a glance of inconsolable wretchedness. Then her head sagged, her hair strung across her face and her shoulders began to heave.

'Her mother left when she was little. Her father was a doctor.' Frank leant in towards Johnny and continued confidentially. 'Both she and her sister had sexual relations with him for many years. She gets it all muddled. Don't you, love?' he said, placing a hand on her back. She was curled up into a ball with her head between her knees, racked with silent sobs.

'Annie? Look at me!' Johnny cried. 'Is this true?' .

'She was whimpering. 'Yes...' Frank looked like a beaten man. He sighed gently. 'I don't suppose she told you any of that. I'm sorry, Johnny, it's my fault. I should have noticed. I need to get her back on the right medication. Please don't be hard on her.'

200

Johnny stared at them both, unable to fathom what the hell was going on. He sucked on his cigarette and looked out at the horizon. *Wind, please come. Get us away from these dreadful people.*

When Clem returned from the rocks, Smudge having run on ahead, she was surprised to find Annie curled up on the blanket crying, with Johnny and Frank sitting near by not taking any notice of her tears. Smudge had tucked her little body tightly into her mother's and was faintly humming a tune. Clem turned to Johnny for some sort of explanation but he didn't meet her eye, he was looking out to sea as always obsessing about the wind. She looked at Frank who was seated on the blanket beside his wife, reading his book, one hand resting comfortingly on her hip. He caught her eye.

'She's just tired and emotional,' he said and Clem looked back at Johnny who shrugged his shoulders dismissively as if he didn't care what the hell was wrong with her and went back to looking out at the horizon.

Clem crouched down beside Annie. 'Are you all right?' she asked, stroking Annie's arm, trying to smooth away the pain. 'Shall we go down to the water, Annie?'

Annie didn't respond. And when she did, she turned slowly to look up at Clem as if she had no idea at all who she was, so lost was she in her own unhappiness.

'Come on, let's freshen you up,' Clem said helping her to her feet. She slowly led her down to the water's edge and sat her in the shallows, gently bathing her, splashing the cool water over her thighs, cupping handfuls and washing her face. It worked; the water seemed to revive her. Soon she stopped crying.

'What's wrong, Annie?' Clemmie asked but Annie shook her head.

They sat there for a while. Eventually Annie mumbled

something and Clem asked her to repeat it, leaning in to hear what she was saying. Annie echoed Frank's words in a whisper, 'I'm just tired and emotional.'

'OK. Do you need to sleep?' Clemmie asked.

Annie nodded and got herself to her feet. 'I think I'll go back to the boat now.'

Annie was a strong swimmer, Clemmie watched her slip into the water, in her clothes, and take powerful, steady strokes towards the *Little Utopia,* leaving only ripples and a peculiar sadness in her wake. Clem stood there at the water's edge watching until she reached the boat. Annie hauled herself up on to the transom out of the water, before disappearing below deck, not once looking back. Soon the dulcet tones of Roberta Flack began to trip across the water and Clem turned back towards the others. How silent and miserable everyone had been after that; all the unsaid things seemed to weigh down the air until one by one they had all lain down and fallen asleep.

The buzz of a fly vaguely woke her. She was dozing on the blanket, feeling the warm sun on the backs of her legs, her shoulders, her arms. Clem prised open her eyelids. Johnny's sleeping body was turned away from her, his brown shoulders moving gently with his breath. She waved her fingers in some sort of dreamy reverie, profoundly comforted by the sight of him at her side; he was as familiar to her as her own body. Sleep had temporarily closed the distance between them. She shut her eyes again, not wanting to think about her own treacherous heart or the oddness of the afternoon.

The light had changed; the sun had moved; new shadows were strewn about the beach. The only sounds were the gentle lapping of the waves on the shore, an occasional distant bird cry and a heavy breathing coming from somewhere behind her. She sleepily turned her head to the side. Frank was propped up under the shade of a tree, a book open on his lap, snoozing in the shade. He looked more fragile asleep; there was a vulnerability to him she rarely saw. He looked old and unfamiliar to her but despite this her disloyal heart stirred a little at the sight. Smudge was soundly sleeping too, lying on her back next to him, half in the sun half in the shade, her little body star-fished out on the sand. It was as if they'd all been struck down, smitten by slumber, here in this bay of tranquillity. Clem closed her eyes, shifted a little closer to Johnny and drifted back into the safety of sleep.

Johnny felt it in his dream: a light movement along the skin of his arm, the caress of a breath. He felt it again and went from sleep to wakefulness in one swift movement. He sat bolt upright. He looked about him. He saw it on the water, in the clouds; he felt it on his face, in his hair. *Oh my God!* His prayers had been answered. They had wind! Yes! There were cotton-wool clouds tiptoeing along the horizon, white wisps above him now. He leapt to his feet to feel the breeze against his chest. It was there, warm and faint. He couldn't remember ever feeling such joy at the arrival of wind. They were saved. They would soon be free, away from all this ghastliness. He could already feel it slipping away from him, the weight of *them* easing. He and Clem were moving on.

'Clem, Clem!' he cried, crouching down over her sleeping form, nudging her awake, whispering into her ear. 'Oh, Clem. My Clem. We're out of here! We're leaving. We're off. We've got wind!' He kissed her cheek again and again. Sleepily she stirred. She opened her eyes and pulled herself up to sitting and smiled at him. She didn't get up and dance with joy as she might have done a week ago. Everything had changed from a week ago and for a moment he wondered whether she even wanted to get away from this place at all.

'Frank!' he cried, running over to the tree where they lay. 'We've got wind! Let's go!' Frank and Smudge shook themselves awake. But no one leapt with joy; he was alone in his jubilation.

'We haven't had the cake yet!' Smudge said, not remotely interested in the wind, rubbing her eyes sleepily. She wandered over to the blanket to look for the cake while Johnny ran down to the water's edge, looking out. The wind had transformed the water: no longer the flat sky-coloured calm, now a dark, rippled blue, the life blown back into it, the wavelets noisily throwing themselves on the shore. It had body and strength again. While they had slept, nature had woken up. The *Little Utopia* had stopped swinging in lazy circles and was now held fast by the anchor rope, nose to the breeze, bobbing about on the surface, ready for action, just like Johnny.

'We have to get Mummy for the cake!' Smudge said, tugging at his hand, pointing at the boat. He looked over at the cake on the blanket, melted now, more of a brown sludge dotted with sunken wonky candles like the old woman's teeth.

'We can have it now,' he said. 'We can take Mummy back a piece.'

'No,' she said, stamping her foot in the sand. It was her birthday after all. The wind had softened him, smoothed the rough edges.

'OK,' he said, ruffling her messy hair, running over to the dinghy, wanting to waste no time. 'I'll go and get her.' She must have slept herself into sobriety by now. They'd eat the cake and then they'd leave and sail through the night. By the morning they might have found a village.

'Get a knife while you're there!' Clem called out to him.

He pulled the tender back down into the water and jumped

in, pushing off from the shore. He rowed towards the *Little Utopia* listening to Smudge's excited cries as she laid the plates out on to the blanket. The wind had lifted his heart; he could put up with anything now that he knew they would be moving, getting out of this awful place, away from these people. He closed his eyes, face to the breeze and felt the steady, warm air on his eyelids. He could feel his love again. They could forget all this, the damage that had been done. Everything was reparable now.

He rowed long, even strokes, keeping the blades at just the right angle for maximum speed. He was always after speed, he realized. He squinted as the sunlight bounced blindingly off the water. He got to the *Little Utopia* as fast as he could, dragging one oar and swinging round to her stern. He could hear the faint white noise of the tape deck being left on: a background scratching. He tied the tender to the stern with a one-handed bowline and climbed on board. She'd left the cockpit doors wide open and he peered down into the saloon. She wasn't in there and the heads door was shut. She'd be passed out on the bed. He went down the companionway steps.

'Annie?' he called, rolling himself a cigarette. 'It's time for the cake. We've got wind. We'll be leaving soon so we've got to have it now.' She didn't respond so he went through the saloon and knocked on the forepeak door.

'Annie?' he said, licking the glue strip of the paper. 'We're going to light the candles.'

He tried the handle but it wouldn't budge so he pushed his weight against the door and it opened slightly, revealing a glimpse of naked flesh. She was crashed out in a crumpled heap beside the toilet.

'Annie?' he cried, now really pissed off with her that she couldn't hold herself together at all, if only for her daughter's sake. What sort of a mother was she? What did he even care any more? What concern was it of his? The wind was here and he and Clem were on their way. He went back out through the saloon and up the steps, glancing back at the others, at the mountains, at an eagle rising in a thermal, as happy as him to have wind again. He went down the deck and lifted open the forehatch and stuck his head through.

'Annie?' he called. 'Get up! Cake time!' She was crumpled up on the floor,, her back to him, wet and naked, unmoving. Then he saw the blood.

He slid through the hatch head first and on to their bed and crawled forwards, falling off the bed on to the floor, reaching for her shoulder and turning her towards him.

'Annie?' She rolled over heavily, a terrible red stripe down the whole left-hand side of her legs, her face white and drained, her eyes rolled back into her head. She was holding the large kitchen knife in her right hand and her left wrist had a deep gash across it. Blood was spilling out in a steady stream, pouring on to the floor and spreading around her body.

'Jesus Christ! Annie! Jesus fucking Christ!'

She moaned. She was still alive; she was still conscious. He grabbed a shirt and, slipping in the warm wetness of her blood, heaved her body up on to his and wrapped the shirt around her wrist, trying to stem the bleeding. 'It's her fucking birthday,' he kept saying. 'It's her fucking birthday.'

He lifted her up in his arms and put her on the bed, put a pillow under her head. She moaned and opened her eyes slightly and tried to focus. When she saw him her face puckered a little, as if she was about to cry but lacked the strength. Her lips were trying to form words that he couldn't make out.

'I can't understand you, Annie,' he said, panicking, pressing his forehead to hers, looking into those dazed, weak eyes. He could taste blood on his lips, rusty and rich on his tongue. 'Just hang on, Annie. Just hang on.'

'Heads…' she whispered. 'Cabinet…' He got off the bed and stepped back into loo area and opened the cabinet door.

'In here?' he asked but she didn't respond. There were two medicine tins in the cabinet. One was locked. The other was the tin they had used on that first night. He pulled it out and put it on the bed. She was moaning now, shaking her head, her eyes rolling back in their sockets. 'Nooo…' she cried.

'Come on, Annie,' he said, holding her head up, utterly terrified that she was going to die on him. 'Stay awake, please. Don't give up… You're not a bad person… Think of Smudge… You're not a bad person…'

Then something inside him switched. The panic took a back seat. He became clinically practical. He moved about the boat efficiently trying to mend her. He bandaged up her wrist. He put a blanket around her. He propped up her arm on a pillow. All the while she was moaning and crying out with the pain. He crushed up four aspirins and made her swallow them with some water. He tried to tidy things up. He didn't really know why he was covering up for her; it wasn't the sort of thing you could hide but he felt he had to do it for Smudge. A child should never see her mother in such a state.

He cleaned the knife and chucked it in the cockpit. He used towels to mop up the blood from the floor and put them in a bin bag. Then he cleaned up himself, wiping her blood from his own body, scrubbing his hands clean in the sink. When he came back through to the forepeak, she was lying there, propped up, her glazed eyes staring out through the hatch at the small patch of sky.

'Annie?' he called but she wasn't listening. She was lost in the sky, perhaps in the wind that might have taken them with it. He told her not to move, but it was perfectly obvious that she wasn't going anywhere. 'I'm going to go back for the others, OK?' She didn't respond. 'I'll be back soon.'

He closed the door and went back through the saloon up into the cockpit, picked up the knife, dropped it into the tender and climbed down on to the transom and into the dinghy. Only then did he notice that his legs and hands were shaking so much he could barely hold the oars.

He rowed, his eyes locked on the knife; he'd missed a bit of blood on the wooden handle. He glanced behind at the shore. The three of them were standing at the edge of the water, shading their eyes from the sun, watching him row back, presumably wondering why Annie was not with him. He gripped hard and carried on rowing until the bottom of the boat ground to a halt on the sand. His knees were shaking so much he could hardly climb out of the boat. He kept his back to them as he pulled it up on to the dry sand.

'Where's Mummy for the cake?' Smudge asked, running over to help him.

'She's not feeling good. She's lying down,' he said, not looking at anyone. And they all believed him, not noticing the fact that his whole being trembled.

'Did you bring the knife?' Clem asked and he looked up at her, momentarily unable to fathom her meaning. She saw it in the boat and bent to pick it up, the sunshine glinting off the wrist-slitting blade. He followed them to the blanket and shortly found himself standing round the cake with its five flaming candles mouthing the words to 'Happy Birthday'. He had no voice. His body juddered. He couldn't eat. He must tell Frank. Up in the sky there were wisps of cloud being blown above his head. There was wind but he was static.

'We must go,' he said. 'We must get moving.' Then he wondered whether he'd said it out loud because no one seemed to have heard him. There was a commotion going on: Smudge was crying, Clem and Frank looking anxious. They knew. They'd guessed. But no, Smudge had lost Granny. *Please stop crying.* They were all running about looking for a tortoise when Annie lay bloodless on the boat. He wanted to reach out and pull Frank back but still his body wouldn't move. He saw Clem and Smudge sprint off and Frank searching around the little tree while he himself stood at the water's edge looking out at the *Little Utopia*, his quivering fingers trying to roll a smoke, unable to comprehend how on earth everything had gone so horribly wrong, how he had not seen any of this coming. It made no sense. Frank's words tumbled about inside his head: *psychotic, delusional, schizophrenic, insane, a mythomaniac…*

He became aware of Frank standing at his side. 'You've got blood on your arm, Johnny.'

Johnny turned sharply, twisting his body to examine his arm; it was true he had a great smear up the back of his left forearm. 'We have to get back to the boat,' Johnny said. 'She cut herself, Frank. She needs a doctor.'

Frank seemed neither surprised nor upset. 'Where did she cut herself?'

'She's OK,' he said even though Frank hadn't asked. 'Across her wrist. She slit her wrist, Frank.' It felt good to tell him, to share the burden. His mouth was so dry the words stuck on his tongue. He thought he was going to cry or scream.

Frank squinted out to sea at the *Little Utopia*, annoyed. 'On her birthday? It's her fucking birthday, for Christ's sake.'

Johnny was glad Frank said that, glad he was angry. He'd felt just the same. 'Why would she do that?' Johnny said, running a clammy hand through his hair, eyes fixed on the boat.

'Vertically or horizontally?'

'What?'

'Her wrist.'

'I don't fucking know, Frank. I've bandaged it up.' His knees were shaking so badly it was as if they were trying to escape. 'Diagonally, maybe.'

'I'm so sorry, Johnny. I should have told you earlier,' he said with a sigh.

'She's fucking crazy…' Johnny said. His words came out in breathy snatches; he couldn't control them. Then very tenderly Frank put his arm around Johnny's shoulder and pulled him in. Johnny couldn't help it. He didn't pull away; he wanted the comfort. He rested his head against Frank's great chest, needing the support of Frank's big, capable bear body to hold him up. They stood there, Frank rocking him gently.

'I'm so sorry you had to see that. I should have gone to get her. She does this from time to time, Johnny. Don't worry. She knows just how far to go.'

Johnny pulled away, trying to regain himself, nodding, taking a drag of his fag. 'I think she might need a doctor. I don't know. I've stopped the bleeding.'

'You're a good lad. I'll go to her,' he said, rummaging for his soft packet of tabs in his back pocket, but going nowhere.

'I've cleared up the mess. Just keep Smudge out of the fore-cabin.'

'Thanks, Johnny.' Frank tapped the packet and caught the cigarette in his customary manner. It seemed somehow inappropriate. 'I presume she told you all those scratches on her thighs were from falling through a glass roof?'

Johnny looked out at the horizon; there were more clouds now. The wind was getting on fine without him. He had a low foreboding feeling that he would never catch it now. He breathed in the faint scent of pine trees that the wind carried: the promise of other things and other times. He shut his eyes and let it wash over him. Annie had indeed told him about falling through a glass roof. He hadn't thought to question her.

'She's always been this way,' Frank said, tapping about his person for a light. Johnny got out his own lighter and passed it to him, still with a faint tremor in his fingers. Frank took Johnny's whole hand in his and pressed it firmly between his own, trying to press the fear out of him. 'She'll be all right,' he said.

They stood there in silence, looking out at the boat, Johnny's trembling hands calmed once Frank had let go. The waves were breaking on the rocks. He listened to the sounds of the sea, at last a language he understood. It calmed him.

'What about when you first met her? Was she like that then?' Johnny asked.

Frank raised his eyebrows, rubbing the back of his neck, his face full of some sweet sadness. ' I heard her before I ever saw her, you know,' he said. 'I heard her singing – singing like an angel – this voice so heavenly it stopped me in my tracks. It quite derailed me, the sound of her unhappiness. Then when they unlocked the door, there she was, this beautiful, tormented creature lying on the floor all strapped up in a white jacket.'

Johnny stared at him. 'I thought you met in a pub in Islington?'

Frank looked at him askance and frowned. 'A pub in Islington? No, she'd been done for assault, found wandering naked in the high street. I met her in Colney Hatch Lunatic Asylum,' he said, flicking his cigarette far out into the water.

8

UNBIDDEN THINGS

THE NEXT DAY, on the way home from the seaside, Clemmie's dad kept tapping the dashboard with his knuckle. He seemed to be in a different mood from yesterday. He was all quiet and serious and annoyed by things, particularly other drivers and the dashboard. He'd asked her not to mention almost falling out of the Waltzer to her mother and she promised that she wouldn't – though it seemed a little unfair not to be allowed to talk about the most dangerous thing that had ever happened to you. He was in no mood for argument. She tried not to do anything that might irritate him. She was slowly working her way through the pear drops in the glove compartment and staring out of the window, watching the way the wind flung itself through the trees and the fields instead of in the litter and the dustbin lids like you see in London. Then, not even an hour into their journey, the car began to judder and her dad began to say rude words and eventually the car ground to a halt in the middle of a long, straight, empty road with barely enough room for another car to get past. Her dad banged the steering wheel so hard that the crows in a nearby tree all flew away and his hand went red. She knew better than to say anything.

He got out of the car, slamming the door, which made the smelling fern tree hanging round the rear-view mirror spin in circles. She watched as he took off his Starsky sunglasses and his suit jacket and had to open the door again to place them neatly folded on his seat. He didn't look at her at all. Then he went to the bonnet and opened it up. She pinched a sneaky handful of pear drops and stared at the shiny blue of the bonnet, which was now the windscreen. After a while her dad reappeared from behind it and walked round to the boot of the car and clanged about a bit before coming round to her side and opening the door. He was holding a plastic red petrol can.

'Fuel gauge has had it. We need petrol. We're going to have to get back to that garage on the main road.' He was looking up and down the road. She did too, for supportive reasons.

It was a beautiful blustery day and she felt as if they were on an adventure, walking down the centre of the deserted road. She had Monkey in one hand and was swinging the petrol can in the other. Her father was still huffing and puffing, turning this way and that, looking for cars and checking his watch. She was jogging a bit to keep up with him and she kept getting distracted by the high tops of the cornfields surrounding them and the way the green leaves waved about angrily in the wind. If she shut her eyes, they sounded like roaring monsters. Her dad said they were sweetcorn. She'd thought sweetcorn was made in a sweetcorn factory by the ho-ho-ho Jolly Green Giant. But it made sense. A giant could easily hide in these dark fields. She peered into the blackness beyond the thick stalks and quickly trotted to catch up with her father, putting Monkey in the can and taking a firm hold of his hand.

After a while, her dad seemed to relax a bit and actually started talking and looking about the countryside. He knew about everything; if there had been a cleverest person in the country competition he would have won it. When they came across a squashed rabbit in the road, he pointed out all the bits of blood and guts, told her what the different things did, how the little heart worked, whether the rabbit had been a smoker or not, all sorts of things. Then he told her how the pylons took the phone calls all over the country, how they laid Tarmac on the roads, how birds sometimes used human hair to make their nests. They were talking so much they missed a car drive past and her dad ran after it. He was cross about that and when she caught up she joined in with his crossness though she didn't really mind. They were a real team.

'I might as well tell you now, Clemmie,' he said after a long, happy silence. 'I was going to stop somewhere nice for tea and tell you...'

He stopped to pull his cigar tin out of his pocket and she saw that there were only two left. She noticed how his hand was all trembly as he lit up, cupping his hands together. She liked the way the smoke slithered up into his nostrils like a slippery blue snake. She wondered whether he was going to tell her she could keep a pony in the garden. She took his hand again, squeezing it, and they walked onwards. 'I'm going to be living somewhere else for a while.'

She looked up at him and followed his gaze. He was watching some birds flying in the V formation that Miss Bradley had taught them about in school. 'Where are we going?' she asked.

'Just me, love.' Briefly he looked down at her.

'And me,' she said, sure that that was what he had meant to say.

'No. You and your mum will stay in the house.'

'Oh. Does Mummy know?' she asked. It seemed a rather odd arrangement.

He nodded. 'I'm going to Somerset.'

'What's Somerset?'

'It's a place.'

'What's so good about Somerset?'

'A friend of mine lives there.'

'Well, why don't we come with you?'

He took another drag. 'You just can't.'

She stopped then and so he had to as well. 'Well, I want to. How long are you going for?'

'I don't know.'

'A weekend?'

'Look, your mum and I... we're not going to be together any more.'

'But if you stayed in the house then you would be.' She smiled at him but he didn't smile back. He looked away, over her shoulder, down the lane and sighed.

'We're getting a divorce, Clemmie,' he said.

'What's a divorce?'

'For God's sake, you know what a divorce is.' He suddenly sounded irritated by her. 'Like Uncle Tim and Sandy. We're splitting up.' He started smoking in a rush, sucking and blowing. She stared at him. She was confused. He must have made a mistake. 'But Uncle Tim and Sandy don't like each other. Sandy threw Mark's Etch A Sketch right through the window. You and Mummy, you don't throw things.'

She expected him to agree, to say, *Yes, that's right, I'm just playing a trick on you.* But he didn't. Instead he kept looking down the lane, this way and then that.

'I'll still see you,' he said and he flashed a smile at her but it wasn't a relaxing smile: it was too quick. Besides, of course he would still *see* her, he was her dad. His words began to worry Clemmie and she didn't like the way he was looking at her in a sad slopey-eyed kind of way. Somewhere inside of her she could feel a horrible falling away, as if she was losing her grip, just like yesterday on the Waltzer. She knew she had to cling on hard. *Don't let go!* She grabbed his hand in both of hers, the panicky feeling taking over.

'Is it me? Is it all the mess I make? My collecting boxes? Don't go to Somerset! I can stop collecting things…'

His eyes had gone all watery in the wind and his voice sounded different. 'No, darlin'. It's not that. You keep collecting things.'

His hand wasn't responding to hers, it felt all clammy and lifeless and the wind whipped the smoke out of his trembling lips. Then he looked straight at her and she didn't like it because in his eyes she could see the ending of things. She got it then. All the dots suddenly joined up to form a monstrous unrecognizable shape. 'You're leaving us,' she said.

He didn't deny it. He just stood there, looking down at the road, his fingers still curled around hers. Then when he looked at her again she could see, just for a second, that he was afraid of her. But that was it. That was all the power she had. Whatever else she said or did meant nothing and would have no effect: her opinion, her needs, her feelings were not relevant. He had already decided. *They* had already decided. She dropped his hand.

'It's going to be all right, Clemmie,' he said, going down on a bended knee as if he was a prince about to ask her to marry him. She stepped back, away from him. He was not a prince at all.

'I hate you.' She spat the words at him and then turned and ran away as fast as she could, her shoes click-clicking like mad on the Tarmac of the road. She could hear him coming after her, walking, then starting to run as she darted off into the cornfield on her right, the rough green leaves towering over her head, not caring if the giant lived there or not. She could feel the wetness of her tears running down her face. Deeper and deeper she ran into the watery darkness still clutching Monkey in the petrol can, darting through the stalks as swift as a little bird, the mud cloying on her Start-rites, slowing her down. She could hear him calling. 'Clemmie! Clemmie! Come back!'

The man from the RAC spent ages looking at the engine and twisting things and taking lids off and putting them back on again. Then after all that he couldn't fix it anyway and he had to tow them back to London. Clemmie could tell that he didn't want them in the van. He kept looking at the state of their clothes. She had managed to get the red mud from the cornfields all over herself and her father. The RAC man gave them his newspaper to lay out on the floor and seats of the Cortina so Clemmie had her Start-rites on a naked lady's bosoms all the way home.

Her dad was sitting in the driving seat, his hands on the wheel, but he wasn't driving. It looked as if he was pretending to drive. Just as he'd been pretending to be happily married to her mother and pretending to be having a wonderful time with her at the seaside when all the time he had wanted to be in Somerset.

She sat back and stared out of the passenger window, watching the raindrops squiggle this way and that, joining up, forming fatter drops, when a thought suddenly struck her: what if *everything* was pretend? What if a great big trick was being played on her and everyone else was in on it? She pressed her face to the cold window pane, looking through the droplets out into the darkening sky. She started to watch the people in the cars overtaking them. Yes, all the drivers were staring at her in a strange way. She could see their lips moving, making comments about her. They all seemed to know something about her. In the back of a red car a little boy stuck out his tongue and laughed. He knew too. It was all a set-up. What if the trees weren't real and the road wasn't real and what if it was all there purely for her benefit, for the big trick against her? She shut her eyes and opened them very quickly, hoping to catch the world out. She blinked quickly but everything remained in place. It was a good trick. The organizers would have planned for this – she thought the best time to check might be in the middle of the night when they took everything down or were doing repairs.

By the time they passed the building with the pouring Lucozade bottle on it another thought was dawning on her: on the journey to the seaside she had forgotten to do the breathing task with the lamp-posts and sure enough, something terrible *had* happened and what was more, today was Friday the thirteenth, just like the lady with the man-voice had said.

'Wake up, Clemmie. We're nearly home.'

'I'm not asleep,' she said, forgetting her promise of never speaking to him again. But she had been asleep. All that crying had made her tired.

He'd carried her back to the car on his shoulders through the cornfield. How different the view had been from up there, the air had felt fresher, the world much bigger. She could see other fields and the patterns the wind was making through the corn. She could even see the shiny blue roof of the Cortina, which was disappointingly close; she thought she'd run a lot further than that. It had certainly taken him ages to find her; she'd run right through this field, through another and on to a steep road. Then she'd stopped crying and got more involved in her own lostness. It was a surprising feeling, being lost. It was her first real taste of freedom and she had liked it very much. She'd looked up at the puffy white clouds whizzing through the sky, the trees shimmering and shaking around her, and she had felt the thrill of the wild as she wondered which way she should go. She tried to imagine what Jesus might have done in her position and decided he would have turned right because he was right-handed. She didn't know that for certain but it seemed most likely because in the painting at church heaven and the angels were all on the right of him, presumably so he could shake hands and sign fan-mail, and hell and the devils were all on the left. She thought Jesus might wander down into that village she could see at the bottom of the hill, where kindly people would wash his feet and praise him. She wasn't expecting that exactly but perhaps a nice old lady might take her in as a mysterious orphan. She didn't think Joseph would have gone to Somerset. Joseph probably liked to be with Jesus and Mary when he got home from a hard day's carpenting; they probably played Scrabble with wooden pieces that he'd made especially. Just then her father had ruined her chances of being orphaned by shouting her name loudly from the field. Then the next thing she knew he was on the road behind her waving frantically. She legged it down the hill as fast as she could, clickety-click-click, but she didn't stand a chance, he was a really fast runner – he'd won the fathers' race at Sports Day. He'd caught her up and grabbed her, scooping her up into his arms from behind, whether she liked it or not. She made her body go rigid but still he clung on to her, not minding the mud she was getting all over his suit and the thumps she was giving him.

When they got back to Putney Clemmie scuttled into the house past her mother, who was standing in the hall looking anxious. 'Look at the state of her, Jim!' she heard her say as she ran up the stairs and into the loo, bolting the door behind her. It was the only safe place, the only room in the house with a lock on it.

She listened to their conversation. Her mum had been *deathly* worried about them. Her father started talking about the Cortina and the journey and her mum said, 'I take it you told her then?' And the strange thing was she *still* gave a little laugh at the end of her question. They were both traitors; they were both in on it. She was the only idiot.

She couldn't make out what her father said and then they went into the kitchen and closed the door so she had to stand on the loo and open the little window and stick her head out. Her mother was asking whether Clemmie had had any tea and what the food was like in the hotel. They were chatting about avocado and prawns as if this was just an ordinary day. Perhaps she had got it all wrong and this was part of the trick. She stayed in the loo though; she wasn't going to risk looking any more stupid unless she heard her dad laughing.

A little while later she heard her dad calling for her. But she didn't move. She carried on sitting on the toilet seat without the light on. The hall light went on and she heard his footsteps coming up the stairs, past the loo and up into her bedroom. 'Clemmie?' he called and she knew that he was checking all the cupboards. She heard him go into their room and open the sliding door of their wardrobe, calling her name. When he came down the stairs again he stopped outside the loo. She could see his trousers through the great big hole he once made sawing off the handle when she'd got locked inside years ago.

He turned the door knob and then gave a little knock on the door. 'Clemmie?' He sounded tired. Maybe he was going to change his mind. 'I've got to go, darlin'. Aren't you going to say goodbye?'

She shook her head.

He knocked again. 'Clembo? You coming out?'

She shook her head again and waited. She wanted him to bash the door down and beg her forgiveness.

'OK, love. Well, I'll see you soon.' She stared through the hole, willing him not to go. The blue of his suit trousers was there and then it wasn't.

That night, Clemmie was awoken by a peculiar sound. She lay in bed listening, blinking up at the ceiling. It was a creaking, dragging sort of a noise that came in short bursts. She sat bolt upright. She knew what it was. It had to be the sound of the pretend world going up. As quietly as she could, she pulled back the bed covers and crept out of bed, tiptoeing across the floorboards towards the curtains where she stood very still. Gingerly she reached out and touched the fabric with her fingertips. Then quite suddenly she whisked back the curtain, fully expecting to catch them red-handed putting up the scenery, lots of men in boiler suits looking round at her guiltily, scurrying down ladders. But the orange London sky and the backs of the gardens were all in the right places. Even the rain had been turned on; she watched it falling in streaks across the glare of the far streetlight. Then she heard the noise again and turned around: it was coming from her parents' room.

She crossed her bedroom and stopped at the door, opening it in that special pushing-pulling way that meant no one could hear. Peering out, she could see that her parents' bedroom door was ajar. She heard the noise again, louder and clearer, so she crept out of her room on to the carpet in the hall, avoiding the squeaky bit. She hovered by their door and then pushed it a little wider. There was a shape in the bed on her mother's side. The other side was empty. Her dad had gone.

The strange noise was coming from her mum, a smothered hiccoughing sound.

Quietly she tiptoed into the room up to the side of the bed where her mother was curled up, facing out, only Clemmie couldn't see her face because it was pressed into a pillow that she was hugging tightly, her body shaking as though she might be laughing. But she wasn't laughing; Clemmie knew that. She had never seen her mother cry before and she stood and watched her for a bit. Slowly it began to dawn on her that this wasn't pretend, it was all real. She pulled back the cover and climbed into the bed, forcing herself into the pillow's place, her mother's sobs all loudened without it, its wetness dampening her neck. She put her arms around her mother as far as she could reach and she felt her mum hold on to her so tightly that on another occasion it might have hurt.

'We'll be all right. We'll be all right,' Clemmie said, wondering whether it was true and slipping her thumb into her mouth. Most alarming of all was that her mother didn't even try to pull it out.

9

DEPARTURE

THE NORTH-EASTERLY blew a steady six and the boat sped through the water. They were running from the wind, the waves hitting them from behind; they were surfing down them at a fair old speed, goosewinging, the mainsail out to the starboard side, the genoa to port. Johnny'd had the spinnaker out earlier, a massive canvas of red and green, ballooning out at the bows. But now the sun had swung across the sky, dipped beneath the waves and left the stars on patrol. Clouds sped by, low and fast, obscuring and revealing them. Johnny was at the helm, standing up, his body balancing, dancing almost, as if he were riding a horse while the boat bucked and kicked in the waves, his eyes fixed on either the compass or the sails, for there was nothing else to see, only the soupy darkness lit by the smudge of the moon, just enough to steer by. All he had to do was keep on sailing, get the maximum out of the boat. He'd been standing there for four hours straight. He was quiet and focused; his only concern the wind and Clem who had been sitting at his side for hours. She knew everything now; she knew everything he knew.

She had stood leaning against the cockpit doors as he tried to explain things that he didn't understand, how Annie was not all that she seemed, how unbalanced her mind was, the accusations she had made against Frank. He'd used Frank's words: *pathological liar, criminally insane*; he spoke of *medi-cation* and *institutions*. He told her not to worry, said they would be gone soon, away from these people. All the while she had stood there listening, pale and shocked, and he fancied that he saw something leave her then, something subtle that he couldn't put his finger on. It was as if she had been dimmed, some of her light stolen.

For an hour or so she took herself off to sit at the bows, watching the sun set, trying to make sense of things. Madness scared her. She'd seen the madness in Annie's eyes; she'd stared it in the face. She'd been reading to Smudge in the saloon, just as Frank had asked, trying to keep her out of the forepeak where Annie was sleeping. She'd brushed Smudge's hair and done her best to comfort her after the loss of Granny on the rocks but just as she was leaning over the table to reach for another book, the saloon door had swung open and what she had glimpsed she couldn't unglimpse: a semi-naked comatose Annie sprawled uncaring on the bed, her great doleful, unblinking eyes staring straight through Clem's, not recognizing her, gone into some distant and private world, her arms outstretched, her wrist red and raw, slashed open, glistening in the hideous intimacy of the side light. Clem had frozen to the spot. Frank was in the heads cutting up a bandage, a packet of pills clamped in his teeth. He'd caught her staring and he had shut the door on her, gently blocking her out.

She had stood there wondering how on earth something like this could have happened, how on earth everything had gone so wrong, what had been going on in Annie's mind to do such a thing. But mostly she had wondered why no one had thought to tell *her*, why no one wanted her help, why she was always to be the last person to know anything.

She and Johnny sat in silence in the cockpit, the blanket of night enveloping them. The only sounds were the thumping of the boat on the waves and the steady rush of movement through the water. She watched him sail the boat, his eyes constantly checking to the port side, into the darkness. She knew he was searching for signs of civilization and she looked too. 'It's not our problem, Clem,' he kept saying as if she'd been asking him. He sat at her side, lit a cigarette and it occurred to her how awful it must have been for him to find Annie lying in a pool of blood.

'We're just getting out of here. We're getting off as soon as we can. The moment I see the lights of a village we're heading in.' Even as he spoke he was looking out for those village lights but there were none, just the hazy blur of the moon up above and the dark shoreline.

'Is that the right thing to do, Johnny?'

'What do you mean *is that the right thing to do?*'

'Should we leave them right now?' she said.

'What?' The clouds briefly parted and his face was lit with a sharp silver glow; the furrow etched on his brow was deep. He looked different, older.

'Shouldn't we wait until Annie's a bit better? It's not really fair on Frank and Smudge.'

'Clem,' he said, looking her in the eye. 'We're leaving.' That was final. He didn't even ask her what she wanted, what she thought. Her opinions meant nothing. She looked away and up at the moon.

Shortly Frank came out. He opened the cockpit doors bearing oilskins and jumpers. He too looked tired. She didn't know what to say. She put on a jumper and an oilskin. He sat down opposite her, blinking a little as his eyes adjusted to the darkness. 'She's out,' he said.

After a while Johnny asked Clem to take the helm, to stay on this course, to keep a lookout; he wanted to check the charts. She felt the chill of his hand as he passed her the tiller. He was freezing; his teeth were chattering. She watched him go below deck, his movements smoothly counterbalancing the sway as he shut the cockpit doors behind him.

She hadn't been alone with Frank since the beach and was wondering what she was meant to say to a man whose wife had just tried to kill herself. 'I'm so sorry, Frank,' was all she could muster and then wasn't quite sure whether he had heard her. He didn't move; his eyes were fixed on the horizon.

'Yes...' he said eventually as if he were still trying to make sense of it. 'She doesn't normally cut quite that deep.'

Clem wanted to ask what it was that Annie *normally* did but it sounded morbid. She could think of nothing to say; her mind kept returning to the gash, the blood shining in the side light, those dazed eyes looking into that different world. 'I just don't understand why she would do that...'

He turned and looked at her and she felt better under his gaze; things made more sense when he looked at her. 'The irony is that cutting herself makes her feel alive.'

Clem tried to understand this, but it was nonsense. 'She has *so* much to live for. She's so lucky... She's got what other people would die for...' She stopped herself short, realizing how insensitive was her turn of phrase.

He was looking at the water, the fuzzy white ribbon leading back to the moon. 'It's not about what you've got on the outside though, is it,' he said and stretched his legs a little.

She glanced up at the sails. She wanted to believe him. 'It is a *bit* though,' she said because surely it was just a little bit. She'd made him smile and it gave her hope. 'If she really thinks you and Smudge are better off without her that's just mad.'

'Well…that's what they say.'

'But she's *wrong*.'

He smiled, but it was half-hearted. 'There you go again, Clem, with your rights and wrongs.'

She pulled in the mainsail a little, not quite sure whether she needed to; she was copying Johnny really, but it was a useful means of punctuating her sentiments. Annie *was* wrong. Smudge and Frank were not better off without her. He should just admit it. Sometimes judgements were necessary.

They sailed in silence, lifting and dipping with the waves. He was stretched out now, his arms behind him, holding on for support, his legs parted, his feet planted firmly on the other cockpit seat, his mind on something new.

'Did you know that most early civilizations considered suicide as a completely honourable means of escaping an unbearable existence?'

She did not know this, but she liked him talking. It normalized all this. Sometimes she just wanted to listen to the sound of his voice, telling her things, educating her, making her see things differently, being objective.

'There never used to be any judgement attached to such a death,' he said, looking back out to sea. She could see that he was more comfortable pondering the ethics of suicide than on the coal face of Annie's misery. 'Not until Socrates did anyone even question the morality of suicide.'

'I'm not saying suicide in itself is wrong,' Clem said, wanting to be a part of his logic, to be of some help. 'Johnny and I once made a pact that if one of us should ever get diagnosed with a terminal illness, we'd get in the car and fume ourselves together.' The idea now sounded slightly ridiculous to her; she couldn't picture it any more. She supposed Frank must think her very childish.

'Why not?' he said, as if he didn't really care one way or the other. 'Suicide is a perfectly noble alternative to suffering.'

Clem stared at him. It seemed an extraordinary thing to say given the state of affairs on the boat. 'But what if Annie had succeeded? Would you still be saying that?'

He held her eye. 'I don't think she wanted to succeed.'

'But if Johnny hadn't got to the boat...'

'She knew someone would. It was a cry for help.'

Sometimes his objectivity made him seem callous. 'But why is she crying for help?' she asked.

'Why do any of us cry for help? Because we want comfort.'

She couldn't imagine him crying for help. It would be an impressive figure whom he sought comfort from; she would like to be privy to that. She wanted to see him weak and vulnerable, needing someone. *Her*, for example. He paused and tapped out a cigarette. He stooped to light it, cupping the flame from the wind. Then he reached out his hand and passed the cigarette to her. She liked it when he did that. She took it from his fingers, feeling the warmth of his skin as he turned his body around to face her. She could feel the hairs on her arm responding to his touch.

'I suppose you're leaving me now,' he said gently and the way he said *me* made her heart beat a little faster and she wondered whether this was it, this was his cry for help. She took a drag of the cigarette.

'Johnny wants to.'

He nodded, looking down at his hands. She knew it was wrong, what with his wife down there with her slashed wrist, but she couldn't help remembering the feel of that hand, those fingers inside her, his touch, moving to her rhythm, digging deep. She shifted at the helm. She could feel a little current running through her breasts to her nipples.

'And you, Clemency? What do you want?'

No one called her Clemency. It felt fiercely intimate. He pinned her with his eyes and the current darted right down her body to between her legs.

'Well?' he said.

'I think I want to stay longer.'

The cockpit doors swung open. Johnny came out with coffees and a small bottle of brandy and the intimacy seamlessly embraced him. 'Johnny,' Frank said, watching the way Johnny's eyes went straight to the shore, forever searching for escape. 'I'm going to miss you guys when you go.'

'You'll find some other couple to enjoy,' Johnny said, taking the tiller from Clem, stooping to the compass to check the bearings. She wished he hadn't said that. She didn't like to think they were replaceable. 'I don't think we'll be entertaining for a while.' Frank said. 'Not after this. And I didn't even tell you about the Australian couple we had on board...'

'What Australian couple?' Clem asked, not liking them already.

'We were on the Yugolsavian coast somewhere near Dubrovnik and we invited this nice couple on board for a barbecue. I nipped off to get another bottle and when I came back Annie had the tongs in her hand, was standing in the cockpit barbecuing the meat and these guys were sitting there right on the edge of the boat, as white as sheets...' Frank laughed. 'It turned out Annie had told them that I'd killed her mother, cut her up into pieces and put her in the freezer.'

Johnny and Clem laughed too, taking their cue from him but their laughter was just a release. It wasn't funny. It was fucked up. They passed around the brandy in silence from one to the other; it felt almost ritualistic, the sharing of the succour. They were soon lulled by the irregular rhythm of the boat, at last offering them some distraction from the day, forcing them into present-moment awareness, rising and falling, falling and rising with the unpredictability of the waves, the salty spray from the crashing bows splashing them every now and then as the wind blew steadily from the stern.

As the night continued the atmosphere up on deck seemed to change. The moon had shrugged off the clouds and was now burning a ferocious white light on to them and the awfulness of the day was slipping further from their consciousnesses, left behind in some dark cove as they sailed onwards. The waves were getting bigger and the bows rose way up into the night and fell thumpingly back down into the water, drenching them, spray dropping like firecrackers on to the decks. Up and down went the *Little Utopia*, ploughing forwards to pastures new, her crew beginning to whoop as they surfed down the silvery slopes, riding the waves as though they were on horseback, on one beast, lifting and falling together, yelling as they sped through the water, heads back, laughing like lunatics as the salt spray soaked their faces. Briefly the absurdity of their little lives was the only thing that mattered.

There was electricity in the air, a kind of buzzing thrill. Johnny could feel it crackling around him. Even the water sparkled with phosphorescence, giving a luminous hue to the night, as it fizzed around the boat. He could feel it – this charged moment, the intensity of the now, the past and the future bearing no weight at all – he felt an extraordinary empathy for Frank and Annie, for everything they had gone through. The craziness of the day was over, Smudge was safely sleeping down below and as much as Johnny cared about the suffering of Annie lying sedated in the bows, they were all up here on the decks busy being alive. He felt quite drunk on life. He'd seen Annie teetering on that gossamer thread between life and death and together they had cheated death. And that deserved celebrating. He felt the blood pumping round his body and the wind blowing on his back and briefly he felt invincible.

Later, the delirium settled into a breezy quiet but no one was tired, no one wanted to go below deck. It was better up here in the fresh, clean air. Clem was looking over at the different shades of darkness between the sea, shore and sky and she felt a sudden dread at the thought of being out there, leaving the *Little Utopia*. She wasn't sure she was ready at all; she wasn't sure she could cope with being just the two of them again. They were a family now, a unit. She thought of Frank and Annie and Smudge travelling on without them, and whether they would pick up other people. She couldn't picture it. She'd forgotten all about other people, the rest of the world. It was the five of them as if no one else had ever existed. They had to wait for Annie to get better; Johnny must see that.

'What happened to Annie, Frank?' she asked.

'Dawn's on its way,' Johnny said. He didn't want to talk about Annie. Couldn't they *not* talk about things, just for once – maybe later, in a week or so, when he and Clem were on the other side of Turkey, they could talk about it. But for now, couldn't they all just keep quiet?

Frank let out a deep sigh and seemed to think hard about the question. 'Some people just have heavier crosses to bear than others.'

'Poor Annie. Having a monster for a father,' Clem said.

'He was a mess of a man,' Frank said sadly. 'But what can I say? She adored him. She insists that for years, as a child, she thought her life was perfect.'

'How on earth could she say that?' Clem asked.

'I know. It's extraordinary but that was the word she used: *perfect*. In her eyes the trouble didn't start until they were about eight and something her sister said at school got social services involved. That was the first time Annie realized that she wasn't *supposed* to feel this way about her father. She was supposed to call herself a *victim* and call him an *abuser*. Society had spoken: he was a *bad* man.'

'But he *was* a bad man. He'd just brainwashed her,' Clem said.

'It was the word *abuse* that bothered her,' Frank said, in his usual analytical manner, 'with all its connotations of pain and suffering – when all she had experienced was love and pleasure.'

'That's just twisted,' Clem said.

He smiled at her and nodded. 'Nevertheless, Clem, that's what she felt. She realized then, as a child, that morally and socially she was not allowed to voice these things. They were unacceptable. So she learnt to keep quiet, to feel guilty about her feelings. She felt different. She was an outsider. Worse than that – a freak. Then Social Services separated her and her sister and put them in different care homes away from the man they loved. *For their own good,* of course, but it didn't feel that way to her.'

'Poor poor Annie,' Clem said.

He sighed. 'I suspect that that was when she first started raging against the world.'

'It's interesting though,' Clem said, 'I hadn't thought of it like that. I know that in some cultures incest is perfectly acceptable. 'The Ancient Egyptians were always marrying their sisters and brothers.'

Johnny glanced at her. This new affected manner she had was really beginning to grate, the way she was trying to impress Frank with her open-mindedness.

'You're absolutely right,' Frank said, duly impressed. 'In fact it was de rigueur in high society.'

'Do you think it's that basic? It's all a question of what is fashionable?' she asked.

Johnny could feel the green-eyed monster raising its head; he hated it when they talked like this. It sounded to him like a pretentious form of foreplay. 'Annie's father was an abuser, whatever confused feelings she had about it,' Johnny said. 'The law is there to protect the children. That's all there is to it.' But they weren't listening to him.

'It's unfashionable in our society to even refer to the fact that children are sexual beings,' Frank said, sounding most aggrieved by society, as ever. 'More so these days than fifty years ago – Huxley talked about it in *Brave New World*. He had young children going off for allotted erotic play-time. Did you ever read it?'

Clem took out her tobacco, casually resting her foot against the portside seat. Johnny knew that she hadn't even heard of *Brave New World*.

'He was making a point. The subject of children's sexuality is a modern taboo. We're absolutely terrified by it. I've always admired Annie's honesty about what she experienced. Must we make children doubly culpable for enjoying the experience? I don't think we should. I think society does children a disservice to react that way.'

'Society doesn't blame *the child*. It blames the abuser,' Johnny said, keeping his eyes on the coast, the dark bay slipping into view. But there were no lights and his disappointed heart sank still further.

'Yes but it *ignores* the child. Freud believed every child is in love with the parent of the opposite sex and that every child experiences sexual jealousy towards the same-sex parent,' Frank continued, tapping himself out a cigarette.

'I wonder if that's true,' Clem said and Johnny really didn't

233

like the way she was demonstrating her wondering, waving her hands about as if she had more to say – when he knew that she didn't.

'Did you never experience sexual jealousy as a child, Johnny?' Frank asked.

'Nope,' he said, looking over at the mountains, which were a sharp black now that the crack of dawn was breaking somewhere over the edge of the planet behind them. He didn't want to bring either his jealousy or his mother into this conversation.

'It's perfectly natural to have had those feelings,' Frank continued. 'We even have words for it. Little princesses, daddy's girls, Oedipus complex…'

Frank was looking at Clem now and she found herself turning to the mountains, looking away from him, ambushed by a dirty kind of embarrassment, for *she* had once been a daddy's girl. And worse than that, if she looked into the whole incest taboo she had to confess that she found something quite titillating about a brother and a sister doing it. She herself had always wanted a good-looking older brother, not to have sex with of course, but one that her friends wanted to have sex with, which didn't seem entirely removed. Frank made her feel as if she had never been entirely honest with herself before and that it was perfectly acceptable to examine the darker side of human nature. Frank passed her the brandy, a smile on his lips. 'You can say what you like on this boat, Clem. We're not going to judge you.'

She took a fleeting glance at Johnny and wasn't so sure. 'Technically *you* were abused,' she said, turning to him. She didn't want to be the only guilty one.

Johnny looked at her, baffled. 'What are you talking about?'

'*You* were abused,' she said. 'You were having sex with a thirty-five-year-old woman from the age of fourteen.'

Johnny laughed and looked up at the sails. 'That wasn't abuse! That was pleasure!'

'Ah!' Frank said, raising a finger, his cigarette glowing as the life was sucked out of it. 'The murky business of drawing lines: *pleasure* or *abuse*?'

Then the boat hit a big wave and the water sprayed about them, landing like shrapnel on the decks, but no one was whooping and hollering now.

Clemmie found the crisp white envelope on the doormat when she got home from school. It was addressed to *Miss Clemency Bailey* in squashy, inky handwriting. Her heart raced about her chest; she had never received a letter that wasn't on her birthday before. She bent down and picked it up from the immaculate doormat. She examined the envelope. The writer had made a spelling mistake and corrected it: *ie* instead of a *y* at the end of *Clemency*. It was obviously from someone who didn't know her, which made it all the more exciting. She sniffed the envelope for clues. It smelt of important things.

She took it through to the kitchen and sat at the table staring at it, enjoying the delicious suspense for as long as she could bear. She thought of waiting until her mother got home from work but that could be another hour or so and there was no way she could hold out that long. She went and got the letter opener from her mother's desk, the one that used to belong to her grandfather, and very carefully she cut the letter open and peered inside. There was a thick card with glittering gold around the edges. She carefully pulled it out of the envelope.

At the top of the card her name was written in the same inky handwriting, only it was spelt the wrong way this time and with no correction. In beautiful swirling print it said: *James and Elizabeth invite you to the christening of Peter*

Arthur Steven Todd-Bailey at St Michael's Church on Saturday July 27th followed by a reception At Home.

At first she thought it must be a mistake, she didn't know any Jameses or Elizabeths or Peter Arthurs. But then of course she remembered and though she should have felt happy for Peter getting blessed by God and all that, she didn't. Everything on the card made her feel *un*happy. James should have been Jim. Elizabeth should have been her mum Jackie, and Peter shouldn't have been there at all. But the worst bit was the *At Home.* He had a new *At Home* and it was a place she didn't know at all. Nowhere near her. She was right out there on the chilly edge of his life when once she had been at the cosy middle.

She was nervous about showing the invitation to her mum. She didn't want her mother to see that her dad had forgotten how to spell her name; she didn't think she could bear the double disappointment in him and so for two whole days she kept it hidden under her pillow and only looked at it at night. She could recite the whole invitation off by heart, the address and all her half-brother's names and everything. On the third day she deliberately left it out for her mother to find. She knew she'd found it because she was doing the washing up with a lot of banging; then when she broke a cup she blurted out that *Two's far too old to be christened.* Clemmie had worked out the maths a while ago. She knew that Liz had been pregnant when her dad left them. She knew that he'd left her for a baby he hadn't even met.

Clemmie pretended that she didn't want to go to the christening, out of loyalty to her mum. But she *did* want to go. She wanted to see where her dad lived. She wanted to see Peter whom she'd only met once when he was a baby in the hospital with a black poo in his nappy. Also, though she would *never* say this to her mother, she wanted Liz to get to know her. She wanted Liz to like her and include her in their plans. She had guilty private thoughts of moving there one day and them all living together happily as a family, of her being really helpful and popular. Something else was bothering her: she was beginning to forget what her dad looked like because what with him being so busy with his new job and the baby and stuff, she hadn't actually seen him for a year and a half. He sent cards at Christmas and on her birthday and she had spoken to him on the phone, but it was difficult to actually make arrangements what with school and them always going on foreign holidays. She could remember his eyes and his mouth but the middle bit was all blurry, probably because the only photograph she had was one where his hand was covering half of his face.

All this aside, there was another major reason she wanted to go to the christening: Sarah's mum, Mrs Love, had said she could pick Clemmie up on their way down to Cornwall and if Jackie wanted, Clemmie could come with them and Jackie could have some time to herself. Clemmie had overheard this on the telephone – she'd been listening in on the phone upstairs. The mums had been organizing pick-ups from Donna's birthday party when the suggestion was made. Clemmie had let out a little squeak and had to clamp her hand over her mouth. She wanted more than anything to go down to Cornwall with Sarah's family especially as she hadn't wet the bed for nearly a month now. She loved everything about the Loves. They were all disorganized and happy. They could spend the whole day deciding what to get at the shop at the bottom of the hill, sitting on each other's laps and making jokes and cups of tea. And no one ever said *what a waste of time*. Sarah's dad was always tinkering around on motorbikes and boats with the boys – he let them do whatever they wanted; once, when Johnny was only eight, they had sailed a dinghy each from Newquay round to Padstow all by themselves. Sarah's mum was the coolest mum at school. She wore black and had clangy jewellery and cooked with garlic. She was always saying things like *The more the merrier* and *Stay the night!* and *I'm sure we can fit in one more* whereas Clemmie's mum wore bright floral dresses and was always counting things up and deciding that there wasn't quite enough.

Clemmie had got the train down to Bridgwater by herself. She kept wandering up and down the carriages, feeling free and grown up, hoping other children would notice how independent she was. It was the first time she had actually used the handbag her nanna had given her, which contained a pound note *for emergencies*. Clemmie was having such fun queuing up in the buffet car – she'd done so four times in the first hour and had already spent the entire pound on crisps – she carried on queuing up for the rest of the journey, as well gathering as many free salt and peppers and plastic cutlery packets as she could. She was collecting souvenirs. She had decided that trains were a fine way to travel; one day she would travel the whole world by train and plane. She had her heart set on those wet serviette sachets people got on aeroplanes.

She saw him before he saw her. He was standing on the Bridgwater platform, his head swivelling quickly from carriage to carriage as he tried to spot her through the windows. Her heart had jumped at the sight of him and his lovely face, all concerned about where she was. Then as the train slowed down she saw Liz and Peter at his side and she'd felt a little less jumpy-hearted because she'd rather hoped it would be just her dad for the first bit.

She got out of the carriage and saw the relief on his face when he recognized her. He held out his arms and she forgot about Liz and Peter and went running down the platform and into his embrace. He lifted her high in the air and hugged her and she felt so happy she thought she might burst. Then he put her down slowly and said things like *What a big girl you are now* and *You've got so grown up*, which was nice but kept reminding them both of all the bits they'd missed. Liz was behind him now with Peter in her arms. She bent down to give Clemmie a kiss and tried to get Peter to say, *Hello, Clemency. How was the journey?* which had seemed both unnecessary and impossible.

As they walked back to the car she had hoped her dad might take her hand but Peter was holding one of them and he had her bag in the other so she walked behind the Todd-Baileys. Her dad looked different. He wasn't like Starsky any more. He was wearing country clothes, one of those jackets that stands up by itself when you're not in it and he had muddy Wellington boots on. Then in the car Liz kept calling him *James* and he didn't correct her or anything so all in all he didn't really seem quite so much like Jim any more.

She could see why her dad liked Liz: she wore Kicker boots and had straight hair and liked making things. She'd made decorations all over the house for the christening, little white angels and paper chains. She wasn't bothered about people spilling things on the carpet or the mess on the kitchen table. Peter had chocolate on his face all day and she didn't mind one bit. She was friendly and asked Clem lots of questions but didn't really have time to listen to the answers because she would have to go off and take Peter to the loo, or give him some food, or pick him up if he'd fallen over, or shake something in his face to stop him crying. Then when she came back she'd usually forgotten what Clemmie was saying and it made her feel a little self-conscious to start all over again. So in the end she just kept her answers short.

It was nice later on when Liz was putting Peter to bed and Clemmie could just sit at the kitchen while her dad cooked. James was a much better cook than Jim. She'd never seen Jim cook at all. But even then Liz kept shouting things down from upstairs and he would say *Hang on a moment, Clemmie*, as he took a bottle or a bib or a baby thing up the stairs to her. *What were you saying?* he'd ask when he got back and she couldn't help but feel a tiny bit hurt that he couldn't remember. It was better after supper when Peter was asleep and the three of them sat in the living room watching telly and chatting.

Her dad and Liz were on the sofa drinking red wine and she was in the armchair not drinking anything. She rather wished she'd sat on the sofa first then he would have sat down next to her and would now be holding her hand like that. Or she could have curled up into him. She supposed she was too big for sitting on him these days even though she was the smallest girl in her class. She was just hoping for one little moment of intimacy with him. From where she was sitting she could pretend to be watching the telly when really she was watching them. He kept touching and stroking Liz and staring at her in a dreamy kind of way that Clemmie recognized. It was the way he used to stare at her sometimes and seeing it used on someone else made her feel wobbly and left out. Liz was his *At Home* now; she could see that. Although Clemmie would most definitely be telling her mum that Liz was not nearly as pretty as she was, she could see that it wasn't about prettiness to Jim and she felt suddenly hugely sorry for her mum, who seemed to be nothing to do with anything any more. She noticed that whenever she mentioned her mum, her dad would mumble something and then Liz and he would exchange a smile or a glance and it made her want to stop mentioning her mother at all. So there were several times

240

when she started talking but would have to fizzle out because most of her stories seemed to involve her mum.

Liz kept yawning and Clemmie hoped she would go to bed and then Clemmie could go and sit on the sofa next to James and he could hold her hand in that special way and rub her shoulder like that and look into her eyes with that very same expression. But Liz didn't go to bed, she just shut her eyes and leant on him in the snugly way Clemmie would have liked to with his arm around her, stroking her. Even when Clemmie was telling him her most exciting news about the finals of the gymnastics competition he just carried on stroking Liz. He was looking at Clemmie but he was loving Liz.

She hated Liz.

'How was the christening?' Sarah's mum asked the next day as they drove down the windy roads out of the village in their big family car. Clemmie could see Sarah's mum's face in the rear-view mirror smiling at her, her ringed fingers on the wheel, the shiny pale pink of her nail varnish. Clem was in the back in the middle, squashed between Sarah and Rob. No one else had wanted to sit there but it was just perfect for Clemmie, right in the middle of things. She had sat at the kitchen window looking out for them for the last couple of hours; they were late and she thought they might have forgotten about her.

'It was fine,' she said, looking out of the window. 'Peter didn't like it when the vicar dunked him in the water.'

It was a lovely sunny evening now but it had poured earlier at the church and the car made swishing sounds as they drove through puddles. Sarah was leaning out of the window letting her hand brush the hedgerows and Johnny, was in the front seat because Sarah's dad was already in Cornwall. She barely recognized Rob beside her; he'd dyed his hair blond and he sounded different.

'Oh, don't mind him, his balls have dropped,' Sarah said and nobody looked shocked.

'Least I've got them,' Rob replied, leaning across Clemmie. 'You're always going to be a *girl*.' He said it as though that was a real insult, a thought that had never occurred to Clemmie.

'What's wrong with girls, *Homo*?' The speed of Sarah's reply was most impressive to Clemmie. But then Sarah had had a lot of practice. Even Johnny, who was looking out of the other window, laughed at that. Maybe one day she and Peter would joke around like this. But it was hard to imagine.

'What's your dad's new wife like?' Sarah's mum asked Clemmie.

'She's nice.'

'Really?' Sarah's mum said as if Clemmie might be lying. She was watching Clemmie from the mirror with a naughty smile on her face. 'You're allowed to say she was horrid, you know. We won't tell.'

Clemmie laughed. 'No, she's nice.'

'You're such a sweetie, Lollipop.' Sarah's mum always called her lollipop. She felt honoured to have a nickname; it was like being part of the family.

'Jonts, I forgot to say,' Sarah's mum said. 'Sally rang. She wants to know if you can babysit the Friday we get back. I said I'd ask.'

'I bet he can,' Rob said, to which Johnny snuck his hand behind the seat and flicked Rob a V-sign. They were slightly scary to Clemmie, Sarah's brothers, in that intimidating teen-agery way.

'I'll babysit,' Sarah said. 'I need the money.' She was so effortlessly grown up; Clemmie felt she should be *needing* money as well.

'I'll give you five p,' Rob said.

'Go on then,' Sarah said, holding out her hand.

'Show us your tits first.'

'Pervert.'

'I'll give you six p,' Rob said.

'Fifty p,' Sarah said.

'Seven,' he said.

'No.'

Clemmie, in the middle, was looking from Sarah to Rob, as if she was watching a tricksy game of tennis. 'Eight.'

'Rob! Stop it!' Sarah's mum said but she didn't sound cross or anything. Clemmie could see her in the mirror and she had a smile on her face.

'Nine p.'

'No.'

'Final offer. Ten.'

'Oh, all right then,' Sarah said and hoiked up her top to reveal one flat little tit.

Rob glanced uninterestedly at his sister. 'Prostitute,' he said. They all fell about laughing, even Sarah. Clemmie joined in, feeling a warm familial happiness consuming her.

'What's a prostitute?' she asked and they all stopped laughing for a moment and then laughed even louder and she wasn't sure why. Johnny was the first to stop. He was looking at her with a kind smile twinkling from his bright green eyes.

'Shut up,' he said to his siblings, his eyes still on her. 'It doesn't matter, Clemmie. He's just stupid.' Then he went back to looking out of the window.

There were no lights. There were no villages. Dawn came and went, bringing nothing but more deserted landscape. So the next day passed sailing and sleeping and all the while Annie lay in the forecabin staring, seemingly in a trance. She could have been in another world altogether. Johnny went down to see her every now and then but she didn't respond to him. She lay there on her back looking up through the hatch at the patch of sky. He tried to get through to her: he'd sit down on the edge of the bed and talk about the wind and how he and Clem would be leaving soon, how she must take good care of herself and Smudge, how he didn't hold anything against her, how sorry he was for her difficulties, but the whole time she remained utterly expressionless, untouched by her surroundings. The boat would roll her here and there and she would let it, she put up no resistance. It was as if her soul had taken flight and vacated her body. He wasn't even sure she could hear him, she was so far removed. A couple of times he just sat there and said nothing.

He had sat like that for hours on his mother's bed near the end. And after all that, none of them were even in the room when she died. It was as if she had deliberately waited to be alone. And of course Johnny had always worried about whether she had panicked at the very end or whether she had been OK. The cats were there, that was some comfort. The cats had sat purring on her cold dead body for two whole days before the undertakers came to take her away. One of the undertakers had picked up one of the cats and his father had reacted so out of character that Johnny had been quite embarrassed. He'd never heard his father shout at anyone before. The man must have been used to it though, he didn't respond at all. But Johnny and Rob had had to hold their dad up, because his legs gave way and he howled like an animal as they carried her body out of the room.

Annie wanted to die, that was the difference. And her eyes weren't shut: they were open and staring. On one occasion he was surprised to see a tear fall down the side of her face and he had wiped it away and said, 'It's going to be all right, Annie.' But he didn't know that, it was just something you said because the thought of it not being all right was too much. At other moments he took her hand and pumped it a little in his own but not once did she respond to anything. Frank had got her heavily medicated.

Smudge was evidently accustomed to her mother in this state. She would go and lie with Annie's limp body, hugging her tight, singing her songs or playing cards on her tummy, but she would soon get bored or distracted and would come out on deck to play or just to sit with Johnny holding his hand. He could feel her tiny paw in his. It was as if she knew that he was going too. Half of him was already gone; his salvation lay on that shore. Once she pressed her lips to his hand and whispered, 'I love you, Johnny,' and his heart had squeezed a little, but he'd looked away because he too would be deserting her the moment that he could. It was in the afternoon of the following day when Johnny saw the village. The other three were all looking down at a great gutted fish. Frank had caught a tuna and had hauled it up on to the deck. It was a baby, with a round silver belly and a beautiful sheen to its skin. It thrashed about on the cockpit sole and Frank had bashed it hard on the head with a block of wood and they all stood there watching it as it lay there stunned and bleeding, its red pain washing down on to the transom and into the water. He killed it calmly and methodically, gutting it efficiently with those great bear hands of his.

Johnny had looked up and seen the smoke rising from the hills. For a moment he couldn't believe his eyes, a part of him had really begun to believe that there was nothing left, civilization had upped and gone. Slowly he stood up, picked up the binoculars and focused in as the boat rounded the bay. He stepped up on to the deck for a better view.

'Yeeeees!' he'd cried and everyone had looked up at him. 'There's a village!'

He jumped with joy. He ran down the deck, leaping and shouting. Smudge trailed him, trotting behind him, not quite sure what was the cause of such merriment but wanting to join in. She jumped up and down too. Frank stood up and he too wandered down the deck, holding on to the lifelines, his eyes following Johnny's. Johnny leapt back down into the cockpit and grabbed the helm from Clem, altering course, heading for land. He wrapped his arm around her and pulled her to him.

'Life!' he kept crying. 'Oh my God! There's human life!' The weight that had been bearing down on his shoulders for so long was suddenly lifted. He felt like a free man. Salvation was here. She let him lift her off the ground, laughing at his wildness. She'd not seen him like this before.

'Human life!' Smudge echoed, jumping down into the cockpit, hugging Clem. 'Where are we going, Johnny?'

He stopped and looked down at her, his smile briefly faltering. 'Clem and I have to get on, Smudge. We have to get on.'

'Get on what?' she asked, not understanding at all.

'We have to get on with our honeymoon,' Johnny said, locking eyes with Clem. Somehow, what with one thing and another, they had both forgotten that this was their honeymoon. Then he picked up the binoculars again and focused in on their new life before disappearing below deck to try and make sense of the rudimentary chart, to see whether this village was marked. He felt such lightness of being, his spirits soared. If it wasn't bad luck, he would have whistled. Instead he began to sing lustily, that same old Beatles song about those words of kindness lingering on, but he couldn't remember the rest of it.

Out of habit he put the kettle on. This would be their final cup of tea. Yes, he would make everyone sweet tea. He could be forgiving and magnanimous now that freedom beckoned. He looked about the saloon making a note of all their belongings; it would only take two minutes to pack up their things. He hummed merrily as he traced the crude outline of the coast on the chart with his forefinger. Then he heard it, very faintly: singing from the forepeak. He stopped in his tracks, just as he had on that very first night on the rocks, drawn in by the haunting sound. She was singing the same song he had been. The others were oblivious to it; he could hear them chatting in the cockpit, Smudge complaining about something.

Slowly Johnny stood up, pushing away the chart. He wanted to hear her better. He quietly crossed the saloon and stood by the door to listen. Even through the mists of her misery she could sing like an angel. She sang slowly and stiltedly, the music almost deconstructed, each note hit perfectly and yet the song almost unrecognizable.

He pressed his ear against the door. He needed to hear more. Although the kettle began to scream from the hob, it didn't disturb her singing. She sang of dead love and eyes that showed nothing.

He would bring her sweet tea. He went to the galley and poured the boiling water into the aluminium pot, stirring the bags and the sugar all in one. He made her a cup and brought it back to the door. He turned the handle and gently pushed it open, stepping in to the forecabin. He could see her lying there at a slight angle, the wrong way round, her head towards the bow, still staring straight up through the hatch, just as she had been when he had last seen her, in some holy communion with the sky, undisturbed by his presence. He closed the door behind him.

'Annie,' he said and he thought she paused a little in her singing. 'I've brought you some tea. There's a village coming up.' She did pause then. Very slowly she blinked and turned her head and looked at him as if she had no idea who he was. Her skin was deathly pale, her eyes transparent pools, her pale lips mouthing lyrics.

'Here,' he said, offering the tea, but she didn't take it. 'Let me help.' He put the cup in the holder and gently lifted her up, propping her up with pillows. She offered no resistance. He sat beside her and fed her the tea.

'Clem and I are going, Annie. You must get better for Smudge. You must.' He tucked some of her hair behind her ears in a feeble attempt at normality. The tea seemed to spill right through her, its hot sweetness loosening something: the tears began to pour from her eyes. She didn't make another sound, nor did she wipe her eyes. She just turned away from him and tucked herself into the hull. He didn't know what he had expected but he felt bad leaving her like this. She made him feel treacherous. Yet he had to. He paused, his hand resting on her side; then he left her.

The village was small, twenty houses or so. There was a café right on the water's edge built of painted red wood with vines hanging from the beams. To Johnny, looking through the binoculars, it was the most wonderful place he had ever seen. There was a road going up into the mountains. There would be people with cars, lifts out of here, options. A small group of men had gathered on the shore to watch the *Little Utopia* sail in.

They dropped the anchor fifty yards out and got themselves ready to go ashore. It felt peculiar preparing for departure, for civilization, getting washed and clothed, brushing hair and teeth, putting shoes on their feet. They looked and felt like strangers to each other. Smudge had dressed up too as if she was coming with them. She was wearing a dress beneath her Captain Hook coat and had put on a pair of socks to go ashore in because she couldn't find her shoes. She sat in the saloon watching them pack and when she began to cry Frank came and took her up on deck.

Johnny chucked his few belongings into the red sail bag, Clem neatly rolling up the prayer mat and folding up the sleeping bags and stuffing them in, bending over to pick up a hair clip, suddenly remembering her flannel. She was looking for all her matchboxes with her collections of beach debris to put in the side panels, slipping pebbles into various pockets and compartments before going through to say goodbye to Annie. There was a certain quiet sadness in the air. Now that they were leaving Johnny allowed himself to indulge in a fondness for the tubby old bucket of a boat and the peculiar adventure they had had in it, accompanied all the while by his heart singing with delight.

They left Annie in the boat and the four of them climbed down into the tender and despite the corks plugging up the holes the water still seeped in. Johnny rowed towards the shore; he felt as strong as an ox, as if he could row for ever. Though his eyes were fixed on the retreating spectacle of the *Little Utopia* the rest of him was concentrated on the land over his shoulder. Clem sat in front of him. She was so brown and her hair bleached so fair, she appeared to have been dunked in the sunshine. She had the red sail bag in her lap and was holding Smudge's hand, trying to cheer her up, saying how they would all meet up again, maybe in Africa. Smudge did not seem cheered by this, she did not want to go to Africa, she wanted to stay here with them. She was suddenly inconsolable at the prospect of their departure and Clem hugged her and she started crying too and Johnny felt bad for not breaking it more gently.

The café was set slightly in the cliff, raised from the beach, in the shade of several trees. There were five or six wooden tables and benches with a bar running along one side and the obligatory portrait of Atatürk hanging on the wall. They were robustly welcomed by the large proprietor with much gesticulating and hand-crushing and squeezing of Smudge's cheeks; the smell of frying garlic and fish almost overwhelmed them. He helped them up the rocky steps and into the bar towards a table. Frank made it clear he wasn't staying but needed to find a few provisions while Johnny went straight to the bar to try and organize a lift. The barman, without being asked, got out several long, tall glasses and a bottle of raki, gesturing for Johnny to go and sit down with Clem and Smudge at a table. Johnny looked about the place. Men seemed to have appeared from every cranny and the other tables were filling up as if their arrival was a curiosity, an excuse to celebrate. Two small boys were staring at Smudge. He hadn't seen her with other children before; she was surprisingly shy, clutching Gilla to her chest as if they might nick him off her. He let his eyes survey the room – there was so much more to take in on land, there were clangings going on in the kitchen and savoury cooking smells in the air and so many close-up things in the room. It was all so intense. His senses would need time to adjust to the immediacy of land life.

He moved over to talk to a young lad with bad skin and a T-shirt that said *Banana Cool* on the front. The café swayed about him as he went; his body not yet in harmony with the land. The boy was probably the same age as he was but seemed much younger. Johnny gesticulated and pointed, mimed driving a car, repeating the word 'Datca' and tried as hard as he could to negotiate a lift out of there. The boy kept pointing at the *Little Utopia* repeating something until Johnny eventually worked out that he was trying to tell him that it would be much quicker to go by boat. Johnny laughed and shook his head. *No way, Banana Cool.* The boy shrugged and said his brother could give him a lift to Datca this afternoon, if he really wanted, dismissing Johnny's offer of lira. Johnny grabbed the boy's hand and shook it heartily, sealing the deal. They were sorted, tthey were on their way! They had come to the right place.

He strolled merrily back over to the table where Frank was involved in a conversation with some of the Turks on the adjacent table. The barman had brought the raki over and was pouring out three generous glasses. Clem sat there watching him pour it, her eyes hidden by shades, Smudge sitting close at her side, her eyes watching the boys.

'Come on, Johnny,' Frank said. 'One for the road!' Smudge got up cautiously to go and investigate where the boys had disappeared to.

He hadn't planned on celebrating their departure but this seemed right, a farewell drink, a proper goodbye to their adventure. How apt that the beverage should be raki – the circle of their journey on the *Little Utopia* was being completed. It seemed such a very long time ago that first night in the thunderstorm, Clem and he scared for their lives, stumbling about on the rocks. He sat down, picked up a glass and chinked it against Frank's.

'To thunderstorms,' he said.

'To thunderstorms,' both Frank and Clem echoed.

The raki burnt pleasantly down his throat.

'They say the mountain road is slow and dangerous,' Frank said. 'By sea it's only a hundred odd miles round the headland, you know...'

Johnny knew this. He didn't care. He smiled and raised his glass to *Banana Cool* over there at the bar. 'Ah well, we're all sorted now.' He stretched out his legs and let the sounds of the bar wash around his head: plates landing on tables, mint tea being stirred, a gabble of Turkish. It sounded heavenly to his ears. The next stage of their adventure was about to begin. He knocked back some more firewater.

Over Frank's shoulder, he caught sight of the boat rocking about in the waves and he thought of Annie lying there, staring or sleeping, and he wondered whether he would always think of her that way: deadened and glazy-eyed, or whether he would think of her under that tree with the cicadas chirruping around them, drinking water from the bottle, taking his hand and placing it on her breast. He looked over at Smudge in her funny dress and socks. She was playing with the boys, hanging upside down from the wooden railing. He would miss her. What a fascinating life she was having and would continue to have, once Annie was well again, back on her medication; Smudge's childhood was exactly what he'd wish for his own children. He looked at Clem – she too was looking over at the boat with nostalgia in her eyes.

As he crossed the room to go to the gents, the bar seemed to sway a little more and this time he couldn't entirely blame his sea legs. He was pretty pissed. So was Frank. When he returned to the table, Frank was holding court. He was talking about where the *Little Utopia* would be going after Turkey – Syria, Lebanon, round to Africa, to Egypt; he wanted Smudge to see the empire of Alexander the Great, the greatest general that ever lived. One of the old men muttered something about Atatürk and some of the men laughed. Frank talked about Libya and Morocco and how eventually they would one day get to Tangiers and back to Spain and Johnny thought that perhaps, one day, they'd cross paths again, maybe in Africa, or some other continent. As the bottle of raki was coming to an end *Banana Cool* appeared at the table with an even spottier version of himself. Johnny leapt up and shook the brothers' hands heartily. They were ready to head off to Datca. The moment had come.

'Time to go!' Johnny said, standing up, fumbling about in his pockets for some money for the raki. 'Clem, we're off.'

She was still seated, looking down at the red sail bag on her lap. 'But, Johnny,' she said. 'If it's quicker and easier by boat I think we should just go on the boat.'

Johnny held her eye. 'But that's not the plan, Clem,' he said.

'We've got wind now,' she said. There was a nervousness in her eye. Smudge had appeared at Clem's side and was tugging at her sleeve.

'Yes, yes, please stay with us, please stay.'

Johnny didn't look at the others at all. He stared at Clem, unable to fathom how she could betray him like that when she knew how badly he needed to get off the boat, how claustrophobic he had become, how their trip had run its course. 'Well, it's all fixed now. We're going by car,' he said, reaching to take the bag out of her hands. He had always decided what they were going to do, where they were going to go, and she had always willingly followed. That was just the way it worked.

'I don't want to,' she said. 'Why can't I meet you in Datca?'

Johnny stood there, frozen to the spot, quite astonished by what she had just said – the idea that they might split up even for a day. He became suddenly aware of everyone in the bar watching them, *Banana Cool* and his brother hovering at his side. He stood and waited for her to get up until his pride could take it no longer. He turned and walked out of the restaurant, tripping fast down the steps. He walked along the beach as fast as he could, his feet making squeaking noises in the fine sand. He didn't turn back and when he got to the privacy of some rocks he slid down into the shade, muttering obscenities under his breath. It was Frank. It was fucking Frank. She didn't want to leave *him*. She had chosen Frank over him. He hated her. He hated Frank. He fucking despised the pair of them. He rolled himself a cigarette but his hands were shaking with anger. He tore the roach from the Rizla packet as he always did, rammed it into the end and lit the fag and he sat there sucking in the bitter smoke, blowing it out like a missile in a line of fire towards the ugly tub of a boat out there in the water. He hung his head and stared at the sand as if the answers might lie there. A shadow darkened the sand and he looked up.

Clem was standing there, holding her shoes in one hand. She was out of breath: she'd been running. Johnny looked away from her, glad she was upset. She *should* be upset: she had done wrong. 'I'm sorry, Johnny,' she said and slowly she slid down the rock and sat at his side. There was nothing to see but sea, sky and the boat, so they both looked out and waited while she got her breath back. Even now when he hated her like this he couldn't help but want her. He was totally at her mercy.

'What's happening to us, Clem?' he said.

'I don't know,' she said, shaking her head as if she had no idea.

'Is this about *him*?'

She kept her eyes on the sunlight bouncing off the water. 'It's not just him,' she said sadly, unaccustomed to being the cause of such cruelty. 'It's Smudge too. And Annie.'

But he wasn't interested in Smudge and Annie. 'Are you in love with him?' he asked and she left a pause long enough for it to speak volumes and for his stomach to curl up into a ball.

'Oh, Johnny, it's not about that,' she said eventually, irritated because he was always trying to put everything into boxes when surely if they'd learnt anything on this trip it was about taking things out of boxes.

'What is it about then?'

She shook her head, trying to find the right words. It was about not letting people down in life, not deserting them when they needed you most, not when their mother or wife was lying comatose in bed; it wasn't right to be there one moment and gone the next. No warning. It just wasn't fair. People couldn't be abandoned like that. They had to give Smudge warning. It *was* about Frank too, of course it was. Maybe she did love him, but it wasn't how Johnny thought, it wasn't in a sordid, exclusive kind of way. They owed him some loyalty for his kindness. But she didn't say any of these things to Johnny. She didn't know how to explain herself any more. He wouldn't understand. Recently she had found herself tiptoeing around his feelings; she had to censor herself and the things she said. She had to keep her thoughts locked up. Sometimes, like now, it felt as if she was being smothered by him. She tucked her knees up to her chest and hugged herself tightly.

Johnny looked beyond her out to sea, at the white diamonds of shining light, almost deliberately blinding himself. He understood that this was one of those pivotal moments that needed acknowledging; the rest of life would hang on it.

'OK, you win,' he said. 'But we leave at Datca.'

When they returned to the boat, all was quiet from the fore-peak. Johnny went below deck and dropped the bag on the saloon seat and looked about at the clutter: the books, the sextant, the hairbrush and clips strewn about the place, the coffee cups in the sink, the utter familiarity of it all. He felt like a criminal returning to the scene of the crime. The other Johnny, the one who made the right decisions, the one who Clem adored, the one without self-doubt, was up in *Banana Cool*'s car somewhere in the mountains on a bumpy road. He'd got the hell out of here. Whereas this Johnny was moving to the rhythm of a different drum – Frank's drum which Clem seemed bound to follow. This Johnny was at Frank's mercy for a little longer, stuck on the *Little Utopia* for another twenty-four hours.

When he pushed open the bathroom door and looked in on Annie, his heart lifted a little. She was sitting upright, her legs crossed, her eyes open, and when she saw him, she looked surprised. He thought the corners of her mouth twitched a little as if she was trying to smile. He had not deserted her after all, that's what her face said. He remembered suddenly how much he had loved to see her face transform with happiness, how her eyes would crease up and the light would fill her. There was just a faint glimmer of that, but at least he could see that she was still connected to the source. He looked away and left, shutting the door behind him. *I'm going, Annie, but just not today.*

He stood in the galley looking around him. Up on deck he could see Frank through the Perspex windows on his knees scrubbing, whistling as he worked. Clem was unperturbed by this; she seemed to have forgotten all about bad luck and omens; it seemed that there was nothing that Frank could do that would meet with her disapproval. She and Smudge were tidying up the decks as if everything was just perfectly normal, she was behaving as if she belonged here, as if they were never going to leave. Smudge was coiling the ropes, completely wrongly, singing as she worked. It was only Johnny and Annie whose hearts had sunk and shrunk; the rest of them were whistling and merrily going about their businesses without a care in the world. He took a deep breath, sat down on the saloon seat and rubbed his head. He had no choice but to accept it. He could see the sense in sailing the last leg and not taking the road. He had been stubborn and had lost the battle. Of course he could put up with Frank for another day, knowing that from

Datca they would take a bus east, get to Cappadocia or Göreme and then hitch onwards. It was only twenty-four hours.

They left in the late afternoon, a gentle wind blowing on the beam. Johnny didn't talk; he had nothing to say. He helmed the boat, glad that everyone was in their own private worlds, snoozing, reading and drinking coffee as the boat slipped through the water, no one expecting anything of him but to sail. Johnny listened as Frank and Clem talked of Annie, how Frank was lessening the sedatives, how he'd order more drugs, get them delivered to various Postes Restantes along the way. He had no doubt she was getting better; it usually took about a fortnight. All the while as they talked, Johnny sailed the boat, getting the most out of every breath of wind, never letting the sail luff, tacking up the coast, getting on with business of getting to Datca. This wouldn't take long. At some stage Clem got up and took her sketch book down to the bows and Frank immersed himself in a book.

Fifty miles later, the moon had risen and was shining silver streaks on to the water, the boat doing a steady four knots in the gentle breeze, Johnny left Frank and Clem for a moment as he went down below deck to try and sort out the spinnaker which had jammed in the forepeak locker. He knocked gently before going in, expecting to find Annie sleeping like Frank had said. Instead, she was still sitting cross-legged, her hands curled together in her lap, looking up through the open hatch, a light spray from the waves coming in. She was covered in a watery ethereal light.

'Sorry, Annie, I thought you'd be sleeping. I need to get to the locker.'

Slowly she dragged her eyes away from the hatch and looked at him; underneath the layers of unhappiness she was definitely more present. She even moved out of his way a little so that he could crawl across the bed and open the locker. He talked to her as he did so, not expecting a reply. 'We probably won't even use it but I want to be prepared. When we round the headland we should get a nice run on the way in to Datca…'

As he sat back up, he felt something hard pressing into his knees. He felt underneath and pulled out a couple of yellow and red pills. He held them out in his hand towards Annie and she took them from him. He watched her slip her hand behind her back and push them underneath the mattress, flashing a glance at the door.

'What are you saving them for?' he asked. She looked at him as if she had been found out. Then she opened her mouth as if to say something but the words wouldn't come out, it seemed like too much effort. Johnny moved closer to her.

'What are you saying?' he said.

'I… want…' Her voice was weak, almost inaudible. He leant in; he could feel her breath on his cheek, but the words wouldn't come.

'You want *what*, Annie?'

'I want to die,' she whispered. She looked away, back out of the hatch, her eyes two wells of sadness. He took her hand in his and smoothed it with his thumb.

'Don't say that, Annie. Think of Smudge.'

Oh God, he thought selfishly. *Please get better. We're leaving you. You have to get better.*

'Smudge.' She seemed to smile a little but in a deadened kind of a way, still staring up at the moon. 'Smudge is *all* I think about.'

Something about the way she said it scared him. 'Annie,' he said, moving forward, cupping her chin with his fingers, forcing her her head to face him. 'What are you planning? You leave Smudge out of this…'

She held his gaze. 'You didn't even look in the cabinet, I told you to look...' she whispered. There was no accusation in it, just a deep weariness. Then she lay back down on the mattress, turning her back on him and curling up into the foetal position.

He paused for a moment, looking at that soft, downy hair on the back of her neck, then slowly he got off the bed and turned on the heads light. He got down on his knees and opened the cabinet doors. He had no idea what he was looking for. He couldn't see properly. He switched on the little light above the basin. The cabinet was full of medicines and plastic bottles: shampoos and sun-block, various lotions and potions. He pulled out the medicine tin and the other locked one. He was pretty sure it was full of Annie's medicines; Frank only kept it locked to protect her from harming herself. He felt around towards the back but there was nothing there. He crouched down as low as he could and peered in. At the very back he could see a red fabric pressed against the hull of the boat behind the plywood. He reached in and felt the sides. It was a book of some sort. It was wedged in, in a fixed position. He got his fingers around the edge and pulled it out and stepped back holding it under the basin light.

It was just an old book with faded gold lettering on the spine: *Gulliver's Travels*. He opened it and flicked through the pages but there was nothing of any interest.

Then right at the back of the book he saw what she had wanted him to see. And as the sickness rose from his stomach, the thought struck him how very nearly he had got away today – he and Clem – they had so very nearly made it.

10

LIGHTS GOING OUT

JOHNNY LIKED IT when the others were all out, when he had the whole house to himself. His dad and Rob had gone to Sarah's school play to try and pretend that life was carrying on as normal while his mum was dying upstairs.

Johnny sat downstairs and watched the snooker while the guinea-pigs flung themselves around the floorboards like they were on a skating rink. They were the only beings in the house that weren't pretending; they just carried on doing what they always had – skating and making more guinea pigs. He kept finding himself staring out at the garden; he'd borrowed a couple of hundred quid off his dad and bought a load of old Lasers and Wayfarers from a sailing school in Datchet and they were strewn about on the grass waiting to be repaired. He should have been sanding them down right now and repairing them but he had found it hard to do anything recently. The four of them were tiptoeing around in a twilight world of sickness.

After a while he made two cups of tea and took them upstairs. He knew her cup was just symbolic, she never drank any but she always said *yes please* – it was part of the whole pretence, she was in on it. Nobody wanted to mention what was really going on, everyone was still talking about getting better and which pills to pop and what a nice day it was. He thought that suffering seemed to separate a family rather than unite it. Or perhaps it was just that suffering was a private affair.

He pushed open their bedroom door and the now-familiar scent of illness hit him; it seemed to have infused everything with its clinical, musty odour, a mixture of medicine cabinet and clothes left in the dryer too long.

She was motionless and his heart skipped a beat as it always did when she was sleeping. He'd overheard the nurse telling his father that she might only have another month, but no one really knew. No one knew anything; they were all totally out of control of the situation pretending not to be. He moved towards the end of the bed and stood quite still until he saw the slow, unsteady rise and fall of her chest. She was breathing. He breathed too. She looked calm, facing away from the window, her face thin and pale, her hands resting at her sides, palms open.

Outside was a bright, sunny day but the curtains were half drawn. They whooshed out a little as a breeze blew through the window and he could see the shimmering leaves outside on the trees. It was a good sailing day. She would have liked it if things were different.

He put her cup down on the bedside table by the alarm clock which ticked and tocked too loudly. He sat himself down on the old leather chair beside the bed and it too breathed out as if it had been waiting to be sat on. It was a good place to sit. He could see the trees outside and at the same time see her, safe in the knowledge that he wasn't going to miss anything should anything happen. Although he wasn't sure that he wanted to be there when she actually went. He wasn't sure he'd be able to handle that. The bed was high and her body was at his eye level and he watched the gentle upping and downing of her tiny frame. The bed had a wooden back and a tall wooden plank at the other end. It was tomblike the way it swallowed her up. It had been his grandmother's bed and one day it would be Sarah's – generations of women had been born in it, made babies in it, given birth in it and now she was dying in it. Why should the bed keep surviving and not her?

He couldn't cope with the ticking of the clock, the horrible rapid countdown to the inevitable. He got up and put it in one of the drawers – what did his mother need a ticking clock for – Time was meaningless now. He looked around the room at the army of pills stacked along the mantelpiece, half-empty glasses of water, cotton wool, flannels: ill-person things. The bowl of fruit on the little table was slowly disintegrating, he'd noticed it change day by day, the subtle smell of decay increasing, and he had begun to think that they were inextricably linked, his mother and the rotting fruit. He should have thrown it out or someone should have, but it felt like a callous thing to do, to dispose of something just because it was no longer fresh and ripe. *She* would have thrown it out; she wasn't sentimental in any way. There were so many things that weren't getting done now that she was lying here. All those little things – he wasn't sure what they were exactly, only that the cumulative effect of them *not* being done had made the house seem like a different space. All the order had gone. There was no longer structure, or clarity, or surprises. And they wouldn't be coming back.

Staring out at the leaves he suddenly felt wildly helpless. He could feel the sadness that had been sitting inside him expanding at such a rate, growing and growing, filling him up until he thought he might burst. His eyes began to sting with tears.

'Hey,' she whispered, her voice dry and husky.

'Mum, you're awake,' he said, quickly wiping his eyes, leaning forward, moving close to her. Her mouth was dry again. Her mouth was always dry. He took a piece of cotton wool and dipped it into the water and dabbed it around her mouth the way the nurse did. She licked at it thirstily then laid her head back down as if the effort of drinking had exhausted her.

'Try not be too sad, darling,' she said.

'I'm not,' he said with the stupid false cheer that they were all using with her.

They stared at each other; words were inadequate and they both knew it. 'You will look after Dad, won't you?'

'Don't say that.' Suddenly he could do nothing about the tears; they began to fall freely down his cheeks.

'Oh love...' she said soothingly trying to make him feel better, squeezing his hand in hers. He took a deep, juddering breath, trying to contain himself but he just couldn't. 'I don't think I can bear it, Mum, without you.'

'Jonts,' she whispered and he could feel the tight grip of her thin, cool hand. 'My brave, kind boy, you've got your whole life ahead of you! You must live it to the full!' It was hard for her to speak; her mouth had dried up again. She closed her heavy lids and he saw a tear fall sideways down her temple. 'You have to be a man now, my love.'

'Yes,' he said, trying so hard to be a man. But then he couldn't help himself, he cried out like a little boy. 'Don't die, Mum!'

He hung his head forwards, sobbing openly, pressed his face to hers, her hand still gripping his. 'I'll live on in you, darling,' she whispered.

'Don't die, Mum. Please don't die,' He laid his head against her chest and his tears fell in streams on to the thin cotton of her nightdress.

'My love,' she said, stroking his hair, waiting for his sobs to cease. 'We'll meet again one day. I promise.'

'We won't.'

He tried to pull himself together. He had to be stronger. He took a deep breath and sat back. Outside birds were singing and the faint chimes of an ice-cream van could be heard. The world was just carrying on. Slowly he felt the sadness subsiding a little as if the tears had emptied some out. He looked at his mother's tired, gaunt face and dabbed her lips again, glad of something to do. She was watching him, a strange expression on her face, a look he hadn't seen before in her eye, her blinks slow and heavy. 'Do you want something?' he said. She managed to shake her head without moving. She was trying to tell him something. 'What is it, Mum?'

But she didn't say anything. He leant in. 'Are you scared?' he asked in a whisper.

She bit her lip and she gave the faintest of nods. 'I am, Jonts. I'm scared.'

And he kissed her hand, her cool hand with the loose rings on it and he didn't let go until she had drifted back to sleep.

Clem lay on the saloon bed with Smudge sound asleep beside her. She could hear Johnny up on deck changing the sails, the squeaks and thumps and rumblings of sailing. He had insisted she sleep down here with Smudge. But she couldn't sleep; her head was whirling, her thoughts tacking all the time but getting nowhere, replaying events from earlier in the day in her mind over and over until she didn't know what she felt at all. In the late afternoon when she had gone down to the bows of the boat to sketch, she had passed the open hatch and caught sight of Annie sleeping peacefully down below in the forepeak, her bandaged wrist limp by her face, the bandage greying and frayed, the dried blood a rusty brown. She'd gone on and sat herself down on the anchor hatch and settled down to draw, looking about at the vista, trying to decide what she wanted to capture: the mast with the sail above billowing out in the wind, or Annie sleeping in the forecabin, or Johnny and Frank in the heeling cockpit, Johnny as ever looking up at the sails or out at the horizon, Frank with his nose in a book. She had decided on the sail, the view directly above, and had opened up her pencil case and begun to sharpen her pencils, watching the shavings drop into the white surf of the bows. A while later Frank had popped his head up through the fore-peak hatch with a cup of sweet tea and passed it to her. 'Hi,' he'd said. 'Let's see your picture!' She had turned the opened sketch pad round so he could see. She was rather pleased with it, the blue of the sky, the great white sail, the shadows where it was luffing a little at the top – Johnny wouldn't have liked that but she'd wanted to make the point that imperfection was part of life. Frank had held it out smiling and nodding, impressed with her work.

'You're seriously good, Clem. Have you thought of art school?' She'd laughed and hadn't responded but she *had* thought of art school actually, before they got married, before she realised that a regimented sort of a life wouldn't really be possible with Johnny. He needed to be on the move. When Frank handed back the sketch, his hand had touched hers, his fingers stealing around her own. 'I nearly lost you back there, Clemency,' he'd said quietly and she'd felt her heart contract a little, his proximity suddenly making her breathless. She'd looked over at Johnny at the helm, his focus on the sails. She hoped Annie was still sleeping and couldn't hear him. 'I don't want that to happen again,' he'd said, his eyes glued to hers, intense and serious and suddenly she hadn't cared whether Annie was listening or not. "I want you, Clem,' he'd said. 'But you know that.' The way he spoke excited her; she'd felt her mouth watering, her breath quickening, that same electric current running through her body. Then, because she felt treacherous and could feel Johnny watching her, she'd pretended to sketch again. 'I promised we'd leave at Datca,' she'd whispered, flashing him a look. He'd nodded and slowly turned away from her, looking out to sea, leaning his weight forward on to his elbows, his palms flat along the deck. He'd sighed and smiled at her. 'It's your decision, Clem. You need to make the decision that is best for you and for everyone around you. Feel it, your gut. You'll know what to do.'

So now she lay there trying to listen to her gut, to make the right decision for herself and for everyone around her. But whichever way she looked at it she couldn't see the right decision and it never worked for *everyone*. Her gut was lurching one way and then the other. Johnny would never be persuaded to stay on this boat; she knew that ultimately it boiled down to a decision between Johnny or Frank. Johnny was a given and yet her thoughts kept going in one direction, *I want you, Clem,* to that warm feeling, those sexual stirrings Frank could trigger with a look or a comment. She had felt a melting in her core, a visceral desire for him that was impossible to ignore. Ever since the night they had all made love in the cockpit, she'd not been near either of them physically. It would be different now if she were to make love with Frank. It would be different with Johnny too because she *did* have feelings for Frank now – big feelings, she could see that; there was no point in denying it and the feelings didn't feel like things that should be covered up: they felt pure and good. Johnny would never understand this. He'd barely said a word since they'd come back on board, since he'd gone down to fix the spinnaker. He'd come back out to the cockpit, no longer bothered about putting it up at all, and had told them to go down and get some kip; he wanted to sail the boat alone. Then he had held her back as she stepped on to the companionway step, gripping her arm, whispering urgently in her ear: 'You sleep with Smudge,' as an order, as if he was worried that she might have slept with Frank. She was tired of his jealousy. She wished lovers could be entirely truthful to each other – the real truth, all the doubts and fears as well as all the love. She could say anything to Frank – anything at all, without fear of judgement. Perhaps that was real love. Perhaps she and Johnny had married too young. Everyone had thought they were too young to get married, too young to be feeling such adult things – maybe they were right. She wished they could all live together – the four of them could be lovers. Now that she was growing and learning she knew that it was perfectly possible to love two people at once; living with several lovers should be normal. Her life had been so sheltered prior to this. She had been so conditioned by society, just like everyone else.

How these thought made her head ache. But she must have dozed off for at some point she woke with the feeling that the boat had stopped, the water was sloshing against the hull and she could hear the flapping of the sails. He was taking a long time changing tack, or perhaps the foresail was caught on the stay. Then, presently, the boat moved off again but heeling over now, on a new tack, landing Smudge's weight almost directly on top of her, and she sat up and looked out at the dark sky through the scuffed Perspex window. She untwined Smudge's arm from around her waist and got up off the saloon seat and went to the galley. She heated up the coffee, opened the cockpit doors and went out.

'Johnny?' she said, blinking as her eyes adjusted. 'I've got you some coffee.' He loomed forward out of the darkness; he was so still he had been indistinguishable from the night itself, the silver glow of the moon coating everything alike. But now she could see him clearly and he looked at her strangely; there was something different about him. Or maybe it was her.

'I can take over if you want to get some rest,' she said. 'You must be tired.'

'I'll be fine.'

He still hadn't forgiven her for making them get back on the boat. He knew her so well. He knew that she loved Frank before she knew it herself; his jealousy was justified. 'Johnny?' she said, moving towards him, looking at his hair; it was wet and shiny. 'Has it been raining?'

He moved slightly away from her, running a hand through his hair.

'I washed it,' he said. 'I got some paint in it.' She looked at him curiously and passed him the coffee and sat down on the dry portside seat, feeling the distance yawning between them. He was lying. She held her tongue; she wasn't going to start accusing him of things when her own guilt was so prevalent. It was one thing *her* having secrets from *him* – she could control that; but she didn't like this, not knowing what was going on in his mind. Perhaps he felt the same about Annie as she was beginning to feel about Frank. It made her feel uncomfortable. She looked back at the horizon. The wind had shifted, or the boat had. She leant over and peered at the compass. 'Have we changed course?' she asked looking carefully round the 360 degrees, unable to spot any land.

'Yes,' he said.

'Are we still heading for Datca?'

'Yes. Just making the most of the wind, going out to sea before heading in,' he said in a quiet voice, not looking at her. 'It might take a little longer.'

She was glad for it She didn't have to make any decisions right now. She would go along with Johnny's decisions for the moment, just as she always had. He didn't say anything else and she knew there were things he wasn't telling her. She wondered when they both started having secrets from each other and whether this was the beginning of the end. It frightened her that thought: the end. She couldn't imagine a life without Johnny in it. The prospect filled her with panic. They were inseparable, like trees grown together, their roots entangled. She suddenly wished for things to be how they were before they had stepped on to this boat. She wanted everything fixed and secure again. She wanted certainty. She reached out for his hand on the tiller. His was cool. He took hers, covering it with his own. Even if their hearts and minds were hiding things, their hands spoke a different language. Her fingers clutched on to his for dear life and his pressed hers hard into the warm wood of the tiller and she wanted to stay like that for ever, squeezed between the wood and him. They sat there for a long time, listening to the boat going through the water, the wind in the sails, the spray hitting the deck, their hands entwined.

'You were right, by the way,' he said eventually.

'Right about what?'

'About the signs.'

'What signs?'

'I should have listened to you,' he said. 'Even that song about the bad moon rising. The green shirt, leaving port on a Friday, the whistling… we should never ever have come on to this boat.'

She stared at him. That all seemed like such a long time ago now. So much had happened since then, she'd forgotten all about signs. *But you don't believe in signs, Johnny*, she wanted to say and then it struck her that maybe she was wrong. Maybe he had changed without her noticing. Perhaps they'd been changing in opposite ways.

Later, she got up and went back down below deck to sleep and Johnny watched her go. He saw the way she turned around as she shut the cockpit doors, the way she looked at him, trying to pretend that everything was all right. She seemed unfamiliar to him. Her dark eyes had shadows the size of saucers underneath them. He saw then how incredibly unhappy she was. But there was nothing he could do about that now. They were all unhappy.

He was glad to be on his own, just him and that sickness in his stomach. He was wide awake. He didn't think he'd ever be able to sleep again. He sailed through the night, looking up at the stars, the empty horizon, the moonlight on the sails. Every so often he glanced down at the compass. The wind was almost on the nose now, still gentle and light, but it felt faster close hauling. He reckoned they were doing a steady three knots. He'd checked the chart; he'd stay on this tack, out into the open sea, and let the wind be his guide. The elements would lead him. The waning moon was in its old guise and he was glad of that: he preferred it white. Earlier, alone at the helm, when he saw it rise out of the darkness, he had known it was an omen. He had watched amazed as it slipped over the horizon, huge and red, like a planet set on a collision course with Earth, like the eye of some monstrous beast on his back. It had spoken to him, that big, bad, blood-red moon – it had told him that it was time for action.

When Clem awoke, it was just before first light. She was still lying on the saloon seat with Smudge head to toe. Without moving she watched the action in the sky swinging about over the cockpit: the day waking up. The yawn of dawn seemed to take for ever, the stretch between first light and the sun's actual appearance was a matter of hours rather than minutes. The sun didn't care what was going on, what decisions had to be made, what towns had to be reached. It was in no hurry. She watched the stars dwindling and the moon slip down the sky. She could see Johnny's shoulder, snatches of him getting up every now and then to see to the sails. She'd watched as he came down and made himself some coffee. His eyes were bloodshot; he'd been at the helm all night. She'd pretended she was sleeping but she needn't have bothered, he hadn't even looked her way.

A little while later, when the night had truly gone and the sun's red light was turning to pink, she had watched amazed as Annie came through from the forepeak in a big woolly jumper, looking pale and fragile, making her way straight up the companionway steps to Johnny. She saw him take her arm and help her up into the cockpit. She could hear the rumble of their voices and she noticed how tenderly he rebandaged her wrist and came down and got her a glass of water and broke a pill in two and pulled out a sleeping bag from the chart-table berth and took it back out into the cockpit for her, not once looking over at herself as she lay pretending to sleep. She felt a sad, swooping kind of envy go through her; all his loving had been redirected. She thought of Frank lying in the fore-peak; he wouldn't be envious. No, he would say that Annie needed Johnny's tenderness more than she did right now. She felt in such a muddle and it was all of her own doing.

Smudge was next to wake. She went from sleeping to wide-awake within seconds. She stepped out of her bed, climbed up the galley steps and snuggled under her mother's sleeping bag, like a puppy looking for milk. Clem sat up next and slowly swung her legs over the seat. She looked towards the fore-cabin. Annie had left the door open; she could see Frank sleeping, lying on his back, his chest rising and falling, and a part of her wanted to go through, shut the door and crawl in with him so he could tell her what to do. Instead she got up, made coffee and joined the others in the cockpit.

They were heading southwest with the wind behind them. No land was visible. Smudge was brushing her mother's hair, rubbing her shoulders, tickling her back, serving her pretend cups of tea, and it seemed perfectly obvious that she was used to this version of a mother. Her diligence paid off; something in Annie must have felt the power of her daughter's love because after a while she wrapped her arms around her and kissed the top of her head again and again.

By the time Frank appeared, looking fresh and clean, clutching some history book, still no shore was visible. Clem was surprised he didn't ask where they were heading, how little interest he had in the charts, how much faith everyone had in Johnny. Johnny seemed different today, aloof from her, and she had no idea what was going on inside his head any more. His face gave nothing away. She herself felt quiet and removed; she sat at the bows with her own book, the Krishnamurti one, which she was struggling with; however interested she was one moment, her mind kept wandering off and she'd have to read each sentence twice. She looked up every now and then wondering when the land would appear, how long they had before they got to Datca, to the place of decision-making.

They all remained in their own separate worlds pretty much the whole day, reading and dozing, making sandwiches, sleeping and playing with Smudge. Later in the afternoon Clem gave Johnny a break at the helm; he was so lost in thought she had to repeat herself before he heard her. He'd got up, told her to stay on this course, taken off his jumper and lain down on the deck on his front and fallen asleep almost immediately. She watched his familiar tanned back, the mole on his right shoulder, the body that had once felt as much hers as his now felt very much his. She could no longer reach out and rest her hand on him. She sailed the boat, lost in her own turbulent thoughts, watching the sun sink lower in the sky; far away she thought she saw land but it could have been clouds. They passed no islands, no boats, nothing at all and she thought of the sea as a kind of wilderness. Annie sat at her side, silent but present. She was sewing, working her way through a pile of clothes that needed mending; sewing for a future with no holes in it.

At the bows Smudge and Frank were playing clapping singing games. '*A sailor went to sea sea sea*,' she sang in her cheery little voice. His was low and rumbling next to hers.

> '*To see what he could see see see,*
> *But all that he could see see see...*'

Clap, clap, clap, salute, salute, salute. '... *Was the bottom of the deep blue sea sea sea.*' Clem's mind wandered as she listened; she tried to imagine the children she might have some day. She had always pictured them fair and skinny with Johnny's green eyes and her copper hair but now she wondered whether they might be dark and strong with brown inscrutable eyes. She didn't know any more.

Later, she watched as Johnny woke up with a jolt, as if from a bad dream. The first thing he did was look up at the sails, checking the wind, then the compass bearing. Then he looked around himself, taking in the empty scenery. Then he looked around the boat, at Annie, at Smudge and Frank and lastly at her. She smiled, but it wasn't a real smile. He smiled back and neither was his; there was an ocean between them now and she was nervous about crossing it. He wandered down the deck into the cockpit and went below without saying anything. He put the kettle on and ate a banana standing there looking out, both she and Annie watching him, both of them wanting something from him.

She noticed the way Annie stopped sewing when Johnny was there, how she looked up at him, with her heavy, sad eyes, how Johnny looked at her with a kind of determination, how he pressed her shoulder as he leant forward to sheet in the genoa and Clem realized then that something was going on between them that she was not party to. He turned on the companionway step and looked down the deck at Frank, who was reading out loud from a book to Smudge. He seemed to watch them for ages, his eyes flicking up at the sails every so often. Clem followed his gaze.

The sails shone like two great golden handkerchiefs billowing out to the starboardside of the boat, the sun slinking down the mint-green sky behind them, the day moon already out. Another day had passed. Where the hell was Datca? She noticed the way Johnny looked around the horizon almost as if he was expecting someone to appear. It was as though he was checking the boat, she thought, as he leant over the stern and then opened the cockpit seat, briefly glancing in. She caught a glimpse of her prayer mat; someone had stuffed it in there. She saw the way Annie's eyes didn't leave Johnny's; she was watching his every move. Yes, something was most definitely going on between them, Clem was sure of that.

'I expect Smudge is thirsty,' Johnny said and Annie looked over to the bows, nodded and put down her sewing.

'Smudge,' Johnny called. 'Your mum wants you.' Annie went down the companionway steps obediently. Clem watched her go through to the bathroom. When Smudge had finished her chapter she came tripping down the deck, stooping to pick up her monster-killing spear before going down into the galley, leaving Frank up there alone.

Johnny took the tiller from Clem, who shifted round to the port side, her back against the coachroof. She picked up her book and began to read, glancing up at Johnny every now and then, watching him letting out a little more sail. The wind had dropped a fair bit, which normally made him anxious, but he seemed unconcerned. His mind was elsewhere and she didn't like it; she liked his mind being where she was.

When she got up a little while later to go to the loo, she was surprised to find Annie putting a very sleepy Smudge into bed in the forepeak. It wasn't even dark yet. Annie was rocking Smudge's little body in her arms, kissing her head again and again, crying, whispering sweet nothings into her ear. Clem watched for a moment, then turned away and made tea for everyone and brought it back out into the cockpit. Annie joined them, pale and red-eyed and returned to her sewing without a word. Johnny was at the helm, smoking, his eyes scanning the horizon as he let the main out a little in the ever-decreasing wind. She sat down next to him, sipping at her coffee, closing her eyes. She had to trust that she would make the right decision when the moment came. When she felt the wind drop suddenly she opened her eyes to see Johnny flicking his cigarette into the water. She looked down at the compass by her side. He'd changed course by twenty degrees, bearing away from the wind.

'Wind's dropped. Frank?' he called down the deck. 'Wind's dropped!'

Frank stopped reading and looked out at the empty sea. He got to his feet, book in his hand, and came down into the companionway, looking up at the sails, the setting sun lighting him up in a golden glow. He was so familiar to her now: his body, the way he moved, the limp, the way he rubbed his beard, the way he spoke, the way he looked at her. She loved two people, she was sure of that. 'It's getting late. Shouldn't we be heading in?' Frank said. He caught her eye then and smiled as if he'd been reading her thoughts. She looked over at Johnny.

'I think we could probably motor to Datca from here,' Johnny replied. 'We shouldn't be that far. Or I'm happy to carry on under sail alone.'

'No, we'll motor,' Frank said, ducking his large frame under the boom and sitting down at the tiller on the other side of her. He reached across for his cigarettes. She was overly aware of his proximity, the size and the smell of him. Next to him, Johnny looked like a young boy. Johnny altered course again, resetting the main and the genny, cleating off the sheets before stepping aside to let Frank take the helm. If the motor was going to be used, Frank liked to helm. The three of them clocked the compass. They were heading due east now, the sun on their backs.

'Stick to this course,' Johnny said, tapping the glass dome. He took his stance in the companionway, leaning against the coachroof, his back to Frank, looking straight ahead out beyond the bows. Sometimes she felt that Johnny deliberately left her alone with Frank; in some way he was wanting her to be with him, pushing her that way. Frank lit his cigarette and then leant towards her. At first she thought he was leaning down to touch her but he was starting the engine, the noise crude and invasive after the watery quiet of sailing. Annie put down her mending and glanced up at him.

Then all of a sudden the engine gave a violent bang and stopped altogether. For a moment Clem thought they had hit something. She had always nurtured a fear of hitting a rock in the middle of nowhere and sinking fast. She clutched the guard rail nervously. 'What the hell was that?' she cried.

'Shit!' Frank said. He turned the key again, only for the engine to clonk into silence. 'That's peculiar.'

Johnny turned around and stepped back out into the cockpit. 'Try again!' he said.

Frank tried the engine once again but nothing happened, not even a clonk this time. 'Sounds like something's caught around the prop,' he said, leaning over the stern.

Johnny joined him, trying to glimpse the propeller through the streaky golden water. 'Could be a net,' he said.

'Could be. Could be anything, damn it.'

Frank tried one more time, determined to get it going, but no joy. 'Something's definitely caught,' he said.

'I'll go in,' Johnny said, taking off his shirt. 'Take the tiller, Clem.'

Clem moved over, heading the *Little Utopia* up into the wind, the sails flapping wildly. 'Careful, Johnny,' she said. He was rummaging around under the cockpit seat looking for a mask. She always hated him swimming in deep water; she thought he might drift away or some creature might grab him from underneath. It was cold and deep in there.

'You'll need a knife,' Frank said, 'It may be a net or a bit of old rope.' Annie went down into the galley and came back out with the very knife she had hacked at her wrist with, this fact escaping nobody as she passed it to him. Johnny put on the mask, took the knife in his right hand and climbed over the guard rail, catching eyes with Clem before he did so. Both of them were anxious now.

She glanced up at the pink and red sky and the sinking orange sun; the light would be gone soon. The water was as black as oil between the streaks of colour.

'Whatever you do, don't turn the engine on!' Johnny said to Frank, smiling through the mask, his brown toes gripping the edge of the stern. 'Clem, keep her head to wind.' She nodded.

Johnny stepped on to the transom step, knelt down and put one hand on the tender for balance as he slipped into the water. He gasped with the cold. He resurfaced, gripping on to the tender. He put his face in the water and looked down at the prop with the three of them on the boat all leaning over the stern trying to get a view of it.

Johnny took a deep breath and dived underneath the hull for a good ten seconds, the others silent as they waited looking down into the darkness beneath. It was impossible to see anything except their own broken reflections and a shimmer of flesh. Johnny resurfaced, panting for breath, grabbing the transom and looking up at their faces, adjusting the mask as he did so. 'Hang on,' he said and dived again. To Clem the seconds felt like minutes, but this time he came up shouting.

'It's a rope caught right round the blades. I can't see it properly – it's too dark down there. Can someone shine a torch from the tender? And I need a screwdriver.'

Frank rummaged around in the cockpit seat, found the torch and a screwdriver, pulled the tender close to the boat and climbed in to get a better view of the propeller. He turned on the torch, placed it in the water and shone it at the prop. Johnny dived again and disappeared, resurfacing not long later, gripping the transom, his back to Frank. Annie was leaning over the stern, as was Clem, with one hand on the tiller, keeping the boat heading into wind.

'OK, Frank,' Johnny shouted above the noise of the sails, turning round to him in the tender. 'Shine it on this side of the prop if you can.'

Clem looked down into the darkness as Johnny dived

down again. She could see bits of frayed rope rising to the surface as Johnny hacked away at it.

'He's doing it!' she cried, keeping her eyes focused on the beam of light from the torch. 'Go on, Johnny!' He was under-water for ages; surely he had to be out of breath. Then up he came bursting into the air holding a short piece of frayed rope.

'Any luck?' Frank asked. Clem looked up at the tender. The sunset behind Frank had begun to shine a rich red; his hair burned as if on fire. He was kneeling, trying to angle the torch correctly through the waves. 'Do you need the screwdriver?' He held it out towards Johnny.

She noticed how Johnny ignored Frank's outstretched arm and slowly pulled himself up on to the transom and out of the water and stood up, wet and dripping in the red light, his face expressionless as he pulled off the mask.

'Have you done it?' Frank asked.

And still Johnny said nothing.

'Have you, Johnny?' she said. She looked over at Frank. The tender had drifted a good ten feet away from the *Little Utopia* and Frank began pulling in the slack rope. Only it wasn't slack: it was loose, no longer tied to the boat at all. He stood there looking confused, holding the wet, frayed end in his hand, the tender drifting further away with each passing second, rising and falling in the tiger-striped swell.

'The knot's come undone!' he said, throwing it back to Johnny on the transom. Johnny didn't move to catch it; he watched as it landed in the water a few feet away from him with a feeble splash.

'Johnny!' Clem cried. 'Pick it up!' But almost as she said the words, it was too late – the end of the rope was out of any reach. Frank began to pull it in again. She stared at Johnny, utterly confused.

'Johnny! Get the rope!' Frank called, throwing it again. But still Johnny didn't move, he continued to stand there on the transom, just staring at the tender as it drifted, maybe twenty feet away now.

'Bring the boat round, Johnny!' Clem called but he did nothing. 'Bring her round, Johnny!' she cried again, letting go of the tiller, looking about for something to throw to Frank instead but Annie was sitting on the cockpit seat where the ropes were and instead of getting out of Clem's way Annie was just staring at Frank, gripping the sides of the seats, going nowhere.

'Get off the seat!' Clem cried. But Annie ignored her, she didn't even look at her.

'Get up! Throw him a rope!' Clem cried, trying to pull Annie off the seat.

Annie reacted then. She let go her grip on the seat and grabbed Clem's shoulders, her nails digging into her back, her grip so hard that Clem saw the fresh red blood seeping through her wound. 'We have to help him, Annie,' Clem said, scared by the look in her eyes. Annie leant forward and whispered into her ear. 'You can't help him,' she said, her voice level and low. 'You can't help us. People like us – we're not fit for this world.'

There was something deeply frightening about Annie, slowly she let go her grip and Clem stepped back, both of them returning their gaze to Frank in the tender. He was panicking now; he started frantically looking about the boat. Water was pouring in. 'Where are the oars? Where are the fucking oars?' he yelled. Clem turned to Johnny because it was dawning on her then that there weren't any fucking oars.

Only then did she understand what was really going on. This was no accident; the rope had been deliberately cast off and the corks removed. This had been organised.

Frank was a good thirty feet away now, maybe more, and

already his voice was sounding distant. She could see that he was thinking of jumping in. He couldn't swim and he would have to rely on her to help him out and she wouldn't be able to. She watched as he scrabbled forwards on his knees and started paddling furiously with his hands; his progress was negligible. 'Go on, Clem, get the boat hook!' Frank yelled. There he was vulnerable and needing her, just as she had wished for, only she couldn't help. She made a dash for the life-belt and tried to unhook it but Johnny was on her. 'Sit down!' he yelled, pushing her back.

'Come back here!' Frank screamed. But nobody moved. 'You leave me here, Johnny, I will find you! You take my daughter I will fucking find you! I swear to fucking God, I will find you and I will kill you!'

Clem stood there aghast. She had never even heard him raise his voice before; he was roaring like a bear.

Johnny was leaning out on the transom shouting right back at him. 'I know what you are! You don't deserve to have a daughter, you monster!'

'You know nothing!'

'I know what you are, Frank! How could you? You don't deserve either of them.' Johnny turned his back on Frank and stepped over the guard rail back into the boat and nudged the tiller with his knee. The sails filled with wind and the *Little Utopia* began to fly away from the tender.

'Annie!' Frank was standing up, yelling but his voice barely carried, he was downwind. 'Annie! I will find you! You know I will!'

Annie stood up slowly, hatred and misery written all over her face. 'We are rotten people, Frank!' she screamed across the water at him, her voice hoarse and breaking. 'We are rotten to the core!'

Clem grabbed hold of Johnny. 'You can't do this!' she cried. 'You've got it all wrong!'

'No, Clem. You listen to me!' He was shouting at her now, as mad and angry as Frank, shaking her off him. '*You've* got it wrong. Wake the fuck up!'

Then behind him Clem saw the blur of Annie leaping from the boat into the water. 'No!' she cried out and Johnny turned round in time to see Annie landing with a splash in the wake of the boat. Johnny slammed the tiller over into a crash-stop heave to. The boat halted dead in the water.

'She jumped, Johnny!' Clem was screaming. 'She just jumped in!'

'Annie?' Johnny cried, straddling the rail. But Annie was making no effort to get back on board; she was floating away from the boat. 'It has to be like this, Johnny!' she cried. 'Smudge is safe with you.'

'Annie, what are you doing? Get in!' he said, one hand on the guard rail, the other leaning out as far as he could. 'Here! Take my hand!'

But she didn't. She was stationary, doggy paddling in the red, fiery water just out of his reach, staring at him with those pathetic eyes as the boat slipped away from her. 'Take my hand! Do it!' If he leant out any further he'd fall in. Clem, trembling all over now, terrified by all of them , opened the cockpit seat and grabbed the boat hook and passed it to Johnny, who held it out to Annie.

'Take it!' he cried. Clem heard the desperation in his voice and it scared her even more. He was trying to hook Annie in but she was too far out.

'Swim to me, Annie!' They could hear Frank shouting at her and the awful thing was that she was obeying him.

'Don't go with him!' Johnny cried. 'The tender won't make

it. Come with us!' She looked back at Johnny, at his outstretched hand, at the boat hook, at the sheer panic in his eyes.

'Annie, get back in! What are you doing?'

But Annie did nothing. She looked up at him with those big, pale eyes full of a resignation, a horrible acceptance of her fate and they both knew that she wasn't coming.

11

LOSS

THE WANING MOON shone brightly, the clouds making silvery shapes as they danced around it and bounced off the waves a hundredfold. Johnny could see, off the starboard bow, a pod of dolphins playing in the surf and he watched them twisting and turning, jumping and diving in their blissful, stupid ignorance. The phosphorescence was so rich and sparkling that when the dolphins leapt out of the water their shapes were perfectly silhouetted as if outlined by millions of liquid diamonds. He sat there staring, but the gap between what he saw and what he felt was now so large that he barely registered it at all.

They had sailed away from the tender until Frank's cries had become indistinguishable from the wind itself and Johnny knew, even as he fled, that he would forever hear him in the wind. Afterwards, his hands had trembled so violently that he had had trouble gripping the sheets. They were still trembling now. His whole body juddered with shock, no matter how many jumpers he put on. That Annie could have thrown herself into the water and swum back to Frank was unfathomable to him; he could not get it out of his head, the sight of her swimming back to the tender, to a certain death. She hadn't even given a backward glance. He had done this for *her*, for her and Smudge. He thought how stupid he had been – she must have thought this up from the moment he'd said he was going to help her, the photographs still in his hands. He recalled how her face had lit up, tears of relief and happiness in her eyes. *Smudge,* she'd kept repeating. *Smudge is going to be all right.* And he had felt full of a focused, dangerous kind of rage. He promised her that Smudge was going to be safe, he would not leave her alone with Frank for one more minute. The solution had been quite obvious to him: sail out into the open sea and leave Frank in the tender far away from any human being. Leave him in the hands of his fucking great god Karma. Frank was an evil man. Then it had just been a question of how to get him in the boat. Now all he could think was that he had saved Smudge from her fate and in so doing had made an orphan of her. He was twenty-one and he had not one but two people's lives on his hands. He looked down at his trembling fingers. His chest was so tight it felt like he had a great weight pressing down on him and he didn't think he was ever going to feel any other way. He could never go back from this.

The sun had dropped fast and now the darkness had swallowed up the light. Perhaps they wouldn't die. There was a slim chance they might make it; they might be rescued or possibly they'd find some sort of paddle or get caught in a favourable current. But these were faint possibilities, he wasn't kidding himself. If they did survive, as long as the *Little Utopia* headed west, there was little chance Frank would find them. He was pretty sure of that; there was no communication between the Greeks and the Turks. He let these thoughts flit to and fro across his mind, but underneath it all, he knew the tender would sink down to the bottom of the sea like all the other things he'd thrown overboard. Once he'd changed course and set the sails, Johnny tried not to look round at where they had come from. They were heading northwest now, eventually towards the Ionian, as far from these troubled waters as was possible. Every time he glanced around, he was half expecting the looming figure of Frank to be upon them but he saw nothing but the zigzagging white path that led to the moon.

Clem had not said a word. She had her back to Johnny; she was refusing to look at him, her eyes permanently fixed on where the tender had been, her body shaking all over, flinching from his touch. She had watched it disappear listening to those cries until there was nothing to see or hear but a wailing dot in the wind. Every now and then she sat up straight, reached for the binoculars and scanned the water but the only sights now were the sea and the dolphins and the only sounds were those of the boat moving through the water. She never turned around, never faced forwards at all; she just stared out at where the ghost of the tender would always be.

'Where's Daddy?'

They both jumped. Smudge, the unknowing victim of all this, appeared just before dawn in the companionway, wearing her Captain Hook coat with a blanket wrapped round her, dragging Gilla in one hand, the moonlight bouncing off his glazed, scratched eye. They were both surprised to see her for somewhere in the drama they had forgotten that she was the unwitting protagonist.

There she stood, with her father's colouring and her mother's face, to remind them lest they should ever forget. She had slept right through the casting off of her parents in a drugged stupor but now she was awake, rubbing her eyes, looking round at them, totally unaware that this day was shape-defining. Her life would always be *before* and *after* this.

'Come and sit here, Smudge,' Johnny said to her.

She rubbed her eyes again and scuffled across the cockpit,

looking about herself. 'Where's my mummy?' she asked, looking down the deck and turning back to Johnny. 'Where's my daddy?

Clem looked at Johnny. He and she hadn't had this conversation yet. They hadn't had any conversation at all. Clem picked up Annie's cardigan, which was lying on the seat, and wrapped it around Smudge. 'Here, put this on!' she said. 'It's cold out here.'

Smudge let Clem wrap the cardigan around the blanket and then knelt on the stern seat and peered over the edge, Johnny and Clem both watching her.

'They've taken the dinghy,' Smudge said.

'Yes,' Johnny said. 'They've gone ashore for a while.'

She looked out to sea. 'Without me?" she asked, confused. 'When are they coming back?'

'I don't know,' he said.

'Have they gone to find Granny?'

He'd forgotten all about Granny. 'I don't know, Smudge. They just left.'

'I think they've probably gone to find Granny,' she said, sitting down next to him, swinging her legs. 'Or maybe...' she added, brightened by some new idea, '... they've gone to find me a *new* pet.'

Johnny put his arm around her, squeezing her gently towards him. 'Maybe,' he said quietly. He had no idea how to handle this.

She looked up into his eyes. 'Do you think it might be a horse?' she asked.

He paused. 'I'm not sure about horses on boats,' he said.

'Horses like boats.' She seemed pretty sure of it.

Clem bit her lip and looked over her shoulder, away from Smudge.

'There were dolphins at the bows just now, Smudge,' he said. 'Go and have a look.' And he watched as she tripped merrily down the deck and lay down on her tummy at the bows talking to the dolphins.

Johnny looked over at Clem. He saw her wipe her cheeks. She was shivering. It was getting very cold up on deck. Shortly she got up and went down the deck to get Smudge and the pair of them went below into the saloon, shutting the cockpit doors behind them, leaving Johnny to sail the boat alone. *We'll get through it*, he said to himself again. But really he was wondering how the hell they were meant to do so. He had done a terrible thing. It had had to be done, there had been no alternative, he knew that, but still, he had done a terrible thing. He would have to live with that. And now he had a child to look after, something that he had never ever anticipated. He had to take deep breaths. *Moment to moment.*

Far away on the horizon he watched a cruise ship making its way somewhere, the row of little lights like lanterns on a wall. He pictured them dancing, sipping cocktails, listening to some old crooner, slipping between clean sheets, and he wanted to be someone on that ship, someone who wasn't him.

He watched the morning star come up. It was so bright and red at first he thought it was the port light of a huge ship but as the hours went on it crawled up the mast and went the way of all the other stars. When it went over the top of the sail he hove to and went down to make some coffee; his eyes were scratchy with tiredness. There was no point in trying to sleep. He knew sleep would evade him now.

Clem was lying motionless on the port side, her back to the saloon, the small reading light on behind her head. He stood next to her and looked down at her. The skin on her temple was so dark now, and even the inside of her upper arm was the same colour as the rest of her body; the sun had forged itself into her very hairline. He would once have been unable to stop himself bending down to kiss her but he couldn't do it now; they had grown so far apart. He knew that they were breaking and he didn't know how to mend them; it seemed so low down on the list of his priorities right at this moment. He went past her and through to the forepeak and opened the door. Smudge had taken her mother's place. Clem had tucked her in, ramming her into the port side with the other pillows. She looked so tiny and vulnerable, her lips parted in sleep, the deep, gentle sounds of her breathing. The full impact of the responsibility he now found himself with hit him like a gybing boom. She was theirs now. She was his. He had to do his best for her. He took her little curled fingers in his own and promised her that he would always put her first and her fingers seemed to tense in response and somewhere in his hardening heart he felt a melting. He bent over and kissed her cheek.

When he came back through the saloon, Clem was sitting up with the blanket tight around her, watching him as he passed. 'I thought you were asleep,' he said as he got to the galley, picking up the kettle.

'How can you look her in the eye?' she whispered in a voice he didn't recognize, as if he disgusted her. He paused a moment before pumping the tap with his foot, looking over at her and deciding to ignore her. He filled the kettle with two cups' worth of water and turned on the hob. He wondered how big the tank was; they'd have to stop at some point.

'You killed her parents,' she said blankly, a statement of fact.

'They've got a chance of making it.' He bent over to light the hob. 'Besides, it was Annie's choice to jump.'

'But it was your choice to kill *him*.'

'I *left* him in the tender, in case you hadn't noticed.'

'You as good as killed him and you know that.'

He banged the kettle down on the flame. 'What choice did I have?' he said.

'You could have *not* killed him. It's not up to you to play God.'

'Could I?' he said, looking over at her. 'Let me tell you something' He took a step towards her and leant on the sink, trying to keep his voice down. 'Do you know how badly Annie wanted to get away from her husband... what lengths she was planning on going to? She'd saved up a stash of pills and this time she was going take Smudge with her.'

Clem stared at him for a moment then shook her head. 'I don't believe you.' But he saw a flash of fear in her eye.

'You tell me why would a woman want to do that? What awful thing must she be trying to escape from?'

'She's insane, Johnny.'

'Tell me what I should have done then, Clem?' He was quiet, fixing her with his eyes.

'You should have just taken us to Datca.'

'I tried but you didn't want to go.'

'No, I mean the second time.'

'Oh, and you'd be OK with that, would you? Leaving him to it? Leaving Smudge in his hands?'

'Yes. Of course I'd be OK.'

He stared at her, incredulous. She was in total denial, deliberately refusing to believe him. 'That man has sex with his five-year-old daughter. Don't you get it?'

She paused. 'She's a lunatic, Johnny. It's all bullshit!' she was shouting now, not caring about Smudge next door.

'Oh my God! Clem!' he said, wiping his brow. 'Open your fucking eyes!'

'She's a mad fucking bitch! You know that!'

He hadn't wanted to tell her this; he hadn't wanted the depths of Frank's depravity to reach her. He had wanted to protect her from him for as long as he could. He leant against the sink and held her eye. 'There's a book in there with a load of photographs of things I don't think you ever want to see. But I think you're going to have to take a look.'

He saw her back away, her lips part, her eyes widen, the blood drain from her cheeks as the ugliness of what he was saying drowned out all other thoughts. She couldn't defend him now.

Eventually she said in a quiet, knowing little voice, 'Is there a picture of *him*?'

Johnny frowned, not understanding what she was asking.

'Is there a photograph of *him* in the book?' she repeated. Then she smiled. 'There's not, is there? Of course there's not. Pictures don't prove anything, Johnny. Annie set him up like a fool and you fell for it.'

He couldn't believe what he was hearing. 'Jesus Christ,' he said. 'He's really got you, hasn't he?'

'And she hasn't got you? You think you're some knight in shining armour rescuing her?'

'She tried to hack her hand off, Clem.'

'It was just a cry for help.'

'Well, I was fucking listening, wasn't I? Annie got some fucking help!' He was shouting at her now. He had never shouted at her before.

'Annie, Annie – it's all I hear from you. It's not up to you to *dispense* with her husband.'

'What would you have done then? Tell me! Reported him to the police?'

'It's not true!' She was blocking her ears trying to drown him out.

Johnny could feel the blood vessels in his head filling with a pure white-hot rage. He was screaming now. 'Who would I report him to? Who gives a shit? There are no laws here! Don't you get it? He can do what the hell he wants. That's why it's called the *Little* fucking *Utopia*!'

Then he punched the crappy wooden panel so hard with his fist that the wood caved in with a crunch and his knuckles went from white to pink and started to bleed. He caught her eye then and they stared at each other, reeling in horrified wonder at what they had become, how everything had got so wrecked so quickly. He turned around and leant his elbows against the companionway steps, hanging his head in his hands, trying not to cry, trying to regain control of himself. Neither one of them dared to speak. He looked up at the night sky, at the vast, aching emptiness around them.

The kettle screamed. He turned and slowly, with meticulous care, he made the coffee, scooping up the grounds as if his whole life depended on these two cups of black stuff. He stirred in the sugar and brought them over to the table. Clem was still sitting there staring blankly ahead, her face drained of all life. He sat down next to her and placed the coffees in front of them on the table, both of them watching the swirling vortexes. They sat like that for a long time.

'I want to go back home,' she said in a small voice.

Home. He hadn't thought of home at all. He looked up at her. He remembered her then, from before, from home, them together. It seemed another world away. He remembered her as a child, back-flipping off the sand dunes, their first date at the Blue Anchor, her in that white shirt and jeans, putting songs on the jukebox, how much he had loved her, *did* still love her. But he couldn't quite reach that love any more. He couldn't reach anything any more. The core of him was numb and the edges were jagged and frayed.

'Yes,' he said in answer to a question no one had asked. 'I'll take you home.'

'How, Johnny?' she said. 'We've got Smudge.'

'We'll take her with us.'

She paused and looked up at him, her dark eyes puffy and swollen. 'How could we ever explain that?'

She was right. They couldn't go home. 'Let's live somewhere else then,' he said, holding her gaze.

She nodded, but tears started to spill from her eyes. 'But I want to go back home, where everything is familiar,' she said.

'Please,' he said, hanging his head, sighing, rubbing his forehead in his hand – he was so phenomenally exhausted. 'I can't do this on my own.' They sat there for a while listening to the waves lapping the boat, eyes on the ghost vortexes now swirled into stillness.

He looked around the boat as if he was only just seeing where they were: the dented wood, the ugly municipal carpet on the floor, Frank's history books, Annie's trashy novels, his pens and gadgets, her bits and bobs of crap, behind the door their sleeping child. They were gone and Johnny and Clem had stolen their life.

12

THE ENDING

THE WEDDING HAD not gone according to plan at all. It was a small affair, there were only about twelve of them waiting at the church in St Mawgan – the same church where Johnny's parents had got married twenty-five years before. Rob had given Clem a lift on the back of the old Tiger Cub because she had insisted they went separately; she was having a hard time keeping to all the superstitions and was picking and choosing along the way. Some were just absurd, like not seeing each other on the wedding morning – nothing would ever induce them to spend a night apart. She did the 'something borrowed, something blue' bit. The dress was borrowed – kind of – she planned on returning it to the charity shop. Sarah had found it in Barnardo's in Newquay in the nightwear section. But it looked like a wedding dress, although it had little blue flowers on it, it was figure hugging and shiny white with long virginal sleeves. She'd also found Johnny a three-piece suit, so they looked the part. No one seemed to have much idea how weddings were meant to be run and Clem had allowed her mother no part at all in the arrangements. She would have wanted everything the traditional way: unknown relatives and flower arrangements, conversations with the vicar and caterers, table names and hired cars until Clem had explained to her that that just wasn't the way things got done with the Loves. So her mother had watched bemusedly as they picked holly and ivy for Clem's bouquet, and bought kegs of beer from the Riv pub. She'd found it hard to conceal her disappointment, especially when she'd found Sarah painting the old Tiger Cub with white emulsion.

It was November and the weather was trying to be everything in one day; a rainbow had even looped the hills earlier on, which Clem had taken as a sign – though she wasn't quite sure what of. She'd hung on tightly to Rob, her knees gripping the bike, her dress hoiked up beneath her, her curls stuffed up under the helmet, letting her body go with the flow, letting Rob's body be her guide as they wound around the country lanes. He was shorter and broader than his brother but otherwise there was a cosy familiarity about him. They smelt similar. She rested her head against his back and her heart seemed so full it might burst. The whole world seemed to be shining in her reflected happiness. When they'd set off from the cottage down the hill, she thought she had never seen the water so blue and the surf so white, the cliffs so sheer and the grass so green. Everything had been intensified for this, their wedding day; nature was putting on a show especially for her – she'd never been able to entirely shake off those childish suspicions that the world had been constructed purely for her benefit.

The weather didn't hold though; as they headed up the hill, the sky darkened dramatically and the heavens opened and it had started to bucket down. She could feel the rain slipping down her neck where the helmet and jacket didn't meet, hear the smacking sound of the rain on Rob's leather jacket, and see the stream of white paint they were leaving behind them – it was coming off all over the road, all over her legs, all over Rob's suit.

The trouble didn't really start until they reached the church where it became apparent that someone else was also having a wedding that day – someone else with a hundred friends. She and Rob had got off the bike and run up the path under the arch to join Johnny and all of their party huddling in the porch out of the rain while, to her bewilderment, hearty singing, coughing and wedding noises were coming from inside. They waited until the other service was over and the multitude had drifted off round to the other side for photographs – something else that they'd forgotten to organize – then they cornered the vicar. He seemed most surprised to find another bride at his church. He said he couldn't possibly marry them, they hadn't confirmed the booking and the banns hadn't been read out, aside from anything else. This was puzzling, not least because they had no idea what banns were. Clem suggested to the vicar that the banns might be read out this very minute. There was much kerfuffle and pleading but the vicar was adamant: no banns, no wedding. Then there was the other business of Clem's dad not turning up. And Rob had left the ring on the kitchen table. So in the end instead of a wedding the lot of them had gone across the road to the Falcon Inn for a pint or five before Johnny's dad had had the brainwave.

The weather had turned again. By the time they got to Padstow harbour, the dark blanket of cloud had slowly slipped off the edge of the sky leaving a chilly sharp blue in its place. The wind was light but biting and the low winter sun cast long shadows across the oily harbour water. Their wedding clothes were now tucked into wellington boots and covered by jumpers and scarves and mismatched oilies that they'd found in the boathouse box. The five of them stood on the steep slope of the jetty ready to launch the old wooden Fireball off the trailer and into the rising tide, its rigging tinkling excitedly in the wind. Sarah and Rob were on one side standing in the freezing shallows and Johnny and Clem on the other while his dad wheeled the trailer back up to the boathouse. Clem hopped into the boat, her white skirt sticking out over the wellies, her make-up fallen in streaks down her face from where she had been crying earlier in the pub. Nobody mentioned it. Everyone pretended they hadn't noticed her crying because it had seemed too callous to point out the reason – but they all knew exactly what it was. And it wasn't the fact that the wedding hadn't happened – they could get married any time – it was the fact that her own father hadn't turned up. Just this once, he might have pulled out the stops. Johnny was so livid he couldn't even say his name. She had been so thrilled when Jim had said yes, that he'd be delighted to give her away and Peter and Tim could definitely do page-boyish things. She had leapt about the flat doing naked dancing. And now the bastard hadn't even shown up. Johnny saw how Clem would not accept the truth – even two hours in she was still making excuses for him, said *he'd probably got lost* and then later when he still wasn't there she'd gone on about *how incredibly busy he was at the moment with his new job*. But Johnny saw how every time the Falcon door opened she turned around expectantly and how later she pretended she had something in her eye when it finally dawned on her that he wasn't going to show up.

Clem sat herself near the mast at the bows of the Fireball, her heart racing with excitement. She zipped up her jacket to the neck and pulled her cuffs down over her fingers. It was colder on the water. Johnny took off his woolly hat and chucked it to her across the boat. She pulled it on and looked up towards the boathouse. Her mother was standing there waving down at them, incongruous in her high heels and puffy blue dress and the yellow oilskin Johnny's dad had given her to keep warm. She was too polite to say no but Clem could see she didn't want to spoil her outfit. But she looked good in it;

she looked as if she was part of them all now. She wanted her mother to see how magical life was with the Loves; something had struck Clem that afternoon when her father hadn't turned up: she had taken for granted the only person who had always been there in her life. She blew her mother a kiss just as Sarah rolled into the boat awkwardly, laughing, and the Fireball rocked from side to side. Johnny's dad jumped in next and Rob and Johnny gave the boat a final shove into the water before neatly stepping on board themselves, Johnny having managed not to get wet at all. After much shuffling about and rope pulling and manoeuvring and leaning out and ducking down and pushing off and fast tacking, the Fireball smoothly slipped along the water and out of the harbour mouth into the estuary beyond, the wind a gentle south-westerly, the sun sharp and golden on her sails. Clem looked back and saw her mother still waving from the harbour wall. She waved back.

They sped through the water, Puffin Island on the sharp horizon ahead, past the cottage on the grey, craggy shore, the sun hiding behind the hills. Despite the squash and the weight the Fireball moved at a lick through the chilly November air. Johnny had Clem wrapped in his arms on the starboard side, kissing her cheek, one eye as always looking up at the sails despite the fact his dad was at the helm. Sarah was shivering, looking up at the sky and Rob was leaning out beside her. They changed tack and Sarah looked at her father. 'Can you get on with it, Dad, it's freezing,' she said.

'Oh yes, sorry. Got carried away. Such a beautiful day! Ready about...' he said. They were almost parallel with the headland now, sheltered a little by the hills. 'Lee ho!' He tacked again; they ducked and the sails shook briefly as they snapped into their new positions. He bore away and the wind took them from behind on to a nice calm, balanced run.

'As captain of this vessel,' Johnny's dad said in his booming voice that both Johnny and Rob had inherited, peering beneath the sails as he spoke in case some other lunatic might be out pleasure sailing today, 'I am about to perform a marriage ceremony.'

'Is it legal, by the way?' Sarah asked.

'Of course it's legal,' he said, looking up at the sail. 'It's more than legal. It's elemental. Now, Sarah, you and Rob are witnesses. Clem, Johnny, you need to be either side of me. Have you got the ring this time, Rob?'

He was a man of eccentric authority. All eyes were on him. He fell quiet for a moment – he often forgot completely what he was talking about and they were all wondering what he was doing when he took his gaze up to the sky. 'I wish your mother was here,' he said. 'She'd know how to do this properly. I can't even remember the vows. I'm going to have to make them up.'

He brought the boat slowly up into the wind and backed the jib to heave to. He cleared his throat. 'Here goes. Jonathan Love,' he boomed above the flapping mainsail. 'Are you crazy about this woman?'

Johnny smiled, looking straight across his father at Clem. 'I am.'

'Louder! We all need to hear. The sky, the sea, we are your witnesses.'

Johnny raised his voice. 'I am!'

'Do you love her more than anything in the world?'

Johnny laughed. 'More than the world,' he said and reached out and took her hands in his.

'Do you promise to cherish, protect and worship her?'

'I do.'

'In sickness and in health?'

'Absolutely.'

'In plain sailing and stormy weather?'

'Yes.'

'Because life is hard, Johnny. Staying together is bloody hard. Walking out is easy.'

'Yes, Dad,' Johnny said, throwing his father a quick glance and then looking back into Clem's beaming dark eyes. 'I'm never walking out, I swear on my life.'

'Where's the poetry in you, lad? A woman needs poetry.'

Johnny smiled. 'I love her. What more do you want?'

'I'll go to the next bit then,' his dad said. 'Do you take this wonderful woman as your wife?'

'I do.'

'Excellent. And you, Clemency Bailey?'

'Oh yes,' she said, leaning forward and kissing Johnny's lips. The make-up was running down Clem's cheeks again in black streams but this time unplugged by happiness.

'No, wait,' his dad said. 'No kissing yet. I have to ask you first. Do you love my son, Jonathan David Love?

'I do.'

'A lot?'

'Dad... get on with it.' Johnny said.

'I love him more than I can bear. I ache with love for him.'

'You say that now, Clem, but are you going to love him when things aren't so rosy? Are you going to love him when life throws slings and arrows at you?'

A shadow seemed to pass over her for she had never considered such an idea. It was inconceivable that anything life could throw at them would ever damage their love. It was indestructible. 'Yes. Oh yes, I am,' she said and turned to his dad, serious and intense. 'I'll love your son until the end of time, until the world has stopped and the sun doesn't rise, until all the stars have gone out. You'll see!'

Johnny squeezed her hand in his; he could feel a kind of burning in his chest and a lump in his throat.

'Oh, I like that,' his dad said. 'That's much more like it. *Until all the stars have gone out.* Clemency Bailey, do you take this man as your husband?'

'I do.'

'Ring, Rob?' Rob leant forward and passed Johnny the ring and he slipped it on to Clem's frozen finger. 'Then I pronounce you man and wife! May the heavens shine on you now and forever!'

The heavens did. At that moment the golden sun peered out over the dip in the hill and lit up the boat. There was a quick little cheer and clap before Sarah said, 'Right, can we go now? I'm frozen solid,' and Rob was quick to grab the jib sheet. But neither Johnny nor Clem moved; they weren't cold at all, they were lit by the same fire from within. They stared at each other. They were married now.

When they got back to the quayside and were pulling the heavy Fireball out of the water, all of them trembling with cold but full up with new warmth, Johnny was surprised to see Clem's father up by the boathouse leaning on a car, smoking a cigarette and waiting for them. He was wearing a brown shoulder-padded suit. Johnny had hold of one of the trailer handlebars and Rob had the far side and the others were pushing up from the rear. Jim was watching them. Johnny turned to see whether Clem had spotted her father but she hadn't; she was at the back, head down, pushing with all her might up the slope. He took a deep breath. Nothing was going to spoil this day. No one was ever going to make his wife unhappy again. He could sense Jim moving towards him but he didn't acknowledge him. As they swung the trailer round back on itself along the quayside, towards Jim and then

301

away from him, Johnny glanced quickly at him as they approached. 'What took you so long?' he said.

'Yeah, so sorry about that,' Jim said, smoothing his hair, hovering, taking a drag of his cigarette. 'Peter fell off the climbing frame and we had to take him to A and E and then…'

He never got the rest of the sentence out. Johnny's right fist came out of nowhere and smacked Jim right between the eyes without his feet missing a single step. The accuracy and ferocity of the punch took even Johnny by surprise. It was so quick that the others, except for Rob, seemed to have missed it altogether and they all just carried on heaving the Fireball up into the car park with their heads down, not one of them noticing the man in a flash suit lying on the cobbles with a bleeding face.

By dawn the rain had begun to fall and Johnny put Frank's oilskins on. The wind had picked up and was blowing so hard it felt personal, as if it was trying to blow the hair right off his head. The bows smack-banged on the water like a frying pan. Smudge, having slept through the pounding in the forepeak, had woken early and crawled up into the cockpit full of tales of her dreams. She had dreamt she had springs instead of legs and she had been jumping hundreds of feet high across the sea, bouncing off the waves. She said she had been very good at wave-jumping and wondered whether she could do it out of her dreams as well. Then she promptly leant over and vomited.

Johnny chucked a bucket of water over the vomit and got her in her oilies and clipped her on with the harness and she'd sat there clinging on to the side puking over the edge every so often but otherwise not unhappy. She didn't ask about Frank and Annie but they permeated everything, they were everywhere, in every cranny of the boat. As the wind blew harder and the sea got rougher there was less and less room for thinking of them; hard sailing demanded present-moment awareness and seasickness was too debilitating for anything other than being sick; there was room for nothing but survival and Johnny was grateful for that. He had decided that they weren't going to risk stopping until the water tank was empty; he was going to get them to Sardinia or Corsica, somewhere very far from here, where they could paint the boat, dump her or sell her and start again.

Clem too crawled up into the cockpit at some stage. She was vomiting as well but she took the helm while he went to lie down for forty winks in the chart-table berth. He didn't bother taking off his oilies or boots, he clambered into the hole of a berth and closed his eyes, hovering at the edge of sleep where the squeaks and thuds of the boat in the water kept turning into Frank's screams and cries. Johnny was beginning to understand that Frank would never let him rest; even when he did drift off and the roll of the boat pushed his body up against the inside of the cockpit, Frank was there. The hardness of the fibreglass became Frank's body pressing up against Johnny's. Twice he'd woken up aroused and ashamed, having dreamt of Frank's tipless fingers brushing the base of his spine. When he heard the low, soft rumble of Frank's voice up in the cockpit talking to Clem he almost flew out of his berth and up into the cockpit ready to take him on. Clem had watched bemusedly as he ran up and down the decks shouting and swearing against the spray of the waves. But there was no one there, just a phantom. And yet Johnny couldn't shake the feeling that he was being watched. *He sees things.* Yes, he could feel those dark, inscrutable eyes following him wherever he went.

He stopped trying to sleep after that and became obsessed with erasing Frank from the boat. He had to get rid of all traces of him. He bagged his clothes. He kept the cash – Frank had hoards of it around the boat. He went through their things: the paperwork, their passports, noticing that Smudge's name was in Frank's passport not Annie's. He wrote Smudge's name beneath his own: Imogen Love. Who would suspect otherwise? A young couple on a boat with a child: he saw no reason for suspicion. He took out the scissors and cut their papers and passports into pieces and bagged them with a couple of tins of soup and chucked them overboard.

On the third day the weather turned for the worse. Clem and Smudge stayed down below, both unable to function now with the seasickness. They lay in a huddle on the lee berth, barely able to raise their heads except to puke bile, looking unbearably grim, almost comatose. All he could do was make sure that they were warm and try to keep them drinking fluids. He never thought of finding an island and stopping. Always lurking at the back of his mind was the thought that Frank was not far behind him. The weather raged; squalls and gusts between forty and fifty knots. All he could do was run downwind under bare poles, but still he refused to seek shelter. Instead he harnessed himself on to whatever was at hand and carried on in a mindset beyond sense. In the distance he saw shadow islands, barely distinguishable from the sky itself, grey smudges in the black cloud. He kept them on the horizon.

By the fourth day, Clem and Smudge were barely keeping water down, and he himself was utterly exhausted. When at last they came to the more westerly Greek islands, the sun began to melt through the white stormy sky and he could at last put up some canvas. When he looked back at the patch-work of caves on the leeward side of one particular island he finally began to feel that Frank was not going to find them. Only then did it hit Johnny quite how exhausted he was.

At last he dropped anchor and went below deck to brew up a saucepan full of ginger for Smudge and Clem. He made a pot of pasta for them to eat before he crashed. He was so tired his eyeballs felt as if they were shaking in his skull. Clem would have to take watch for a while. But there was still one more thing to do before he could rest.

The late-afternoon sun shone softly down on the boat as he painted over the looped lettering of the *Little Utopia* on with some gloss paint he had found underneath the cockpit seat. It felt good to wipe over those wretched words; Frank's sick little utopia was no more. He let it dry a little, dipped the brush in the paint and leant over the stern again.

'What are you doing?' He turned around. Clem was up. She was standing in the companionway looking pale and tired. She'd not eaten a thing for forty-eight hours, nor spoken a word for longer.

'How are you feeling?' he asked, paintbrush in hand. 'There's some ginger tea down there for you both and some pasta.'

'What are you doing?' she said again looking at his paintbrush.

'I'm painting over the name.'

Her face was expressionless. 'You can't do that.'

'Clem, we can't risk it. We have to change the name.'

'Johnny,' she said, shaking her head. 'You can't change the name of a boat. You must never do that.'

He turned his body round to face her, pot in one hand, brush in the other, his eyes red and scratchy with sleeplessness. 'How much more bad luck could we possibly get?' he said. But he was glad to see she cared about such things again.

'OK. OK,' he said. 'What if we leave her with no name?'

She nodded and looked away. He finished painting over the letters and put the lid back on the pot and wrapped the brush in an old bit of plastic bag with an elastic band and went down to the galley. Smudge was feeling better too; they drank their ginger tea and ate the pasta slowly, their empty stomachs fragile. Smudge was sitting on the companionway step looking just like her mother but pale and tired, even Gilla hanging at her side seemed to have taken on the general air of misery. She sat there watching as Clem washed up and Johnny unclicked the kitchen table .

'I want my daddy,' Smudge said and Johnny paused as he slotted the table into a bed. 'Are they coming back soon?' she asked. He would rather have this conversation when his brain was working. He just needed a little tiny sleep; forty minutes, half an hour, that was all, then he would be able to cope.

'Not yet,' Clem said. Johnny turned around and caught her eye then. Lying to Smudge wouldn't help matters. After he had slept he would tell her that they weren't coming back.

'Do you think they found the horse?' Smudge said, coming down the steps.

Clem took the plate from her hands. 'Maybe,' she said and Smudge jumped on to the saloon seat, grabbed a handful of books from the shelf and took herself through to the forepeak, shutting the heads door behind her. She often took herself off for hours at a time to look at her books – she was her father's daughter after all. Clem stood there at the sink still staring at the closed door as Johnny pulled out the bedding and started taking off his oilskins. 'She knows, Johnny.' He turned around.

'She knows what?' he said, taking off his two jumpers in one move.

'She knows what we've done.' Her big, dark eyes had huge shadows all around them; she looked so delicate, so vulnerable.

'Don't be silly. Of course she doesn't.'

He stopped what he was doing and slowly came towards her, gently putting his arms around her and he pressed her body to his, feeling his own need as well as hers. He felt her arms go around his waist as she leant her head against his shoulder. This was the first time he had held her in a long time. He could feel her chest rise and fall as she took deep breaths. He kissed her forehead and she lifted her face up to his. He kissed her cheek, her nose, her eyelids, her mouth, her tears. Then she started to kiss him back. It was as though they were remembering each other, their bodies getting reacquainted; their lips were their fingers. They kissed urgently, as if time itself was running out. They pulled off each other's clothes and there against the sink they fucked hard because they had to, it was the only way of reaching each other.

The tenderness came afterwards as they lay down together on the saloon bed, still and satiated. He ran his fingers over her smooth brown skin, over the bleached blond hairs, the dimples at the base of her spine, up the ridges of her back, breathing in the woody smell of her, the softness of her shoulder on his lips, feeling the wonderful fullness of love again, the promise of peace at last. But it was a brief respite; even as his eyelids closed and sleep dragged him under, he could feel her slipping away from him. She had turned her head aside and was staring up through the hatch, her thoughts a million miles from his. He wanted to turn her face to his, to look her in the eyes and tell her that everything was going to be OK but his body was leaden and the words never made it to his lips. He fell into a deep and exhausted sleep.

He woke slowly, his body in just the same position as when he'd fallen asleep but the world around him changed. Clem was no longer in his arms. The light was different; it was a new day. He turned and glanced at the clock; he'd slept for eleven hours straight. His neck was stiff; he hadn't moved a muscle all night. He blinked and stretched, his eyelids and fingers still swollen with sleep. His head and his eyeballs no longer ached. The exhaustion had at last left him. He knew by the lazy roll of the boat and the half-hearted flop of the sail that they were becalmed and he didn't care – they should be far enough away now. He turned towards the cockpit where he could see Smudge's crossed legs on the portside seat, a book in her lap; he could hear her faintly singing some song, and above her the boom was swinging indecisively across the coachroof with a heavy thud, one way then the other.

He got up on his knees and peered out of the window, rubbing his neck. The sea was glassy still, the island barren and craggy, uninhabited. He wondered vaguely where on earth they were. No boats. No Frank. It wasn't until he turned back that he saw Clem sitting in the corner of the bed, totally motionless, knees up to her chin, arms wrapped around them, watching him.

'Hello,' he said, smiling, slowly sitting back down as he rubbed his neck.

She didn't move. 'I have to go, Johnny,' she said, her voice low and calm.

He looked at her, puzzled. 'You have to go where?'

'I have to go back.'

'Home?'

She shook her head. He waited for her to say something else, trying to read her features as he did so, but her face was expressionless. She was giving nothing away.

'Where then?' he heard himself ask but he knew exactly where she meant and he didn't want to hear her say it. He wanted to lean forward and put his hand over her mouth and seal up her lips to stop the words coming out; he wanted to press as hard as he could and not stop pressing until she could no longer even think those thoughts. *Don't say it.*

'To Frank.'

Everything stopped except one muscle pulsating in his jaw.

'We did wrong,' she said. 'I'll take Smudge with me. We'll wait at Datca. Go up to Bodrum. He's a survivor. I have to find him.'

She'd got it all worked out; she already had a plan. Her mind was made up. She had been thinking about this while he had been resting falsely in the arms of sleep. He wondered when she'd first hatched this plan – before they'd had sex up against the sink? It had been nothing but a mercy fuck. He was way behind her.

'Why?' he said.

She looked away then, out through the Perspex window and he felt a chill slink over his skin. He pulled the sleeping bag up around him, but the silky sheen offered no protection. He didn't want to hear what she had to say; he had to put a stop to this right now before she could think any more. 'It's all right, Clem,' he said, the words tumbling out. 'We're going to carry on. We're going to head up to Sicily, Sardinia, Corsica. We're going to dry dock the boat, it's going to be just—'

'I have to find him,' she said, his words petering out into nothing.

'Why?'

She said nothing.

'Are you in love with him?'

She shrugged, unable to meet his eye. 'I don't know.'

She might just as well have got out the old kitchen knife and stuck it in his guts. He shook his head, snatching at the air for breath. He thought he was going to be sick.

'I'm sorry, Johnny,' she said, biting her lip. A single tear slipped from her eye and rolled down her cheek briefly giving him comfort; he saw it as a salty drop of hope but then as she wiped it away with her arm it struck him that she wasn't crying for him, she was crying because her love was dead. And he thought of Annie's voice, how her song had sung of this.

'Why?' he heard himself say, for he was reeling now, not quite feeling the impact of her blow. 'Why are you doing this?'

She shook her head and looked up out through the window, searching for the right things to say, her face red and tangled with misery. 'I feel dead inside, Johnny... like I'm being suffocated.'

He tried to speak, to say *no, it wasn't so*, but all he could feel was that icy chill whistling around his insides.

' I miss him,' she said, heedless of Johnny.

'But we're married...' he said. He sounded pathetic even to himself. 'You made promises... until the world ends...'

'I know, I know...' she said, waving her hands with irritation as if she didn't need him to remind her of that dreadful fact. 'I don't know what I feel any more... You've changed, Johnny. You're always criticizing me. I can see it in your eyes. You're always judging me. You don't actually even *like* me any more... and I've changed too. I've stopped seeing things in the same way, I've got this new inner life now...'

'*I've* got an inner life!' he cried. 'I have so much inner fucking life. You're wrong, I love you so much, Clem.' His voice was breaking, his throat closing up, trying to plug the pain.

'I know you do,' she said as if his love didn't really count, as if it was cheap.

There was nothing more to offer her. She didn't want his everything. She was prepared to gamble his love for Frank's. She was cutting him off and he didn't know what to do because he was still attached, hanging on. The pain really got him now; it sliced across his belly, sharp and deep; he found himself rocking back and forth clutching his stomach, suddenly aware of Smudge up there in the cockpit, swinging her legs, oblivious to this carnage. He tried to take deep breaths to steady himself, to regain some composure, to keep his pride. *Fuck you, Clemency Bailey. Fuck you.*

He wiped his face on the sleeping bag and sat himself up, mustering what was left of his dignity. 'You'd better be sure about this, Clem, because I won't have you back,' he said, almost believing it himself. 'You leave me and I swear to you, I won't take you back. Do you understand?'

She turned her bloodshot eyes to his, her lids red and swollen. Then she nodded. The final blow. He could see it then: she had already severed her connection to him and he hated her for her complete and utter betrayal.

'By the way,' he said, the chill had reached his voice now; the words came out all curt and cold. 'Does it even bother you that he's a paedophile? Because I'm beginning to think that it doesn't.'

She glared at him for a moment and then got off the bed as if *he* was the one saying the terrible things. Despite himself, he didn't want her to go. He wanted her back in the bed naked and close and cruel. She stepped into the heads and closed the door firmly behind her.

It was much later on when Smudge came up into the cockpit and sat herself on Johnny's lap. 'I don't like Clem,' she said.

Good, he thought, I don't like her either. I don't even recognize her. He held on to Smudge and tried to smile. How odd it was that the muscles in his face were still working, that he could sail the boat and make tea and look out for other boats when inside he had been quite felled.

He swept her hair over her head, as a parent might, smoothing out the matted wildness. *He would not let Clem take Smudge back to him. He would not let it happen.*

'I need Gilla and Clem won't let me in the forepeak,' she said crossly. So Johnny reluctantly found himself going down to the forecabin. He stopped outside the door catching sight of himself in the mirror hanging above the basin and got a shock. He looked old and hardened, with lined, dark skin and black stubble on his chin, his hair long and bleached, sticky with salt; his eyes looked different: they were tinged with bitterness. This was a Johnny he didn't yet know and behind the door was another stranger. He pushed the door open. 'Smudge needs Gilla,' he said perfunctorily. Clem was sitting there in the middle of the bed, her back to him, cross-legged, her shirt slipped off one shoulder, her heart necklace hanging the wrong way round against her skin. It seemed symbolic that it was all back to front.

He looked about for Gilla, who was leaning against the spinnaker hatch right at the very bows of the boat. Clearly Clem wasn't going to pass Gilla so he got on the bed and leant forwards to pick him up, glancing at her as he did so. She had a piece of paper in her hands, her hair was hanging down but he could see that she was in a terrible state. And he was glad. Her mouth was open, a drool of spit hanging from her lip, her eyes dazed looking down at her lap and he thought for a moment that she had changed her mind, that she had realised what a mistake she had made and he found that almost immediately he was ready to have her back. Then he saw the book open upon her lap. At first he didn't recognize it, but when he did, he understood. She had found the *Gulliver's Travels*. It wasn't paper she was clutching in her fingers; it was a photograph. He reached out for it but her grip was claw like and he had to tug it free from her grasp. He hadn't looked closely at any of this filth when he'd first found it, not from the moment he'd realized the nature of it. But he had to look now: in the photograph was a fair-haired little girl, no more than seven or eight years old, lying naked on a bed, her wrists and ankles tied to the bed posts, a look in her eyes of total puzzlement. In front of the little girl, right on the edge of the frame, a man's hand was perfectly visible clutching the bedstead – a familiar right hand with the tips of two of the fingers missing.

Slowly Johnny sat back against the inside of the hull, letting the photograph fall from his fingers.

Well, now she knew.

It was a still, hot night. They were moored amongst a cluster of small islands north of Sicily; they avoided the big places these days, they only moored in harbours or marinas when they had to fill up with diesel and water, otherwise they would find a small bay and avoid authorities and crowds. Even so, there was always someone there to remind them, some garment of clothing, some gait or limp, the sound of a laugh, or a song, or sometimes just a word that would send a flutter to their hearts. Smudge had been prone to run up to total strangers and ask them if they'd seen her mummy or daddy with Clem and Johnny standing right there beside her. But she hadn't done that in a while, not since Johnny had told her that they weren't coming back, they were staying in Turkey, and Clem and Johnny were her new guardians. He'd made it as matter-of-fact as he could and to his surprise she had seemed to take it on board without too much apparent dismay. Yet she still saw them everywhere; they haunted her just as they haunted him and Clem. He understood that this was the cross he had to bear: he would always need eyes in the back of his head, he would never be free of them, he would forever be waiting for that tap on the shoulder, to turn and see the big bear man standing there ready to claim his life back. Clem was the same; he saw the way she jumped at the sight of a particular shirt, or the size of a particular man, how she cowered, how everything seemed to startle her, how her free spirit had been contained and crushed, her confidence shot. She never spoke of *him*. She barely spoke at all.

For Frank had killed a part of her; it sat inside her, a dead, heavy thing sunk into her gut. She could feel it, cold and solid. She had bared herself to him and given of herself and all the time he had been doing those unspeakable things. She felt like she was drowning in shame, it clung to her, it was in her hair, in her eyes and her nose, she would never escape it. And to think that she had thought herself in love with him – she was a stupid, stupid girl. It made her skin crawl and her stomach twist into knots: those hands that had touched her were the same hands on that bedpost. Everything he'd said had been a lie. All those wondrous feelings she had felt were now negated. No wonder he didn't want judgements – he was a charlatan, a sham, a monster. She had been duped. And now she had lost Johnny's love. Oh, he *loved* her, she knew that, but he would never love in the way he *had*, with such unconditional totality; from now on there would always be shadows, lesions in their love. She could see it in his eyes when he looked at her, the light had gone out. She had treated their love with callous disregard and above everything else she hated Frank for that the most. She was getting everything she deserved, she was unworthy of Johnny. She vowed never to mention Frank's name again.

Her silence suited Johnny, for the time being. The damage Frank had done was irrevocable and ever-present. There was nowhere to run to, he was always there, wherever they went. He was on the boat, in the wind, in every port, on every horizon. And so the silence and the gulf between Clem and

Johnny grew and grew and he watched as she retreated further and further into herself. She didn't paint any more, or read. She just sat there staring out at the water when they sailed, a shadow of her former self. When they were on dry land, she pulled her hat down and put her glasses on and barely raised her head. She looked different too. Her hair had grown thin and long over the months. It had lost its curl, as if depression had reached the very tips of her. *At least she's still there. She hasn't left.* Johnny liked to imagine that she was getting better, that her old self would re-emerge, that they would get through it. He didn't like to admit that he was playing a part in her unhappiness but some proud and crooked part of him couldn't help but feel that she deserved to be suffering. She should have to pay for her blindness, for her treachery. Yet he still wanted her back to how she used to be; he wanted everything to go back to how it once had been; only he didn't know how it was going to happen for not once had she reached out for him. And if he thought about it, not once had he reached out for her.

'Johnny,' she whispered. He opened his eyes; he had been fast asleep. It was the dead of night. Clem was crouching by the bedside. 'Wake up!'

Usually when he awoke, it was to her back and he would have to remember afresh the void between them. But here she was: her face right beside his, her eyes with that old spark in them. He thought she might have slipped into his dream, for in his dreams their love was untainted. He sat up. 'What is it?' he asked.

'Come up into the cockpit!'

He heard it then, a kind of snarling, sighing, monstrous noise, a dragon's breath, a distant rumbling war, gunshot and explosion. He threw off the covers and rushed up the galley steps out into the night.

'Oh my God!' he cried, blown backwards by the sight.

They had anchored beside an active volcano. The mountain right in front of them, that yesterday had been smoking, tonight turned out to be alive. The earth was spewing red fire from its belly into the night, angry jets of white and orange molten rock bursting high up into the night sky, belching jets of fire that landed softly and rolled back down the mountain top like liquid jewels disappearing into blackness before another burst of activity. They watched in awe, climbing up on to the decks as high as they could, their own private spectacular. They gazed in utter wonderment as the earth groaned and heaved before them. Then something quite extraordinary happened. Moved by the earth itself, he felt Clem slip her hand into his and his heart nearly bubbled over with its own fire for he had waited so long for this. And it felt so good. It felt like being home again.

It would have been easy then to squeeze that hand in his, for his fingers to have responded to her gentle touch, to have pressed his palm against hers and made the peace that he had been so craving. But he couldn't do it. He needed to punish her; she had to be rejected, to understand the hurt. He needed to make her suffer just a little more, as she had made him suffer. He wanted her to beg for forgiveness, to make amends for all the damage she had done before they could become whole again. And so he didn't respond to that small warm hand that had sought his out. He let it sit there for just a moment before he punished her. Then he let it go. He dropped it from his own, hating himself as he did so, turning away, saying, 'Smudge needs to see this,' before disappearing below deck to get her.

When he came back out, he could see that she had been crying: there were wet golden tracks on her cheeks glinting with reflected volcanic light and he felt the full cruelty of this new Johnny. Miserable, he sat down and watched the earth pour out its guts for the rest for the night but it wasn't the same. It had lost its magic.

The following day they chugged into the marina of a neighbouring island. They had to buy diesel and do a supermarket shop: they were running low on everything they would need before they sailed north. Johnny checked out the other boats, as he always did, his eyes not missing a thing, every name of every boat, every laundered shirt hanging on every line, every size of every shoe sitting on the decks. He moored them on the end of a pontoon with no immediate neighbours and they got themselves together to go down to customs. They hadn't been on land for a week or so and it felt strange underfoot as it often did, swaying and rolling beneath them as they wandered down the pontoon, Smudge swinging on their hands, looking to all intents and purposes like a perfect little family.

This island was another volcanic one, towering mountains and black sand; it was lush and green, a beautiful, unspoilt place for unspoilt people; he wouldn't be here long. He paid their dues at the customs house, handed over their false documentation with his heart beating fast as it always did, his eyes as ever on the move, Smudge as usual bribed into silence, this time with the promise of climbing to the top of the hill where she could see people leaning over a wall.

She took Johnny's hand as they climbed the hill, Clem lagging behind. They went up the steep streets, their hats tucked low over their heads, their dark glasses impenetrable. They wandered down shaded alleyways, past tall, coloured houses with high balconies, washing waving like bunting crisp in the harsh sunlight, at the end of every alley a view of sea and sky, a high, dark line sorting blue from blue, Smudge darting here and there chasing manky dogs and scrawny kittens. A while ago he'd cut her hair short and as she wore her dungarees whenever they were on land she looked like exactly like a boy. She didn't mind this. She'd spent ages practising peeing standing up like Johnny did over the edge of the boat.

'I prefer it just you and me,' she whispered as they neared the top of the hill and found themselves in an old Greek amphitheatre with a few fellow tourists. He'd looked down at her then and back at Clem who was on a lower level leaning on a wall, looking far out to sea as if the answers all lay out there. He tried to see things from Smudge's point of view. Clem had not been good company. Her depression infected everything; it sucked the pleasure out of life and Smudge was such a creature of pleasure. He had been so preoccupied by the state of play between himself and Clem he had not really taken her into account. The atmosphere was bad. It was strange how easily they had slipped into a functional animosity, how the war had become the norm and the little moments of peace had become memorable. He had been offered a moment of peace last night and he had spurned it – his own foolish pride.

'She'll be her old self again soon,' he said and something about standing there on top of the world looking down on the sea, at the town, at the islands, at the beauty of this place gave him a fresh perspective. He had to try and make things right again. He would surprise her. He would cook her favourite supper; he would get the ingredients at the supermarket and a bottle of wine and he would play 'These Arms of Mine' again and again on the loop. He would fix them. But the trouble was, no sooner than he had had the thought, the nagging doubt was back: how could he fix things when every time he felt love he felt betrayal and sickness. His head would fill with twisted images. When he looked at her he could only see *him*. And he wondered how on earth that was ever going to change. Or if not change, at least be repaired, for he already knew that they could never be what they were. He sighed and closed his eyes and asked her God that he might be a better, stronger man. He would bring out the prayer mat again.

They wandered back down the hill, Smudge chasing a cat all the way down from the ruins to the ice-cream shop, Clem walking ahead of him, in flip flops and her old ripped jeans. She was thin; the jeans sagged on her now. She turned and asked for the cockpit key, she wanted to get a cardigan from the boat before they went to the supermarket. It wasn't even cold. He bought Smudge an ice cream as they waited at the marina entrance. He watched Clem walking back towards them down the pontoon, the green shopping bag flung across her shoulder, heavy with all her bits and bobs, her hat low on her head, a cigarette dangling from her lips. There was something different about the way she looked that he couldn't quite put his finger on. It was hard to tell through her sunglasses whether she was looking at him but he smiled anyway when she reached the gate. 'Ready for the supermarket?' he said, trying to sound like a man full of new beginnings, and she stood and stared at him as if she couldn't take his kindness. He saw her lips quiver. Then, to his surprise, she leant forwards and kissed him lightly on the lips as she gave him back the key. Even then, with forgiveness stirring in his heart, he was unable to kiss her back.

It was an ordinary-looking small supermarket: bright fluorescent lights, bargains written in thick felt tip on cardboard hanging from the cheap white panels above the aisles of shelves. Johnny surveyed the occupants as a matter of procedure and then he and Smudge went up and down the aisles filling the trolley. He'd promised her sherbet sweets so she was really just pushing the trolley as fast as she could until she found the sweet shelf. They got to the end of the third aisle and she found them; they were deliberating over which packets to buy when he

319

spotted some pear drops. He hid them in the trolley beneath the alcohol and the biscuits, peering down the aisle as he did so. Clem was standing there, the bag over her shoulder, one strap slipped down, doing absolutely nothing, staring at a shelf, gone, in another world. A large man was trying to get past her and she didn't move; she didn't even notice him.

'Clem?' Johnny said, but she didn't hear him. He looked down; Smudge was tugging at his wrist, talking about sweets, and he let her drag him away, turning back just as he reached the end of the aisle, but Clem had disappeared and the large man was now trying to push past him. He looked out for her down the next aisle, loading up cereals and pasta as he went, but she had moved elsewhere.

When he got to the checkout he was surprised she hadn't joined them and he left Smudge with the trolley and wandered the width of the supermarket but he couldn't see her. The girl at the till began totting up his wares so he sent Smudge off to look for her. It took the girl a while to put everything into bags; he'd bought food enough for the trip to Corsica where his plan was to stop for a while, to get their lives back on track.

He was paying with Frank's cash when Smudge came sliding down the aisle saying she couldn't find Clem anywhere. He left her with the bags and went to look again himself, walking up and down the aisles, this time a little quicker, but to no avail. He and Smudge picked up the bags and went outside. She wasn't there either. He looked up and down the main street but there was no sign of her anywhere so he presumed that she must have returned to the boat. Between them they carried the heavy bags all the way back to the marina, with much complaining and stopping from Smudge. When they got to the gate and entered the marina they could see from the end of the pontoon that the boat was still locked up, that she wasn't on it. He walked down the decking, eyes scanning the place – she might be sitting down somewhere, staring into the water, taking a look at the other yachts. But she wasn't there. He checked the boat. She was not on the decks and the door was still locked. He had the only key. He thought of the last moment he had seen her in the supermarket staring into space. His heart started to beat fast as a terrible idea took hold in him: she had gone.

He dropped the bags on the wooden pontoon decking, told Smudge to wait on the boat for Clem while he ran back out of the marina and along the road towards the supermarket. He ran as fast as he could, his chest aching. He knocked a woman out of his way as he ran inside, double-checking the aisles – running up and down. He paused at the very place where he had last seen her and turned to see what she had been staring at. Cereals. *Cornflakes*. Home, she was trying to get *home*. But he was her *home*. There was nothing at home for her. But maybe *nothing* was preferable to this.

He ran out into the street and down the road into town, his legs shaking beneath him. It was late afternoon now and the shops were all opening, the streets filling up. He wove his way between the people. He was looking out for the green bag, looking left and right, inside shops, down side streets. He came to a crossroads, looked up and down all ways and ran towards the sea. Eventually he found himself at the port, where ferries were coming and going, people were embarking and disembarking, going to Sicily and the other islands. He ran through a queue, crying out, '*Chica, bolsa verde,*' useless Spanish words coming into his head. He jumped on to a small ferry, knocking people out of his way.

'Clem!' he was calling, 'Clemency!' his voice rising with increasing panic.

People were looking at him as though he was mad and the ticket man asked for his ticket and ushered him off the boat. He jumped on to another one and ran up and down, calling out her name, searching the faces, banging on the toilet door. People were shouting back at him now, shuffling about around him, out of his way. '*Mi femme*,' he kept saying. He was causing such chaos a policeman on the quayside stepped down on to the pontoon. He couldn't have the police involved – he jumped off the boat, darted back down the main street, calling out, crying, running until his legs could move no more.

Night was falling by the time he hobbled breathlessly back to the boat, his last hope extinguished as he got to the edge of the pontoon and saw Smudge alone on the cockpit sole surrounded by sweetie wrappers – Clem was long gone now. Smudge was looking up at him expectantly. He hadn't even opened the cockpit doors for her. He looked down at her, shaking his head, the dreadful reality sinking in.

'Oh dear, Johnny,' she said. 'Why do we keep losing people?'

He found the key and opened the cockpit doors. 'Clem?' he called forlornly, knowing full well there would be no response.

It was a few hours later, he was at the kitchen table, his head in his hands, when he looked up and saw the matchbox sitting right in front of him. It was a Swan Vestas matchbox, one from her collection. He reached out and took it in his hands. His name was written in tiny writing along the edge. He stared at it and then slid it open. Inside there were tiny pieces of broken shells and lying on them was the heart necklace, the heart he had given her all those years ago when she was just a child. That was it – that's what he had noticed when he saw her walking down the pontoon – she'd taken off his heart. That was why she had kissed him. A kiss goodbye. He took it out and smoothed the slate in his fingers, just as he had done on the beach when he'd first fallen in love with her. There was something else in the box, beneath the broken shells: a tiny scrap of paper. He took it out and unfolded it. In tiny lettering she had written: *I can't do this anymore, J. I can't wait until the stars have all gone out for you to forgive me.* Very slowly he put the matchbox back down on the table. He stood up, turned around and pulled open the chart-table drawer – at least she'd taken some money with her. Her passport was missing. He shut the drawer again and climbed the companionway, stepping out into the cockpit. She wasn't coming back. Their love was broken; he knew it as well as she did. She was right: he would never forgive her, not properly, not entirely. He didn't have it in him. Tears welled up in his eyes as he looked out at the watery night sky and for a moment he thought the sun had flung itself out of orbit for he hadn't noticed it getting dark. It seemed quite natural that Time itself should have stumbled to a halt – he could see no reason for the Earth to spin right now.

The human spirit is cursed with survival and after what might have been days or weeks, he must have stopped waiting for her to come back, he must have got himself up off the saloon berth, stopped staring into the yellow flower on the fabric of the cushion covers and started functioning again, because he left the island, the wind took them west and the sun set and rose as if everything was exactly the same. He watched aimlessly as it journeyed across the timeless sky. At night the stars carried on their usual business prickling the sky with false hope. Meaningless days passed. Alcohol was his only friend. He drank all the hours he could.

He had no idea what month it was. It might have been August or September: it meant nothing. He saw other boats, day trippers. Some sailed close and he stared dazed and confused at their smiling, waving faces. He wondered what they saw. He remembered Smudge then, but she was a stranger to him. She was as brown as a nut, her once dark hair now streaked by the sun. He knew he wasn't fit to look after himself, let alone her. Truly, he just didn't care; where there should have been a hot and sentient heart, there was nothing, only numbness. He watched Smudge feeding herself, opening jars, eating jam with her fingers, licking biscuit crumbs from the floor, squeezing cartons of old juice that she had ripped open, scooping out powdered milk with her fingers, her face covered in the white powder like something out of *Scarface*. She would sit at the bows clutching her spear, looking as feral and as crazy as he presumed he did, but he couldn't feel anything about it. Sometimes he caught her staring at him and once or twice he thought he had heard her whispering in his ear, singing songs, but on the whole she left him alone and mainly he just didn't notice her at all. He knew he frightened her with his mumbling. Sometimes, in his sleep, the numbness was pierced by a hot white fury and he would rant and rave and wake himself up in a furious sweat. Frank, Annie, Clem – all three of them had fucked him over. He was full of loathing.

And yet he couldn't rid himself of all the love. What was he meant to do with this left-over love inside of him, where was it meant to go. Her absence hit him again and again, a hundred times a day, never lightening its touch. There was no point to anything. Nor would there ever *be* any point, he knew that. He kept his eyes focused on the horizon because that was all he could do – he kept moving because there was no other choice.

Only when Smudge spotted the island did it strike him that perhaps he did have a choice. The choice had been there all along. He'd taken the binoculars from her and had a look. They were a long way off. He could see that it was like most of the islands they had passed: mountainous, the tip of some ancient volcano exposed to the air, the landscape so dry and scorched that human life seemed an impossibility. He wondered vaguely where they were, what island this was, what language the people spoke, but not enough to find out. He was better off not knowing. They were somewhere off Africa, that was all he needed to know. It crossed his mind to start working out the longitude and latitude, perhaps he should drag the sextant out – it was probably about midday, perfect for a bearing. But ultimately, he saw no point.

All afternoon he tacked towards the island, then the wind swung round and he found himself approaching it on a gentle run. As they got closer it became clear that he had been wrong about human life: the occasional stone house stood on the hillsides and his idea began to grow roots. He kept checking through the binoculars and soon saw a small port, which he avoided; he had no desire to be seen or to see people, he barely felt human himself any more. Instead he sailed around to the western side. The coastline was sheer, punctuated by the occasional turquoise cove, but mainly the beaches were made of black volcanic sand: the kind the tourists didn't like.

The moon had begun to rise now and it was huge and yellow, stealing the light from the sun as it slipped down the other side of the sky, both of them glinting in competition.

When he saw the church everything fitted into place. At least one of them could be saved. A cross, even at a subliminal level, is a strangely comforting sign. It stood out, propitious and blaring above the small arched building at the top of a hill. Beneath the church a few houses were scattered about around a sheltered bay. Ten or so colourful fishing boats bobbed up and down by a pontoon in the golden evening light. They were still a good couple of miles out and he sat there at the tiller knowing what he had to do; he was filled, for the first time since she'd gone, with a purpose.

He sailed past the church and took refuge in a small inlet on the other side near a natural arch in the rocks. The moon had won the battle for the sky. It was shining up high, had got smaller and turned silver but was glowing brighter than ever. In fact it was so bright, the water so clear and the seabed so sandy, he watched the anchor sink and take hold beneath him. The boat swung round into a comfortable position and Johnny sat on deck and rolled the last of the cigarettes. He picked up the binoculars and studied every cranny of the shoreline, spotting a path over beyond the rocks on the far side of the beach.

He told Smudge that they were going to dress for dinner on the boat. She looked up, surprised to hear him speak directly to her. Her face lit up, so like her mother's he felt the hairs on the back of his neck stand up on end. He told her that they would wait until tomorrow to go ashore; in the meantime they would have a dinner party.

Below deck, Smudge wandered down to the forepeak while Johnny examined the non-contents of the food cupboard. There was one packet of pasta left. He rifled around for more edibles and found a tin of sardines under the saloon seat. He didn't think either of them had had anything resembling a meal for a long time so he pulled up a bucket of seawater and got it on the boil over the weak gas flame.

He went through the saloon, where Smudge was now taking off her filthy clothes, and into the heads where he found a hairbrush lying by the sink. He noticed little specks of blood on the mirror. Annie's blood. He picked them off with his thumbnail, looking through them into the reflection beyond, which shocked him. He was terribly thin and wasted with a look in his eye so grim that he wasn't surprised that Smudge cowered from him.

He went through into the forecabin and leant over the planks of the bed and opened one of the lockers. He rummaged around and grabbed a few handfuls of Smudge's clothes, picking up the hairbrush from the washstand as he came back through. He chucked the clothes in the corner and tried to brush her hair but she didn't like it so he didn't bother, instead he put her old woolly hat on her head. He ran a flannel over her filthy face and it turned out that most of her tan was dirt. Her freckles emerged one by one like the first stars of the night. He couldn't avoid her big, watery stare as he wiped clean her little heart-shaped face.

'Hello, Johnny,' she said quietly and he felt an unfamiliar tugging at his heart.

He tried to smile but the muscles in his face felt strange and unused. 'I'm so sorry,' he said.

'What are you sorry for?' she asked as he concentrated on getting the dirt off her neck. 'Why are you cleaning me?' she said.

'Can't have a dinner party looking like shit, can we?' he said.

'You look like shit too,' she said.

'Yes,' he said. 'You're right. Shall I shave?'

'Daddy has a suit you could wear.'

'Does he?'

'And a twiddly tie. I think he met the Queen in it.'

Johnny nodded. 'Did he now?' He tweaked her cheek. 'Well, what's good enough for the Queen should be good enough for you. I'll put it on.'

He went back through for a shave. He could see her in the saloon going through her bag of clothes with great deliberation, humming all the while. He marvelled at her capacity for happiness, the resilience of childhood, for she too had lost everything. He saw her pick out her blue, stripy pyjamas and he watched as she carefully put them on back to front and went up into the cockpit to wait for him.

Smooth-faced and paler beneath the beard, Johnny looked inside the forepeak locker again and found Frank's suit, black and creased. He put it on with a white shirt and the dicky bow and stared at himself in the mirror. He looked ridiculous, as though he was getting married or something. He rolled up the trouser legs and the sleeves and tied a belt around the waist. He put on his old trainers but his feet felt strange in shoes, he'd been barefoot for so long.

'OK, my lady,' he said to her as he put the pasta in the pot. 'Before we eat we must have a toast!'

She was enjoying the game, or perhaps was just enjoying some attention for a change. He could see her stripy legs banging against the cockpit seat as she waited impatiently for him to come up and join her. Inside the silver medicine box, he found the bottle of sleeping medicine that Annie had used, which he took out and brought up along with two tumblers and a bottle of wine. She laughed with delight when she saw him dressed up like that. He paused, listening to that crackly little laugh that he hadn't heard for a long while. *She's five years old, for Christ's sake. Five years old.*

He placed the tumblers between them on the seat and poured her a shot of the sleeping medicine and himself a tumbler full of wine. They chinked glasses. He noticed how she mimicked the way her mother held her glass, with her little finger raised.

'To you, Smudge!' he said, a lump in his throat, and they both knocked it back. He refilled the tumblers and they repeated the toast several times until the medicine bottle was nearly empty and he thought to himself surely that had to be enough. He watched her eat her salty pasta in silence. She was ravenous; she couldn't get it into her mouth fast enough. He took courage from that. She would be all right, he thought. She was a survivor.

An hour later, the moon beaming down on them, Smudge sound asleep on his lap, he gently rubbed her little fingers in his hand and stared out at the silver water with his vacant eyes. There were no other options. He looked up at the stars; they were trying to tell him where they were, trillions of them splashed about the heavens like arrows, but he didn't want to know.

The time had come. He pressed her little hand to his lips, looking at the grubby long nails, the dimples on her hands. In her sleep she gave his hand a little squeeze in response. He closed his eyes and kissed her fingers. He prised himself out from under her sleeping body and laid her flat on the cockpit seat. She was wearing a jumper of Clem's now, the small blue one with holes at the elbows and the sleeves rolled up.

He went down into the saloon and clicked the light on. He opened the portside seat and pulled out their big maroon sail bag. For a moment he stood there holding it, unable to move, filled with an intense but fleeting anger towards Clem for leaving him in this situation. Then he hurriedly unzipped it and glanced inside. It was full of all her bits of crap: papers, tickets, pear drops, pebbles and stuff that she'd been dragging round for months. He couldn't bear to look at it. Instead he turned it inside out and shook out all the contents on to the floor. He folded a blanket and laid it out on the base of the bag like a mattress, putting in a few clothes at the sides to pad it out.

He took it up into the cockpit and picked up Smudge's drugged little body, carefully placing her inside the bag on to the blanket, fitting her in as snugly as he could. He wrapped the sides of the blanket around her and folded her arms across her body. He picked up Gilla, with his shining button eyes, and tucked him under her arm and did up the zip to her chest. He went down into the saloon and filled one of her beakers with water and put it in the bag with her. Then he clicked off the lights and shut the cockpit door behind him.

He pulled the inflatable life raft from the deck, wondering how old it was, hoping it would still work. He chucked it in the water. He'd never opened one of these before but it did exactly what it said it would. He pulled the rope and it unfolded into air-filled life like that blow-up doll Rob had once bought. He tied it to the cleat and then carefully leant overboard and lowered Smudge into the raft, surprised at how small and light she was: the bag was no heavier than it had been with all Clem's stuff. He climbed into the boat after her and undid the painter.

He began to paddle shorewards. The moon was so bright he felt extremely visible but was pretty sure he was safe from prying eyes; there was nothing habitable on this side. Once on the shore, he pulled the raft up high on to the sand behind a small rock and lifted the bag over his shoulder and carried little Smudge like a piece of luggage. He trudged across the sand and clambered up over the rocks towards the path, noticing the shells that were embedded in the volcanic rock as if artfully placed and he couldn't help but wonder where he was. He became aware of a cacophony of noise ahead of him, birds or frogs, he wasn't quite sure.

The church was up high on the left of the bay, he'd noticed that as they'd passed, and he headed up towards it, the moon lighting up every cranny in the rocks as he carried her gently on to the path. He must have disturbed whatever was making the noise for it stopped abruptly as he got there and in the silence he could hear faint sounds of a guitar; it took him by surprise, he hadn't been near other humans for ages. He paused on the rocks and listened but the warmth of the music made him ache for Clem and his old life so acutely he bit his lip until he could taste blood. He could hear laughter and applause from the same direction as the guitar music. The laughter sounded displaced, utterly alien to him; the idea that there could be joy and happiness in the world when she was gone confirmed to him that he had no place here any more.

He stood stock-still, taking in his surroundings. He was on the westerly edge of the bay; there were barely a dozen houses dotted about it and, to his left, the highest point of the village was the church. The music was coming from one of the houses nearer the water, a bar perhaps. A single frog ribbited from close by; he must have been near a pool, but he couldn't see it. Then the lot of them joined in, he had never heard frogs en masse before and the noise was deafening. He peered at Smudge under his arm, sleeping peacefully despite the racket, her mouth open, her cherubic lips a little parted, and he set off up the sandy path towards the church.

The church was a small building with an arch and a bell at the top, its rusty tongue hanging out above him. The door was ajar and he pushed it wide open. It creaked loudly and he stepped inside. The space was functional and to the point, Christ on a cross at the pulpit and ten or so rows of chairs. Moonlight flooded in through an arched window at the back of the church casting Christ's shadow across the stone floor in the aisle, his left hand almost brushing Johnny's trainer. He looked around carefully, trying to fix it in his memory; he didn't know why, but it seemed important. And then he turned briskly and stepped out. Not a soul was about. He carefully took the bag off his shoulder and placed it gently on the ground in the porch with only the moonlight looking on. He undid the zip a smidgeon and tucked Gilla in close under Smudge's arm.

He bent over her and kissed her soft, smooth cheek and squeezed her little fingers. The tightness in his throat came out as a stifled sob. 'God, you bastard,' he said. 'If you have any mercy at all, look after her.'

Then he crept off stealthily back towards the boat with no name without looking back, just glad that she hadn't cried out. He ran down on to the beach and dragged the life-raft back into the water and rowed as fast as he could back to the boat. He tied it up, got on board, pulled up the anchor, got the main up and set off at a lick. He didn't look back once, he didn't want to know where he was, what island this was, what bay he was in. It didn't matter to him. Nothing mattered to him at all any more. He had no attachments; he was just ghosting now.

He sailed out into the night, over the water into the nothingness, and didn't stop until the sun had set and risen again and crossed the sky and set and risen and he was sure that he had no chance of being rescued.

DROWNING

THERE HAD TO be worse ways of dying. This was unbelievably good. He hadn't envisaged this at all. He had never imagined death to be such a peaceful affair. What was all the fuss about? Death had had a bad press. Death was nothing but a refuge for the tired, a pillow at the end of an exhausting day. And now that the pillow was so tangible, so plumped and comfortable, all the pain inside him had subsided. He was a man with absolutely nothing left to lose. He was a free man.

The surface of the water was flickering silver and black ribbons in the moonlight. The waves had abated a little; they were his friends again. He hadn't noticed when everything had stopped hurting. He must have been too busy dying. It couldn't be long now; he felt as though he'd been drowning for days. He wanted to roll over face down into the water and slip away. But even that felt like too much effort. He turned his head slightly, or maybe he didn't but his eye looked up at the moon, which was so bright and so beautiful that he had to squint a little. His salted lips cracked as he smiled up at her. He must have turned again for now he seemed to be lying on his back looking up at the stars. They took his breath away, sparkling like jewels in the dark blanket of the night: Orion's belt pointing to the west, the plough, the North Star, Betelgeuse. There they all were, eternally glittering and dancing, regardless of anything, all for nothing, all for no one. It was so fucking beautiful he wanted to weep.

He let his head fall back until he was looking at the world upside down; he was swimming in the stars. He knew his place in the universe.

He heard it first, something coming up out of the water. At his upside down three o'clock he saw a shape looming out of the sea up into the moonlight about ten yards away. He blinked and stared, lifting his head as high as he could, trying to turn around, to spin the world back into shape. He thought it was a fish or a whale or a dolphin. Then he thought of Smudge and her sea monsters. Maybe it was a sea monster come to gobble him up. *Oh, Smudge.* But to his utter amazement he realized that it was a human being. He watched, with some wonder, as the person slowly began to swim towards him, a steady breaststroke unnaturally high in the water. How on earth had they found him?

He recognized the garment first, the old crocheted poncho. He'd forgotten all about that poncho, the one with holes in it big enough for him and Rob to put their arms through and pretend they were fish trapped in a net. He realized who it was then and his heart leapt like a flying fish and he knew for sure that he wasn't dead yet. She swam towards him, smooth and fast, smiling at him all the while, her face silver in the moonlight.

'Mum!' he cried, filling up with the exquisite warmth of his mother's love.

Her eyes were glinting in the moonlight and when she got near enough, she dipped under the water and came out as elegantly and easily as an otter up on to the fender. She was slightly out of breath, the water streaming down her pale face. He stared into her eyes, which were green with dark lashes, just like his own; she was so utterly familiar to him it was like looking at himself.

'Mum,' he said, overcome with happiness, and she laughed and leant forward a little, her bare elbow underneath the spider-web fabric of the poncho brushing his skin.

'Hello, Jonty,' she said, bending her head down and kissing his hand, her lips cool against his skin. He was burning up. If he had the energy he would like to have taken off his clothes.

'Oh, Mum,' he said a catch in his throat. Her eyes were full of water; he could see the moonlight dancing inside them. 'I missed you.'

She was smiling. ' I told you I'd see you again,' she said, her cold fingers against his cheek. 'I told you so. I live in you. You came from me.'

'That's right,' he said, puzzled. 'I was born in the caul, wasn't I?'

She nodded and smiled with those eyes that could have been his.

'Then how can I be drowning?' he asked, remembering then how horribly wrong everything was.

'You mustn't give up,' she said, droplets of water falling down her face, little moons running down her cheeks.

'But I *have* given up, Mum. That's why I'm here,' he croaked because he was crying now. 'I lost her.'

She put her arm around him and he rested his head against her shoulder and cried. 'Shhh,it's not over yet,' she said, her fingers running through his hair, the coolness of her palm pressing against his forehead, the hardness of her rings. 'Stay awake, you're going to be all right!'

But I don't want to be all right, he thought, but he was so tired, he could barely keep his eyes open. He could feel her pushing him away from her, lifting his head, her fingertips on his chin.

'You mustn't sleep, Jonty, my love,' she said and he could feel her kisses on his face. He tried to focus; he opened his eyes. He'd forgotten the way her eyebrows went up like that, the little freckle on her forehead. But it was no good; his eyelids were too heavy, he was drunk with the tiredness.

He was asleep.

When he first heard the music he barely registered it as music at all, for the place he was in was so remote and beyond all sensation, a delicious worm hole of peace that he had fallen into, that it took a long time for him to realize that the music was not part of him but was a separate thing and in so being demanded something other from him, an outline perhaps, an edge or an acknowledgement.

The music, so implausibly faint, was right on the circumference of his consciousness; he had to listen with every cell of his being to be sure it was there at all. When he did recognize it as music – it wasn't that he heard the tune, for it seemed to bypass his senses altogether, heading straight into his essence, to the dot that he had become – he felt it drag him outwards to the periphery where the rest of the world must surely be lurking. Then when he understood what the notes were doing, a flame lit up in his darkness and the vast void that he had always known existed – even as a child – was suddenly filled with *her* love again, just as he had been filled that very first time, on the beach, in the waves, holding her in his arms. It was Otis. It was Otis Redding singing 'These Arms of Mine'.

The trembling guitar, the crescendo, it filled his entire being with boundless love, which was music. The music *was* her; he knew that. She was there and he felt her love and his whole body smiled. It spread beyond him, up into the sky, out into the whole universe.

There was something else there too, something aside from the music. He could hear it faintly: water. And the moment he knew that it was water he remembered that she was gone, that he was left without her and the music stopped abruptly.

He opened an eye. He listened. No music. No mother. No Clem. And yet something of them all lingered. He tried to turn his head but nothing happened. He couldn't feel his face any more, or his hands, or any part of his body; he was solid all over, without sensation anywhere except one eye, which still looked and saw the rolling heavens as he rose and fell with the waves. Two large moons bounced about him, one high above and one in the water nestling by his face, linked only by the jagged white path of his mind. The red morning star was rising up the hem of the sky, twinkling promises of dawn.

Then he saw it, just beneath the star on the horizon: a tiny slash of a sail, white in the moonlight. He blinked and blinked again. He was still hallucinating. No, it was there, a boat on the horizon. He watched the sail move onwards, quite subjectively, as a thing of beauty, wondering who was on the boat, where they were going, what they were talking about. It struck him that he had never seen anything so beautiful in his life as this boat gliding through the water with the wind on her shoulder, governed by nature's breath and nothing more.

It was not until the boat changed tack and he realized that she was coming towards him that his heart began to stir. His mouth filled with a sweet sharpness. Hope had a taste. It tasted of pear drops. He couldn't deny it – somewhere in the very core of him he had not given up. His lips moved faintly, soundless words of need tumbled out of him on to the prayer mat.

He tried to pull himself higher up the fender, his blue fingers twitching a little but it was no good, his body was useless. He could barely keep his eye open. He watched through a slit as the waves lifted and dropped him, hiding and revealing the yellowing flag like a cruel game of peek-a-boo.

The sail was no longer a slash now but a triangle, perhaps half a mile away, glowing a brilliant blood-orange, reflecting the rising sun behind him. She was stunning, this boat, truly she was. She was the boat he had always dreamt of: the wooden, double-ended, Scandinavian ketch, flying through the water, her sails shining against the dark blue of the sky. When she changed tack again, heading south now, he thought he glimpsed a man in a red jumper at the helm. The boat was going to pass him on the beam, but with the sun behind his lifeless body, there was a chance the man might not see him.

The flicker of hope had become a flame now. He wanted to live. He needed to live. He made a deal with a god he didn't believe in: if he lived he would make amends. He promised that if that boat rescued him, he would go back and rescue Smudge. He swore on that prayer mat, he would find that island.

Then something extraordinary happened. Although he couldn't move a muscle and his eye would no longer open and the breath had left his body, inside he felt movement of a kind he had never experienced before. It was as if he were being reached into; there were hands on his heart, gently opening him up like an unfolding flower, turning him inside out. Love and peace and forgiveness were being poured into him and he was filled with a lucidity that he had never encountered before, a total absence of fear. With all fear gone, there was nothing left but love. An all-encompassing love – it was without attachment or judgement; there were no criteria, no barriers, no divisions. He thought of Frank and

Annie and the love permeated them too. He thought of Smudge, of his mother, of Clem, all of them were enshrouded by it. They were all safe; he knew that. All was well. The boat hadn't seen him. The last thing he saw before he slipped away was the elegant port bow pass by not fifty yards away, close enough for him to catch the name: The *Maid Marion*. And somewhere deep inside his rigid body, he laughed and wept and believed. *Maid Marion*.

EPILOGUE

STU WAS THE skipper. He was a sandy-haired Irishman, a fine sailor and a fine linguist. He rarely bathed, had often crossed whole oceans without changing his clothes and had an unfortunate skin condition because of it. His first mate was a Spaniard named Emilio and they worked for a Frenchman who ran his yacht-delivery business from a bar in Bermuda. Together they had delivered boats all over the globe through all kinds of seas and all types of weather. This was their eighteenth joint delivery. Their French boss knew he could rely on them to turn up on time with minimum damage. Most of the boats they delivered were standard charter boats but they'd lucked out with this one: a forty-eight-foot Scandinavian wooden double-ended ketch that sailed like a dream and even had a state-of-the-art autopilot on board. She belonged to a wealthy German racing driver who was expecting her in Crete within the next week for his holiday.

They had left Narbonne in the south-west of France later than expected due to foul weather. In the end, with the wind showing no signs of abating, the Mistral coming off the Pyrenees being a tricky customer, they'd had to depart in a force nine. So they were slightly behind schedule by the time they hit the Tyrrhenian Sea. They had stopped once en route at Bonifacio on the southern coast of Corsica where they'd got so shit-faced Emilio hadn't made it back to the boat at all and Stu, who had consumed his own body weight in alcohol, had to be pulled out of the marina by the port authorities.

Emilio was a few years Stu's junior and a different character altogether. He liked the ladies, as did Stu, but the ladies liked him in return. They liked the way he danced and they liked the way he looked and they liked the way he smelt as fresh as the morning breeze. And Stu liked the way the ladies all piled back to their boat of an evening and they both liked the way their boat moved on pretty sharpish the next day. Aside from both being formidable sailors and lovers of women, they shared an unbridled passion for rum and Moroccan hashish.

They'd left Bonifacio a couple of days before and were enjoying the calmer weather. The boat was moving beautifully under full sail on a comfortable beam reach. Emilio had been on watch for the last four hours until dawn and was now down in the galley making some coffee for Stu, dancing about the kitchen to the Jackson Five on the all-mod-con stereo system. He stuck his head into Stu's cabin. Stu was sound asleep on his back fully clothed, snoring and snorting.

'Rise and shine, Stu baby,' Emilio said in his thick Spanish accent, discoing back out over to the chart table to turn up the weather report. He never stopped dancing. He had once danced for three weeks solid from the Azores to Barbados.

Stu staggered out of his berth and stood in the doorway looking wild and haggard, his hair standing upright, his red-veined eyes blinking blearily. He headed straight to the fancy fridge and pulled out an early-morning heart-starter. The can opened with a click and a fizz and he took a long, thirsty gulp of cold beer.

'Any traffic?' he asked.

'Couple of trawlers and a cruise ship. *Pero nada màs.*'

Stu stretched out his limbs and sat down at the chart table to listen to the melodic tones of the woman reading the weather report, one ear cocked, a dreamy smile resting on his lips.

'I'd give her one,' he said and belched violently. He stood up, ran a hand through his mop of hair with one eye on Emilio, who was doing a nifty half-turn with jazz hands. He listened to the woman's soft voice warning of a change of wind coming their way.

'Easterlies, you big feckin' poof. We're changing course. We're going south of Sicily instead.'

'Aye aye, skipper,' Emilio said, shimmying out of his way.

Stu leant across the table, grabbed his red jumper, which was so salty and dirty it still held his form. He put it on, lit himself a fag and took his can of beer out into the cockpit. He had a quick look about. It was a beautiful morning; the red rising sun was so bright he had to squint. He yawned again, finished the beer, crushed the can in his hand and chucked it overboard. Then he reset the autopilot to head due south for the next hundred miles or so, sat down by the tiller, farted loudly, and got out his little silver box of hashish as the boat sped off across the water.

He spent a while adjusting the sails before sprinkling some of the finest Moroccan hash all over the entrails of a Marlborough cigarette. He called down to Emilio.

'Come and have a little smoke with me before you lay down your sweet head, Emilio.'

Emilio finished making the coffee in the galley and brought it out into the cockpit. 'Beautiful day,' he said, his face a golden red in the morning light. He sheltered his eyes, looking over at the fiery sun bouncing off the water. Stu passed him the big fat reefer and Emilio took it up on to the deck, leaning against the boom to appreciate the full glory of the morning.

His eye was caught by something in the water. He stood up to get a better look.

'Stu?' he called down. 'Your nine o'clock. What's that in the water?' he said, pointing due east.

Stu stood up and looked out. It was hard to see anything because of the glare of the sun. He leant forward and picked up the binoculars from the coachroof and peered through them. 'A turtle maybe?' he said, passing the binoculars to Emilio, who took another look.

It wasn't a turtle. Emilio was pretty sure about that. He stood up and steadied his feet for a better look.

'*Joder!*' he said, lowering the binoculars and squinting out. He checked again. 'Get the engine on!'

Stu leant down and turned the engine on and spun the wheel, the bows shifting round, heading towards the object in the water.

By the time they came up alongside, they knew exactly what they were dealing with. A human body was strapped face down to a fender. It wasn't moving. Emilio had the boat hook ready and leant out and hooked the body in by the trousers, pulling it in towards the hull.

Stu rushed along the deck and the pair of them got down on their stomachs and hauled the heavy soaked corpse up on to the boat. He lay motionless face down on the deck, his rigid arms clinging on to a scrap of carpet.

Emilio heaved the body over on to his back and they both sat back at the sight of his lifeless face.

'Holy mother of God,' Stu cried, crossing himself. The expression on the boy's face was extraordinary; he looked like an angel dropped from the sky. He appeared to be in some blissful sleep. Despite the blue hue of his skin, he had a beatific smile on his lips as if lost in some divine reverie, peace emanating from him.

Emilio too crossed himself and stared. 'Is he dead?' he asked. 'I'd say so.'

Stu got on to his knees and picked up the boy's cold grey wrist and felt for a pulse. 'Jesus, he's just a wee boy,' he said. He looked up at Emilio and shook his head.

Emilio leant over the body and pressed his lips to the boy's smile and tried to give him mouth to mouth, his fingers pinching his icy blue nose. Nothing happened.

Stu started to pump the boy's chest. *One two three four. One two three four.* But there was no response. He stopped pumping and looked up at Emilio. There was no need to say anything. They lifted the corpse, the water pouring on to the deck from his clothing, noticing then that he wearing a suit and bow tie. He must have fallen from a cruise ship. They carried him along the deck, down the companionway and into the saloon, Stu sweeping the table clear with his elbow as they laid him out. They cut off the fender and the ragged little mat that was attached to it and ripped off his soaking wet clothes to reveal a thin, grey, ice-cold body. His hands, lips and feet were a pale but vivid blue. Stu dashed through to the cabin and returned with an armful of blankets and towels.

'Come on, lad,' he said, covering the boy's naked body with the bedding whilst Emilio filled water bottles with hot water and proceeded to put them underneath the blankets against the boy's skin. Emilio tried again with the mouth to mouth and they pumped his chest several times but still the boy didn't respond.

After what felt like a long time, they stopped trying and sat down either side of the body, staring at each other, shocked by what the sea had coughed up. Stu reached round for the rum from the shelf behind. He unscrewed the cap and knocked back a glug. He leant forward and poured a little into the dead boy's mouth and watched as it dribbled down his chin.

'I should have seen him earlier,' Emilio said eventually, reaching across the body and taking the rum from Stu.

'Poor kid,' Stu said, lighting up a cigarette, staring at the boy's fine-featured face. 'Look at him. Why's he so feckin' happy?'

Emilio shook his head. 'What do we do? Chuck him back in?'

Stu shrugged and nodded.

Then, all of a sudden, the corpse coughed and spluttered. They both jumped to their feet, staring down at him, turning him on to his side, watching the colour creep back into his parted lips, his skin changing from blue to grey to a pale yellow as the blood began to flow.

Then the corpse opened his vivid green eyes and sat up suddenly and took a great gasp of air. 'The stars have all gone out!' it cried, looking from one man to the other. 'The stars have all gone out!'